Take one daring agent of SCENT (Society for the Conversion of Extraterrestrial Nascent Totalitarianisms) and send him on orders of DDT (Decentralized Democratic Tribunal) to seek out and root out any remaining pockets of PEST (Proletarian Eclectic State of Terra).

Give him for assistance one FCC (Faithful Cybernetic Companion) in the guise of a talking horse, equipped with computer feedback and a faulty capacitor making it the only epileptic robot in the universe.

Land him on a planet inhabited by devotees of Creative Anachronisms, meaning witchcraft, the supernatural, and medieval mummery propped up by scientific materialism.

And the result is a fun novel of breathless excitement guaranteed to be one of the best fantasies of the year.

CHRISTOPHER STASHEFF used to be in educational television and may be again, but at the moment he is in college. He has a fondness for science fiction, theater, puns, and thinking up new answers to "How are you?"

He comes of an old and distinguished line. One ancestor had to leave Ireland in a bit of a hurry—sheriff trouble, he'd been shooting landlords out of season. Another ancestor was sent to Siberia for teaching peasants to read and write.

Consequently, Mr. Stasheff has an inborn love for freedom and public attention and, therefore, for America. His main ambition is to live up to the family traditions.

THE WARLOCK
IN SPITE
OF HIMSELF
Christopher Stasheff

AN ACE BOOK

Ace Publishing Corporation
1120 Avenue of the Americas
New York, N.Y. 10036

THE WARLOCK IN SPITE OF HIMSELF

Cover art by Jack Gaughan.

Dedication:

To JEANIE D.

PART ONE

VISIT TO A SMALL PLANTAGENET

THE ASTEROID HURTLED in from Capricorn, nosed around a G-type sun, swerved off toward the fifth planet. Such a trajectory is somewhat atypical for asteroids.

It slapped into the planet's gravity net, swooped around the globe three times in three separate orbits, then stabbed into atmosphere, a glorious shooting star.

At a hundred feet altitude it paused, then snapped to the surface—but only *to* the surface. No fireworks, no crater—nothing more drastic than crushed grass. Its surface was scarred and pitted, blackened by the friction-heat of its fall; but it was intact.

Deep within its bowels echoed the words that would change the planet's destiny.

"Damn your bolt-brained bearings!"

The voice broke off; its owner frowned, listening.

The cabin was totally silent, without its usual threshold hum.

The young man swore, tearing the shock-webbing from his body. He lurched out of the acceleration chair, balanced dizzily on the balls of his feet, groping till his hand touched the plastic wall.

Steadying himself with one hand, he stumbled to a panel on the other side of the circular cabin. He fumbled the catches loose, cursing in the fine old style of galactic deck-hands, opened the panel, pressed a button. Turning, he all but fell back to the chair.

The soft hum awoke in the cabin again. A slurred voice asked, with varying speed and pitch, "Izzz awwl (Hic!) sadizfagtoreee . . . M'lorrr' Rodney?"

"All the smooth, glossy robots in the galaxy," muttered Milord, "and I get stuck with an epilepic!"

"Ivv ut bleeezz m'lorr', thuh c'passsider c'n be—"

"Replaced," finished Rodney, "and your circuits torn out and redesigned. No, thank you, I like your personality the

5

way it is—except when you pull off a landing that jars my clavicles loose!"

"Ivv m'lorrd will vorgive, ad thuh cruzhial momend ovvv blanetfall, I rezeived zome very zingular radio waves thad—"

"You got distracted, is that what you're trying to say?"

"M'lorrrd, id was imberative to analyze—"

"So part of you was studying the radio waves, and part of you was landing the ship, which was just a wee bit too much of a strain, and the weak capacitor gave. . . . Fess! How many times do I have to tell you to keep your mind on the job!"

"M'lorrd egzbressed a wizh to be like thuh—"

"Like the heroes of the Exploration Sagas, yes. But that doesn't mean I want their discomforts."

Fess's electronic system had almost recovered from the post-seizure exhaustion. "But, m'lorrd, the choncebt of heero-izm imblies—"

"Oh, forget it," Rodney groaned. Fess dutifully blanked a portion of his memory banks.

Fess was very dutiful. He was also an antique, one of the few remaining FCC (Faithful Cybernetic Companion) robots, early models now two thousand years out of date. The FCC robots had been programmed for extreme loyalty and, as a consequence, had perished in droves while defending their masters during the bloody Interregnum between the collapse of the ancient Galactic Union and the rise of the Proletarian Eclectic State of Terra.

Fess (a name derived from trying to pronounce "FCC" as a single word) had survived, thanks to his epilepsy. He had a weak capacitor that, when overstrained, released all its stored energy in a massive surge lasting several milliseconds. When the preliminary symptoms of this electronic seizure—mainly a fuzziness in Fess's calculations—appeared, a master circuit breaker popped, and the faulty capacitor discharged in isolation from the rest of Fess's circuits; but the robot was out of commission until the circuit breaker was reset.

Since the seizures occurred during moments of great stress —such as trying to land a spaceship-*cum*-asteroid while analyzing an aberrant radio wave, or trying to protect a master from three simultaneous murderers—Fess had survived the Interregnum; for, when the Proletarians had attacked his masters, he had fought manfully for about twenty-five seconds, then collapsed. He had thus become a rarity—

the courageous servant who had survived. He was one of five FCC robots still functioning.

He was, consequently, a prized treasure of the d'Armand family—prized as an antique, but even more for his loyalty; true loyalty to aristocratic families has always been in short supply.

So, when Rodney d'Armand had left home for a life of adventure and glory—being the second son of a second son, there hadn't been much else he could do—his father had insisted on his taking Fess along.

Rod had often been very glad of Fess's company; but there were times when the robot was just a little short on tact. For instance, after a very rough planetfall, a human stomach tends to be a mite queasy; but Fess had the bad sense to ask, "Would you care to dine, m'lord? Say, scallops with asparagus?"

Rod turned chartreuse and clamped his jaws, fighting back nausea. "No," he grated, "and can the 'm'lord' bit. We're on a mission, remember?"

"I never forget, Rod. Except on command."

"I know," growled his master's voice. "It was a figure of speech."

Rod swung his legs to the floor and painfully stood up. "I could use a breath of fresh air to settle my stomach, Fess. Is there any available?"

The robot clicked for a moment, then reported, "Atmosphere breathable. Better wear a sweater, though."

Rod shrugged into his pilot's jacket with a growl. "Why do old family retainers always develop a mother-hen complex?"

"Rod, if you had lived as long as I have—"

"—I'd want to be deactivated. I know, 'Robot is always right.' Open the lock, Fess."

The double doors of the small air lock swung open, showing a circle of black set with stars. A chill breeze poured into the cabin.

Rod tilted his face back, breathing in. His eyes closed in luxury. "Ah, the blessed breath of land! What lives here, Fess?"

Machinery whirred as the robot played back the electron-telescope tapes they had taken in orbit, integrating the pictorial data into a comprehensive description of the planet.

"Land masses consist of five continents, one island of note-worthy dimensions, and a host of lesser islands. The continent and the minor islands exhibit similar flora—equatorial rain forest."

"Even at the poles?"

"Within a hundred miles of each pole; the ice caps are remarkably small. Visible animal life confined to amphibians and a host of insects; we may assume that the seas abound with fish."

Rod rubbed his chin. "Sounds like we came in pretty early in the geologic spectrum."

"Carboniferous Era," replied the robot.

"How about that one large island? That's where we've landed, I suppose?"

"Correct. Native flora and fauna nonexistent. All lifeforms typical of Late Terran Pleistocene."

"How late, Fess?"

"Human historical."

Rod nodded. "In other words, a bunch of colonists came in, picked themselves an island, wiped out the native life, and seeded the land with Terran stock. Any idea why they chose this island?"

"Large enough to support a good-sized population, small enough to minimize problems of ecological revision. Then too, the island is situated in a polar ocean current, which lowers the local temperature to slightly below Terran normal."

"Very handy; saves them the bother of climate control. Any remains of what might have been Galactic Union cities?"

"None, Rod."

"None!" Rod's eyes widened in surprise. "That doesn't fit the pattern. You sure, Fess?"

The developmental pattern of a lost, or retrograde, colony —one that had been out of touch with Galactic civilization for a millennium or more—fell into three well-defined stages: first, the establishment of the colony, centered around a modern city with an advanced technology; second, the failure of communications with Galactic culture, followed by an overpopulation of the city, which led to mass migrations to the countryside and a consequent shift to an agrarian, self-sufficient economy; and, third, the loss of technological knowledge, accompanied by a rising level of superstition, symbolized by the abandonment and eventual tabooing of a coal-and-steam technology; social relationships calcified, and a caste system appeared. Styles of dress and architecture were usually burlesques of Galactic Union forms: for ex-

8

ample, a small hemispherical wooden hut, built in imitation of the vaulting Galactic geodesic domes.

But always there were the ruins of the city, acting as a constant symbol and a basis for mythology. Always.

"You're sure, Fess? You're really, really sure there isn't a city?"

"I am always certain, Rod."

"That's true." Rod pulled at his lower lip. "Sometimes mistaken, but never in doubt. Well, shelve the matter of the city for the time being; maybe it sank in a tidal wave. Let's just make a final check on the life-forms' being Terran."

Rod dove head-first through the three foot circle of the lock, landed in a forward roll, rose to his knees. He unclipped the guerilla knife from his belt—a knife carefully designed so that it could not be attributed to any one known culture—and drew the dagger from its sheath.

The sheath was a slender cone of white metal, with a small knob at the apex. Rod plucked several blades of grass, dropped them into the sheath, and turned the knob. The miniature transceiver built into the sides of the sheath probed the grass with sonics to analyze its molecular structure, then broadcast the data to Fess, who determined if any of the molecules were incompatible with human metabolism. If the grass had been poisonous to Rod, Fess would have beamed a signal back to the sheath, whereupon the white metal would have turned purple.

But in this particular case, the sheath stayed silver.

"That ties it," siad Rod. "This is Terran grass, presumably planted by Terrans, and this is a Terran colony. But where's the city?"

"There is a large town—perhaps thirty thousand souls—in the foothills of a mountain range to the north, Rod."

"Well . . ." Rod rubbed his chin. "That's not exactly what I had in mind, but it's better than nothing. What's it look like?"

"Situated on the lower slopes of a large hill, at the summit of which is a large stone structure, strongly reminiscent of a Medieval Terran castle."

"Medieval!" Rod scowled.

"The town itself consists of half-timbered and stuccoed buildings, with second stories overhanging the narrow streets —alleys would be a better term—along which they are situated."

"Half-timbered!" Rod rose to his feet. "Wait a minute, *wait a minute!* Fess, does that architecture remind you of anything?"

The robot was silent a moment, then replied, "Northern European Renaissance."

"That," said Rod, "is *not* the typical style of a retrograde colony. How closely do those buildings resemble Terran Renaissance, Fess?"

"The resemblance is complete to the last detail, Rod."

"It's deliberate then. How about that castle? Is that Renaissance too?"

The robot paused, then said, "No, Rod. It would appear to be a direct copy from the German style of the 13th Century A.D."

Rod nodded eagerly. "How about styles of dress?"

"We are currently on the night side of the planet, and were upon landing. There is a good deal of illumination from the planet's three satellites, but relatively few people abroad. . . . There is, however, a small party of soldiers, riding Terran horses. Their uniforms are—uh—copies of English Beefeaters'."

"Very good! Anyone else in the streets?"

"Um . . . a couple of cloaked men—uh—doublet and hose, I belive and . . . yes, a small party of peasants, wearing smocks and cross-gartered buskins. . . ."

"That's enough." Rod cut him off. "It's a hodgepodge, a conglomeration of styles. Somebody has tried to set up his idea of the ideal world, Fess. Ever hear of the Emigrés?"

The robot was silent a moment, mulling through his memory banks. Then he began to recite:

"Malcontents abounded toward the end of the 22nd Century A.D. Bored with their 'lives of quiet desperation,' people turned primarily to mysticism, secondarily to escapist literature and entertainment. Gradually the pseudo-Medieval became the dominant entertainment form.

"Finally, a group of wealthy men pooled their funds to buy an outmoded FTL liner and announced to the world that they were the Romantic Emigrés, that they intended to reestablish the glory of the Medieval way of life on a previously-uncolonized planet, and that they would accept a limited number of emigrants in the capacities of serfs and tradesmen.

"There were, of course, many more applicants than could be accommodated. Emigrants were selected 'for the poeticness of their souls'—whatever that may mean."

"It means they loved to listen to ghost stories," said Rod. "What happened?"

"The passenger list was swiftly completed. The thirteen tycoons who had organized the expedition announced that they thereby rejected their surnames and adopted instead the family names of great Medieval aristocrats—Bourbon, di Medici, and so forth.

"Then the ship departed, with its destination carefully unspecified, so that there would be 'no contamination from the materialist world.' Nothing more was ever heard of them."

Rod smiled grimly. "Well, I think we've just found them. How's *that* set with your diodes?"

"Quite well, Rod. In fact, a statistical analysis of the probability of this being the Emigrés' colony reveals the following—"

"Skip it," Rod said quickly. Statistics was Fess's hobby; given half a chance, he could bore you for hours.

Rod pursed his lips and eyed the section of the hull that housed Fess's brain. "Come to think of it, you might send the statistics back to SCENT with our educated guess that we've found the Emigrés' colony. Might as well get at that right now; I'd like them to know where we are in case anything happens."

SCENT, the Society for the Conversion of Extraterrestrial Nascent Totalitariansims, was the organization responsible for seeking out the lost colonies. The Proletarian Eclectic State of Terra had shown remarkably little interest in any colony that was lacking in modern technology; so that the lost colonies had stayed lost until the totalitarian rule of PEST had been overthrown by DDT, the Decentralized Democratic Tribunal. DDT had quickly consolidated its rule of Terra, governing in accordance with the almost-unattainable goals of Athenian democracy.

It had long been known that the inefficiency of democratic governments was basically a problem of communication and prejudice. But, over a period of two centuries, DDT cells had functioned as speakeasy schoolrooms, resulting in total literacy and masters' degrees for seventy-two percent of the population; prejudice had thus joined polio and cancer on the list of curable diseases. The problems of communication had been solved by the development, in DDT laboratories, of sub-molecular electronics, which had lowered the bulk and price of electronic communication gear to the point where its truly extensive use became practical for the first

11

time. Every individual was thus able to squawk at his Tribune at a moment's notice; and, being educated, they tended to do a lot of squawking just on general principles—all very healthy for a democracy.

Squawking by radio had proved singularly effective, due largely to an automatic record of the squawk. The problems of records and other bureaucratic red tape had been solved by red oxide audio recording tape, with tracks a single molecule in width, and the development of data-retrieval systems so efficient that the memorization of facts became obsolete. Education thus became exclusively a training in concepts, and the success of democracy was assured.

After two centuries of preparing such groundwork, the DDT revolution had been a mere formality.

But revolutionaries are always out of place when the revolution is over, and are likely to prove an embarrassing factor to the police forces of the new government.

Therefore, DDT had decided not to be selfish; rather, they would share the blessings of democracy with the other remnants of the old Galactic Union.

But democrats are seldom welcome on planets run by totalitarian governments, and scarcely more welcome on planets where anarchy prevails—this due to the very nature of democracy, the only practical compromise between totalitarianism and anarchy.

What was needed was a permanent organization of revolutionaries, subversive republican democrats. Since there was a large supply of out-of-work revolutionaries on hand, the organization was quickly formed, and christened the Society for the Conversion of Extraterrestrial Totalitarianisms. The "Nascent" was added a century later, when all the known inhabited planets had been subverted and had joined DDT. The old revolutionaries were still a problem, the more so since there were more of them; so they were sent out singly to find the Lost Colonies.

Thus was formed SCENT, the organization whose mission it was to sniff out the backward planets and put them on the road to democracy.

Since Rod had found a medieval planet, he would probably have to foster the development of a constitutional monarchy.

Rod, born Rodney d'Armand (he had five middle names, but they make dull reading) on a planet inhabited exclusively by aristocrats and robots, had joined SCENT at the tender

12

age of eighteen. In his ten years of service, he had grown from a gangling, ugly youth to a lean, well-muscled, ugly man.

His face was aristocratic; you could say that for it—that, and no more. His receding hairline gave onto a flat, sloping forehead that ran up against a brace of bony brow-ridges, somewhat camouflaged by bushy eyebrows. The eyebrows overhung deep sockets, at the back of which were two, somewhat hardened gray eyes—at least Rod hoped they looked hardened.

The eye sockets were thresholded by high, flat cheekbones, divided by a blade of nose that would have done credit to an eagle. Under the cheekbones and nose was a wide, thin-lipped mouth which, even in sleep, was twisted in a sardonic smile. Under the mouth was a square jawbone and a jutting chin.

Rod would have liked to say that it was a strong face, but it tended to soften remarkably when/if a girl smiled at it. Dogs and children had the same effect, with a great deal more frequency.

He was a man with a Dream (There had been a Dream Girl once, but she was now one with his callow youth.)— Dream of one unified Galactic government (democratic, of course). Interstellar communications were still too slow for a true democratic federation; the DDT was actually a loose confederation of worlds, more of a debating society and service organization than anything else.

But adequate communication methods would come along some day, Rod was sure of that, and when they did, the stars would be ready. He would see to that.

"Well, let's be about our business, Fess. No telling when someone might wander by and spot us." Rod swung up and into the air lock, through and into the cabin again. He went to the plate in the wall, released the catches. Inside was a control panel; above this was a white metal sphere with a dull finish, about the size of a basketball. A massive cable grew out of the top of the sphere and connected to the wall of the shop.

Rod unscrewed the connection, released the friction clamp that held the sphere in place, and carefully lifted it out.

"Easy," Fess's voice said from the earphone implanted in the bone behind Rod's right ear. "I'm fragile, you know."

"A little confidence, please," Rod muttered. The micro-

13

phone in his jawbone carried his words to Fess. "I haven't dropped you yet, have I?"

"Yet," echoed the robot.

Rod cradled the robot "brain" in the crook of one arm, leaving one arm free to negotiate the air lock. Outside again. he pressed a stud in the side of the ship. A large door lifted from the side of the pseudo-asteroid. Inside, a great black horse hung from shock webbing, head between its forelegs, eyes closed.

Rod pressed a button; a crane extended from the cargo space. The horse swung out on the crane, was lowered till its hooves touched the ground. Rod twisted the saddlehorn, and a panel in the horse's side slid open.

Rod placed the brain inside the panel, tightened the clamp and the connections, then twisted the saddlehorn back; the panel slid shut. Slowly the horse raised its head, wiggled its ears, blinked twice, gave a tentative whinny.

"All as it should be," said the voice behind Rod's ear. The horse champed at the bit. "If you'll let me out of this cat's cradle, I'll check the motor circuits."

Rod grinned and freed the webbing. The horse reared up, pawing the air, then sprang into a gallop. Rod watched the robot run, taking a good look at his surroundings in the process.

The asteroid-ship had landed in the center of a meadow, shaggy with summer grass, ringed by oak, hickory, maple, and ash. It was night, but the meadow was flooded with the light of three moons.

The robot cantered back toward Rod, reared to a halt before him. Forehooves thudded on the ground; the great indigo eyes turned to look at Rod, the ears pricked forward.

"I'm fit," Fess reported.

Rod grinned again. "No sight like a running horse."

"What, none?"

"Well, almost none. C'mon, let's get the ship buried."

Rod pressed studs on the side of the ship; the cargo hatch closed, the air lock sealed itself. The ship began to revolve, slowly at first, then faster and faster as it sank into the ground. Soon there was only a crater surrounded by a ring-wall of loam, and the roof of the asteroid curving three feet below.

Rod pulled a camp shovel from Fess's saddlebags, unfolded it, and bent to his task. The horse joined in, flashing

14

out with its heels at the ring-wall. In ten minutes the wall had been reduced to six inch height; there was a large mound of earth in the center, twenty feet across and two feet high.

"Stand back." Rod drew his dagger, twisted the hilt 180 degrees, pointed the haft at the earth-mound. A red light lanced out; the loam glowed cherry red, melted, and flowed.

Rod fanned the beam in a slow arc over the whole of the filled-in crater till the soil had melted down a foot below ground level. He shoveled the rest of the ring-wall into the hole, making a slight mound, but the next rain would take care of that.

"Well, that's it." Rod wiped his brow.

"Not quite."

Rod hunched his shoulders; there was a sinking feeling in his belly.

"You have still to assume clothing appropriate to this society and period, Rod."

Rod squeezed his eyes shut.

"I took the precaution of packing a doublet in my left-hand saddlebag while you were testing the grass, Rod."

"Look," Rod argued, "my uniform will do well enough, won't it?"

"Skintight trousers and military boots will pass, yes. But a pilot's jacket could not possibly be mistaken for a doublet. Need I say more?"

"No, I suppose not." Rod sighed. He went to the saddle-bag. "The success of the mission comes first, above and before any considerations of personal comfort, dignity, or—hey!" He stared at something long and slender, hanging from the saddle.

"Hey what, Rod?"

Rod took the strange object from the saddle—it had a handle on one end, he noticed, and it rattled—and held it up where Fess could see it.

"What is *this?*"

"An Elizabethan rapier, Rod. An antique sidearm, a sort of long knife, designed for both cutting and thrusting."

"Sidearm." Rod eyed the robot as if doubting his sanity. "I'm supposed to wear it?"

"Certainly, Rod. At least, if you're planning to adopt one of your usual covers."

Rod gave a sign appropriate to a Christian martyr and

pulled the doublet from the saddlebag. He wriggled into it and belted the rapier to his right side.

"No, no, Rod! Belt it to your *left* side. You have to cross-draw it."

"The things I go through for the sake of democracy. . . ." Rod belted the rapier to his left hip. "Fess, has it ever occurred to you that I might be a fanatic?"

"Certainly, Rod. A classic case of sublimation."

"I asked for an opinion, not an analysis," the man growled. He looked down at his costume. "Hey! Not bad, not bad at all!" He threw his shoulders back, lifted his chin, and strutted. The gold and scarlet doublet fairly glowed in the moonlight. "How do you like it, Fess?"

"You cut quite a figure, Rod." There was, somehow, a tone of quiet amusement in the robot's voice.

Rod frowned. "Needs a cape to top it off, though."

"In the saddlebag, Rod."

"Think of everything, don't you?" Rod rummaged in the saddlebag, shook out a voluminous cloak of the same electric blue as his uniform tights.

"The chain passes under the left armpit and around the right-hand side of the neck, Rod."

Rod fastened the cloack in place and faced into the wind, the cloak streaming back from his broad shoulders.

"There, now! Ain't I a picture, though?"

"Like a plate from a Shakespeare text, Rod."

"Flattery will get you a double ration of oil." Rod swung into the saddle. "Head for the nearest town, Fess. I want to show off my new finery."

"You forgot to seed the crater, Rod."

"What? Oh! Yeah." Rod pulled a small bag from the right-hand saddlebag and sprinkled its contents over the circle of raw earth. "There! Give it a light rainstorm and two days to grow, and you won't be able to tell it from the rest of the meadow. Let's hope nobody comes this way for two days, though. . . ."

The horse's head jerked up, ears pricked forward.

"What's the matter, Fess?"

"Listen," the robot replied.

Rod scowled and closed his eyes.

Distant, blown on the wind, came youthful shouts and gay laughter.

"Sounds like a bunch of kids having a party."

"It's coming closer," Fess said softly.

16

Rod shut his eyes and listened again. The sound *was* growing louder . . .

He turned to the northeast, the direction the sound seemed to be coming from, and scanned the horizon. There were only the three moons in the sky.

A shadow drifted across one of the moons. Three more followed it.

The laughter was much louder now.

"About seventy-five miles per hour," Fess murmured.

"What?"

"Seventy-five miles per hour. That's the speed at which they seem to be approaching."

"Hmmm." Rod chewed at his lower lip. "Fess, how long since we landed?"

"Almost two hours, Rod."

Something streaked by overhead.

Rod looked up. "Ah, Fess?"

"Yes, Rod."

"They're flying, Fess."

There was a pause.

"Rod, I must ask you to be logical. A culture like this couldn't possibly have evolved air travel yet."

"They haven't. *They're* flying."

Another pause.

"The people themselves, Rod?"

"That's right." Rod's voice held a note of resignation. "Though I'll admit that one who just flew over us seemed to be riding a broomstick. Not too bad-looking, either. Matter of fact, she was stacked like a Las Vegas poker deck . . . Fess?"

The horse's legs were locked rigid, its head swinging gently between its legs.

"Oh, hell!" Rod growled. "Not again!"

He reached down under the saddlehorn and reset the circuit breaker. Slowly, the horse raised its head and shook it several times. Rod caught the reins and led the horse away.

"Whaddappend, RRRawwwd?"

"You had a seizure, Fess. Now, whatever you do, *don't* whinny. That airborne bacchanalia is coming our way, and there's an off chance they might be out to investigate the shooting star. Therefore, we are heading for the tall timber—and *quietly*, if you please."

Once under the trees at the edge of the meadow, Rod looked back to check on the flying flotilla.

The youngsters were milling about in the sky half a mile away, emitting joyful shrieks and shouts of welcome. The wind tossed Rod an intelligible phrase or two.

"Rejoice, my children! 'Tis Lady Gwen!"

"Hast thou, then, come at last to be mother to our coven, Gwendylon?"

"Thy beauty hath but waxed, sweet Gwendylon! How dost thou?"

"Not yet robbing cradles, Randal. . . ."

"Sounds like the housemother dropping in on a party at the Witches' College," Rod grunted. "Sober, Fess?"

"Clearheaded, at least," the robot acknowledged, "and a new concept accepted in my basic programming."

"Oh." Rod pursed his lips. "My observation is confirmed?"

"Thoroughly. They *are* flying."

The aerial sock-hop seemed to have rediscovered its original purpose. They swooped toward the meadows with shouts and gales of laughter, hovered over the ring of newly-turned earth, and dropped one by one to form a circle about it.

"Well, not too many doubts about what they're here for, is there?" Rod sat on the ground, tailor-fashion, and leaned back against Fess's forelegs. "Nothing to do but wait, I guess." He twisted the signet on his ring ninety degrees, pointed it at the gathering. "Relay, Fess."

The signet ring now functioned as a very powerful, very directional microphone; its signal was relayed through Fess to the earphone behind Rod's ear.

"Ought we to tell the Queen of this?"

"Nay, 'twould fash her unduly."

Rod frowned. "Can you make anything out of it, Fess?"

"Only that it's Elizabethan English, Rod."

"That," said Rod, "is why SCENT always sends a man with a robot. All right, let's start with the obvious: the language confirms that this is the Emigré's colony."

"Well, of course," Fess muttered, somewhat piqued.

"Now, now, old symbiote, no griping. I know you don't consider the obvious worth reporting; but overlooking obvious facts does sometimes lead to overlooking secrets hidden right out in plain sight, doesn't it?"

"Well . . ."

"Right. So. They mentioned a Queen. Therefore, the government is a monarchy, as we suspected. This teenage in-group referred to themselves as a coven; therefore they consider themselves witches. . . . Considering their form of loco-motion, I'm inclined to agree. But . . ."

He left the *but* hanging for a few minutes. Fess picked up his ears. `

"They also spoke of telling the Queen. Therefore, they must have access to the royal ear. What's this, Fess? Royal approval of witchcraft?"

"Not necessarily," said Fess judiciously. "An applicable precedent would be the case of King Saul and the Witch of Endor. . . ."

"But chances are they've got an in at court."

"Rod, you are jumping to conclusions."

"No, just coming up with a brilliant flash of insight."

"That," said Fess, "is why SCENT always sends a robot with a human."

"Touché. But they also said that telling the Queen would 'fash her unduly.' What's *fash* mean, Fess?"

"To cause anxiety, Rod."

"Um. This Queen just might be the excitable type, then."

"*Might* be, yes."

Music struck up in the field—Scottish bagpipes playing the accompaniment to an old Gypsy tune. The young folk were dancing on the cleared earth, and several feet above it.

"Bavarian peasant dance," Fess murmured.

" 'Where the ends of the earth all meet,' " Rod quoted, stretching his legs out straight. "An agglomerate culture, carefully combining all the worst Old Earth had to offer."

"An unfair judment, Rod."

Rod raised an eyebrow. "You *like* bagpipes?"

He folded his arms and let his chin rest on his sternum, leaving Fess the sleepless to watch for anything significant.

The robot watched for a couple of hours, patiently chewing his data. When the music faded and died, Fess planted a hoof on Rod's hip.

"Gnorf!" said Rod, and was instantly wide awake, as is the wont of secret agents.

"The party's over, Rod."

The young folk were leaping into the air, banking away to the northeast.

One broomstick shot off at right angles to the main body; a boyish figure shot out after it.

"Do thou not be so long estranged from us again, Gwendylon."

"Randal, if thou wert a mouse, thou wouldst woo oli-

19

phants! Farewell, and see to it from now thou payest court to wenches only six years thy elder!"

The broomstick streaked straight toward Rod, climbed over the trees and was gone.

"Mmm, yes!" Rod licked his lips. "Definitely a great build on that girl. And the way she talks, she's a wee bit older than these birdbrains. . . ."

"I had thought you were above petty conquest by now, Rod."

"Which is a nice way of saying she wouldn't have anything to do with me. Well, even if I haven't got the buying power, I can still window-shop."

The junior coven sailed over the horizon; their laughter faded away.

"Well, that's that." Rod gathered his feet under him. "The party's over, and we're none the wiser." He rose to his feet. "Well, at least we're still a secret; nobody knows there's a spaceship under that circle of earth."

"Nay, not so," chuckled a pixie voice.

Rod froze, turned his head, stared.

There, among the roots of an old oak, stood a man, broad-shouldered, grinning, and all of twelve inches tall. He was clad in doublet and hose in varying shades of brown, and had very white teeth and a general air of mischief.

"The King of the Elves shall be apprised of your presence, Lord Warlock," said the apparition, chuckling.

Rod lunged.

But the little man was gone, leaving only a chortle behind him.

Rod stood staring, listening to the wind commenting to the leaves and the last faint snicker dying away among the oak roots.

"Fess," he said. "Fess, did you see that?"

There was no answer.

Rod frowned, turning. "Fess? Fess!"

The robot's head swung gently between its fetlocks.

"Oh, hell!"

A deep-toned bell was proclaiming the advent of nine o'clock somewhere in the large, ramshackle town that was, as near as Rod and Fess could figure from speed and bearing, the juvenile witches' home base. In view of their remark about the Queen, Rod had hopes the town would turn out to be the capital of the island.

20

"Only a guess, of course," he added hurriedly.

"Of course," Fess murmured. The robot voice gave the distinct impression of a patient sigh.

"On a more immediate level, what name should I go by in this culture?"

"Why not Rodney d'Armand VII? This is one of the few cases where your natural name is appropriate."

Rod shook his head. "Too pretentious. My forebears never did get over their aristocratic aspirations."

"They *were* aristocrats, Rod."

"Yeah, but so was everybody else on the planet, Fess, except the robots. And they'd been in the family so long they had a right to claim some of the honors."

"It was honor enough to—"

"Later," Rod cut him off. Fess had a standardized sermon on the *noblesse oblige* tradition of the Maxima robots, which he would gladly deliver at the drop of anything resembling a cue. "There's a small problem of a name, remember?"

"If you insist." Fess was disgruntled. "Mercenary soldier, again?"

"Yes. It gives me an excuse to travel."

Fess winced. "You could pose as a wandering minstrel . . ."

Rod shook his head. "Minstrels are supposed to be up on the current news. Might not be a bad idea to pick up a harp, though—especially if the ruler's a woman. Songs can get you places where swords can't. . . ."

"We go through this every time. . . . Would 'Gallowglass' suit you, Rod? It was the Irish term for a mercenary soldier."

"Gallowglass . . ." Rod rolled the word over his tongue. "Not bad. That's got some dash to it."

"Like yourself."

"Do I detect a touch of irony there? But it *is* a good, solid word . . . and it's not exactly what you'd call pretty. . . ."

"Definitely like yourself," the robot murmured.

"I daresay it'll do. Rod Gallowglass it is. *Whoa!*"

Rod sawed back on the reins, frowning. From someplace ahead of them came the low mutter of a mob.

Rod frowned. "What's all the commotion?"

"Rod, may I recommend caution . . ."

"Not a bad idea. Gee-up again, but lightly with the hooves, please."

Fess went at a walk through the narrow moonlit street, sidling up against the weathered wall of a building. He stopped at the corner, thrust his horse's head around the angle.

"What do you see, Sister Ann?"

"A mob," said Fess.

"Astute observation, Watson. Anything else?"

"Torchlight, and a young man climbing up on a platform. If you'll pardon the analogy, Rod, it closely resembles a pep rally at your alma mater."

"Just might be what it is." Rod swung out of the saddle. "Well, you stay here, big fella. I'll scout the terrain."

He rounded the corner and let himself fall into a soldierly swagger, one hand on the pommel of his sword.

Not a bad idea, from the look of the crowd. Must be a meeting of the local Vagabond's Union. Not an unpatched doublet among them. He wrinkled his nose; a washed body seemed to be even more rare. Definitely a seedy lot.

The meeting-place was a large, open square, bordered by a wide river on one side; there were wharves with wooden ships riding at their moorings. On the other three sides of the square were cheap, decaying lodging-houses; sea-tackle stores and other cheap shops, and warehouses. The warehouses, at least, were in good repair. All the buildings were half-timbered, with the characteristic overhanging second story.

The shouting, jostling mob filled the whole square. Flaming pine knots lent a demonic light.

A closer look at the crowd revealed patched eyes, shriveled limbs, heads minus ears—an odd contrast to the figure that stood on the jury-rigged platform.

He was young, broad-shouldered and blond-headed. His face was clean and unscarred, snub-nosed and blue-eyed. It was a round, almost innocent face, open and honest, filled with the eerie light of a Man with a Mission. His doublet and hose were clean, for a wonder, and well-tailored from good cloth. A sword hung at his hip.

"A kid from the right side of the tracks," Rod mused. "What in the Seventh Hell is he doing in this rathole?"

The youth threw up his hands; the crowd roared, pine-knot torches surged forward to light him.

"Whose shoulders have borne up the weightiest burdens?" the boy shouted.

"Ours!" roared the crowd.

"Whose hands are worn hard and scarred with rough toil?"

"Ours!"

"Who is it have built all the wealth that the noblemen squander?"

"We!"

"Who is it have reared up their lofty castles of granite?"

"We!"

"Shall you not have a share in these riches and luxuries?"

"We shall!"

"Why," roared the young spokesman, "there is wealth enough in even one of these castles to make each one of you a king!"

The crowd went wild.

"You catching this, Fess?"

"I am, Rod. It sounds like a mixture of Karl Marx and Huey Long."

"Strange synthesis," Rod muttered. "And yet, maybe not so strange, when you come to think of it."

"This is your wealth!" shouted the youth. "You have a *right* to it!"

The crowd went wild again.

"Will they give you your due?"

The crowd went suddenly quiet. An ugly murmur began.

"No!" the young man bellowed. "You must therefore demand it, as is your right!"

He threw up his arms. "The Queen has given you bread and wine when the famine was upon you! The Queen has given meat and good wine to the witches whom she harbors!"

The crowd fell deathly still. A whisper ran through the ranks: "The witches! The witches!"

"Aye," roared the spokesman, "even the witches, the outcast and spurned. How much more, then, will she give to you, who have borne the heat of the day?

"She will give you your due!"

The crowd echoed his roar.

"Where do you go?" yelled the young Demosthenes.

"To the castle!" someone shouted, and other voices took up the cry. "To the castle! To the castle!" It became a rhythmic chant. "To the castle! To the castle! To the castle!"

A high, keening wail cut across the chant. The crowd fell silent. A narrow, twisted figure hobbled to the edge of a warehouse roof and called out over the square:

"Soldiers, a company or more!"

"Out through the alleys and wharves!" bellowed the young

man. "At the House of Clovis we shall meet, within the hour!"

To Rod's amazement, the crowd remained silent. Streams of people began to pour down the twisted alleys. There was no panic, no crush.

Rod shrank into a doorway and watched as the torches were grounded. Score upon score of beggars ran past him, light-footed and silent, to be swallowed up by the dark mouths of the byways.

The square emptied; the light sounds of scampering faded away. In the sudden quiet, Rod heard the drum of approaching hooves—the soldiers, coming to check up on the Queen's loyal subjects.

Rod stepped out onto the cobbles, running on the balls of his feet, around the corner where Fess stood waiting.

He was into the saddle without breaking stride. "The good part of town," he whispered, "fast and quiet."

Fess could extrude inch-thick rubber pads from his hooves when silence was called for; he had also memorized a photo-map of the city from their aerial survey. There are advantages to a robot horse.

They fled through the town; the ground rose beneath them, building into the hill crowned by the royal castle. The quality of the buildings improved gradually; they were coming to the more affluent districts.

"What do you make of all that, Fess?"

"A totalitarian movement, beyond question," the robot replied. "A rabble-rouser, no doubt power-hungry, who will lead the people to make demands on the goverment, demands which cannot be met. The crown's refusals will be used to incite the mob to violence, and you have your revolution made."

"Couldn't be just an ambitious nobleman trying to usurp the crown?"

"Usurpation derives its support from the upper classes, Rod. No, this is a proletarian revolution—a prelude to a totalitarian government."

Rod pursed his lips. "Would you say there was evidence of outside intervention from a more advanced society? I mean, proletarian revolutions aren't usually found in this kind of culture, are they?"

"Rarely, Rod, and the propaganda is rudimentary when they do occur. Persuasion in a medieval society never refers

24

to basic rights; the concept is alien to the culture. The probability of intervention is quite strong. . . ."

Rod's lips pulled back in a savage grin. "Well, old mechanism, it looks like we've come to the right place to set up shop."

At the uphill edge of the town, they came on a rambling, two-storied structure built around three sides of a torchlit courtyard. A timber palisade with a gate closed the fourth side. A party of laughing, well-dressed young men sauntered out of the gate; Rod caught a snatch of drunken song. Tableware rattled, and voices called for meat and ale.

"I take it we've found one of the better inns."

"I would say that was a warranted assumption, Rod."

Rod leaned back in the saddle. "Looks like a good place to spend the night. Is garlic sausage possible in this culture, Fess?"

The robot shuddered. "Rod, you have the most unearthly tastes!"

"Make way, make way!" a voice trumpeted behind him.

Turning, Rod saw a party of soldiers, cavalry, trotting toward him. Behind them rolled a gilded, richly-carved carriage.

A herald rode in front of the soldiers. "Stand aside from the road, fellow!" he called. "The Queen's coach passes!"

"Queen!" Rod's eyebrows shot up. "Yes, yes! By all means, let's stand aside!"

He nudged Fess with his knee. The horse whirled off the road and jockeyed for a position on the shoulder that would give Rod a good look at the royal party.

The curtains on the coach were half drawn, but there was looking space. A lantern cast a warm yellow glow inside the coach, affording Rod a brief glimpse as the coach spun by.

A slender, frail form wrapped in a dark, hooded traveling cloak; a pale, small-boned face framed with blond, almost platinum hair; large, dark eyes; and small, very red lips drawn up in a pout.

And young, very young—scarcely past childhood, Rod thought.

She sat ramrod straight, looking very fragile but also very determined—and, somehow, forlorn, with the hostile, chip-on-the-shoulder attitude that so often goes with fear and loneliness.

Rod stared after the retreating party.

"Rod."

Rod started, shook his head, and realized that the coach had been out of sight for a while.

He glowered at the back of the horse's head. "What is it, Fess?"

"I wondered if you'd fallen asleep." The black head turned to Rod, the great eyes laughing gently.

"No." Rod twisted, looking back at the turn where the coach had disappeared.

Fess schooled his voice to patience. "The Dream again, Rod?"

Rod scowled. "I thought robots didn't have emotions."

"No. But we *do* have an innate dislike of a lack of that quality which has often been termed common sense."

Rod threw him a sour smile. "And, of course, an appreciation for that quality called irony, since it's basically logical. And irony implies—"

"—a sense of humor, yes. And you must admit, Rod, that there is something innately humorous in a man's chasing an object of his own invention over half a galaxy."

"Oh yeah, it's a million yuks, sure. But isn't that the difference between a man and a robot, Fess?"

"What? The ability to form imaginary constructions?"

"No, the ability to get hung up on them. Well, let's see if we can't find you a quiet stall where you can chew your data in peace."

Fess turned and trotted through the inn-yard gate.

A hostler came running from the stables as Rod dismounted. Rod tossed him the reins, said, "Don't give him too much water," and strolled into the big common room.

Rod hadn't known that rooms could be smoky without tobacco. Obviously, chimney-building was numbered among the underdeveloped sciences on this planet.

The customers didn't seem to mind, though. The room was filled with laughter, coarse jokes, and coarser voices in loud conversation. The great room was taken up by twenty or so large, round tables; there were several smaller tables, occupied by people whose dress marked them above the common (but not high enough to be staying at the castle). Lighting consisted of pine torches, which added to the atmosphere; tallow candles, dripping nicely on the guests; and a huge fireplace, fit to roast an ox, which was exactly what it was doing at the moment.

A small horde of boys and stocky peasant girls kept a

steady stream of food and drink passing between the tables and the kitchen; many of them displayed considerable skill at broken-field running.

A large balding man with an apron tied around his ample middle burst out of the kitchen with a great smoking platter —the landlord, at a guess. Business was good tonight.

The man looked up, saw Rod, took in the gold and scarlet doublet, sword and dagger, the general air of authority, the well-filled purse—most especially the purse—and shoved the platter at the nearest serving girl. He bustled up to Rod, rubbing his hands on his apron.

"And how may I serve you, good master?"

"With a tankard of ale, a steak as thick as both your thumbs, and a table alone." Rod smiled as he said it.

The innkeeper stared, his lips forming a round O—Rod had apparently done something out of the ordinary.

Then the old man's eyes took on a calculating look, one that Rod had seen before; it was usually accompanied by a remark to the waiter, *sotto voce*, "Soft touch. Soak him for all he's worth."

Rod had smiled.

He should have known better.

Some things can be undone, though. Rod let his smile droop into a scowl.

"Well, what are you waiting for?" he barked. "Be quick about it, or I'll dine on a slice off your backside!"

The landlord jumped, then cringed, bowing rapidly.

"But of course, m'lord, of course! Quickly it will be, good master; yes, quickly indeed!" He turned away.

Rod's hand clamped onto his shoulder. "The table," he reminded.

The landlord gulped and bobbed his head, led Rod to a table beside an upright log that served as a pillar, and scurried away—cursing under his breath, no doubt.

Rod returned the courtesy, but enlarged the object to include all that the landlord stood for, namely the mercenary ways of mankind.

And, of course, wound up cursing himself for having catered to Mammon by getting tough.

But what could he do? SCENT agents were supposed to remain inconspicuous, and a softhearted medieval bourgeois was a contradiction in terms.

But when the landlord said quickly, he meant it. The steak and ale appeared almost before Rod had sat down. The landlord stood by rubbing his hands on his apron and looking very worried. Waiting for Rod to accept the cooking, probably.

Rod opened his mouth to reassure the man, and stopped with a word not quite past his larynx. His nosed twitched; a slow grin spread over his face. He looked up at the landlord.

"Do I smell garlic sausage?"

"Oh yes, your worship!" The landlord started bobbing again. "Garlic sausage it is, your worship, and very fine garlic sausage too, if I may say so. If your worship would care for some . . . ?"

"My worship would," said Rod, "and *presto allegro*, sirrah."

The landlord shied, reminding Rod of Fess regarding a syllogism, and ran.

Now, what was that all about? Rod wondered. Must have been something he said. And he'd been rather proud of that sirrah. . . .

He sampled the steak, and had just washed it down when a plate of sausage *thunked!* onto the table.

"Very good," said Rod, "and the steak is acceptable."

The landlord's face broke into a grin of relief; he turned to go, then turned back.

"Well, what is it?" Rod asked around a mouthful of sausage.

The landlord was twisting his hands in his apron again. "Beg pardon, my master, but . . ." His lips twisted too, then the words burst out. "Art a warlock, m'master?"

"Who, me? A warlock? Ridiculous!" For emphasis, Rod jabbed his table knife in the landlord's general direction. The huge belly shrank in amazingly; then it bolted, taking its owner along.

Now where did he get the idea I was a warlock? Rod mused as he chewed a mouthful of steak.

Never had a better steak, he decided. *Must be the smoke. Wonder what wood they're using?*

Must have been the presto allegro *bit. Thought they were magic words, probably. . . .*

Well, they *had* worked wonders.

Rod took a bite of sausage and a swig of ale.

Him, a warlock? Never! He might be a second son of a second son, but he wasn't *that* desperate.

Besides, being a warlock involved signing a contract in

28

blood, and Rod had no blood to spare. He kept losing it in the oddest places. . . .

He drained his tankard, set it down with a thump. The landlord materialized with a jug and poured him a refill. Rod started a smile of thanks, remembered his station, and changed the smile to a sneer. He fumbled in his purse, felt the irregular shape of a gold nugget—acceptable currency in a medieval society—remembered the quickness of the house to gyp the generous, and passed over the nugget in favor of a sliver of silver.

The landlord stared at the small white bar in the palm of his hand, his eyes making a valiant attempt to turn into hemispheres. He made a gargling sound, stuttered elaborate thanks, and scurried away.

Rod bit his lip in annoyance. Apparently even so small a chunk of silver was enough to excite comment here.

The touch of anger dissipated quickly, though; a pound or two of beef in the belly *did* tend to make the world look better. Rod threw his legs out in the aisle, stretched, and slumped backward in the chair, picking his teeth with the table knife.

Something was strangely wrong in this common room. The happy were a little too professional about it—voices a shade too loud, laughter a trifle strained, with a dark echo. The glum, on the other hand, were *really* glum; their brown studies were paneled in walnut.

Fear.

Take that pair at three o'clock on the third table from the right, now—they were awfully earnest about whatever it was they were hashing over. Rod gave his ring a surreptitious nudge and pointed it at the twosome.

"But such meetings do no good if the Queen is continually sending her soldiers against us!"

" 'Tis true, Adam, 'tis true; she won't hear us, for, when all's said and done, she won't let us close enough to speak."

"Why, then, she must be forced to listen!"

"Aye, but what good would that do? Her nobles would not let her give what we demand."

Adam slammed his open hand on the table. "But we've a right to be free without being thieves and beggars! The debtors' prisons must end, and the taxes with them!"

"Aye, and so must the cutting off of an ear for the theft of a loaf of bread." He rubbed the side of his head, with a hangdog look on his face. "Yet she hath contrived to do summat for us . . ."

"Aye, this setting-up of her own judges now! The great lords will no longer give each their justice, by style and taste."

"The nobles will not bear it, and that thou knowest. The judges will not stand long." One-Ear's face was grim; he traced circles on the wet tabletop.

"Nay, the noblemen will stand for naught that the Queen designs!" Adam plunged his knife into the tabletop. "Will not the Loguire see that?"

"Nay, speak not against the Loguire!" One-Ear's face darkened. "If 'twere not for him, we would still be a ragtag horde, with no common purpose! Speak not against Loguire, Adam, for without him, we would not have the brass to sit in this inn, where the Queen's soldiers are but guests!"

"Oh, aye, aye, he pulled us together and made men of us thieves. Yet now he holds our new manhood in check; he seeks to keep us from fighting for that which is ours!"

One-Ear's mouth turned down tight at the corners. "Thou hast hearkened too much to the idle and envious chatter of the Mocker, Adam!"

"Yet fight we must, mark my words!" Adam cried, clenching his fist. "Blood must be shed ere we come to our own. Blood must answer for blood, and 'tis blood the nobles have ta'en from—"

Something huge slammed into Rod, knocking him back against the table, filling his head with the smell of sweat and onions and cheap wine.

Rod braced an arm against the table and shoved with his shoulder. The heavy form swayed away with a *whuff!* of breath. Rod drew his dagger and thumbed the signet ring to off.

The man loomed over him, looking eight feet tall and wide as a wagon.

"Here now!" he growled. "Why doncha look where I'm going at?"

Rod's knife twisted, gleaming light into the man's eyes. "Stand away, friend," he said softly. "Leave an honest man to his ale."

"An honest man, is it!" The big peasant guffawed. "A sojer, callin' hisself an honest man!" His roaring laughter was echoed from the tables.

On an off bet, Rod decided, strangers weren't popular here.

The laughter stopped quite suddenly. "Nay, put down your plaything," said the big man, suddenly sober, "and I'll show you an honest villager can outfight a sojer."

A prickle ran down Rod's spine as he realized it was a put-up job. The landlord had advised the big ox of the whereabouts of a heavy purse. . . .

"I've no quarrel with you," Rod muttered. He realized it was the worst thing he could have said almost before the words were off his tongue.

The big man leered, gloating. "No quarrel, he says now. He throws hisself in the path of a poor staggering man so's he can't help but ran into him. But, 'No quarrel,' sez he, when he's had a look at Big Tom!"

A huge, meaty hand buried itself in the cloth at Rod's throat, pulling him to his feet. "Nay, I'll show you a quarrel," Big Tom snarled.

Rod's right hand lashed out, chopping into the man's elbow, then bouncing away. The big man's hand loosened and fell, temporarily numbed. Big Tom stared at his hand, a look of betrayal.

Rod pressed his lips together, tucked his knife into the sheath. He stepped back, knees flexed, rubbed his right fist in his left palm. The peasant was big, but he probably knew nothing of boxing.

Life came back into Tom's hand, and with it, pain. The huge man bellowed in anger, his hand balling into a fist, swinging at Rod in a vast roundhouse swipe that would have annihilated anything it struck.

But Rod ducked under and to the side and, as the fist went by him, reached up behind Tom's shoulder and gave a solid push to add to the momentum of the swing.

Big Tom spun around; Rod caught the man's right wrist and twisted it up behind Tom's back. Rod jerked the wrist up a little higher; Big Tom howled. While he was howling, Rod's arm snaked under Tom's armpit to catch the back of his neck in a half nelson.

Not bad, Rod thought. So far he hadn't needed boxing.

Rod planted a knee in Tom's backside as he released his holds; Tom blundered into the open space before the hearth, tried to catch his balance, and didn't make it. Overturned tables clattered and thudded as the patrons scuttled back, all too glad to leave the fireside seat to Big Tom.

He came to his knees, shaking his head, and looked up to see Rod standing before him in a wrestler's crouch, smiling grimly and beckoning with both arms.

Tom growled low in his throat and braced a foot against the fieldstones of the hearth.

He shot at Rod head-first, like a bull.

Rod sidestepped and stuck out a foot. Big Tom went flailing straight for the first row of tables. Rod squeezed his eyes shut and set his teeth.

There was a crash like four simultaneous strikes in a bowling alley. Rod winced. He opened his eyes and forced himself to look.

Big Tom's head emerged out of a welter of woodwork, wide-eyed and slack-jawed.

Rod shook his head sadly, clucking his tongue."You've had a rough night, Big Tom. Why don't you go home and sleep it off?"

Tom picked himself up, shin, wristbone, and clavicle, and put himself back together, taking inventory the while.

Satisfied that he was a gestalt again, he stamped a foot, planted his fists on his hips, and looked up at Rod.

"Here now, man!" he complained. "You don't half fight like an honest gentleman!"

"Not hardly a gentleman at all," Rod agreed. "What do you say we try one more throw, Tom? Double or nothing!"

The big man looked down at his body as if doubting its durability. He kicked at the remains of an oak table tentatively, slammed a fist into his own tree-trunk biceps, and nodded.

"I'll allow as I'm fit," he said. "Come on, little man."

He stepped out onto the cleared floor in front of the hearth, walking warily around the perimeter, keeping one baleful eye on Rod.

"Our good landlord told you I had silver in my purse, didn't he?" said Rod, his eyes snapping.

Big Tom didn't answer.

"Told you I was an easy mark, too," Rod mused. "Well, he was wrong on both counts.

Big Tom's eyes bulged. He gave a bellow of distress. "No silver?"

Rod nodded. "I thought he told you." His eyes flicked over to the landlord, ashen and trembling by a pillar.

And looked back to see Big Tom's foot heading right toward his midriff.

Rod fell back, swinging both hands up to catch Big Tom's heel and inspire it to greater heights.

Tom's foot described a neat arc. For a moment, he hung in the air, arms flailing; then he crashed howling to the floor.

Rod's eyes filled with pain as Big Tom floundered about, struggling for the breath that the floor had knocked out of him.

Rod stepped in, grabbed the front of Tom's tunic, braced his foot against Tom's and threw his weight back, hauling the big man to his feet. Tom immediately sagged forward; Rod shoved a shoulder under Tom's armpit and pushed the big man back to the vertical.

"Ho, landlord!" he shouted. "Brandy—and fast!"

Rod liked to think of himself as the kind of man people could lean on, but this was ridiculous.

When Big Tom had been somewhat revived and commended to the gentle jeers of his booze buddies, and the guests had somewhat restored the room and resumed their places, and Rod had still not wreaked anything resembling vengeance on the landlord, that worthy's eyes sparked with a sudden hope. He appeared again before Rod, his chin thrust out and the corners of his mouth drawn down.

Rod hauled himself out of the depths of a rather cynical contemplation of man's innate goodness and focused on the landlord. "Well, what do you want?"

The landlord swallowed thickly. "If it please your worship there's a little matter of some broken chairs and tables. . . ."

"Chairs," said Rod, not moving. "Tables."

He slammed to his feet and coiled a hand around the innkeeper's neck. "Why, you slimy little curmudgeon! You set that ox on me, you try to rob me, and you have the gall to stand there and tell me I owe you money?" He emphasized each point with a shake of the landlord's neck, slowly pushing him back against the pillar. The landlord made a masterful attempt to blend into the bark, but only succeeded in spreading himself thin.

"And to top it all off, my ale's gotten warm!" Rod shouted. "You call yourself a landlord, and you treat a gentleman of arms like *this?*"

"Forgive, master, forgive!" the landlord rattled, clawing at Rod's hand with commendable effort and negative effect. "I meant no harm, your worship; I meant only—"

"Only to rob me, yes!" Rod snorted, letting him go with

a toss that fetched him up backward over a table. "Beware the kind, for they tend to grow cruel when you cross them. Now! A goblet of hot mulled wine by the time I count three, and I may refrain from stretching your ears out and tying them under your chin. Git!"

He counted to three, with a two second pause between numbers, and the goblet was in his hand. The landlord scuttled away with his hands clapped over his ears, and Rod sat down to sip at the wine and wonder what a curmudgeon was.

Looking up, he saw half a garlic sausage sitting on the table. He picked it up with a heavy hand and tucked it into his purse. Might as well take it along; it was about the only good thing that had happened today.

He surged to his feet and called, "Ho, landlord!"

Mine host came bobbling up.

"A chamber alone, with heavy blankets!"

"A chamber alone, sir! At once, sir!" The landlord scuttled away, still bobbing his head. "Heavy blankets, sir! Quite surely, sir!"

Rod ground his teeth and turned away to the door. He stepped out and leaned back against the jamb, letting his head slump forward onto his chest, eyes closed.

"The law of the jungle," he muttered. "If it looks weak, prey upon it. If it turns out to be strong, bow to it; let it prey upon you and hope it won't devour you.'"

"Yet all men have pride," murmured a voice behind his ear.

Rod looked up, smiled. " 'Art there, old mole?' "

" 'Swear! Swear!' " Fess answered.

Rod let loose a stream of invective that would have done credit to a sailor with a hangover.

"Feel better?" Fess asked, amused.

"Not much. Where does a man like mine host hide his pride, Fess? He sure as hell never lets it show. Obsequiousness, yes; avarice, yes; but self-respect? No. I haven't seen that in him."

"Pride and self-respect are not necessarily synonymous, Rod."

Someone tugged at Rod's elbow. He snapped his head around, muscles tensed.

It was Big Tom, his six-foot-five bent strangely in a valiant attempt to put his head below the level of Rod's.

"God e'en, master."

34

Rod stared at him for a moment without answering.

"God e'en," he replied, his voice carefully neutral. "What can I do for *you?*"

Big Tom hunched his shoulders and scratched at the base of his skull. "Eh, master," he complained, "you made a bit of a fool of me back a while."

"Oh?" Rod lifted an eyebrow. "Do tell!"

"I do," the big man admitted, "and . . . well . . ." He pulled off his cap and twisted it in his great hands. "It *do* seem like . . . well, master, you've finished me here, and that's gospel."

Rod felt his back lifting. "And I'm supposed to make it up to you, is that it? Pay you damages, I suppose!"

"Eh, no, master!" Big Tom shied away. " 'Tisn't that, master, not that at all! It's just . . . well . . . I was a-wonderin', I was, if you might . . . that is . . . I . . ."

He twisted the hat through some gyrations that would have astounded a topolgist; then the words came out in a rush.

"I was wonderin' if you might be needin' a servin'-man, you know—a sort of groom and lackey, and . . ." His voice trailed off. He eyed Rod sidewise, fearful and hopeful.

Rod stood frozen for a moment or two. He searched the big man's open, almost worshipful face.

He crossed his arms and leaned back against the jamb again. "Why, how's this, Big Tom? Not half an hour agone, you sought to rob me! And now *I* am supposed to trust *you* for a squire?"

Big Tom caught his nether lip between his teeth, frowning. " 'Tain't right-seeming, master, that I know, but—" His hands gestured vaguely. "Well, the fact of it is, you're the only man what I ever raised hand against, could beat me, and . . ."

His voice ran out again. Rod nodded slowly, his eyes on Big Tom's.

"And therefore you must serve me."

Tom's lower lip thrust out, pouting. "Not must, my master —only that I *wants* to."

"A robber," said Rod. "A cutpurse. And I'm to trust you." Big Tom's hat twisted again.

"You've got an open face," Rod mused, "not the kind of face that hides its feelings."

Big Tom smiled widely, nodding.

"Of course, that doesn't mean anything," Rod went on.

"I've known quite a few gentle-seeming girls that turned out to be first-class bitches."

Tom's face fell.

"So you might be honest—or you might be a thorough rogue. It's a *Fess*-cinating puzzle."

The voice behind his ear murmured, "Preliminary interpretation of available data indicates basically simplistic personality structure. Probability of individual serving as reliable source of information on local social variables exceeds probability of individual practicing serious duplicity."

Rod nodded slowly. He would have settled for an even chance.

He fished a scrap of silver from his purse—it smelt slightly of garlic—and slapped it into the big man's hand.

Tom stared at the silver in his palm, then at Rod, then back at the metal.

Abruptly, his hand closed into a fist, trembling slightly. His staring eyes came up to Rod again.

"You've accepted my coin," said Rod. "You're my man."

Big Tom's face split from ear to ear in a grin. He ducked his head. "Yes, master! I thanks you, master! Forever I thanks you, master! I—"

"I get the message." Rod hated to see a grown man grovel. "You go on duty right now. Tell me, what are the chances of getting a job with the Queen's army?"

"Oh, most excellent, master!" Big Tom grinned. "They're always needing new sojers."

A bad omen, Rod decided.

"Okay," he said. "Duck back inside, find out which room we've been assigned, and check it to make sure there isn't a cutthroat in the closet."

"Yes, master! Right away!" Big Tom bustled back into the inn.

Rod smiled, closed his eyes, and let his head fall back against the jamb. He rolled his head from side to side, laughing silently. He would never cease to be amazed at the bully psychology; how a man could go from arrogance to servility in less than ten minutes, he would never understand.

A low, quavering wail cut the night air, soaring into a shriek.

Rod's eyes snapped open. Sirens? In *this* culture?

The sound was coming from the left; he looked up, and saw the castle, there on its hilltop.

And there, at the base of the tower, something glowed,

36

and keened like a paddy wagon lamenting the death of some squad cars.

The guests tumbled out of the inn to stand in the courtyard, staring and pointing.

" 'Tis the banshee!"

"Again!"

"Nay, all will be well. Hath it not appeared thrice before? And yet the Queen lives!"

"Fess," Rod said carefully.

"Yes, Rod."

"Fess, there's a banshee. On the castle battlements. A banshee, Fess."

There was no answer.

Then a raucous buzz snarled behind Rod's ear, swelled till it threatened to shake his head apart, and cut off.

Rod shook his head and pounded his temple with the heel of his hand.

"I'm going to have to have that boy overhauled," he muttered. "He used to have *quiet* seizures."

It would have been unwise for Rod to go to the stables to reset Fess while the inn-yard was full of gawkers; he would have been thoroughly conspicuous.

So he went up to his room, to lie down till things had quieted down a bit; and, of course, by the time the courtyard was clear, Rod was too comfortable to take the trouble of going down to the stables. No real reason to reset the robot, anyway; it would be a quiet night.

The room was dark, except for a long swathe of light streaming in the window from the largest moon. There was a subdued murmur and clatter from the common room—night-owl guests drinking late. Rod's chamber was very peaceful.

Not quiet, though. Big Tom, curled up on a pallet at the foot of the bed, snored like a bulldozer on idle, making more noise asleep than he did awake.

Now there was a riddle—Big Tom. Rod had never before been in a fight where he hadn't been hit at least once. Big Tom had left himself wide open, every time; and sure, he was big, but he didn't have to be *that* clumsy. Big men *can* be quick. . . .

But why would Big Tom have thrown the fight?

So Rod would take him on as a serving-man?

And what about Adam and One-Ear? Their talk would seem to indicate they'd been at the pep rally down by the

wharf, which would mean they were members of the proletarian party. What had the young rabble-rouser called it?
The House of Clovis, yes.

But if Adam and One-Ear were a representative sample,
the House of Clovis was a house divided against itself. There
seemed to be two factions, one backing the Loguire—the
juvenile orator?—and one led by the Mocker, whoever that
might be. The usual two factions, nonviolent and violent,
tongue and sword.

Now, why would Big Tom have wanted a butler job?
Social climber, maybe? No, he wasn't the fawning type.
Better wages? But he'd seemed to be moderately prosperous
as the neighborhood heavy.

To keep an eye on Rod?

Rod rolled over on his side. Tom just might be a member
in good standing of the House of Clovis. But why would
the House want to keep tabs on Rod? They couldn't suspect
anything, could they?

If Fess's guess was right, and the House was backed by
an off-planet power, they definitely might suspect something
—never mind how.

But wasn't Rod letting his paranoia show again?

He was wide awake, every muscle tense. He sighed and
rolled out of bed; he couldn't sleep now. Better reset Fess
and have a talk. Rod needed the robot's electronic objectivity;
he had very little of his own.

Big Tom stirred and wakened as Rod lifted the rusty
door latch.

"Master? Where dost thou go?"

"Just got a little worried about my horse, Big Tom. Think
I'll run down to the stables and make sure the hostler's treat-
ing him right. Go back to sleep."

Big Tom stared a moment.

"Certes," he said, "thou'rt a most caring one, master."

He rolled over and burrowed his head into the folded
cloak he used for a pillow. "To be so much concerned for a
horse," he muttered, and snored again.

Rod grinned and let himself out of the room.

He found a stairway a few paces away—dark and musty,
but closer to the stables than the main door.

There was a door at the bottom of the stair, one that was
not very often used; it groaned like a bullfrog in heat when
he opened it.

The inn-yard was flooded with the soft, golden light of

the three moons. The largest was only a little smaller than Terra's, but much closer; it filled a full thirty degrees of sky, a perpetual harvest moon.

"Great planet for lovers," Rod mused; and, because his eyes were on the moon, he didn't notice the gray strand of cord stretched a little above the doorstep. He tripped.

His arms swung up, slapping the ground to break his fall. Something hard struck the back of his head, and the world dissolved in a shoal of sparks.

There was a ruddy glow about him, and a throbbing ache in his head. Something cold and wet moved over his face. He shuddered, and came wide awake.

He lay on his back; a limestone roof vaulted over him, glimmering with bits of captured light. Pinch-waisted limestone columns stretched from the roof to a green carpet—stalactites and stalagmites joined. The green carpet stretched away in all directions for at least a mile. He was in a vast underground cavern. The light seemed to come from everywhere, a dancing, wavering light, setting the sparks in the ceiling into an intricate ballet.

The green carpet spread under him; he could feel it, cold and springy, damp, under his back: moss, three inches thick. He tried to put out a hand to touch the moss, and discovered that he couldn't move his arms or legs. Lifting his head, he looked for ropes binding him, but there was not so much as a thread.

He shook his head, trying to get the ache out of it so he could think clearly.

"Fess," he muttered, "where am I?"

There was no answer.

Rod bit his lip. "Come on, iron horse! Are you asleep at the switch?"

Switch . . .

Fess had had a seizure. Rod had been en route to reset him.

Rod was on his own.

He sighed and lay back on the green moss carpet.

A deep voice bgan singing, off to his right. Rod looked.

A fire fluttered in a bare stone circle. A tripod stood over it, supporting a cauldron—a covered cauldron, bubbling merrily, with a tube leading from a hole in the cover. Drops of water fell from the roof, striking the tube; and a beaker sat under the far end of the tube, collecting drops.

A primitive still.

And a moonshiner, a moonshiner perhaps eighteen inches high, very broad-shouldered and generally stocky, clad in doublet and hose. He had a round, cheerful face, twinkling green eyes, a snub nose, and a very wide mouth curved in an impish smile. To top it off, he wore a Robin Hood hat with a bright red feather.

The green eyes looked up and caught Rod's. "Ha!" said the little man in a buzzing baritone. "Tha'rt come to thy senses, warlock!"

Rod scowled. "Warlock? I'm not a warlock!"

"To be sure," said the little man, "tha'rt not. Thou comest in a falling star, and thou hast a horse made of cold iron. . . ."

"Just a minute, there," Rod interrupted. "How'd you know the horse was made of cold iron?"

"We are the Wee Folk," said the little man, unperturbed. "We live by Oak, Ash, and Thorn, by Wood, Air, and Sod; and those who live by cold iron seek the end of our woodlands. Cold iron is the sign of all that cannot abide us; and therefore we know cold iron, no matter what form or disguise it may be in."

He turned back to the kettle, lifting the lid to check the mash. "Then, too, thou canst hear what is said a good half mile off; and thy horse can run as silent as the wind and faster than a falcon, when it has cause to. But tha'rt not a warlock, eh?"

Rod shook his head. "I'm not. I use science, not magic!"

"Assuredly," said the little man, "and a rose by any other name . . . Nay, tha'rt a warlock, and as such tha'rt known already, throughout the length and the breadth of Gramarye!"

"Gramarye? What's that?"

The little man stared in surprise. "Why, the world, warlock! The world we live in, the land between the Four Seas, the realm of Queen Catharine!"

"Oh. She rules the whole world?"

"Certes," said the elf, giving Rod a sidelong glance.

"And the name of her castle? And the town around it?"

"Runnymede. In truth, tha'rt a most untutored warlock!"

"That's just what I've been trying to tell you," and Rod sighed.

The little man turned away, shaking his head and muttering. He opened a pippet on the collection beaker and drained some of the distillate into a shot-glass-sized mug.

Rod suddenly realized he was very thirsty. "Uh, say—

40

what're you brewing up there? Wouldn't be brandy, would it?"

The elf shook his head.

"Gin? Rum? *Aqua Vitae?*"

"Nay; 'tis spirits of another sort." He bounced over to Rod and held the miniscule mug to the man's lips.

"Thanks." Rod took a sip. He looked up at the roof, smacking his lips. "Tastes like honey."

"Where the wild bee sucks, there suck I." The little man hopped back to the fire.

"Not bad at all. Could you spare the recipe?"

"Aye, assuredly." The elf grinned. "We would do aught within our power for a guest."

"Guest!" Rod snorted. "I hate to impugn your hospitality, but immobililizing me isn't exactly what I'd call a welcome."

"Oh, we shall make amends ere long." The little man lifted the cauldron lid and stirred the mash.

Something clicked in Rod's mind. The hairs at the base of his skull began to prickle.

"Uh, say, uh . . . I don't belive we've been introduced, but . . . your name wouldn't be Robin Goodfellow, would it? Alias Puck?"

"Thou speakest aright." The elf replaced the lid with a clang. "I am that merry wanderer of the night."

Rod fell back onto the moss carpet. It'd make a great story to tell his grandchildren; nobody else would believe it.

"Say, Puck—you don't mind if I call you Puck?"

"Oh, nay."

"Thanks, uh . . . I'm Rod Gallowglass."

"We ha' known it."

"Well, just thought I'd make it official. Now, you don't seem to spare me any particular ill-will, so, uh, may I ask . . . uh . . . why am I paralyzed?"

"Ah, that," said Puck. "We must find if you are a white warlock, or black."

"Oh." Rod chewed the inside of his cheek for a moment. "If I'm a white warlock, you'll, um . . . let me go?"

Puck nodded.

"What happens if you decide I'm a black warlock?"

"Then, Rod Gallowglass, you shall sleep till the Trump of Doom."

Rod felt as though a weak electric current had been applied to his jaw. "Great. The Trump of Doom. And I never was much good at bridge."

Puck frowned. "How . . . ?"

"Skip it. 'Sleep till the Trump of Doom.' A very neat euphemism. Why don't you just come right out and say you'll kill me?"

"Nay." Puck thrust his lower lip out, shaking his head. "We would not kill you, Rod Gallowglass. Thou shouldst but sleep forever, and with pleasant dreams."

"I see. Suspended animation?"

Puck's brow wrinkled. "I know not that word. Yet rest assured, thou shalt not be suspended. The Wee Folk have no fondness for a hanging."

"Well, I suppose that's something of a comfort. So how do I prove I'm a white warlock?"

"Why," said Puck, "by our enlarging you."

Rod stared. "How's that again?"

"Aren't I big enough already?"

The elf's face split into a broad grin. "Nay, nay! Enlarging you! Removing the spell that binds you!"

"Oh." Rod lay back with a sigh of relief. Then he jerked back up. "*Freeing* me? That's going to prove I'm a white warlock?"

"By itself, no," said Puck. " 'Tis a question where we free you."

He clapped his hands. Rod heard the scurrying of scores of small feet coming from behind him; a fold of dark cloth was drawn over his eyes, knotted behind his head.

"Hey!" he protested.

"Peace," said Puck. "We do but bear you forth to your freedom."

A host of tiny hands lifted Rod. He resigned himself and lay back to enjoy the trip.

It was a rather pleasant way to travel, actually—like an innerspring mattress with four-wheel drive.

His feet tilted up higher than his head and the pace of the scuttling feet under him slowed—they were mounting an incline.

Damp night air struck his face; he heard the breeze sighing in the leaves, accompanied by a full complement of crickets, with an owl and maybe a curlew providing the harmony.

He was dropped unceremoniously; the blindfold was whipped from his eyes.

"Hey!" he protested "What do you think I am, a sack of potatoes?"

He could hear a stream gurgling off to his left.

"Tha'rt free now, Rod Gallowglass," Puck's voice husked in his ear. "May God be with you!" And the elf bounded away.

Rod sat up, flexing his limbs to make them realize they could move again. He looked about.

It was a moonlit forest glade, with a silver stream trickling past on the left. The trees were bright steel trunk and tinsel leaf, and black shadow among the trunks.

One of the shadows moved.

It stepped forward, a tall figure in a dark, hooded monk's robe.

Rod scrambled to his feet.

The figure moved slowly toward Rod, halted ten feet away, and threw back the hood.

Wild, disordered hair over a long, thin face, with hollows under the cheekbones and caves for eye sockets, with two burning coals at their backs—and the whole face twisted, curdled with bitterness.

The voice was flat and thin, almost a hiss. "Are you, then, so tired of life that you come to a werewolf's cage?"

Rod stared. "Werewolf!"

Well, why not? If elves were a basic assumption. . . .

Then Rod frowned. "Cage?" He looked around. "Looks like the great outdoors to me."

"There is a wall of magic around this grove," hissed the werewolf. " 'Tis a prison the Wee Folk have made me—and they do not feed me in my proper fashion."

"Oh?" Rod looked at the werewolf out of the corner of his eye. "What's your proper fashion?"

"Red meat." The werewolf grinned, showing a mouthful of canines. "Raw, red meat, and blood for my wine."

Something with lots of cold little feet ran down Rod's spine.

"Make peace with your God," said the werewolf, "for your hour has come."

Fur appeared on the backs of his hands, and his fingernails grew, curving outward. Forehead and cheeks sprouted fur; nose, mouth, and chin slipped together and bulged, tapering outward to a muzzle. His ears moved upward to the top of his head and stretched into points.

He flung off the dark cloak; his whole body was silvery fur, his legs had become haunches.

He dropped to all fours. His upper arms shortened and

his forearms lengthened; his hands had become paws. A tail sprouted and grew into a long, silvery plume.

The silver wolf crouched close to the earth, snarling, growling low in its throat, and sprang.

Rod whirled aside, but the wolf managed to change course in mid-air just enough; its teeth ripped Rod's forearm from elbow to wrist.

The wolf landed and spun about with a howl of joy. It crouched, tongue lolling out, then it sprang again.

Rod ducked, dropping to one knee, but the wolf checked itself in mid-leap and fell on top of him. Its hindlegs clawed at his chest; the great jaws fumbled for a hold on his spine.

Rod surged to his feet, bowing forward and shoving against the wolf's belly with all his strength. The wolf went flying, but its claws had raked Rod's back open.

The wolf landed on its back, hard, and howled with the pain. It scrambled to its feet and stalked around Rod in a circle, growling with blood-lust.

Rod pivoted, keeping his face toward the wolf. How do you handle a werewolf? Fess would know, but Fess was still out of order.

The wolf snarled and leaped for Rod's throat.

Rod crouched low and lunged with his hand stiffened. His fingers caught the wolf right in the solar plexus.

Rod leaped back, falling into a crouch. The wolf clawed at the ground, struggling to regain its breath as life poured back into its nerves. Rod circled around it, widdershins for luck.

How do you fight a werewolf?

Wolfbane, obviously.

But Rod couldn't tell wolfbane from poison ivy without a botany text.

The wolf dragged in a long, grating breath and rose into a crouch. It snarled and began to prowl, widdershins around Rod, watching for an opening.

So much for widdershins, Rod thought, and reversed direction, circling clockwise in an attempt to get behind the wolf.

The wolf sprang.

Rod pivoted aside and let fly a right jab at the wolf's jaw; but the wolf caught his fist in its teeth.

Rod bellowed with pain and kicked the beast in the belly. Fang went down for a breather again, freeing Rod's hand as the toothy jaws gaped for air.

Silver bullets. But chemical sidearms had been out of vogue for thousands of years, and the DDT had gone off the silver standard quite a while before.

A crucifix. Rod made a firm resolution to take up religion. He need a hobby, anyway.

His furry friend had meanwhile pulled itself back together. Haunches tensed, it sprang.

Rod sidestepped, but the wolf had apparently counted on his so doing. It landed full on his chest, slavering jaws snapping for Rod's jugular vein.

Rod fell on his back. He pulled up his legs, planted his feet in the wolf's belly, and shoved, catapulting the canine clear of his corpus. The wolf fell hard and squirmed, getting its feet under its body.

What else didn't werewolves like?

Garlic.

Rod circled around the wolf, fumbling in his purse for the garlic sausage left over from dinner.

The wolf spread its jaws wide and hacked a cough.

Rod munched a mouthful of sausage.

The wolf came to its feet with an ugly, very determined growl. It tensed and sprang.

Rod caught the beast under the forelegs, staggering back under the weight of its body, and breathed full in its face. He dropped the wolf and sprang away.

The wolf rolled, spitting and coughing, drew in a shuddering gasp, and collapsed.

Its form stretched, relaxed, and slowly stretched again—and a tall, lean wiry man lay naked, facedown, in the grass, unconscious body heaving with great panting breaths.

Rod sank to his knees. Saved by garlic sausage!

Grass whispered by his knee; he looked into the smiling eyes of Robin Goodfellow.

"Return with us if you will, Rod Gallowglass, for our paths are yours, to walk at your pleasure, now."

Rod smiled wearily. "He might have killed me," he said, with a nod at the unconscious werewolf.

Puck shook his head. "We looked on, and would have prevented death to either of you; and as for your wounds, why! we shall quickly have them mended."

Rod rose, shaking his head in disbelief.

"Then, too," said Puck, "we knew you to be a warlock of such potency that you could defeat him . . . if you were a white warlock."

"Oh?" Rod raised an eyebrow. "What if I wasn't? What if I was black?"

"Why, then," Puck said, grinning, "you would have leagued with him against us, and sought to fight loose of the prison."

"Um." Rod gnawed at his lower lip. "Wouldn't that have put you in a rather delicate position?"

"Nay." Puck grinned again. "The magic of a score of elves has never yet been equaled by two warlocks."

"I see." Rod rubbed his chin. "Hedged your bets, didn't you? But you couldn't let me know, of course. As long as I was in the dark, fighting the werewolf proved I was one of the good guys?"

"Partly."

"Oh? What's the other part?"

"Why, Rod Gallowglass, there were several times when you had rendered the werewolf helpless, but you did not kill him."

"And that shows I've got a good heart."

"That," Puck agred, "and also that you are sure enough of your own power that you dare be merciful. And *there* is proof that you are white, but greater proof that you are a warlock."

Rod squeezed his eyes shut. With exaggerated patience, he said, "Of course, it *might* just be that I'm a trained fighter."

"It might," Puck agreed, "but it was by sorcery that you overcame him."

Rod took a deep breath. "Look," he said carefully, "I am not a warlock. I have never been a warlock. I never want to be a warlock. I'm just a mercenary soldier who happens to know a few tricks."

"Assuredly, Master Warlock," said Puck cheerfully. "Will you come back to the cavern? We shall guide you forth to your inn."

"Oh, all right," Rod grumbled.

But he turned to look at the miserable collection of bone and sinew that was the sleeping werewolf, lying in the center of the glade.

"Master Gallowglass?" Puck's voice was puzzled, disturbed. "What troubles you?"

Rod shook his head, coming out of his reverie. "Nothing," he said, turning away. "Just wondering."

"What of, warlock?"

"They used to call me a lone wolf when I was a schoolboy . . . Never mind. Which way did you say the cavern was?"

The stars wheeled toward dawn as Rod stumbled, foot-sore and weary, across the inn-yard and into the stable.

A single candle-lantern lit the row of stalls, serving only to deepen the shadows.

Rod flung an arm across Fess's back to steady himself, his other hand groping across the robot's withers till he found the enlarged vertebra that was the reset switch. He pressed; the steel body stirred under its horsehair camouflage. The velvet black head lifted, shook twice, turned to look back over its shoulder, great brown eyes focusing on Rod. The robot was silent a moment; then the voice behind Rod's ear spoke with a touch of reproach:

"You have left me inactive a long time, Rod. I have no aftereffects from the seizure."

"Sorry, old iron." Rod kept his arms across the horse's back; his legs felt a trifle wobbly. "I was on my way to reset you when I got clobbered."

"Clobbered!" Fess's voice writhed with shame. "While I slept! May my casing lie forever corroding on the junkpile! May my germanium be consigned to the Converter for re-clamation! May my—"

"Oh, stow it!" Rod growled. "It wasn't your fault." He stepped away from the horse, straightening his shoulders. "I wasn't in any real danger, anyway. Just a busy night, that's all."

"How so, Rod?"

Rod started to answer, then changed his mind. "I'll tell you in the morning, Fess."

"I have reoriented my circuits to accept the discrepancies between accepted theory and actual occurrence, Rod. You may confide in me without fear of overload."

Rod shook his head and turned to stumble out of the stall. "In the morning, Fess. You might be able to believe it right now, but I'm not sure I could."

Rod sat down to a whopping breakfast, but he was on a starvation diet compared to Big Tom. The man was sur-rounded by unbelievable stacks of food.

Some of it was familiar to Rod—the eggs, pancakes, and ham. The 'cakes had a subtly alien flavor, though, and the eggs had three inch yolks. There was some sort of grain on

47

any human-inhabited planet, usually a descendant of Terran cereals; but the soil of another planet sometimes produced weird variations in the grain. There was always some sort of domesticated fowl; but more often than not it was a local life-form. Hogs, of course, were ubiquitous; they were found on Terran planets even more consistently than dogs. Rod sometimes wondered about his species.

The food was all digestible, of course, and probably nourishing: genetic drift couldn't change human metabolism all that much. But trace elements were another matter; Rod swallowed an all-purpose pill just to be on the safe side.

Big Tom noticed it. "What was that, master?"

Rod forced a smile. "Just a minor spell. Don't let it worry you, Big Tom."

Tom stared, then looked down at his plate, muttering a quick prayer under his breath. He attacked the pancakes with a shaking fork.

The big man started to speak, but his voice cracked. He cleared his throat and tried again.

"What doth the new day bring, good master?"

"A trip to the castle," said Rod. "We'll see if the Queen's in the market for a new soldier."

Tom wailed a protest. "A Queen's sojer! Nay, master, that's no trade for a honest man!"

Rod cocked an eyebrow. "Are you trying to tell me that one of us might be honest?"

Big Tom shut up.

The landlord had a spare horse, or so he suddenly remembered when Rod rested a hand on the hilt of his dagger. It was an old, swaybacked gray gelding with a slightly longer neck and smaller ears than the Terran-standard animal. That was bad, since it would call a certain amount of attention to Fess; but then, the great black horse wasn't exactly inconspicuous anyway.

The church bells were ringing as they rode out of the inn-yard, Rod on Fess and Tom on the equine antique. The sound of the bells reminded Tom of the early hour; he began to grumble at masters who kept unreasonable hours.

But his gripes trailed off as they mounted the slope above the town, where they could look out to the horizon and see the east pregnant with the morning sun.

Tom took a deep breath of the dawn and grinned back over his shoulder at Rod. "Eh, master! 'Twill be a fine day!"

"And a chill one," said Rod, turning up his collar, for the wind was at his back.

"Aye, aye! Did I not say 'twould be fine?"

"I don't quite share your enthusiasm for low thermometer readings," Rod growled. "Look alive, Tom; we're almost to the castle."

"Stand and declare yourselves!" cried the sentry on the drawbridge.

"Oh, ye gods!" Rod rolled his eyes upward.

"Your name and your concern at the Queen's castle."

"Overdoing it a bit, aren't you?" Rod eyed the sentry sidewise.

The footman's mouth turned down sharply at the corners. "None of your mouthings," he barked. "I'm a Queen's man, and you'll speak with respect."

"Not likely," said Rod, smiling benignly. "My name is Rod Gallowglass."

"Gallowglass?" The sentry frowned. "Your time is wasted; the Queen already has a fool."

"From the look of you, I'd say she has many." Rod grunted. "My trade is soldier, and my manservant's, too. Call the master-at-arms, and let him enroll me."

The sentry glowered. "Enlisting in the Queen's army is not so easily done as that."

"Why, how now!" Rod scowled. "Must I prove I'm a soldier?" He dismounted, swinging out of the saddle to land just a yard from the sentry.

"If you're a soldier, you're a poor one," the sentry said with a sneer, "or you'd not leave your horse untethered."

Rod threw him a saccharine smile and called out, "Fess, back up four feet, take a half step to the left, come forward four and a half feet, then stand till I call you."

The sentry stared, mouth gaping open, as Fess executed the maneuver with machine-like precision.

"I'm a soldier," said Rod, "and a good one."

The sentry's mouth opened and closed like a fish's. His eyes bulged slightly as they flicked over Rod's lean frame, the black-gloved hand on the pommel of the sword.

"You see," Rod explained, "I might have need of my horse. It's easier to let him come to me."

His right hand jumped out in a feint. The soldier grunted with surprise and stepped back as Rod's foot snaked out to catch him behind the ankle. The sentry went down in a clatter of tinware.

Rod twisted the pike from the sentry's hands as he fell and threw it back under the portcullis.

"Now," he said, "let's try it again, shall we?"

"Well done, oh! Well done, my master!" Big Tom pounded his nag's withers, grinning from ear to ear.

The sentry staggered to his feet, shouting, "A rescue! A rescue!"

"Oh, no!" Rod dropped his forehead into his palm. "Oh, no!"—shaking his head.

He leaned back against Fess' shoulder and folded his arms. Three guardsmen came running up, pikes at the ready. The leader looked from Rod to the sentry, back to Rod, then back to the sentry. He frowned. "What need for a rescue?"

The sentry fluttered a hand in Rod's general direction. "This man . . ."

"Yes?" Rod smiled.

"Why, he knocked me down, that's what he did, and took my pike from me!"

"I wouldn't brag, if I were you," Rod murmured. Big Tom bent low over his saddlebow, convulsed with silent laughter.

"Is that the truth of it, man?" The leader glowered at Rod.

"True." Rod bowed his head.

"Well, then!" The leader straightened, planting his fists on his hips and scowling.

"Well, what?" Rod raised an eyebrow.

The sergeant was beginning to get flustered. "Well, what's your reason?"

"I wish to enlist in the Queen's army. This man-at-arms indicated I should prove myself."

The sergeant looked from the flabbergasted sentry to Rod, and nodded.

"You'll have your chance," he said. "Come."

The chance consisted of a hulking sergeant equipped with a broadsword and buckler.

"Will you not take a buckler, man?" growled the old knight who was Master of the Guard.

"No thanks." Rod slipped his dagger from its sheath. "This will do me quite well."

"Naught but a poniard and a wisp of a sword 'gainst

50

broadsword and buckler!" Sir Maris shook his head sadly. "You must truly wish to die young!"

Rod's eyes widened in surprise. "Thank you," he said. "I haven't been told I looked young since I was thirteen."

"Well, cross your swords," Sir Maris sighed. Rod and the sergeant complied; Sir Maris limped forward, his own broadsword coming up to separate their blades.

The sergeant's broadsword swung up for a full-armed chop. Rod took advantage of the moment's delay to feint once at the sergeant's belly. The buckler dropped down to catch the sword-tip, and Rod's blade leaped over the sergeant's arm to rip the cloth over his heart.

"Hold!" cried Sir Maris, and the sergeant's broadsword paused in mid-chop. He dropped his buckler, staring about him. "Wot 'appened?"

"Had this Gallowglass not fought in sport alone," said Sir Maris, "thou wert a dead man this day, Sergeant Hapweed."

He scowled at Rod, puzzled. "Who would ha' thought to use a sword's point?"

"Shall we have at it again?" Rod's blade whined through the air and slapped against his leg.

Sir Maris studied Rod's face, his brow furrowing.

"Nay," he said, lifting his head. "I'll warrant you're a swordsman."

"Aye," muttered Big Tom, and Sir Maris glanced over at him; but the big man was only beaming with pride.

The Master of the Guard turned and caught up a quarterstaff. "Here!" He tossed it to Rod. "We'll try you with this."

Rod sheathed his dagger and caught the staff by the middle. He slipped his sword into its scabbard.

The big sergeant was practicing quick one-two-three blows with his quarterstaff.

"Have at it!" Sir Maris called, and the big sergeant stepped forward, knees bent, quarterstaff on guard. Rod followed suit.

Then he was in the middle of an oaken rain, blows from the sergeant's staff drubbing about his head and shoulders, seeking an opening, a half second drop of Rod's guard.

Rod set his jaw and matched the sergeant's pace, catching the blows as quick as they came—just barely. His stomach sank as he realized he was on the defensive.

He blocked a swing at his shin, caught the rebound toward his head, swung the lower end of his staff to catch the answering blow at his belly—but the blow never came. It had been a feint.

Frantically, he tried to recover to guard his head, but the sergeant had gained his half second opening. Rod saw the heavy oak staff swinging at him out of the corner of his eye.

He sank back, rolling with the blow. It cracked on his skull like a thunderclap. The room darkened, filled with dancing motes of light; there was a roaring in Rod's ears.

He gave ground, blocking the sergeant's blows by sheer reflex, and heard the onlooking soldiers yell with triumph.

Won't do at all, Rod's thoughts whirled. He'd been trained at quarterstaff; but he hadn't had a bout in a year, whereas the sergeant had all the skill of a devout hobbyist. It was just a game to him, probably, as the swordplay had been to Rod. The sergeant was in the driver's seat, and he knew it.

There was one chance. Rod leaped back, his hands slipping to the middle of the staff. It began to turn end-over-end, twirling like a baton.

Rod set his jaw and put some muscle into it. His staff leaped into a whirling, whining blur.

It was French single-stick play, *le moulinet.* The sergeant probably knew it as well as Rod; but chances were he wasn't any better practiced at it than Rod was. It was rather exotic form, unless you were French. And with a name like Sergeant Hapweed . . .

Sir Maris and Co. gaped. The sergeant stepped back, startled. Then a wariness came into his face, and his staff jumped into a whirl.

So he knew the style. But he wasn't a master; in fact, Rod had the advantage. The sergeant's staff was a blur, but a quiet blur. Rod's staff was doing a very nice imitation of a buzz saw. He had the edge on the sergeant in angular velocity, and consequent greater striking power.

Sergeant Hapweed knew it too; the muscles of his neck knotted as he tried to speed up his wing.

Now! Rod leaped forward. His staff snapped out of its whirl, swinging down counter to the rotation of the sergeant's.

The sticks met with the crack of a rifle and a shudder that jarred Rod's back teeth. He recovered a half second ahead of the sergeant and brought his staff crashing down on the sergeant's in two quick blows, knocking the other's staff out of his hands.

Rod straightened, drawing a deep breath and letting the tension flow out of him as he grounded the butt of his staff.

The sergeant stared at his hands, numb.

Rod reached out and tapped the man's temple gently with the tip of his staff. "Bang! You're dead."

"Hold!" cried Sir Maris, making things official. Rod grounded his staff again, and leaned on it.

Sir Maris scowled at Rod, eyes bright under bushy eyebrows.

Rod gave him a tight smile.

Sir Maris nodded slowly. "Shall I try you with a longbow?"

Rod shrugged, bluffing. With a crossbow, maybe. But a longbow . . .

A deep, skirling laugh rolled from the rafters. The Master of the Guard and all his men jumped. Big Tom fell on his knees, arms flung up to protect his head.

Rod's head snapped out, eyes searching for the source of the laugh.

On one of the great oaken beams crossing the hall sat a dwarf, drumming his heels against the wood. His head was as large as Rod's, his shoulders broader, his arms and legs as thick as Rod's. He looked as though someone had taken a big, normal man and edited out three feet here and there.

He was barrel-chested, broad-shouldered, and bull-necked. The shaggy black head seemed strangely large for such a truncated body. Black, curly hair hung down to the point of the jaw and the nape of the neck; bushy black eyebrows jutted out from a flat, sloping forehead. The eyes were large, coal-black, and, at the moment, creased with mirth. They were separated by a hawk-beak nose under which thick, fleshy lips grinned through a bushy black beard, jutting forward at the chin. Square, even teeth gleamed white through the beard.

Someone had tried to cram a giant into a nail-keg, and had almost succeeded.

"Longbow!" he cried in a booming, bass voice. "Nay, I'll wager he's as fair a shot as the county ram in springtime!"

Sir Maris glowered up at the dwarf. "A plague on you and your stealthy ways, Brom O'Berin! Is there not enough salt in my hair already, but you must whiten it all with your pranks?"

"Stealthy ways!" cried the dwarf. "Forsooth! Had you

53

some pride in your calling, Sir Maris, you would thank me for showing you your own lack of vigilance!"

"Brom?" muttered Rod, staring "O'Berin?"

The dwarf turned to Rod, glowering. "Black Brom O'Berin, aye!"

"That's, uh, a combo of Dutch, Irish, and Russian, if I've got it right."

"What words of nonsense are these?" growled the dwarf.

"Nothing." Rod looked away, shaking his head. "I should have seen it coming. I should expect something else, on this crazy—uh . . . in Gramarye?"

The dwarf grinned, mischief in his eyes. "Nay, unless I mistake me, that hath the sound of a slur on the great land of Gramarye!"

"No, no! I didn't . . . I mean . . ." Rod paused, remembering that apologies were unbecoming for a fighting man in this culture.

He straightened, chin lifting. "All right," he said, "it was an insult, if you want it that way."

The dwarf gave a howl of glee and jumped to his feet on the rafter.

"You must fight him now, Gallowglass," Sir Maris rumbled, "and you shall need every bit of your skill."

Rod stared at the Master of the Guard. Could the man be serious? A dwarf, give Rod a hard fight?

The dwarf chuckled deep in his throat and slipped off the beam. It was a twelve foot drop to the stone floor, more than three times Brom's height, but he hit the floor lightly, seeming almost to bounce, and wound up in a wrestler's crouch. He straightened and paced toward Rod, chuckling mischief.

There was a roar behind Rod, and Big Tom blundered forward. " 'Tis a trap, master!" he bellowed. "Witchcraft in this land, and he is the worst witch of all! None has ever beaten Black Brom! Yet I shall—"

Every soldier in the room descended on Big Tom in a shouting chaos of anger and outrage.

Rod stood a moment in shock. Then he dropped his staff and waded into the melee, hands flashing out in karate punches and chops. Soldiers dropped to the floor.

"*Hold!*" thundered Brom's voice.

Silence gelled.

Brom had somehow gotten up on the rafters again.

"My thanks, lads," the miniature Hercules growled. "But the big fellow meant no harm; let him go."

"No harm!" yelped half a dozen outraged voices.

Brom took a deep breath and sighed out, "Aye, no harm. He meant only defense of his master. And this Gallowglass meant only defense of his manservant. Stand away from them now; they're both blameless."

The soldiers reluctantly obeyed.

Rod slapped Tom on the shoulder and murmured, "Thanks, Big Tom. And don't worry about me; that Dutch Irishman is only a man, like you and me. And if he's a man, I can beat him."

The dwarf must have had very keen ears, for he bellowed, "Oh, can you, now? We'll see to that, my bawcock!"

"Eh, master!" Big Tom moaned, rolling his eyes. "You know not what you speak of. That elf is the devil's black own!"

"A warlock?" Rod snorted. "There ain't no such beasts."

Sir Maris stepped back among his men, ice-eyed and glowering. "Harm a hair of his head, and we'll flay you alive!"

"No fear," Brom O'Berin chuckled. "No fear, Gallowglass. Try all that you may to harm me. Be assured, you shall fail. Now look to yourself."

He jumped on the rafter, bellowed *"Now!"*

Rod dropped into a crouch, hands drawn back to chop.

Brom stood on the beam, fists on hips, great head nodding. "Aye, hold yourself ready. But"—his eyes lit with a malicious gleam; he chuckled—"Brom O'Berin is not a light man." He leaped from the rafter feet-first, straight at Rod's head.

Rod stepped back, startled at the suddenness of the dwarf's attack. Reflex took over; his hand swung up, palm upward, to catch Brom's heels and flip them up.

Then, expecting the dwarf to land flat on his back on the granite floor, Rod jumped forward to catch; but Brom spun through a somersault and landed bouncing on his feet.

He slapped Rod's hands away with a quick swipe. "A courtly gesture," he rumbled, "but a foolish one; your guard is down. Save gentleness for those who need it, man Gallowglass."

Rod stepped back, on guard again, and looked at the little man with dawning respect. "Seems I underestimated you, Master O'Berin."

"Call me not master!" the dwarf bellowed. "I'm no man's master; I'm naught but the Queen's fool!"

Rod nodded, slowly. "A fool."

He beckoned with both arms, and a savage grin. "Well enough then, wise fool."

Brom stood his ground a moment, measuring Rod with a scowl. He grunted, mouth snapping into a tight smile, and nodded.

He sprang, flipped in mid-air, feet heading straight for Rod's chin.

Rod swung a hand up to catch Brom's heels again, muttering, "I'd've thought you'd learn."

He shoved the dwarf's feet high; but this time Brom flipped his head up under Rod's chin. He had a very solid head.

Rod rolled with the punch, wrapping his arms tightly around Brom O'Berin's body in the process.

The dwarf shook with merriment. "How now?" he chortled. "Now that you've got me, what shall you do with me?"

Rod paused, panting.

It was a good question. If he relaxed his grip for a moment, he could be sure Brom would twist a kick into his belly. He could drop the little man, or throw him; but Brom had a tendency to bounce and would probably slam right into Rod's chin on the rebound.

Well, when in doubt, pin first and think later. Rod dropped to the floor, shoving Brom's body out at right angles to his own, catching the dwarf's knee and neck for a cradle hold.

But Brom moved just a little bit faster. His right arm snaked around Rod's left; he caught Rod's elbow in a vise-like grip and pulled.

Rod's back arched with the pain of the elbow lock. He now had a simple choice: let go with his left hand, or black out from pain.

Decisions, decisions!

Rod took a chance on his stamina; he tightened his hold on Brom's neck.

Brom grunted surprise. "Another man would have yelped his pain and leaped away from me, man Gallowglass."

Brom's knee doubled back; his foot shoved against Rod's chest, slid up under the chin, and kept on pushing.

Rod made a strangling noise; fire lanced the back of his neck as vertebrae ground together. The room darkened, filled with points of colored light.

"You must let hold of me now, Gallowglass," Brom murmured, "ere sight fails, and you sleep."

Did the damn half-pint *always* have to be right?

Rod tried a furious gurgle by way of reply; but the room

was dimming at an alarmingly rapid rate, the points of light were becoming pinwheels, and a fast exit seemed indicated.

He dropped his hold, shoved against the floor with his arms, and came weaving to his feet, with a throaty chuckle filling his ears.

For Brom had kept his hold on Rod's arm and had wrapped his other hand in the throat of Rod's doublet, his weight dragging Rod back toward the floor.

Brom's feet touched the ground; he shoved, throwing Rod back.

Rod staggered, overbalanced, and fell, but habit took over again. He tucked in his chin, slapped the floor with his forearms, breaking his fall.

Brom howled with glee at seeing Rod still conscious, and leaped.

Rod caught what little breath remained to him and snapped in his feet. He caught Brom right in the stomach, grabbed a flailing arm, and shoved, letting the arm go.

Brom flipped head over heels, sailed twenty feet past Rod, and landed on the stone flags with a grunt of surprise. He landed on his feet, of course, and spun about with a bellow of laughter. "Very neat, lad, very neat! But not enough . . ."

Rod was on his feet again, panting and shaking his head. Brom hopped toward him, then sprang.

Rod ducked low, in a vain hope that Brom might be capable of missing once; but the little man's long arm lashed out to catch Rod across the throat, stumpy body swinging around to settle between Rod's shoulders.

One foot pressed into the small of Rod's back, both arms pulled back against the base of his throat.

Rod gurgled, coming to his feet and bending backward under Brom's pull. He seized the dwarf's forearms, then bowed forward quickly, yanking Brom's arms.

Brom snapped over Rod's head and somersaulted away. He crowed as his feet hit the floor.

"Bravely done, lad! Bravely done!"

He turned about, the glint of mischief still in his eyes. "But I grow weary of this game. Let us be done with it."

"Tr-try," Rod panted.

Brom hunched forward, his long arms flailing out, slapping at Rod's guard.

He grabbed for Rod's knee. Rod dropped his right hand to block Brom's attempt, then threw his left about Brom's shoulders, trying to shove him forward to lose his balance;

but the dwarf's hands seemed to have gotten tangled in Rod's collar again.

Rod straightened, trying to throw Brom off, hands chopping at the little man's elbows; Brom's grip only tightened.

The dwarf kicked out, throwing all his weight forward. Rod stumbled, saw the floor coming up at him.

Brom leaped past him, catching Rod's foot on the way. Rod did a bellywhopper on the stone floor, but he slapped out with his forearms and kept his head from hitting.

He tried to rise but someone had tied a millstone across his shoulders. A snake coiled under his left arm and pressed against the back of his neck.

Rod tried to roll to break the half nelson, but a vise closed on his right wrist and drew it up into a hammerlock.

"Yield, lad," Brom's voice husked in his ear. "Yield, for you cannot be rid of me now."

He shoved Rod's arm higher in the hammerlock to emphasize his point. Rod ground his teeth against the pain.

He struggled to his feet somehow, tried to shake the little man off. But Brom's feet were locked around his waist.

"Nay," the dwarf muttered, "I told you you'd not be rid of me."

Rod shook himself like a terrier, but Brom held on like a bulldog. For a moment, Rod considered falling on his back to crush Brom under him. It was galling to be beaten by a man one-third your size. He discarded the idea quickly, though; there were many times in this bout where Brom could have played equally shabby tricks on Rod.

So Brom had a strong sense of fair play; and Rod was damned if he'd come off as smaller than a dwarf.

Brom's voice was a burr in his ear. "Will you not yield, man?" And Rod gasped as his right hand tried to touch the nape of his neck.

Then Brom shoved hard on Rod's neck, forcing his chin down to touch his collarbone. Rod staggered, lurched forward, and threw out a leg to keep himself from falling. The muscles across his back and neck screamed at the torture; his right arm begged him to give in. His diaphragm folded in on itself, stubbornly refusing to pull in another breath of air. His windpipe crooked into a kink, and his lungs called for air. In a weird, detached moment he noted that night seemed to have fallen all of a sudden; and, stranger yet, the stars were tumbling . . .

Water splashed cold on his face. The mouth of a bottle

thrust between his lips, feeling as large as a cartwheel. Liquid trickled over his tongue and down to his belly, where it exploded into fire.

He shook his head, and noticed that there was cold stone under his back. Now, what the hell was he doing, trying to sleep on a stone floor?

Voices echoed in his head. He opened his eyes, saw a round face with great brown eyes framed in shaggy black hair and beard, peering down at him.

The head swam away, and gray stone blocks reeled about him. He gasped, stared at the glint of light from a spearhead, and the room slowly steadied.

A voice thundered in his ear. "He is a miracle, Sir Maris! He made me sweat!"

A massive arm cradled Rod's head and shoulders, lifting them from the stone. Big Tom's great round face swam into view, brows knit with concern.

"Be you well, master?"

Rod grunted something, waving a hand and nodding.

Then the shaggy head was there, too, a shaggy head with a chimpanzee's body, and a hand heavy with muscle clasped his.

"Well fought, lad," rumbled Brom O'Berin. "I've not had such a bout since I came to my manhood."

Rod gripped the dwarf's hand and tried to grin.

Then Sir Maris' scarred, white-bearded face bowed over him, his old hand clasping Rod's upper arm, lifting him to his feet. "Come, lad, stand tall! For you're a man of the Queen's army now!"

"Queen's army!" boomed Brom, somehow up on the rafters again. The room rocked with his laughter. "Nay, Sir Maris, I claim this lad! 'Tis the Queen's own bodyguard for him!"

"No, dammit, Big Tom! Get away from me with that thing!"

"But, master!" Tom chased after him, holding up the breastplate. "You must wear *some* armor!"

"Give me one good reason why," Rod growled.

"Why, to turn away arrows and swords, master!"

"Swords I can turn easily enough with my own. Arrows I can duck. And against crossbow quarrels, it won't do a damn bit of good anyway! No, Big Tom! All it'll do is slow me down."

The guard room door groaned on its hinges, boomed shut.

Brom O'Berin stood watching them, fists on his hips, a silver glimmer draped over one shoulder. "How is this, Rod Gallowglass? Will you not wear the Queen's livery?"

"I'll wear livery when you do, you motley manikin!"

The dwarf grinned, teeth flashing white through the wilderness of beard. "A touch, a distinct touch! But I'm not a Guardsman, Rod Gallowglass; I'm a fool, and motley is fool's livery. Come, soldier, into your colors!"

"Oh, I'll wear the Queen's colors well enough. Fact is, I'm kinda partial to purple and silver. Only thing I've got against them is that they're livery; but I'll wear 'em. But, dammit, Brom, I absolutely refuse to have anything to do with that damn sweatbox you call armor!"

The dwarf's face sobered; he nodded slowly, his eyes holding Rod's. "Oh, aye. I had thought you to be of such persuasion."

The silver cloth flew jingling from his shoulder, slapped against Rod's chest. Rod caught it, held it up, inspected it with a frown.

"Will you wear a mail shirt, Rod Gallowglass?"

"I'd as soon wear a hair shirt," Rod growled; but he wriggled into the iron vest. "Good fit," he muttered, and gave the mail shirt a baleful eye; but his chest expanded and his shoulders came back, almost as though he were strutting.

His glance stabbed out at Brom O'Berin. "How is this, Brom? How come you'll let me get away without a breastplate? Out of uniform, aren't I?"

"Not so," Brom rumbled, "for the armor is hidden under the livery. And you are the only man of the Guard who would not wish plate armor."

Rod looked at the little man out of the corner of his eye. "How'd you know I didn't want the breastplate?"

Brom chuckled, deep in his beard. "Why, I've fought you, Rod Gallowgalss, and 'twas well you fought me, in my own manner!" His smile disappeared. "Nay, you'd no sooner wear armor than I would."

Rod scowled, studying the great bearded face. "You don't quite trust me yet, do you?"

Brom smiled, a tight grimace of irony. "Rod Gallowglass, there's no man I trust, and I regard any Queen's Guard with suspicion till he has given his life to save hers."

Rod nodded. "And how many is that?"

Brom's eyes burned into his. "Seven," he said. "In the last year, seven Guards have I come to trust."

Rod jerked the left side of his mouth into a hard smile.

He caught up the silver-on-purple doublet, shrugged into it. "So if you really come to think highly of me, you may let me taste the Queen's food to see if it's poisoned."

"Nay," Brom growled. "That pleasure is mine, mine to me alone."

Rod was silent a moment, looking into the little man's eyes.

"Well," he said, and turned away to buckle on the purple cloak. "I notice you're still alive."

Brom nodded. "Though 'tis several times I've been ill—ill for fair, my lad. But I seem to have the knack of telling poison by taste; I need not wait for death's proof."

He grinned, and strode across the floor to slap at Rod's iron-clad belly. "But come, there's no cause to be glum! All you'll have to face is swords, and perhaps now and again a crossbow, so be of good cheer."

"Oh, I'm just trembling with eagerness," Rod muttered.

Brom pivoted, headed for the door. "But now to the Queen's council chamber! Come, I'll show you your station."

He spun, arm pointing at Big Tom. "You there, man Tom! Back to the barracks with you; your master will call you at need."

Tom looked to Rod for confirmation; Rod nodded.

Brom slammed the door open and strode through. Rod shook his head, smiling, and followed.

The Queen's council chamber was a large, round room, mostly filled with a great round table twenty feet in diameter. There were ponderous doors at the south, east, and west points of the compass; the north point was taken up by a yawning fireplace, crackling with a small bonfire.

The walls were hung with gaudy tapestries and rich furs. A great shield blazoned with the royal arms hung over the fireplace. The ceiling arched concave, almost a dome, crossed by great curving beams.

The table was polished walnut. Around it sat the twelve Great Lords of the realm: the Duke Di Medici, the Earl of Romanoff, the Duke of Gloucester, the Prince Borgia, the Earl Marshall, Duke Stewart, the Duke of Bourbon, the Prince Hapsburg, Earl Tudor, the Baronet of Ruddigore, the Duke of Savoy, and the great grizzled old Duke of Loguire.

All were there, Rod saw, listening to a herald read their names from a scroll—all except the Queen, Catharine Plantagenet. Mulling over the list of names the elite of the

Emigrés had chosen for themselves, Rod decided that they had been not only romantics, but also geniune crackpots. Plantagenet forsooth!

Next to each of the great lords sat a slight, wiry, wizened little man, an old man; each had an almost emaciated face, with burning blue eyes, and a few wisps of hair brushed flat over a leathery skull.

Councillors? Rod wondered. Strange that they all looked so much alike. . . .

All sat in massive, ornately carved, dark-wood chairs. A larger, gilded chair stood vacant at the east point of the table.

A drum rolled, a trumpet sneezed, and the lords and councillors rose to their feet.

The great double leaves of the east door boomed wide, and Catharine stepped into the chamber.

Rod was stationed at the side of the west door; he had an excellent view, one which gave his heart pause.

A cloud of silver hair about a finely chiseled, pouting face; great blue eyes and rosebud lips; and a slender child's body, budding breasts and kitten hips under clinging silk, molded tighter to her by the wide belt of her girdle, a Y from hips to floor.

She sat in the vacant chair, hands gripping the arm rests, back braced stiff against the gilded wood.

Brom O'Berin hopped up onto a stool at her right. Directly across from her, at the west point of the table, sat the Duke Loguire. His councillor leaned close, whispering. The Duke shushed him impatiently.

Brom O'Berin nodded to a herald.

"The Queen's Grand Council is met," the herald cried. "The high and great of the land of Gramarye are gathered. Let all among them who seek redress of wrongs petition now the Queen, in the presence of their peers."

Silence filled the room.

The Duke of Bourbon stirred uneasily and coughed.

Brom's head swiveled to the man. "My lord of Bourbon," he rumbled, "will you address the Queen?"

Slowly, the Duke rose. His doublet was blazoned with fleurs-de-lis, but his hair and moustache were blond.

"Your Majesty," said the Duke, bowing gravely to the Queen, "and my brother lords." He nodded his head toward the table in general, then lifted his chin, straightening his shoulders. "I must protest," he growled.

Catharine tilted her back so that she gave the impression of looking down her nose at the tall nobleman. "What must you protest, my lord?"

The Duke of Bourbon looked down at the walnut table-top. "Since our ancestors came from beyond the stars, the peasants have been subject to their lords; and the lords have been subject to the Great Lords. The Great Lords, in their turn, are subject to the King . . . the Queen," he amended, with a slight bow to Catharine.

Her lips pressed into a tight, thin line, but she took the slight with good grace.

"This," the Duke resumed, "is the natural order of mankind, that each man be subject to the man above him; that justice and order be the concern of the lord; within his demesne, he is, and should be, the law, subject, of course, to the Queen."

Again the polite nod to Catharine, and again, she accepted the slight; but her hands pinched the arms of the chair so tightly the knuckles turned white.

"Yet now your Majesty would overturn this great and lasting order, and force upon us judges of your own appointing to dispense justice within our demesnes, judges subject only to yourself. This, though it be contrary to the wisdom of your father, noble Queen, and his father before him, and all your ancestors from the beginning of your line. If I may speak plainly, I find it almost a mockery of your great and noble forebears; and, speaking for myself, I cannot abide this peasant underling of yours, who thinks to lord it over me in my own manor!"

He finished almost in a shout, glaring red-faced at the Queen.

"Are you done?" asked Catharine in a tone she'd been keeping in cold storage for just such an occasion.

Slowly, the Duke of Bourbon bowed his head. "I am." He sat.

Catharine closed her eyes a moment, then looked to Brom O'Berin and nodded, almost imperceptibly.

Brom stood. "Do any speak in support of my lord of Bourbon?" A young man with fiery red hair came to his feet. "I agree with all that my lord of Bourbon has said. I will add, moreover, that the Queen might do well to consider the question of the corruptibility of her appointed judges; for a man without lands or means, and no family name to uphold, might easily be tempted to sell his justice."

"If they do," Catharine snapped, "they shall be hanged from the highest gallows; and the men they have wronged shall serve for their executioners."

She was silent for the space of three breaths, eyes locked with the young nobleman's; then Brom O'Berin growled, "Our thanks to the noble Duke of Savoy."

The young man bowed, and sat.

"Who else will speak in favor of my lords of Bourbon and Savoy?"

One by one, the other ten lords rose to second the Duke of Bourbon. The Queen's Grand Council was unanimously against her.

Catharine held her eyes closed a moment; her lips pressed tight. She looked up to sweep the table with a glare. "My lords, I am deeply grieved to find you all so much opposed to the Queen's justice." She gave them a brittle smile. "I thank you for your *honest* council. Yet I am constant in my purpose; my judges shall remain on your estates."

The noblemen stirred in their seats, muttering to one another in low, husky voices. They seemed to comprise one large, restless animal, growling.

The old Duke of Loguire rose slowly, and leaned heavily on the table. "My Queen," he rumbled, "consider: even kings may fault in judgment, and you are young in statecraft yet. It is known that many minds together may come to clearer knowledge than one mind alone; and here are gathered with you twelve men of most ancient and honorable lineage, of families grown hoary in statecraft; old men of old families; and, it is to be hoped, wise with the weight of their years. Will you persist in your course, when so many are so sure that you are wrong?"

Catharine's face was pale, almost dead white. Her eyes were burning. "I will," she said quietly.

The Lord Loguire held her eyes for a long moment, then slowly sat.

Catharine surveyed the faces around her, taking time to look deep into each pair of eyes.

Then, lifting her chin, she said, "My judges will remain on your estates, my lords. As to their corruptibility, you will find them almost saintly in their disregard for money, wine, and . . . comforts. They care for one thing only, and that is justice."

She paused to let her words sink in; and Rod noted that there were several beet-red faces among the great lords. At a rough guess, he decided, justice had not been quite as pure as it might have been on some of their estates.

The Duke Loguire did not have a red face. The only emotion Rod could read in him was grief.

"This whole matter of the judges is, however, secondary to the purpose for which I have called you here today." Catharine smiled, with more than a hint of malice.

Heads jerked up in alarm, all around the board. Brom O'Berin looked more shocked than any. Apparently Catharine had not consulted with her Prime Councillor; even Brom was due for a surprise.

Each lord bent his head for a quick, whispered conference with his councillor; and the looks of alarm on their faces deepened into sullen anger.

"On each of your estates," said Catharine, "there is a monastery. You have been accustomed to appointing the priests for the parishes of your demesnes from your own monasteries."

She looked down at the tabletop for a moment, then lifted her head again. "Here in this castle I am gathering the best theologians of all the monasteries. You shall choose young brothers from your monks, one for each of your parishes, and send them here to me, to be trained by my monks. If in any case I do not approve of your choice in young men, I shall send them back to you, and demand others in their places. When they have finished their studies and taken their Orders, I shall return them to you, to be your parish priests."

The lords slammed to their feet, shouting and gesturing, fists thudding on the table.

Catharine's voice crackled into the uproar. "Enough! Be still!"

Slowly, one by one, the Great Lords fell into sullen silence and sank back into their seats, glaring.

But their councillors' faces seemed lit with a suppressed joy; their eyes were burning, and each face held a smile just short of a grin.

"I have spoken," Catharine said, voice and eyes both chill. "It shall be done."

Trembling, the old Lord Loguire rose. "Will your Majesty not—"

"I will not."

Brom O'Berin cleared his throat. "If your Majesty will permit—"

"I will not."

Silence sat over the council chamber. Once again, Catharine surveyed the faces of her lords and their councillors.

Then, turning to her left, she bowed her head. "My Lord Loguire."

The old nobleman rose, his jaw clamped tight under the grizzled beard, his liver-spotted fist palsied with barely-held anger.

He drew back the great, gilded chair, and Catharine rose. He stepped back to his place. Catharine turned away, and the great oak doors were thrown wide. Guardsmen fell in before and behind her.

She paused in the doorway, and turned. "Consider, my lords," she said, "and consent; for you cannot stand against me."

The great doors slammed behind her.

The council chamber burst into pandemonium.

"Oh, come off it! It's the classic pattern, right down to the last look of outrage!"

His day's duty done, Rod was riding Fess back to the inn, bent on picking up a little gossip and a lot of beer. Big Tom was tending the home fires at the Royal Castle, with orders to keep his ears open for juicy tidbits of information.

"I disagree, Rod. It's the classic pattern with something added."

"Bull! It's a simple, premature attempt at centralization of authority. She's trying to unify Gramarye under one law and one ruler, instead of twelve near-independent dukedoms. This business with the judges is that, and nothing more. Five'll get you ten some of those dukes have been playing god on their estates, forcing half the women to sleep with them and overtaxing everybody and anything else that occurred to them. Catharine's a reformer, that's all; she's trying to cure all the evils she can find by making herself the only law in Gramarye—and she won't make it. The noblemen just won't stand for it. She might have gotten away with the judges; but this business with the priests'll bring on a rebellion for sure. Priests have more influence over the people than any other officials in this kind of society. If she makes them responsible to her, and only her, she's really pulling the noblemen's teeth, and they know it. And they won't give up without a fight."

"So far, I'll agree with you," the robot said. "So far, it is the classic pattern, closely resembling the attempt of the

English King John to centralize his nation before such a project could succeed."

"Yes." Rod nodded. "And we can hope that, like King John's noblemen, the great dukes will insist on a Magna Carta."

"But . . ."

Rod assumed a look of martyr-like patience. "But what, Fess?"

"But there is a foreign element: a group of councillors to the Great Lords, a group that seems to be very cohesive."

Rod drowned. "Well, yes. There is that."

"And from what you tell me of the scene after Catharine left . . ."

"Yii!" Rod shuddered. "It was just as though she'd thrown down a gauntlet, and all the dukes were out to see who'd get the honor of taking it up. The girl might know some elementary political science, but she sure doesn't know any diplomacy! She was just daring them to fight her!"

"Yes, and the councillors were egging them on very nicely —each one councilling his lord not to fight, because he was too weak . . . and then telling them that if he must fight, he'd better ally with the other lords, because each was too weak to stand alone. Expert use of reverse psychology. One would almost think the councillors were out to eliminate central authority completely."

"Yes . . ." Rod frowned, musing. "That's not quite normal to this kind of society, is it, Fess?"

"No, Rod. The theory of anarchy does not usually arise until the culture has attained a much higher degree of technology."

Rod chewed at his lip. "Outside influence, maybe?"

"Perhaps. And that brings us to the popular totalitarian movement: another anomaly. No, Rod, this is not the classic pattern."

"No, dammit. We've got three groups contending for power: the peasants, the dukes and their councillors, and the Queen and whoever supports her. That support seems to be limited to Brom O'Berin at the moment."

"Totalitarians, anarchists, and the Queen in the middle," Fess murmured. "Which one do *you* support, Rod?"

"Catharine, dammit!" Rod grinned. "I'm out to plant the seeds of democracy; and it looks like the only chance to do that is to engineer a constitutional monarchy."

"I might be mistaken," Fess murmured, "But I do believe you're delighted to find you must support her."

Around them the few lights were dimmed by the night mist, a wall of fog thirty feet away. Rod rode alone through a world of smoke; Fess's hooves rang strangely weird in the echoing silence.

A long yell split the night, followed by the slapping clash of swords. "A rescue, a rescue!" a young voice cried.

Rod froze, hand on the pommel of his sword; then he dug his heels into Fess's metal sides, and the great black horse sprang toward the ruckus.

A torch smoldered red through the fog at the mouth of an alley. There, under its smoky light, one man battled three, his back against the wall.

Rod bellowed and landed horse and all in the middle of the melee. He laid about him with the flat of his sword, howling like an Indian studying to be a Confederate soldier. He yanked the dagger from the small of his back, just in time to catch a rapier coming at him from his left. His own sword swung in an arc over his head and clashed against steel as his opponent caught the blow.

Then steel points were jabbing up at him like sawgrass. Rod was forced back on the defensive, swatting the blades aside.

But the intended victim let loose a yell that would have shamed a banshee and waded in from the rear.

All at once the three swords fell away, their owners pelting down the alley. Rod sat a moment dazed; then he yelled, and Fess sprang after the retreating figures.

But they gained the dark at the end of the alley; and when Rod caught up, the stones were empty. It was a dead end; they had gone through one of the shadowed, evil-smelling doorways.

Their would-be victim came running up behind, looked about, and panted.

"Gone, and no use to seek them further. They'll be five leagues away in as many minutes."

Rod swore and slapped his sword back into its scabbard. He winced, and touched his forearm gingerly; one of the rapier-points had slashed through his doublet and sliced his skin.

He turned to the stranger. "You all right?"

The young man nodded, sheathing his sword.

Rod looked down into an open, snub-nosed, blue-eyed face

68

with a grin that flashed white through the fog. The cheek-bones were high, and the eyes large and wide, with a look of innocence. Blond hair was cropped round in a bowl cut. It was a young, inexperienced, very handsome face—Rod felt a surge of resentment.

He swung down from his horse. The top of the youth's head was about on a level with Rod's eyes; but what the boy lacked in height, he made up in bulk. A barrel chest swelled into bull shoulders, a good six inches wider than Rod's. The arms would have looked more appropriate on a bear or gorilla; and the legs were two small tree trunks, rammed into narrow hips.

He wore a leather jerkin over a white shirt, a wide black belt, hose, and high, soft boots.

He frowned, seeing the blood on Rod's sleeve. "You're hurt."

Rod snorted. "A scratch," he said, and fumbled in Fess's saddlebag for an antiseptic bandage. He wound the bandage around his forearm, threw the youth a hard grin. "You can pay the tailor bill, though."

The boy nodded, blue eyes sober. "That will I gladly; for they would have cut my heart out, had it not been for your timely rescue. Tuan McReady stands in your debt."

Rod looked him up and down, nodding slowly. A good kid, he thought.

He held out his hand. "Rod Gallowglass, at your service; and there's no debt involved. Always glad to help one against three."

"Ah, but debt there is!" said the boy, clasping Rod's hand with a grip like a sentimental vise. "You must, at the least, let me buy you a tankard of ale!"

Rod shrugged. "Why not? I was on my way to an inn just now, anyway; come on along!"

To his surprise, Tuan hesitated. "By your leave, good Master Gallowglass . . . there is only one house in this town where I am welcomed. All others have known my custom of old, and"—the round face suddenly broke into a grin—"my manner of living does not please the peaceful and proper."

Rod grimaced, nodding. *"Post jocundum juventutem.* Well, one inn's as good as another, I guess."

The route to Tuan's inn was somewhat out of keeping with his well-bred looks. They dogged down two dark alleys, wriggled through a weathered brick wall, and came out in a wide, moonlit courtyard that had been elegant in its day.

That day must have been a century or two in the past. The remains of a fountain burbled in the center of cracked flagstones, sending up a stench redolent of primitive plumbing. Weeds, themselves in a state of dire poverty, poked through the paving everywhere. The brick of the walls was cracked and split, the mortar crumbling. Heaps of garbage lay by the walls and in the corners, with stray mounds of refuse here and there about the yard.

The inn itself was a rotting granite block with tumbledown eaves. The overhanging second story was propped up with roughhewn timbers, not to be trusted due to the infirmities of age. The windows were boarded over, the boards split, moldy, and fungoid. The massive oak door was the only sound piece of wood in sight, and even it was sagging.

"Ah, they tolerate your behavior here?" Rod asked, surveying the stagnant courtyard as Tuan knocked on the door with the hilt of his dagger.

"Tolerate, yes," said Tuan, "though even their hospitality is sometimes strained."

Rod felt a chill between his shoulder blades and wondered just what kind of mild-mannered youth he'd run into.

Tuan knocked again. Rod wondered that he expected an answer; not a gleam of light showed through the sagging window boards. By the look of it, the place must be totally deserted.

But the door began to move, and groaned that it was going on strike for an oil break, till it was open just wide enough to admit the two men.

"Your host," said Tuan cheerily, "the Mocker."

A gnarled, hunched, dessicated travesty of a human being peered around the door, making gobbling sounds in its throat. One ear was cauliflower, and the other was gone; a few strands of greasy hair straggled over a scabby skull. The nose was bulbous, the mouth a slash in a mass of warts, the eye malevolent, gleaming slits. It was dressed in a collection of tatters and patches that might once have laid claim to being a doublet and hose, sagging badly on the scarecrow figure.

The troll scurried away into the foul-smelling dark of its lair. Tuan strode through the door, following. Rod took a deep breath, squared his shoulders, and looked back over his shoulder to make sure Fess was still standing there, by the fountain, head lowered in a good imitation of a horse grazing. For a moment, Rod envied the robot his ability to cut off his olfactory receptors.

Then, lifting his chin, he followed Tuan into the inn.

The door ground shut behind him; there was a scurrying sound as the Mocker ran ahead to open another door.

This one opened easily, slammed back against the wall, flooding them with a blaze of torchlight and gales of coarse, bawdy laughter. Rod stared.

They stepped through the door, and Rod looked about him. It was a great common room, with four roaring open fires and score upon score of torches bracketed along the walls. Roasting meat hung over the fires; waiters wove their way through the crowd with tankards of ale and wine from two huge, flowing kegs that dominated the far side of the room.

The clientele were the lees of the city. Their clothes were crusted, patched castoffs. Their bodies bore the marks of primitive justice: this one was missing an ear, that one an eye. Their faces were disfigured and scarred by disease. Yet here in their own den they roared merrily; all of them grinned, though malice glinted in their eyes as they looked at Rod.

But the malice faded, was transmuted into something almost like worship, as they looked at young Tuan.

"It is said," and the boy smiled, "that there is no honor among thieves; but there is at least kinship here, among the beggars of Gramarye. Welcome, Rod Gallowglass, to the House of Clovis."

The hair at the base of Rod's skull prickled. He remembered the torchlight mob he had seen on the waterfront the night before.

His eyes widened; he stared at Tuan. He couldn't be. He couldn't be.

Oh, but he could. Yes, he could.

Tuan McReady was the young rabble-rouser who'd been haranguing the mob to march on the castle.

This apple-cheeked, wholesome youth was top rat in the local sewer.

The crowd broke into a raucous, cheering clamor, welcoming their Galahad. Tuan grinned and waved. A slight flush crept up from his collar. He seemed almost embarrassed by the reception.

He led Rod to a dark corner at the back of the hall. He hadn't said a word to the Mocker, but two steaming mugs of mulled wine thumped down on the table almost as they sat. The landlord scuttled away without pay.

Rod watched him go, one eyebrow lifted in cynicism. He turned to Tuan. "You don't use money here?"

"None." Tuan smiled. "All who come to the House of Clovis bring what little money they have. It is put into a common chest, and meat and wine given out to all according to their needs."

"And a place to sleep, I suppose?"

"Aye, and clothing. It is poor fare by a gentleman's standards; but it is great wealth to these my poor brethren."

Rod studied Tuan's face and decided the boy might have meant it when he said brethren.

He sat back and crossed his legs. "Would you call yourself a religious man?"

"I?" Tuan tried to choke back a laugh and almost succeeded. "Oh, nay! Would that I were; but I have not seen the inside of a church for three score and more Sundays!"

So, Rod noted, his motive for helping the poor probably wasn't too hypocritical, whatever else it might be.

He looked into his mug. "So you feed and clothe all these people out of the pennies they bring you, eh?"

"Nay; that is but a beginning. But with that much earnest proof of our good intentions, our noble Queen found us worthy of a livelihood."

Rod stared. "You mean the Queen is putting the lot of you on the dole?"

Tuan grinned with mischief. "Aye, though she knows not whom she aids. She knows not the House of Clovis by name, knows only that she gives the good Brom O'Berin moneys to care for her poor."

"And Brom gives it to you."

"Aye. And for his part, he is grateful that there are fewer thievings and murders among the dark alleys."

Rod nodded. "Very shrewd. And this whole setup is your idea, is it?"

"Oh, nay! 'Twas the Mocker who thought of it; but none would give ear to him."

Rod stared. "The Mocker? You mean that twisted fugitive from the late show is boss of this operation?"

Tuan frowned, shaking his head. "Men will not follow him, friend Gallowglass; there is nothing of governance in him. He is host, keeping the inn, doling out goods as they are needed—a steward, and only a steward, but a good one.

72

You will find him a sharper clerk than any; aye, even the Queen's Lord Exchequer."

"I see, just a steward." *But also the man who holds the pocketbook,* Rod added mentally. *The brains of the outfit, too. Tuan might know how to make people do what he wanted; but did he know what he wanted?*

Yes, of course he did. Hadn't the Mocker told him? Which made the Mocker the local political economist, and probably Tuan's speech-writer.

Rod leaned back, rubbing his chin. "And you manage to keep them in this decadent luxury with only the alms the beggars bring in? Plus the Queen's shilling, of course."

Tuan grinned sheepishly and leaned forward, nodding. " 'Tis not easy done, friend Gallowglass. These beggars are loath to let any man rule them. It is tedious labor, cajoling, threatening, flattering—a man grows a-weary of it. Yet it is well worth the doing."

Rod nodded. "It would take a man with no false pride, and less false humility, and one who could see into his fellow's heart."

Tuan blushed.

"Such a man," said Rod, "could make himself king of the beggars."

But Tuan shook his head, eyes closed. "No, there is no king here, friend Gallowglass. A lord of the manor, perhaps, but naught more."

"You don't want to be king?"

Tuan's shoulders shrugged with a snort of laughter. "The beggars would not hear of it!"

"That wasn't what I asked."

Tuan's eyes locked with Rod's, the smile fading from the boyish face. Then Tuan caught Rod's meaning, and his eyes hardened. "Nay!" he spat. "I do not seek the throne."

"Then why are you trying to lead the beggars against the Queen?" Rod rapped out.

The smile eased across Tuan's face again; he sat back, looking very satisfied with himself. "Ah, you know of my plotting! Then may I ask of you outright, friend Rod, will you join with us when we march on the castle?"

Rod felt his face setting like plaster. His eyes locked with Tuan's again; his voice was very calm. "Why me?"

"We shall have need of as many friends in the Queen's Guard as we may have. . . ."

"You must already have quite a few," Rod murmured, "if

73

you know already that I joined the Queen's Guard today."

Tuan's grin widened; his eyelids drooped.

A stray fact clicked into place in Rod's mind.

"If I were to search through this hall," he said carefully, "would I find the three men who attacked you tonight?"

Tuan nodded, eyes dancing.

"A put-up job," Rod said, nodding with him. "A small performance, arranged solely for my benefit, with the single purpose of maneuvering me in here for a recruiting lecture. You *do* know how to manage people, Tuan McReady."

Tuan blushed, and looked down.

"But what if I don't want to join you, Tuan McReady? Will I leave the House of Clovis alive this night?"

Tuan's head came up, eyes boring into Rod's.

"Only," he said, "if you are an excellent swordsman, and a warlock to boot."

Rod nodded slowly, the events of the past two days whirling through his mind. For a moment, he was tempted to join; he had no doubt that he could maneuver himself into the throne after the revolution.

But no; what Tuan said was true. It took a man with an inborn gift of mass hypnotism to control the beggars. Rod might take the throne, but the beggars—and the Mocker, and whoever was behind him—would not let him keep it.

No, the power structure had to stay the way it was; a constitutional monarchy was the only hope for democracy on this planet.

Then, too, there was Catharine. . . .

Then the jarring note in the score of events caught Rod's ear. He was hung up on Catharine, probably; she was the Dream.

But he had liked Tuan at first sight. How could he like them both if they were really working against one another?

Of course, all Tuan's forthright charm might be an act, but somehow Rod doubted it.

No. If Tuan had really wanted the throne, he could have wooed Catharine, and could have won her—Rod had no doubt about that.

So Tuan was supporting the Queen. How he figured his demagoguery could help her, Rod couldn't figure, but somehow it made sense that Tuan believed he was.

Then why the elaborate plot to get Rod into the House of Clovis?

To test Rod, of course; to find out if he was to be trusted next to the Queen.

Which made sense, if this kid had dealings with Brom O'Berin. It would be just like Brom to try to drum up popular support for the Queen in just this way—but why the propaganda for a march on the castle?

Tuan probably had an answer to that one, and speaking of answers, it was about time Rod came up with one.

He gave Tuan a savage grin and rose, with his hand on his sword. "No thanks. I'll take my chances with swordcraft and sorcery.

Tuan's eyes lit with joy; he caught Rod's arm. "Well spoken, friend Gallowglass! I had hoped you would answer thus. Now sit, and hear the truth of my plot."

Rod shook his hand off. "Draw," he said between his teeth.

"Nay, nay! I would not draw 'gainst a friend. I have played a low trick on you, but you must not hold anger; 'twas for a good purpose. But sit, and I shall tell you."

"I've heard all I want." Rod started to draw his sword.

Tuan caught Rod's forearm again, and this time his hand wouldn't shake off. Rod looked into Tuan's eyes, jaw tightened and arm muscles straining; but slowly and steadily, his sword was forced back into its scabbard.

"Sit," said Tuan, and he forced Rod back into his chair as easily as though Rod had been a child.

"Now hear my plot." Tuan let go of Rod's arm and smiled, as warmly as though nothing had happened. "The Queen gives us money, and the beggars know that she gives it; but the taking of a gift raises only burning anger in the taker. If we would win friends for the Queen, we must find a way to transmute this anger to gratitude."

Rod nodded, frowning.

"Thus we must make the Queen's shilling something other than a gift."

"And you found a way to do it."

"Not I," Tuan confessed, "but the Mocker. 'When is a gift not a gift?' he riddled me, and answered, 'Why, when 'tis a right.' "

Tuan leaned back, spreading his hands. "And there you have it, so easily done. The beggars shall march to the castle and cry to the Queen that she owes them bread and meat, because it is their right. And she will give it to them, and they will be grateful."

Rod smiled, rubbing his chin. "Very shrewd," he said, nodding, but to himself he added: *If it works. But it won't; people who have money enjoy giving for charity, but they won't give a cent if you tell them they must. And how grateful will the beggars be when she refuses them, and calls out the army to drive them away?*

And even if she did yield to their demands, what then? What about the sense of power it would give them? Beggars, forcing a Queen's hand! They wouldn't stop at bread and meat; no, they'd be back with more demands in a week, with or without Tuan.

Oh, yes, it was a very shrewd plan; and Tuan had been sucked into it beautifully. The Mocker couldn't lose; and neither could the off-planet totalitarians who were behind him.

But Tuan meant well. His intentions fairly gleamed. He was a little weak on political theory; but his intentions were fine.

Rod raised his mug for a deep draught, then stared into it, watching the swirl of the heated wine. "Yet some say that the House of Clovis would pull Catharine off her throne."

"Nay, nay!" Tuan stared, appalled. "I love the Queen!"

Rod studied the boy's sincere, open face and made his own interpretation of the statement.

He looked back into his mug. "So do I," he said, with more truth than he liked. "But even so, I'd have to admit she's, shall we say, not acting wisely."

Tuan heaved a great sigh and clasped his hands. "That is true, most true. She means so well, but she does so badly."

Have you looked in a mirror lately, Mr. Kettle? Rod wondered. Aloud, he said, "Why, how is that?"

Tuan smiled sadly. "She seeks to undo in a day what ages of her grandsires have wrought. There is much evil in this kingdom, that I will gladly admit. But a pile of manure is not moved with one swing of a shovel."

"True," Rod admitted, "and the saltpeter under it can be explosive."

"The great lords do not see that she is casting out devils," Tuan went on. "They see only that she seeks to fill this land with one voice, and only one—and that hers."

"Well"—Rod lifted his mug, face bleak with resignation—"here's to her; let's hope she makes it."

"An' you think it possible," said Tuan, "tha'rt a greater

fool than I; and I am known far and wide as a most exceptional fool."

Rod lowered the mug untasted. "Are you speaking from a general conviction, or do you have some particulars in mind?"

Tuan set one forefinger against the other. "A throne rests on two legs: *primus*, the noblemen, who are affronted by anything new, and therefore oppose the Queen."

"Thanks," said Rod with a bittersweet smile, "for letting me in on the secret."

"Left to themselves," said Tuan, "the nobles might abide her for love of her father; but there are the councillors."

"Yes." Rod caught his lower lip between his teeth. "I take it the lords do whatever their councillors tell them?"

"Or what they tell the lords *not* to do, which comes to the same thing. And the councillors speak with one voice—Durer's."

"Durer?" Rod scowled. "Who's he?"

"Councillor to my Lord Loguire." Tuan's mouth twisted, bitter. "He hath some influence with Loguire, which is a miracle; for Loguire is a most stubborn man. Thus, while Loguire lives, Catharine may stand. But when Loguire dies, Catharine falls; for Loguire's heir hates the Queen."

"Heir?" Rod raised an eyebrow. "Loguire has a son?"

"Two," said Tuan with a tight smile. "The younger is a fool, who loves his best enemy; and the elder is a hothead, who loves Durer's flattery. Thus, what Durer will say, Anselm Loguire will do."

Rod raised his mug. "Let us wish the Loguire long life."

"Aye," said Tuan, fervently. "For Anselm hath an ancient grievance against the Queen."

Rod frowned. "What grievance?"

"I know not." Tuan's face sagged till he looked like a bloodhound with sinus trouble. "I know not."

Rod sat back, resting one hand on the hilt of his sword. "So he and Durer both want the Queen's downfall. And the other nobles'll follow their lead—if old Loguire dies. So much for one leg of the throne. What's the other one?"

"*Secundus*," said Tuan, with a Cub Scout salute, "the people: peasants, tradesmen, and merchants. They love her for this newfound easing of their sorrows; but they fear her for her witches."

"Ah. Yes. Her . . . witches." Rod scowled, managing to look sharp-eyed and competent while his brain reeled. *Witches as a political element?!*

"For ages," said Tuan, "the witches have been put to the torture till they forswore the Devil, or have undergone the trial of water or, failing all else, been burned at the stake."

For a moment, Rod felt a stab of compassion for generations of espers.

"But the Queen harbors them now; and it is rumored by some that she is herself a witch."

Rod managed to shake off his mental fog long enough to croak, "I take it this doesn't exactly inspire the people with unflagging zeal for the Queen and her cause."

Tuan bit his lip. "Let us say that they are unsure. . . ."

"Scared as hell," Rod translated. "But I notice you didn't include the beggars as part of the people."

Tuan shook his head. "Nay, they are apart, frowned and spat upon by all. Yet of this flawed timber, I hope to carve a third leg for the Queen's throne."

Rod digested the words, studying Tuan's face.

He sat back in his chair, lifted his mug. "You just may have what the Queen needs, there." He drank. Lowering the mug, he said, "I suppose the councillors are doing everything they can to deepen the people's fear?"

Tuan shook his head, brow wrinkled in puzzlement. "Nay, they do nothing of the sort. Almost, one would think, they do not know the people live." He frowned into his mug, sloshing the wine about inside. "Yet there is little need to tell the people they must fear."

"They know it all too well already?"

"Aye, for they have seen that all the Queen's witches cannot keep the banshee off her roof."

Rod frowned, puzzled. "So let it wear a groove in the battlements if it wants to! It's not doing any harm, is it?"

Tuan looked up, surprised. "Dost not know the meaning of the banshee, Rod Gallowglass?"

Rod's stomach sank; nothing like displaying your ignorance of local legends when you're trying to be inconspicuous.

"When the banshee appears on the roof," said Tuan, "someone in the house will die. And each time the banshee has walked the battlements, Catharine hath escaped death by a hair."

"Oh?" Rod's eyebrows lifted. "Dagger? Falling tiles? Poison?"

"Poison."

Rod sat back, rubbing his chin. "Poison: the aristocrat's

weapon; the poor can't afford it. Who among the great lords hates Catharine that much?"

"Why, none!" Tuan stared, appalled. "Not one among them would stoop to poison, Rod Gallowglass; 'twould be devoid of honor."

"Honor still counts for something here, eh?" Seeing the scandalized look on Tuan's face, Rod hurried on. "That lets out the noblemen; but someone on their side's up to tricks. Wouldn't be the councillors, would it?"

Understanding and wary anger rose in Tuan's eyes. He sat back, nodding.

"But what do they gain by her death?" Rod frowned. "Unless one of them wants to crown his lordling and be the King's Councillor. . . ."

Tuan nodded. "Mayhap all wish that, friend Gallowglass."

Rod had a sudden vision of Gramarye carved up into twelve petty kingdoms, constantly warring against one another, each run by a warlord who was ruled by his councillor. Japanese usurpation, the man behind the throne, and anarchy.

Anarchy.

There was an outside force at work in Gramarye, agents with a higher technology and sophisticated political philosophies at work. The great nobles were slowly being divided, and the people were being set against the nobility, by means of the House of Clovis. The twelve petty kingdoms would be broken down to warring counties, and the counties to parishes, and so on until real anarchy prevailed.

The councillors were the outside force, carefully engineering a state of anarchy. But why?

Why could wait for later. What mattered now was that skulduggery was afoot, and it sat next to the Lord Loguire; its name was Durer.

And his top-priority goal was Catherine's death.

The castle loomed up black against the sky as Rod rode back, but the drawbridge and portcullis were a blaze of torchlight. Fess's hooves thudded hollow on the drawbridge. A blob of shadow detached itself from the larger shadow of the gate, a shadow that reached up to clamp a hand on Rod's shin.

"Hold, Rod Gallowglass!"

Rod looked down and smiled, noding. "Well met, Brom O'Berin."

"Mayhap," said the dwarf, searching Rod's face. "Thou must come before the Queen for this night's work, Rod Gallowglass."

Rod was still wondering how Brom could have known where he'd been as they came to the Queen's audience chamber. Brom had a spy in the House of Clovis, of course; but how could the word have gotten back to Brom so fast?

The door was massive, oak, iron-studded, and draped with velvet, the green and gold of the Queen's house. Brom ran a practiced eye over the two sentries, checking to see that all leather was polished and all metal gleaming. Rod gave them a nod; their faces turned to wood. Was he under suspicion of high treason?

At Brom's nod, one Guardsman struck the door backhanded, three slow heavy knocks, then threw it wide. Rod followed Brom into the room. The door boomed shut behind them.

The room was small but high-ceilinged, paneled in dark wood, lit only by four great candles that stood on a velvet-draped table in the center of the room, and by a small fire on the tiled hearth. A rich carpet covered the stone floor; tapestries hung on the walls. A huge bookcase filled the wall at the far end of the room.

Two heavy carved armchairs stood at either side of the fireplace; two more were drawn up at the table. Catharine sat in one of these, head bent over a large old leather-bound book. Five or six more lay open on the table about her. Her blond hair fell unbound about her shoulders, contrasting with the dark russet of her gown.

She lifted her head; her eyes met Rod's. "Well come." Her voice was a gentle, slightly husky contralto, so different from the crisp soprano of the council chamber that Rod wondered, for a moment, if it could be the same woman.

But the eyes were wary, arrogant. It was Catharine, all right.

But the heavy crown lay on the table beside her, and she seemed smaller, somehow.

"Hast been to the House of Clovis?" she demanded. Her eyes read like a subpoena.

Rod showed his teeth in a mock-grin and inclined his head in a nod.

" 'Tis even as you said, my Queen." Brom's voice had a grim overtone. "Though how you knew—"

"—is not your affair, Brom O'Berin." She threw the dwarf a glare; Brom smiled gently, bowed his head.

"How?" Rod snorted. "Why, spies of course. A very excellent spy service, to get the word back to her so fast."

"Nay." Brom frowned, puzzled. "Our spies are few enough, for loyalty is rare in this dark age; and we keep no spies at all at the House of Clovis."

"No spies," Catharine agreed, "and yet I know that thou hast had words with Tuan of the beggars this day."

Her voice softened; her eyes were almost gentle as she looked at the dwarf. "Brom . . . ?"

The dwarf smiled, bowed his head, and turned to the door. He struck the wood with the heel of his hand. The door swung open; Brom turned with one foot on the threshold, and a malevolent glare stabbed at Rod from under the bushy eyebrows; then the door slammed behind him.

Catharine rose, glided to the fireplace. She stood staring at the flames, hands clasped at her waist. Her shoulders sagged; and for a moment, she looked so small and forlorn—and so beautiful, with the firelight streaming up like a mist about her face and shoulders—that Rod's throat tightened in an old, familiar way.

Then her shoulders straightened, and her head snapped around toward him. "You are not what you seem, Rod Gallowglass."

Rod stared.

Catharine's hand strayed to her neck, playing with a locket at her throat.

Rod cleared his throat, a trifle nervously. "Here I am, just a simple blank-shield soldier, just carrying out my orders and taking my pay, and three times in thirty hours I get accused of being something mysterious."

"Then I must needs think that it is true." Catharine's mouth twisted in a mocking smile.

She sat in one of the great oaken chairs, grasping the arms tightly, and studied Rod for a few moments.

"What are you, Rod Gallowglass?"

Rod spread his arms in a shrug, trying to look the picture of offended innocence. "A blank shield, my Queen! A soldier of fortune, no more!"

" 'No more,' " Catharine mimicked, malice in her eyes. "What is your profession, Rod Gallowglass?"

Rod scowled, beginning to feel like the rodent half of a game of cat-and-mouse. "A soldier, my Queen."

"That is your avocation," she said, "your pleasure and your game. Tell me now your profession."

The woman was A) uncanny; and B) a bitch, Rod decided. Trouble was, she was a beautiful bitch, and Rod had a weakness.

His brain raced; he discarded several lies and chose the most obvious and least plausible.

"My profession is the preserving of your Majesty's life."

"Indeed!" Catharine mocked him with her eyes. "And who hath trained you to that profession? Who is so loyal to me that he would send you?"

Suddenly, Rod saw through the mocking and the belligerence. It was all a mask, a shield; behind it lay a very frightened, very lonely little girl, one who wanted someone to trust, craved someone to trust. But there had been too many betrayals; she couldn't let herself trust any more.

He looked into her eyes, giving her his gentlest, most sincere gaze, and said in his best couch-side manner, "I call no man master, my Queen. It is myself who has sent me, out of love for Catharine the Queen and loyalty to the nation of Gramarye."

Something desperate flickered in her eyes; her hands clutched at the chair arms. "Love," she murmured.

Then the mockery was back in her eyes. "Yes, love—for Catharine *the Queen.*"

She looked away, into the fire. "Be that as it may. But I think you are in most comely truth a friend—though why I believe that, I cannot say."

"Oh, you may be sure that I am!" Rod smiled. "You knew that I was at the House of Clovis, though you couldn't say how, and you were right about that."

"Be still!" she snapped. Then slowly her eyes lifted to his. "And what affairs took you to the House of Clovis this night?"

Was she a mind reader, maybe?

Rod scratched along his jaw; the bone-conduction microphone would pick up the sound. . . .

"There's some confusion *Fess*tering in my mind," he said. "How did you know I was at the House of Clovis?"

"Here, Rod," a voice murmured behind his ear.

Catharine gave him a look that fairly dripped with contempt. "Why, I knew you spoke with Tuan Loguire. Then where could you be but the House of Clovis?"

Very neat—only how had she known he was with Tuan . . . Loguire?

Loguire!

Rod stared. "Excuse me, but—uh—did you say Tuan *Loguire?*"

Catharine frowned.

"I thought his name was, uh—McReady."

Catharine almost laughed. "Oh, nay! He is the second son of Milord Loguire! Did you not know?"

Second son! Then Tuan was himself the man he had been condemning for a fool!

And his big brother was the man who had "an ancient grievance 'gainst the Queen," and was a major threat to the throne.

"No," said Rod, "I did not know."

Fess's voice murmured, "Data indicate existence of excellent intelligence system."

Rod groaned mentally. Robots were a great help!

He pursed his lips, staring at Catharine. "You say you have no spies in the House of Clovis," he said, "and if I assume that you speak the truth, then that means . . ."

He left the sentence hanging; Fess would fill in the blank. There was a moment of silence; then a loud hum behind Rod's ear, ended in a sharp click.

Rod cursed mentally. If Catharine had no spies, she logically couldn't have known what she did know. He'd given Fess another paradox, and the robot's circuits had overloaded. Epileptic robots could be very inconvenient.

Catharine glared at him. "Of a certainty, I speak truth!"

"Oh, I never doubted!" Rod held up a hand. "But you *are* a ruler, and you were reared to it; one of the first lessons you must have learned was lying with a straight face."

Catharine's face froze; then, slowly, she bent her head, looking down at her hands. When she looked up, her face was drawn; the mask had been stripped away, and her eyes were haunted. "Once again, my knowledge was true," she murmured. "You know more than soldiering, Rod Gallowglass."

Rod nodded heavily. He'd made another slip; blank-shield soldiers don't know politics.

"Then tell me," she murmured, "how you came to the House of Clovis, this night."

"My Queen," Rod said gravely, "one man was set upon by three, in an alley. I helped him out; he took me to the House of Clovis to tell me his thanks with a glass of wine. That is how I came to meet Tuan Loguire."

Her brows drew together in an anxious little frown. "If

I might but credit your words with truth," she murmured.

She rose and went to the fireplace. All at once, her shoulders slumped, her head bowed forward. "I shall need all my friends in this hour that comes upon us," she murmured, voice husky, "and I think thou art the truest of my friends, though I cannot say why."

She raised her head to look at him, and he saw with a shock that her eyes swam with tears. "There are still some to guard me," she said, her voice so low he could scarcely hear; but her eyes shone through the tears, and an invisible band tightened around Rod's chest. His throat tightened, too; his eyes were burning.

She turned away, biting her clenched fist. After a moment, she spoke again, her voice trembling. "The time shall come soon when each of the Great Lords shall declare himself for or against me; and I think they will be few who ride to my standard."

She turned, came toward him again, eyes alight and a shy, trembling smile on her lips. Rod rose to meet her, staring, fascinated, heart pounding in his ears.

She stopped just before him, one hand touching the locket at her throat again, and whispered, "Will you stand by my side in that day, Rod Gallowglass?"

Rod nodded awkwardly and garbled out something affirmative. At that particular moment, his answer would probably have been the same if she'd requested his soul.

Then, suddenly, she was in his arms, lithe and squirming, and her lips were moist and full on his own.

Some timeless while later, she lowered her head and moved reluctantly away, holding to his arms as if to steady herself. "Nay, but I am a weak woman," she murmured, exultant. "Go now, Rod Gallowglass, with the thanks of a queen."

She said something else, but Rod didn't quite follow it; and, somehow, he was on the other side of the door, walking down a wide, cold, torchlit corridor.

He stopped, shook himself, made a brave try at collecting his wits, and went on down the hall with a step that was none too firm.

Whatever else you might think of her political abilities, the gal sure knew how to bind a man to her service. . . .

He stumbled and caught himself; his stumbling block shoved a hand against his hip to steady him.

84

"Nay, mind thy great feet," grumbled Brom O'Berin, "ere thou trip headlong and foul the paving."

The dwarf studied Rod's eyes anxiously; he found whatever he was looking for someplace between iris and cornea, and nodded, satisfied.

He reached up to grab Rod's sleeve and turned away, guiding him down the hall.

"What had you from Catharine, Rod Gallowglass?"

"Had from her?" Rod frowned, eyes unfocused. "Well, she took my pledge of loyalty . . ."

"Ah!" Brom nodded, as though in commiseration. "What more could you ask, Rod Gallowglass?"

Rod gave his head a quick shake, eyes opening wide. What the hell more could he ask, anyway? What in heaven's name had he expected? And what, in the seventh smile of Cerebus, was he getting moon-eyed for?

His jaw tightened, sullen anger rising in him. This bitch was nothing to him—just a pawn in the Great Game, a tool that might be used to establish a democracy. And what the hell was he getting angry about? He had no right to that, either. . . .

Hell! He needed a little objective analysis! "Fess!"

He meant it as a mutter, but it came out as a shout. Brom O'Berin scowled up at him. "What is a fess?"

"An unreliable gear train with a slipped cam," Rod improvised. Where the hell was that damn robot, anyway?

Then he remembered. Fess had had a seizure.

But Brom had stopped, and was studying Rod's face with his ultra-suspicious look. "What are these words, Rod Gallowglass? What is a gear train? And what is a cam?"

Rod pressed his lips together and mentally recited the books of the Bible. *Careful, boy, careful! You're at the brink! You'll blow the whole bit!*

He met Brom's eyes. "A gear train is the pack mule a knight uses to carry his armor and weapons," he growled, "and a cam is a half-witted squire."

Brom scowled, puzzled. "Half-witted?"

"Well, some kind of an eccentric. In my case, it all adds up to a horse."

"A horse?" Brom stared, completely at sea.

"Yes. My horse, Fess. The sum and total of my worldly goods and supporting personnel. Also the only soul—well, consciousness, anyway—that I can tell my troubles to."

Brom caught at the last phrase and held to it with all

the vigor of a drowning man. His eyes softened; he smiled gently. "You are of us now, Rod Gallowglass, of we few who stand by the Queen."

Rod saw the sympathy in Brom's eyes and wondered what bound the deformed little man to Catharine's service—and suddenly hated Catharine again for being the kind of bitch that enjoyed using men.

He set off down the hall, striding long. Brom marched double-time to keep up with him.

"Unless I miss in my judgment of a man," Rod growled through his teeth, "the Queen has another friend in the House of Clovis; yet she calls him her enemy. Why is that, Brom? Is it just because he's the son of her enemy the Duke of Loguire?"

Brom stopped him with a hand on his hip and looked up into Rod's eyes with a half-smile. "Not enemy, Rod Gallowglass, but one that she loves well: her uncle, blood-kin, who gave her sanctuary and cared for her five years while her father tamed the rebel Northern lordlings."

Rod raised his head slowly, keeping his eyes on Brom O'Berin's. "She chooses strange ways to show her love."

Brom nodeed. "Aye, most truly strange, yet doubt not she loves them, both the Duke and his son Tuan."

He held Rod's eyes a moment, not speaking.

He turned away, pacing slowly down the hall. Rod watched him a moment, then followed.

"It is a long tale, and a snarled one," Brom murmured as Rod caught up with him. "And the end and beginning and core of it is Tuan Loguire."

"The beggar king?"

"Aye." Brom nodded heavily. "The lord of the House of Clovis."

"Ane one who loves the Queen."

"Oh, aye!" Brom threw his head back, rolling his eyes upward. "One who loves her right well, be certain; he will tell you as much!"

"But you don't believe him?"

Brom locked his hands behind his back and stamped as he walked, head bowed. "He is either truthful, Rod Gallowglass, or a most excellent liar; and if he lies, he has learned the way of it right quick. He was trained only in truth, in the house of his father. Yet he is lord of the House of Clovis, of they who claim the ruler should be chosen as the ancient

King Clovis was, or as they say he was—by the acclamation of those whom he rules."

"Well, they've warped history a little bit there," Rod muttered. "But I take it their plans calls for pulling Catharine off her throne?"

"Aye; and how can I then believe him when he says that he loves her?" Brom shook his head sadly. "He is a most worthy young man, high-minded and honest; and a troubador who will sing you the beauties of milady's eyetooth as quick as he will twist the sword from your hands with his rapier. He was always a gentleman withal, and in him was nothing of deception."

"Sounds like you knew him pretty well."

"Oh, aye! I did, most surely I did! But do I know him now?" Brom heaved a sigh, shaking his head. "They met when she was but seven years of age, and he but eight, at the keep of Milord Loguire in the South, where her father had sent her for safety. There two children met and frolicked and played—under my eye, for I was ever a-watch over them. They were the only two of their age in the whole of the castle, and"—he smiled, and gave a bitter laugh—"I was a miracle, a grown man who was smaller than they."

Brom smiled, throwing his head back, looking past the stones of the hall into the years that were dead. "They were so innocent then, Rod Gallowglass! So innocent, aye, and so happy! And he worshiped her; he would pluck the flowers for her crown, though the gardener scolded him. Did the sun chasten her? He would put up a canopy of leaves! Had she broken milady's crystal goblet? He would claim the fault for his own!"

"Spoiled her rotten," Rod muttered.

"Aye; but he was not the first to play Tom Fool for her; for even then, she was a most beautiful princess, Rod Gallowglass.

"Yet over their happiness stood a dark, brooding shadow, a lad of fourteen, heir to the keep and estates, Anselm Loguire. He would look down from the tower, watch them at play in their garden, his face twisted and knotted all sour; and he alone in the land hated Catharine Plantagenet—why, no man can say."

"And he still hates her?"

"Aye; and let us therefore wish my lord of Loguire long life.

"For near to five years Anselm's hatred did fester; but then at long last he did stand triumphant. For the lords of the North were subdued, and her father called for her to be brought again to his side, here in his castle. And then did they vow, Tuan and Catharine, she at eleven and he twelve, that they would never forget, that she would wait till he came for her."

Brom shook his great shaggy head sadly. "He came for her. He came for her, a lad of nineteen, a golden prince riding out of the South on a great white charger—broad-shouldered, golden-haired and handsome, with muscles that would thicken any woman's tongue and make it cleave to her palate. A troubador, with a harp on his back and a sword by his side, and a thousand extravagant praises for her beauty. And his laugh was as clear, his heart as open, and his temper as frolicsome as when he was twelve."

He smiled up at Rod. "She was eighteen, Rod Gallowglass, and her life had been as still and smooth as a summer stream. Eighteen, and ripe for a husband, and her head filled with the giddy gossamer dreams that a girl learns from ballads and books."

He peered sharply, but his voice was gentle, echoing strangely in the emptiness of his years. "Was there never a dream of a princess for you, Rod Gallowglass?"

Rod glared at him and swallowed, hard. "Go on," he said.

Brom turned away, shrugging. "What need to say it? She loved him, of course; what woman would not? He knew not what a woman was for, and I'll swear it, and neither did she; but it may be that together, they learned; you may be sure that they had golden chances."

He shook his head, scowling. "If 'twas so, 'twas the crown of the last days of her youth; for it was that spring that her father died, and the scepter was set in her hands."

He fell still, measuring the hall with his stride, and was silent so long that Rod felt the need to say something.

"Here is no matter for hating, Brom O'Berin."

"Oh, aye! But hear the end of the tale, for only when the crown was on her head did Catharine come to see that Tuan was a second son; that he thus inherited his family's honor, but no more. She swore then that he loved her not, that he coveted only her throne. She would not have him; but in wrath and scorn she sent him away—without due cause, it seemed, though only they two could know the truth of that. She banished him to the Wild Lands with a price on his head, to dwell midst the beast-men and elves, or to die."

He fell silent again.

Rod prodded him. "And Milord Loguire rose up in wrath?"

"Aye," grated Brom, "and all his liegemen with him, and half the nobles of the kingdom besides. If Tuan failed in his courting, wrath and scorn were his due, quoth Loguire; but banishment comes only for treason.

"And was it not treason, Catharine answered hotly, to conspire for the crown?

"Then Loguire stood tall in cold pride and declared that Tuan had sought only the love of Catharine; but his words rang hollow, for he whom the Queen marries must reign; and this Catharine told him.

"Then did Loguire speak in sorrow, that his son was no traitor but only a fool, a fool to be courting a silly, spoiled child; and then would Catharine have cried 'Treason!' again, had I not prevented her."

"And yet you say she loves them, Loguire and Tuan?"

"Aye; why else such harshness?"

Brom lapsed into silence again. Rod cleared his throat and said, "Tuan doesn't seem to have stayed banished too well. . . ."

"Aye." Brom's mouth drew back at the corners. "The fool would be near her, he swore, though his head should be forfeit. But with a price on his life, he must live like a murderer or thief."

Rod smiled sourly. "And, somewhere, he got hold of the idea that the beggars would cause less trouble if someone took care of them."

Brom nodded. "And thus the beggars became somewhat a power; but Tuan swears he will throw all his forces to guard the Queen's back. He professes that he still doth love her; that he will love her though she hew off his head."

"And she, of course," Rod mused, "claims there isn't a reason in the world why he shouldn't hate her."

"And in that she is right; yet I think Tuan loves her."

They had come to the guard room door; Rod put a hand on the latch and smiled down at Brom O'Berin, smiled and shook his head sadly. "Brainless," he said. "The pair of them."

"And most tender loving enemies they are," Brom smiled, with a touch of exasperation. "And here is your lodging; good night."

Brom turned on his heel and stalked off.

Rod looked after him, shaking his head and cursing himself silently. "Fool that I am," he murmured; "I thought he stood by her because he was in love with her. Oh, well, Fess makes mistakes too. . . ."

The great candle in the barracks was burned down to a stub. Time in Gramarye was kept by huge candles banded in red and white, six rings of red and six white. One candle was lit at dawn, the other twelve hours later.

According to this candle, it was three A.M. Rod's eyelids suddenly felt very heavy. They seemed downright leaden when he remembered that an hour on Gramarye was roughly equal to an hour and twenty minutes Galctic Standard.

He staggered toward his bunk and tripped. The object underfoot gave a muffled grunt; Rod had forgotten that Big Tom would be sleeping at the foot of the bed, on the floor.

The big man sat up, yawning and scratching. He looked up and saw Rod. "Oh, gode'en, master! What's the time?"

"Ninth hour of the night," Rod said softly. "Go back to sleep, Big Tom. I didn't mean to wake you."

" 'S what I'm here for, master." He shook his head to clear it of sleep.

Which was somewhat strange, Rod suddenly realized, since the man's eyes had been wide awake. A synapse flicked in Rod's brain, and he was wide awake and wary, once again the subversive agent.

So, to keep from arousing Big Tom's suspicions, he tried to appear even more sleepy than he had been.

"It was a great night, Big Tom," he mumbled, and fell face forward into his bunk. He hoped Big Tom would leave matters as they were and go back to sleep; but he heard a deep, warm chuckle from the foot of the bed, and Big Tom started pulling off Rod's boots.

"A bit of folly in you, hadn't you, master?" he muttered. "Aye, and a wench or two under your belt, I'll warrant."

"Wake me at the lighting of the candle," Rod mumbled into his pillow. "I'm to wait on the Queen at breakfast."

"Aye, master." Big Tom worried loose the other boot and lay down, chuckling.

Rod waited till Tom began to snore again, then propped himself up on his elbows and looked back over his shoulder. Generally, the big oaf seemed thoroughly loyal and superbly stupid; but there were times when Rod wondered . . .

He let his head slump down onto the pillow, closed his eyes, and willed himself to sleep.

Unfortunately, the mind-over-matter bit wasn't working to-night. All his senses seemed boosted past maximum. He would've sworn he could feel every thread in the pillow under his cheek, could hear the mouse gnawing at the base-board, the frog croaking in the moat, the festive laughter wafted on the breeze.

His eyelids snapped open. Festive laughter?

He rolled out of bed and went to the high slit window. Who the hell was partying at this hour of the night?

The moon stood behind the castellated north tower; silhouettes flitted across its face, youthful figures in a three-dimensional dance; and some of them seemed to be riding on broomsticks.

Witches. In the north tower. . . .

Rod climbed the worn stone steps of the tower, toiling up the spiral. The granite walls seemed to crowd closer and closer the higher he went. He reminded himself that, having been declared a warlock by the elves—unreasonable little bastards!—he qualified for membership in this group.

But his stomach didn't get the message; it was still suing for a Dramamine. His mouth was bone-dry. Sure, the elves approved of him; but had they gotten the word to the witches?

All the old tales of his childhood came flooding back, liberally interspersed with chunks of the witch scenes from Macbeth. Now that he stopped to think about it, he couldn't remember one single instance of a philanthropic witch, ex-cept Glinda the Good, and you couldn't really call her a witch.

One thing in his favor: these witches seemed happy enough. The music floating down the stairwell was an old Irish jig, and it was salted with laughter, buoyant and youthful.

The wall glowed with torchlight ahead of him. He turned the last curve of the spiral and came into the great tower room.

A round, or rather globular, dance was in progress, a sort of three-dimensional *hora*. Through the clouds of torch-smoke he could make out couples dancing on the walls, the ceiling, in mid-air, and occasionally on the floor. Here and there were knots of chattering, giggling people. Their clothes were bright to the point of—well, hell, they were downright gaudy. Most of them held mugs, filled from a great cask near the stairwell.

They were all young, teenagers. He couldn't spot a single face that looked old enough to vote.

He paused on the threshold, possessed of a distinct feeling that he didn't belong. He felt like the chaperon at a high school prom—a necessary evil.

The youngster tapping the keg saw Rod and grinned. "Hail!" he cried. "You are laggard in coming." A full tankard slapped into Rod's hand.

"I didn't know I was coming," Rod muttered.

"Be assured that we did." The youth grinned. "Molly foresaw it; but she said you would be here half an hour agone."

"Sorry." Rod's eyes were a trifle glazed. "Ran into a couple delays . . ."

"Eh, think naught of it. 'Twas her miscalling, not yours; the wine, no doubt. Yet we have expected you since you set foot in the castle; the elves told us last night you were a warlock."

Rod's mind snapped clear. "Baloney! I'm no more a warlock than you . . . I mean . . ."

"Oh, thou art a warlock." The boy nodded sagely. "A warlock, and a most puissant one. Did you not come in a falling star?"

"That's science, not magic! And I'm not a warlock!"

The youth smiled roguishly. "Knowing or not, thou'rt most surely a warlock." He saluted Rod with the mug. "And therefore one of us."

"Uh . . . well, thanks." Rod returned the salute and took a draft from the mug. It was mulled wine, hot and spicy.

He looked around the room, trying to grow accustomed to the constant clamor and the flagrant violations of Newton's Laws.

His eyes lit on a couple seated under one of the windows, deep in conversation, which is to say, she was talking and he was listening. She was a looker, fairly bursting her bodice; he was thin and intent, eyes burning as he watched her.

Rod smiled cynically and wondered about the boy's motives for such steadfast devotion.

The girl gasped and spun around to glare outraged at Rod.

Rod's mouth sagged open. Then he began to stammer an apology; but before it reached his lips, the girl smiled, mollified, bowed her head graciously at him, and turned back to her one-man audience.

Rod's mouth sagged again. Then he reached out, groping for the tapster's arm, his eyes fixed on the girl.

The boy threw an arm around his shoulders, his voice worried. "What troubles thee, friend?"

"That—that girl," Rod stammered. "Can she read my mind?"

"Oh, aye! We all can, somewhat; though she is better than most."

Rod put a hand to his head to stop it from spinning. Telepaths. A whole room full of them. There were supposed to be about ten proven telepaths in the whole of the known galaxy.

He looked up again. It was a mutation, or genetic drfit, or something.

He drew himself up and cleared his throat. "Say, pal . . . uh, what's your name, anyway?"

"*Ay de mi!*" The boy struck his forehead with the heel of his hand. "A pox upon my lacking courtesy. I am Tobias, Master Gallowglass; and thou must needs meet us all."

He whirled Rod away toward the nearest group.

"But—but I just wanted to ask—"

"This is Nell, this is Andreyev, this Brian, this Dorothy . . ."

A half hour and fifty-three introductions later, Rod collapsed on a wooden bench. He swung his tankard up and swallowed the dregs. "Now," he said, slamming it down on his knee, "we're both drained."

"Ah, let me fetch you another!" Toby snatched the mug from his hand and flew away.

Literally.

Rod watched him drift across the room, ten feet off the floor, and shook his head. He was beyond astonishment now.

It seemed what he had on his hands was a budding colony of espers—levitative, precognitive, and telepathic.

But if they could all teleport, how come the girls all rode broomsticks?

Toby appeared at Rod's elbow, with a slight *poof!* of displaced air. Rod goggled at him, then accepted the refilled mug. "Uh, thanks. Say, you can, uh, levitate *and* teleport?"

"Pardon?" Toby frowned, not understanding.

"You can—uh—fly? And, uh—wish yourself from one place to another?"

"Oh, aye!" Toby grinned. "We all can do that."

"What? Fly?"

"Nay; we all can wish ourselves to places that we know. All the boys can fly; the girls cannot."

Sex-linked gene, Rod thought. Aloud, he said, "That's why they ride broomsticks?"

"Aye. Theirs is the power to make lifeless objects do their bidding. We males cannot."

Aha! Another linkage. Telekinesis went with the Y-chromosomes, levitation with the X.

But they could all teleport. And read minds.

A priceless colony of espers. And, if their lives were anything like those of the rare telepaths outside this planet . . .

"And the common people hate you for this?"

Toby's young face sobered to the point of gloom. "Aye, and the nobles too. They say we are leagued with the Devil. 'Twas the trial by water, or a most thorough roasting for us, till our good Queen Catharine came to reign." Turning away, he shouted, "Ho, Bridgett!"

A young girl, thirteen at the most, spun away from her dance partner and appeared at Toby's side.

"Friend Gallowglass would know how the people do like us," Tob informed her.

All the joy went out of the child's face; her eyes went wide and round; she caught her lower lip between her teeth.

She unbuttoned the back of her blouse from neck to bodice and turned away. Her back was a crisscross of scars, a webbing of welts—the sign of the cat-o'-nine-tails.

She turned back to Rod as Toby buttoned her blouse again, her eyes still round and tragic. "That," she whispered, "for naught but suspicion; and I but a child of ten years at the time."

Rod's stomach tried to turn itself inside out and climb out through his esophagus. He reprimanded it sternly, and it sank back to its ordinary place in the alimentary tract. Bile soured the back of Rod's tongue.

Bridgett spun and disappeared; a nano-second later she was back with her partner, giddy and exuberant again.

Rod frowned after her, brooding.

"So you may see," said Toby, "that we are most truly grateful to our good Queen."

"She did away with the fire and/or water bit?"

"Oh, she revoked the law; but the witch-burnings went

on, in secret. There was only one way to protect us, and that she chose: to give sanctuary to any of us who would come here and claim it."

Rod nodded, slowly. "She's not without wisdom, after all."

His eyes wandered back to Bridgett where she danced on the ceiling.

"What troubles you, friend Gallowglass?"

"She doesn't hate them," Rod growled. "She has every reason in the world to hate the normal folk, but she doesn't."

Toby shook his head, smiling warmly. "Not she, nor any of us. All who come to shelter in the Queen's Coven swear first to live by Christ's Law."

Slowly, Rod turned to look at him. "I see," he said after a moment. "A coven of white witches."

Toby nodded.

"Are all the witches of Gramarye white?"

"Shame to say it, they are not. Some there are who, embittered through greater suffering than ours—the loss of an ear or an eye, or a loved one, or all—have hidden themselves away in the Wild Lands of the mountains, and there pursue their vengeance on all mankind."

Rod's mouth pulled back into a thin, grim line, turned down at the corners.

"They number scarce more than a score," Toby went on. "There are three in the prime of life; all the rest are withered crones and shrunken men."

"The fairy-tale witches," Rod growled.

"Of a truth, they are; and their works are noised about just sufficient to cover report of any good works that we may deal."

"So there are two kinds of witches in Gramarye: the old and evil ones, up in the mountains; and the young white ones in the Queen's castle."

Toby shook his head and smiled, his eyes lighting once again. "Nay, there are near threescore white witches beside us, who would not trust to the Queen's promise of sanctuary. They are thirty and forty years aged, good folk all, but slow indeed to be trusting."

Understanding struck with all the power of Revelation. Rod leaned back, his mouth forming a silent O; then nodding rapidly, he leaned forward and said, "*That's* why you're all so young! Only the witches who still had some trust and recklessness left in them took the Queen's invitation! So she got a flock of teenagers!"

Toby grinned from ear to ear, nodding quick with excitement.

"So the mature witches," Rod went on, "are very good people, but they're also very cautious!"

Toby nodded. His face sobered a trifle. "There are one or two among them who had daring enough to come here. There was the wisest witch of all, from the South. She grows old now. Why, she must be fair near to thirty!"

That line caught Rod right in the middle of a drink. He choked, swallowed, gagged, coughed, wheezed, and wiped at his eyes.

"Is aught wrong, friend Gallowglass?" Toby inquired with the kind of solicitousness usually reserved for the octogenarian.

"Oh, nothing," Rod gasped. "Just a little confusion between the esophagus and the trachea. Have to expect a few quirks in us old folk, you know. Why didn't this wise witch stay?"

Toby smiled, fairly oozing understanding and kindess. "Ah, she said that we made her feel too much her age, and went back to the South. If thou shouldst come to trouble there, but call out her name, Gwendylon, and thou'lt right quick have more help than thou needst."

"I'll remember that," Rod promised, and immediately forgot as he had a sudden vision of himself calling a woman for help. He almost went into another coughing fit, but he didn't dare laugh; he remembered how sensitive he'd been in his teens.

He took another swig of the wine to wash down his laughter and pointed the mug at Toby. "Just one more question, now: why is the Queen protecting you?"

Toby stared. "Didst thou not know?"

"Know I didst not." Rod smiled sweetly.

"Why, she is herself a witch, good friend Gallowglass!"

Rod's smile faded. "Hum." He scratched the tip of his nose. "I'd heard rumors to that effect. They're true, eh?"

"Most true. A witch unschooled, but a witch nonetheless."

Rod raised an eyebrow. "Unschooled?"

"Aye. Our gifts need a stretching and excercising, a training and schooling, to come to their full. Catharine is a witch born, but unschooled. She can hear thoughts, but not at any time that she wishes, and not clearly."

"Hm. What else can she do?"

"Naught that we know of. She can but hear thoughts."

"So she's sort of got a minimum union requirement." Rod scratched in back of his ear. "Kind of handy talent for a Queen. She'd know everything that goes on in her castle."

Toby shook his head. "Canst hear five speak all at once, friend Gallowglass? And listen to them all the hours of the day? And still be able to speak what they spoke?"

Rod frowned and rubbed his chin.

"Canst repeat even one conversation?" Toby smiled indulgently and shook his head. "Of course thou can'st not—and neither can our Queen."

"She could write them down. . . ."

"Aye; but remember, she is unschooled; and it needs high training of an excellent good gift to make words of thoughts."

"Hold on." Rod's hand went up, palm out. "You mean you don't hear thoughts as words?"

"Nay, nay. An instant's thought suffices for a book of words, friend Gallowglass. Must you needs put words to your thoughts in order to have them?"

Rod nodded. "I see. Quantum thought mechanics."

"Strange . . ." murmured a voice. Looking up, Rod found himself the center of a fair-sized group of young witches and warlocks who had apparently drifted over to get in on an interesting conversation.

He looked at the one who had spoken, a burly young warlock, and smiled with a touch of sarcasm. "What's strange?" He wondered what the kid's name was.

The boy grinned. "Martin is my name." He paused to chuckle at Rod's startled look; he still hadn't gotten used to the mind-reading. "And what is strange is that you, a warlock, should not know the ins and outs of hearing thoughts."

"Aye." Toby nodded. "You are the only warlock we have known, friend Gallowglass, that cannot hear thoughts."

"Uh, yes." Rod ran a hand over the stubble on his cheek. "Well, as I mentioned a little earlier, I'm not really a warlock. You see . . ."

He was cut off by a unanimous burst of laughter. He sighed, and resigned himself to his reputation.

He reverted to his former line of questioning. "I take it some of you can hear thoughts as words."

"Oh, aye," said Toby, wiping his eyes. "We have one." He turned to the ring of listeners. "Is Aldis here?"

A buxom, pretty sweet-sixteen elbowed her way through to the front rank. "Who shall I listen to for you, sir?"

A spark arced across a gap in Rod's mind. A malicious gleam came into his eyes. "Durer. The councillor to Milord Loguire."

Aldis folded her hands in her lap, settled herelf, sitting very straight. She stared at Rod; her eyes lost focus. Then she began to speak in a high-pitched nasal monotone.

"As you will, milord. Yet I cannot help but wonder, are you *truly* loyal?"

Her voice dropped two octaves in pitch but kept the monotonous quality. "Knave! Have you the gall to insult me to me face?"

"Nay, milord!" the high voice answered hurriedly. "I do not insult you; I do but question the wisdom of your actions."

Durer, Rod thought. The high voice was Durer, practicing his vocation—the care and manipulation of the Duke Loguire.

"Remember, milord, she is but a child. Is it kindness to a child to let her have her willful way? Or is it kindness to spank her when she needs it?"

There was a silence for a moment; then the deeper voice of the Lord Loguire answered, "There is some measure of truth in what you say. Certain, there is something of the wanton child in her taking up the power to appoint the priests."

"Why," murmured the high voice, " 'tis an act against tradition, milord, and against the wisdom of men far older than herself. 'Tis in bitter truth the act of a rebellious child."

"Mayhap," Loguire rumbled. "Yet she is the Queen, and the Queen's Law shall be obeyed."

"Even should the Queen make evil laws, milord?"

"Her actions are not evil, Durer." The deep voice took on an ominous quality. "Reckless, perhaps, and thoughtless, and ill-considered; for the good they bring today may bring havoc down upon our heads tomorrow. Foolish laws, perhaps; but evil, no."

The high voice sighed. "Mayhap, milord. Yet she threatens the honor of her noblemen. Is that not evil?"

"Why," rumbled Loguire, "how is this? She has been haughty, aye, taking to herself greater airs than ever a Queen may own to, mayhap; but she has never yet done aught that could be construed as insult."

"Aye, milord, not yet."

"Why, what do you mean?"

"The day shall come, milord."

"What day is that, Durer?"

"When she shall put the peasants before the noblemen, milord."

"Have done with your treasonous words!" Loguire roared. "On your knees, slight man, and thank your God that I leave you with your head!"

Rod stared at Aldis' face, still not recovered from the shock of hearing two disembodied male voices coming from the mouth of a pretty girl.

Slowly, her eyes focused again. She let out a long breath and smiled up at him. "Did you hear, friend Gallowglass?"

Rod nodded.

She spread her hands, shrugging. "I cannot recall a word of what I said."

"Don't let it worry you, I remember it all." Rod rubbed the stubble on his chin. "You were acting as a channel, a medium in the purest sense of the word."

He threw his head back, drained his mug, and tossed it to one of the young warlocks. The youth caught the tankard, disappeared, and reappeared. He handed the tankard, brimming full, to Rod, who shook his head in mock despair.

He leaned back and sipped at the wine, looking up at the young faces around him, smiling and fairly glowing with the knowledge of their power.

"Have you ever done this before?" he asked, with a wave of the mug that took them all in. "Listened to skull sessions like that one, I mean."

"Only of the Queen's enemies," Aldis answered with a toss of her head. "We often listen to Durer."

"Oh?" Rod raised an eyebrow. "Learn anything?"

Aldis nodded. "He is much concerned with the peasants of late."

Rod was very still for a moment. Then he learned forward, elbows on his knees. "What's his interest in the peasants?"

Toby grinned knowingly. "Hark now to his latest exploit! He hath brooded trouble 'twixt two serfs on the Queen's own estate. A young peasant wished to marry an old farmer's daughter, and the old man said nay. And the youth would've thrown up his hands in despair and let himself waste away with a broken heart."

"But Durer stepped in."

"Aye. He was after the young one night and day; for knowledge of the boy's suit spread throughout all the villages, and saw to it that the rumor was told with one question appended: Could the youth be a man who would let a doddard idiot rob him of the girl he loved?"

Rod nodded. "And the other peasants started throwing that up to the kid."

"Most certainly. Taunts and jeers and mocking—and the lad stole the girl away by night and got her with child."

Rod pursed his lips. "I imagine Papa was a trifle perturbed."

Toby nodded. "He hauled the boy before the village priest and demanded the lad be hanged for a rapist."

"And the priest said . . . ?"

"That it was love, not rape, and the fitting punishment was marriage, not hanging."

Rod grinned. "Bet the two kids were real sad about that."

"Their grief was so great it set them to dancing." Toby chuckled. "And the old man gave a heavy sigh, and would have judged it the widom of God, and blessed them."

"And Durer stepped in again."

"Most certainly. He was up before the Queen, when she was at table before all her lords and her ladies, crying that the Queen must prove the justice of her new order by declaring herself what was just in this case; for were these not peasants on the Queen's own estates?"

Rod grinned and slapped his thigh. "She must have been ready to spit in his eye!"

"Oh, you know not the Queen!" Toby rolled his eyes up toward the ceiling. She would most cheerfully have slipped a knife 'twixt his ribs. But the challenge must needs be answered; she must needs hear the case herself, when next she held General Court."

"General Court?" Rod scowled. "What the hell is that?"

"One hour each month the Queen opens her court to all in her realm who wish her ear; and peasants, nobility, and clergy come to her Great Hall. Mostly the great lords but look on while the petty nobility and peasantry bring forth their grievances. And with the great ones watching, you may be sure the grievances brought up are petty indeed."

"Like this case." Rod nodded. "When's this next General Court?"

"Tomorrow," said Toby, "and I think the great lords shall have their tame clergy and peasantry protest the Queen's new judges and priests. The lords shall lodge their protest first, of course; and the other, more common folk shall be echoing them."

Rod nodded. "Put the whole matter on public record. But what does Durer hope to gain by bringing in this seduction case?"

Toby shrugged. "That, only Durer may know."

Rod leaned back, frowning, and pulled at his mug. He studied the young faces around him and scratched at the base of his skull. "Sounds to me like this is information the Queen would like to have. Why don't you tell her?"

The faces sobered. Toby bit his lip and looked down at the floor.

Rod scowled. "Why don't you tell her, Toby?"

"We have tried, friend Gallowglass!" The boy looked up at Rod in mute appeal. "We have tried; yet she would not hear us!"

Rod's face turned to wood. "How's that again?"

Toby spread his hands in helplessness. "The page we sent to her returned to tell us that we should be thankful for the protection she accorded us, and not be so ingracious and insolent as to seek to meddle in her governing."

Rod jerked his head in tight, quick nods, mouth drawn back in grim agreement. "Yeah, that sounds like Catharine."

"Mayhap," one of the boys murmured thoughtfully, "it is all to the best; for she hath cares enough without warnings of doom from us."

Rod grinned without humor. "Yeah. Between the noblemen and the beggars, she's got more than enough worries to keep her busy."

Toby nodded, eyes wide and serious. "Aye, she hath troubles sufficient, between the councillors, the House of Clovis, and the banshee on her roof. She hath great cause to be most afeard."

"Yes." Rod's voice was tight, rasping. "Yes, she hath good cause; and I think that she is thoroughly afeard."

Big Tom must have been a very light sleeper; he sat up on his pallet as Rod came tiptoeing up to his bunk.

"Art well, master?" he whispered in a rasping voice that had about as much secrecy as a bullfrog in rut.

Rod stopped and frowned down at his manservant. "Yes, very well. Why shouldn't I be?"

Big Tom smiled sheepishly. "Thou hast small use for sleep," he muttered. "I had thought it might be a fever."

"No." Rod smiled with relief, shaking his head. He pushed past Big Tom. "It's not a fever."

"What is it, then?"

Rod fell backward onto the bed, cupping his hands under his head. "Did you ever hear of a game called cricket, Tom?"

"Cricket?" Tom scowled. " 'Tis a chirping creature on the hearth, master."

"Yeah, but it's also the name of a game. The center of the game is a wicket, see, and one team tries to knock down the wicket by throwing a ball at it. The other team tries to protect the wicket by knocking the ball away with a paddle."

"Strange," Big Tom murmured, eyes wide with wonder. "A most strange manner of game, master."

"Yes," Rod agreed, "but it gets worse. The teams trade sides, you see, and the team that was attacking the wicket before is defending it now." He looked down over his toes at Tom's round beehive face.

"Nay," the big man muttered, shaking his head in confusion. "What is the point to it all, master?"

Rod stretched, let his body snap back to relaxation. "The point is that no matter who wins, it's going to be hard on the wicket."

"Aye!" Big Tom nodded vigorously. "Most certain true, master."

"Now, I get the feeling that there's a colossal game of cricket going on around here; only there's three teams in the game: the councillors, the beggars . . ."

"The House of Clovis," Tom muttered.

Rod's eyebrows went up in surprise. Yes, the House of Clovis. And, of course, the Queen."

"Then who," asked Big Tom, "is the wicket?"

"Me." Rod rolled over on his side, thumped the pillow with his fist, and lowered his head onto it with a blissful sigh. "And now I am going to sleep. Good night."

"Master Gallowglass," piped a page's voice.

Rod closed his eyes and prayed for strength. "Yes, page?"

"You are called to wait upon the Queen at her breakfast, Master Gallowglass."

Rod forced an eyelid open and peered out the window; the sky was rosy with dawn.

He squeezed his eyes shut and counted to ten, amost dozing off in the process. He drew in a sigh that would have filled a bottomless pit, swung his legs over the side of the bed, and sat up. "Well, no rest for the wicket. What'd I do with my damn uniform, Tom?"

Rod had to admit that Catharine Plantagenet had a good dramatic instinct and, moreover, knew how to use it on her court. The guards were at their stations in the dining hall before sunrise. The lords and ladies who were privileged—or, more accurately, cursed—to share the Queen's dawn breakfast arrived right after the cock's crow. Not till they were all assembled, and all waiting some time eyeing the breakfast meats, did Catharine make her entrance.

And she definitely made an entrance, even at that hour. The doors of the hall were thrown wide, revealing Catharine standing in a pool of torchlight. Six buglers blew a fanfare, at which all the lords and ladies rose and Rod winced (pitch was more or less a matter of taste in that culture).

Then Catharine stepped into the hall, head high and shoulders back. She paced a quarter way around the wall to the great gilded chair at the head of the table. The Duke of Loguire stepped forth and pulled the chair back. Catharine sat, with the grace and lightness of a feather. Loguire sat at her right hand, and the rest of the company followed suit. Catharine picked up her two-tined fork, and the company fell to, while liveried stewards invaded from the four corners of the hall with great platters of bacon and sausage, pickled herring, white rolls, and tureens of tea and soup.

Each platter was brought first to Brom O'Berin, where he sat at the Queen's left hand. Brom took a sample of each platter, ate a morsel of it, and placed the remainder on a plate before him. Then the huge platters were placed on the table. By this time Brom, finding himself still alive, passed the filled plate to Catharine.

The company fell to with gusto, and Rod's stomach reminded him that all that had hit his digestive tract that night had been spiced wine.

Catharine picked daintily at her food with the original bird-like appetite. Rumor had it that she ate just before the formal meal in the privacy of her apartments. Even so, she was so thin that Rod found it in himself to doubt the rumor.

The stewards wove in and out with flagons of wine and huge meat pies.

Rod was stationed at the east door; he thus had a good view of Catharine, where she sat at the north end of the table, Milord Loguire at her right hand, Durer, at Loguire's right hand, and the back of Brom O'Berin's head.

Durer leaned over and murmured something to his lord. Loguire waved a hand impatiently and nodded. He tore the meat off a chop with one bite, chewed, swallowed, and washed it down with a draft of wine. As he lowered the cup to the table, he turned to Catharine and rumbled, "Your Majesty, I am concerned."

Catharine gave him the cold eye. "We are all concerned, Milord Loguire. We must bear with our cares as well as we may."

Loguire's lips pressed tight together, his mouth almost becoming lost between moustache and beard. "My care," he said, "is for your own person, and for the welfare of your kingdom."

Catharine turned back to her plate, cutting a morsel of pork with great care. "I must hope that the welfare of my person would indeed affect the welfare of my kingdom."

Loguire's neck was growing red; but he pushed on obstinately. "I am glad that your Majesty sees that a threat to your welfare is a threat to this kingdom."

The skin furrowed between Catharine's eyebrows; she frowned at Loguire. "Indeed I do."

"Knowing that the Queen's life is threatened, the people grow uneasy."

Catharine put down her fork and sat back in her chair. Her voice was mild, even sweet. "Is my life, then, threatened, milord?"

"It would seem so," Loguire murmured carefully. "For the banshee was upon your roof again last night."

Rod's ears pricked up.

Catharine's lips turned in, pressed between her teeth; her eyes closed. Silence fell around the table. Brom O'Berin's voice rumbled into the sudden quiet. "The banshee hath often been seen upon her Majesty's battlements; yet still she lives."

"Be still!" Catharine snapped at him. Her shoulders straightened; she leaned forward to take up her goblet. "I do not wish to hear of the banshee." She drained the goblet, then held it out to the side. "Steward, more wine!"

Durer was out of his seat and at the Queen's elbow in an instant. Plucking the goblet from her hand, he turned to the steward who had come running up. He held the goblet up while the steward filled it from his ewer and the court stared; such courtesy to the Queen was, from Durer, somewhat unusual.

He swung back to the Queen, dropping to one knee and holding up the goblet. Catharine stared, then slowly accepted it. "I thank you, Durer; yet must I confess that I had not expected such courtliness from you."

Durer's eyes glinted. He rose with a mocking smile and bowed very low. "Drink deep in health, my Queen."

But Rod was a trifle less trusting than Catharine; moreover, he had seen Durer pass his left hand over the goblet just before the steward poured.

He left his post and caught the goblet just as Catharine raised it to her lips. She stared at him, face paling, rage rising in her eyes. "I did not summon you, sirrah."

"Your Majesty's pardon." Rod unclipped his dagger from his belt, shook the blade out onto the table, and filled the conical sheath with wine. Thank Heaven he'd taken the precaution of resetting Fess before he went on duty!

He held up the silver horn and said, "I con*Fess*, with apologies to your Majesty, that I cannot *analyze* my actions; it is only that I fear for your Majesty's life."

But all Catharine's anger had vanished in fascination at Rod's action. "What," she said, pointing to the silver horn, "is that?"

"Unicorn's horn," Rod answered, and looked up to see Durer's eyes, burning with rage at him.

"Analysis complete," murmured the voice behind his ear. "Substance poisonous to human metabolism."

Rod smiled grimly and pressed the knob at the apex of the horn with his little finger.

The "unicorn's horn" turned purple.

A gasp of horror went up from the whole court; for they all knew the legend, that a unicorn's horn will turn purple if poison is placed in it.

Catharine turned pale; she clenched her fists to conceal their trembling.

Loguire's hand balled into a huge fist; his eyes narrowed as he glared at Durer. "Slight man, if any part of this treachery was yours . . ."

"Milord, you saw." Durer's voice crackled. "I but held the cup."

But his burning eyes were fixed on Rod's, seeming to suggest that Rod could save himself a lot of trouble and agony if he would just drink the wine right there and then.

Rod was assigned as one of the four guards who would escort Catharine from her apartments to the Great Hall for the General Court. The four of them waited outside her chambers till the door opened, and Brom O'Berin stepped out, preceding the Queen. Two soldiers fell in before the Queen and behind Brom; Rod and another Guardsman fell in behind her.

They moved down the corridor slowly, matching their pace to Catharine's; and the Queen, draped in a heavy fur cloak and weighed down by the great gold crown, moved very slowly. Somehow, she contrived to look stately rather than clumsy.

As they drew near the Great Hall, a slight, emaciated, velvet-clad figure came scurrying up—Durer.

"Your pardon," he said, bowing three times, "but I must speak with your Majesty." His lips were pressed tight, anger in his eyes.

Catharine stopped and drew herself up to her haughtiest. *Chip on her shoulder as large as a two-by-four*, Rod thought.

"Speak, then," she said, looking down her nose at the cringing little man before her; "but speak quickly, sirrah."

Durer's eyes flared at the word of contempt; "sirrah" was a term reserved for peasants.

He managed to keep his manner respectful, though. "Your Majesty, I beg you to brook no delay in hearing the Great Lords' petition, for they are most greatly overwrought."

Catharine frowned. "Why should I delay?"

Durer bit his lip, looking away.

Catharine's eyes kindled in anger. "Speak, sirrah," she snapped. "Or do you mean to imply that the Queen fears to hear her noblemen?"

"Your Majesty . . ." Durer spoke with great reluctance; then the words came in a rush. "I had heard there were two peasants to be heard in Court today . . ."

"There are." Catharine's mouth hardened. " 'Tis the case you recommended to me, Durer."

The little man's eye shot a malevolent gleam at her; then he was all fawning humility again. "I had thought . . . I had heard . . . I had feared . . ."

"What hast thou feared?"

"Your Majesty hath been most concerned for your peasants

106

of late. . . ." Durer hesitated, then stumbled on. "I had feared . . . that your Majesty might . . . perhaps . . ."

Catharine's eyes hardened. "That I might hear these two peasants before I gave ear to the petitions of my noblemen?"

"Your Majesty must not!" Durer dropped to his knees, hands clasped in supplication. "Thou must not risk offense of the Great Lords today! Fear for thy very life if thou—"

"Sirrah, do you call me coward?"

Rod closed his eyes; his heart sank.

"Your Majesty," cried Durer, "I meant but to—"

"Enough!" Catharine turned away, spurning the meager form of the councillor. Brom O'Berin and the Guardsmen moved with her. The great oaken doors swung open before them.

Rod risked a glance back over his shoulder.

Durer's face was contorted with malevolent glee; his eyes glittered with triumph.

The best way to get a teenager to do something is to tell her not to. . . .

Brom led the Queen's entourage into a great vaulted room, lighted by a row of clerestory windows on each side. Fifty feet above, the roof-beam ran through the hall like a spine, with oaken ribs running down to the granite walls. Two great wrought-iron chandeliers hung from the ceiling, with candles burning in the sconces.

They had come in onto a raised dais, ten feet above the floor of the hall. A huge gilded throne rose before them.

Brom led them in a swing around the lip of the dais to the throne. There the Guardsmen lined up on either side, and Catharine mounted the last half-step to stand slender and proud before the throne, gazing out over the multitude gathered below.

The multitude looked like a sampling of the population. They filled the great hall, from the steps of the dais to the triple doors at the far end of the hall.

In the first rank were the twelve great nobles, seated in wooden hourglass-shaped chairs in a semicircle twelve feet out from the steps of the throne.

Behind them stood forty or fifty aging men in brown, gray, or dark green robes with velvet collars and small, square, felt hats. Chains of silver or gold hung down over their ample bellies. Burghers, Rod guessed—local officials, merchants, guildmasters—the bourgeoisie.

Beyond them were the black, cowled robes of the clergy;

and beyond them were the dun-colored, patched clothing of the peasantry, most of whom, Rod felt moderately certain, had been sent up from the castle kitchen so that the Great Court would have representatives of all classes.

But in the center of the peasants stood four soldiers in green and gold—the Queen's colors—and between them stood two peasants, one young and one old, both looking awed and scared almost to the point of panic, caps twisting in their horny hands. The oldster had a long, grizzled beard; the youngster was clean-shaven. Both wore dun-colored smocks of coarse cloth; more of the same material was bound to their legs, to serve as trousers. A priest stood by them, looking almost as much out of place as they did.

All eyes were on the Queen. Catharine was very much aware of it; she stood a little taller, and held her pose until the hall was completely quiet. Then she sat, slowly, and Brom sank cross-legged at her feet. Pike-butts thudded on stone as Rod and the other three Guardsmen stood to rest, pikes slanting outward at twenty degrees.

Brom's voice boomed out over the hall. "Who comes before the Queen this day?"

A herald stepped forward with a roll of parchment and read off a list of twenty petitions. The first was that of the twelve noblemen; the last was Durer's two peasants.

Catharine's hands tightened on the arms of the throne. She spoke in a high, clear voice. "Our Lord hath said that the humble shall be exalted, the last shall be first; therefore let us first hear the testimony of these two peasants."

There was a moment's shocked silence; old Lord Loguire was on his feet bellowing.

"Testimony! Have you such great need of their testimony that you must set these clods of earth before the highest of your nobles?"

"My lord," Catharine snapped, "you forget your place in my court."

"Nay, it is you who forget! You who forget respect and tradition, and all the law that you learned at your father's knee!"

The old lord drew himself up, glaring. "Never," he rumbled, "would the old king have disgraced his liegemen so!"

"Open thine eyes, old man!" Catharine's voice was chill and arrogant. "I would my father still lived; but he is dead, and I reign now."

"Reign!" Loguire's lips twisted in a sour grimace. " 'Tis not a reign, but a tyranny!"

The hall fell silent, shocked. Then a whisper began and grew: "Treason! TreasontreasontreasonTreason!"

Brom O'Berin rose, trembling. "Now, Milord Loguire, must thou kneel and ask pardon of milady the Queen, or be adjudged forever a traitor to the throne."

Loguire's face turned to stone, he drew himself up, back straightening, chin lifting; but before he could answer, Catherine spoke in a tight, quavering voice.

"There shall be no forgiveness asked, nor none given. Thou, Milord Loguire, in consideration of insults offered our Royal Person, art henceforth banished from our Court and Presence, to come near us nevermore."

Slowly, the old Duke's eyes met the Queen's. "How then, child," he murmured, and Rod saw with a shock that there were tears in the corners of the old man's eyes. "Child, wilt thou serve the father as thou hast served the son?"

Catharine's face went dead white; she half rose from her throne.

"Hie thee from this place, Milord Loguire!" Brom's voice shook with rage. "Hie thee from this place, or I shall hound thee hence!"

The Duke's gaze slowly lowered to Brom. "Hound me? Aye, for thou art most surely our gentle Queen's watchdog!" He raised his eyes to Catharine again. "Lady, lady! I had hoped to grace thee with a greyhound ere I died."

Catharine sat again, drawing herself up proudly. "I have a mastiff, milord; and let my enemies beware!"

The old man nodded slowly, his grieving eyes never leaving her face. "Thou wilt, then, call me enemy. . . ."

Catharine tilted her chin a little higher.

Loguire's eyes hardened; the grief was swept from his face by cold pride.

He spun on his heel, stalking down the length of the great hall. A lane through the crowd opened before him. The Guardsmen at either side of the great central door snapped to attention and threw the portals open.

The Duke stopped short under the lintel and pivoted to look back over the throng at Catharine. His heavy old voice filled the hall one last time.

And his voice was somehow gentle, almost kindly.

"Yet take this of me, Catharine, whom once I called my

niece—thou shalt not fear the armies of Loguire while I live."

He stood motionless a moment, holding Catharine's eyes.

Then he swung about, cape swirling, and was gone.

The court was silent for the space of three breaths; then, as a man, the eleven remaining Great Lords rose and filed down the lane to the great central door, and followed Loguire into exile.

"So how did she decide the case of the two peasants?" Fess asked.

Rod was riding the robot horse on the slope outside the castle, "for exercise," or so he had told the stableboy. Actually, he needed Fess's advice as to What It All Meant.

"Oh," he answered, "she upheld the parish priest's decisions: the fitting punishment for the kid was marriage. The old man didn't like that too well, but Catharine had an ace up her sleeve—the kid would have to support his father-in-law in his old age. The old man grinned at that, and the kid walked out looking like he wasn't quite so sure he'd come out on top after all."

"An excellent decision," Fess murmured. "Perhaps the young lady should seek a career in jurisprudence."

"Anything, so long as it keeps her out of politics. . . . Glorious sunsets on this planet."

They were riding into the setting sun; the dying globe painted the sky russet and gold halfway around the horizon and nearly to the zenith.

"Yes," the robot supplied, "the excellence of the sunsets is due to the density of the atmosphere, which is nearly one point five Terra-normal. At this latitude, however, due to the inclination of the planet's axis, which is—"

"Yes, yes, I wrote it all down in the logbook when we landed. Have the grace to let it rest in peace. . . . I notice the sun's rays turn almost blood-red . . ."

"Appropriate," Fess murmured.

"Hmm, yes. That brings us back to the point, doesn't it? What's this about another assassination coming up?"

"Not an assassination, Rod—an attempt."

"All right, an attempt. Pardon my denotations, and get on with it."

Fess paused a moment to set up the readout for a pre-fabricated report.

"The political situation on the island of Gramarye is comprised of three definite factions, one Royalist and two Anti-Royalist. The Royalist faction consists of the Queen, her chief councillor—one Brom O'Berin—the clergy, the Royal Army, the Queen's Bodyguard, and a group of espers known by the local term 'witches.' "

"How about the judges?"

"As I was about to say, the civil servants may also be included in the Royalist faction, with the exception of those officials whose corruption leaves them opposed to the Queen's reforms."

"Hmm, yes. I'd forgotten that hitch. Anybody else on the Plantagenet side?"

"Yes, a subspecies of Homo sapiens characterized by extreme dwarfism and referred to by the local term 'elves.' "

"Well, they sure don't seem to be against her, anyway," Rod murmured.

"The Anti-Royalist factions are significantly *not* united by their common opposition to the Throne. The first of these factions is the aristocracy, led by twelve dukes and earls, who are in turn led by the Duke Loguire. It is worth noting that the aristocrats are unanimous in their opposition to the Queen. Such unanimity among the aristocrats of a feudal culture is totally without precedent, and must therefore be regarded as an anomaly."

"And just where did this strange united front come from?"

"The unanimity may be attributed to the presence of a group termed the councillors, each member of which serves in an advisory capacity to one of the twelve great lords. The physical coherence of this group indicates—"

Rod jerked his head around, staring at the robot horse's ears. "How's that again?"

"Each of the councillors is physically characterized by a stooped posture, extreme leanness, sparse cranial hair, pale skin, and a general appearance of advanced age."

Rod pursed his lips. "Ve-ry interesting! I hadn't caught any significance in that."

"Such a physical appearance is characteristic of an extremely advanced technological society, in which the problems of longevity, metabolic adjustment, and exposure to ultraviolet have been controlled."

"Modern medicine and a barroom pallor." Rod nodded. "But how do you account for the hunched-over posture?"

"We may assume that is a part of the obsequious manner

employed by this group. The extremeness of this behavior would seem to indicate that it is not natural to the men in question."

"Finagle's Law of Reversal." Rod nodded. "Go on."

"The goal of the Royalist faction is to increase the power of the central authority. The goal of the councillors seems to be the elimination of the central authority, which will result in that form of political organization known as warlordism."

"Which," said Rod, "is a kind of anarchy."

"Precisely; and we must therefore entertain the possibility that the councillors may pursue the pattern of political breakdown from warlordism through parochialism to the possible goal of total anarchy."

"And that's why they're out to kill Catharine."

"An accurate observation; any chance to eliminate the central authority will be taken."

"Which means she's in danger. Let's get back to the castle."

He pulled on the reins, but Fess refused to turn. "She is not in danger, Rod, not yet. The mythos of this culture requires that preliminary to a death, an apparition known as a banshee must be seen on the roof of the dwelling. And the banshee cannot appear until nightfall."

Rod looked up at the sky. It was twilight; there was still some of the sunset's glow around the horizon.

"All right, Fess. You've got fifteen minutes, maybe a half-hour."

"The evidence of the councillor's origin in a high-technology society," the robot droned on, "indicates that the group derives from off-planet, since the only culture on the planet is that of Catharine's realm, which is characterized by a medieval technology. The other Anti-Royalist faction also bears indications of off-planet origin."

"I think I've heard that before," Rod mused. "Run through it again, will you?"

"Certainly. The second Anti-Royalist faction is known as the House of Clovis, a name deriving from the supposedly elective process of choosing ancient kings. The rank and file of the House of Clovis consists of beggars, thieves, and other criminals and outcasts. The titular leader is a banished nobleman, Tuan Loguire."

"Hold it a moment," said Rod. "*Titular* leader?"

"Yes," said Fess. "The superficial structure of the House of Clovis would seem to verge on the mob; but further analysis discloses a tightly-knit sub-organization, one function of which is the procurement of nourishment and clothing for the members of the House."

"But that's what Tuan's doing!"

"Is it? Who supplies the necessities of life at the House of Clovis, Rod?"

"Well, Tuan gives the money to the innkeeper, that twisted little monkey they call the Mocker."

"Precisely."

"So you're saying," Rod said slowly, "that the Mocker is using Tuan as a fund-raiser and figurehead, while the Mocker is the real boss."

"That," said Fess, "is what the data would seem to indicate. What is the Mocker's physical appearance, Rod?"

"Repulsive."

"And how did he earn his nickname of 'the Mocker'?"

"Well, he's supposed to be a sort of Man of a Thousand Faces. . . ."

"But what is his basic physical appearance, Rod?"

"Uh . . ." Rod threw his head back, eyes shut, visualizing the Mocker. "I'd say about five foot ten, hunched over all the time like he had curvature of the spine, slight build—very slight, looks like he eats maybe two hundred calories a day—not much hair . . ." His eyes snapped open. "Hey! He looks like one of the councillors!"

"And is therefore presumably from a high-technology society," Fess agreed, "and therefore also from off-planet. This contention is reinforced by his political philosophy, as indicated in Tuan Loguire's speeches to the rabble. . . ."

"So Tuan is also the mouthpiece," Rod mused. "But of course; he never could have thought up proletarian totalitarianism by himself."

"It is also worth noting that the Mocker is the only member of the House of Clovis of this particular physical type."

"Ye-e-e-s!" Rod nodded, rubbing his chin. "He's playing a lone game. All his staff are locals trained to back him up."

"His long-range goal," said Fess, "may be assumed to be the establishment of a dictatorship. Consequently, he would wish someone on the throne whom he could control."

"Tuan."

"Precisely. But he must first eliminate Catharine."

"So the councillors and House of Clovis are both out for Catharine's blood."

"True; yet there is no indication that they have joined

113

forces. If anything, they would seem to be mutually opposed."

"Duplication of effort—very inefficient. But, Fess, what're they doing here?"

"We may assume that they derive from two opposed societies, both of which wish to control some commodity which may be found on Gramarye."

Rod frowned. "I haven't heard of any rare minerals aroundabout . . ."

"I had in mind human resources, Rod."

Rod's eyes widened. "The espers! Of course! They're here because of the witches!"

"Or the elves," Fess reminded.

Rod frowned. "What would they want with the elves?"

"I have no hypothesis available; yet the logical possibility must be entertained."

Rod snorted. "All right, you stick with the logical possibility, and I'll stand by the witches. Anyone who could corner the market on telepaths could control the galaxy. Hey!" He stared, appalled. "They probably *could* control the galaxy."

"The stakes," Fess murmured, "are high."

"I'll have mine . . ." Rod began; but he was cut off by a ululating, soaring wail that grated like nails on glass.

Fess swung about; Rod looked back at the castle.

A dim shape glowed on the battlements, just below the east tower, like a fox-fire or a will-o'-the wisp. It must have been huge; Rod could make out detail even at this distance. It was dressed in the rags and tatters of a shroud, through which Rod could see the body of a voluptuous woman; but the head was a rabbit's, and the muzzle held pointed teeth.

The banshee began to wail again, a low moan that rose to a keening cry, then stabbed up the scale to a shriek, a shriek that held, and held, and held till Rod's ears were ready to break.

"Fess," he gasped, "what do you see?"

"A banshee, Rod."

Rod rode down, ran into, through and over five pairs of sentries en route to the Queen's chambers. But there, at her doors, he met an insurmountable roadblock about two feet high—Brom O'Berin, standing with feet set wide and arms akimbo.

"Thou hast been long in coming," the little man growled.

His face was beet-red with anger, but fear haunted the backs of his eyes.

"I came as fast as I could," Rod panted. "Is she in danger?"

Brom grunted. "Aye, in danger, though there is as yet no sign of it. Thou must stand watch at her bedside this night, warlock."

Rod stiffened. "I," he said, "am not a warlock. I am a simple soldier-of-fortune who happens to know a little science."

Brom tossed his head impatiently. "This is a poor time to bandy words. Call yourself what you will, cook, carpenter, or mason, thou hast still warlock's powers. But we waste time."

He rapped back-handed on the door; it swung in, and a sentry stepped out. He saluted and stood aside.

Brom bowed Rod into the room. "After you, Master Gallowglass."

Rod smiled grimly and went through the door. "Still don't trust me behind your back, eh?"

"Nearly," said Brom.

"That's what I said."

The sentry entered behind them and closed the door.

The room was large, with four shuttered slit windows on one side. The floor was covered with fur rugs; the walls were hung with silk, velvet, and tapestries. A fire crackled on a small hearth.

Catharine sat in a huge four-poster bed, covered to the waist with quilts and furs. Her unbound hair flowed down over the shoulders of a velvet, ermine-trimmed dressing gown. She was surrounded by a gaggle of ladies-in-waiting, several serving-girls, and two pages.

Rod knelt at her bedside. "Your Majesty's pardon for my tardiness!"

She gave him a frosty glance. "I had not known you were called." She turned away.

Rod frowned, looked her over.

She sat back against eight or ten fluffy satin pillows; her eyelids drooped in languid pleasure; there was a half-smile on her lips. She was enjoying the one spot of real luxury in her day.

She might be in mortal danger, but she sure didn't know about it. Brom had been keeping secrets again.

She held out a hand to one of her ladies; the woman gave her a steaming goblet of wine. Catharine brought it to her lips with a graceful flourish.

"*Whoa!*" Rod jumped to his feet, intercepted the goblet on its way to her lips, and plucked it away with his left hand while his right brought out his "unicorn's horn."

Catharine stared, amazed; then her eyes narrowed, her face reddened. "Sirrah, what means this?"

But Rod was staring at the "unicorn's horn" dagger-sheath; Fess's voice spoke behind his ear: "Substance with the analysis unit is toxic to human metabolism."

But Rod hadn't poured the wine into the horn yet. There was nothing in it.

Except air.

Rod pressed the stud that turned the horn purple.

Catharine stared in horror as the violet flush crept over the surface of the dagger-sheath.

"Sirrah," she gasped, "what means this?"

"Poison air," Rod snapped. She shoved the goblet at a servant-girl and looked about the room. Something in here was emitting poison gas.

The fireplace.

Rod crossed to the hearth and held the horn upside-down over the flames; but the color of the sheath dimmed to lavender.

"Not there." Rod spun about, coming to his feet. He paced about the room, holding the horn before him like a candle. It stayed lavender.

He frowned, scratched at the base of his skull. What would be the best place to put a poison-gas cartridge?

As close to the Queen as possible, of course.

He turned, moving slowly to the four-poster. As he came to Catharine's side, the horn's color darkened to violet.

Catharine stared at the horn in fascination and horror.

Rod knelt, slowly. The horn's color darkened to purple and began to shade toward black.

Rod threw up the bedskirts and looked under the four-poster. There before him, on the stone floor, steamed a warming-pan.

Rod grabbed the long handle and yanked the pan out. He inverted the horn over one of the holes in the cover—if his memory was correct, warming-pans didn't usually have holes. . . .

The horn turned dead black.

He looked up at Catharine. She had the knuckles of one hand jammed between her teeth, biting them to keep from screaming.

Rod turned, holding the pan out to the sentry. "Take this," he said, "and fling it into the moat."

The sentry dropped his pike, took the warming-pan, and rushed out, holding it at arm's length.

Rod turned slowly back to Catharine. "We have cheated the banshee again, my Queen."

Catharine's hand trembled as she took it away from her mouth. Then her lips clamped shut, her eyes squeezed tight, little fists clenched so hard the knuckles were white.

Then her eyes opened, slowly; there was a wild light in them, and a faint smile crept over her lips. "Master Gallowglass, stay by me. All else, remove yourselves!"

Rod swallowed and felt his joints liquefy. She was, at that moment, the most beautiful woman he had ever seen.

The Guardsmen, ladies, and pages were already in motion, heading for an incipient traffic jam at the door.

Brom bawled orders, and the jam failed to develop. In thirty seconds, the room was clear, except for Rod, the Queen, and Brom O'Berin.

"Brom," Catharine snapped, eyes locked on Rod's face. Her teeth were beginning to show through her smile. "Brom O'Berin, do you leave us also."

Brom stared a moment, outraged; then his shoulders slumped, and he bowed heavily. "I will, my Queen."

The door closed quietly behind him.

Slowly, Catharine lay back against the pillows. She stretched with a luxurious, liquid grace. One hand snaked out to clasp Rod's. Her hand was very soft.

"It is twice now you have given me my life, Master Gallowglass." Her voice was a velvet purr.

"My—my privilege, my Queen." Rod cursed himself, he was gawking like an adolescent with a copy of *Fanny Hill.*

Catharine frowned prettily, tucking her chin in and touching a forefinger to her lips.

Then she smiled, rolled over onto her side. The velvet gown fell open. Apparently it was the custom to sleep nude.

Remember, boy, Rod told himself, *you're just a traveling salesman. You'll wake up in the morning and be on your way. You're here to peddle democracy, not to court a Queen. Not fair to take advantage of her if you're not going to be here to take advantage of it. . . . Did that make sense?*

Catharine was toying with a pendant that hung from her neck. Her teeth were worrying her lower lip. She looked him over like a cat sizing up a canary.

"Blank-shield soldiers," she murmured, "have a certain repute . . ."

Her lips were moist, and very full.

Rod felt his lips moving, heard his own voice stammering, "As—as my Queen seeks to reform the ills of her land, I . . . hope to reform the reputation of soldiers. I would do . . . only good to your Majesty."

For a moment, it seemed Catharine's very blood must have stopped, so still she lay.

Then her eyes hardened, and the silence in the room stretched very, very thin.

She sat up, gathering her dressing gown about her. "Thou art much to be commended, Master Gallowglass. I am indeed fortunate to have such loyal servitors about me."

It was much to her credit, under the circumstances, Rod thought, that there was only a faint tone of mockery to her voice.

Her eyes met his again. "Accept the Queen's thanks for the saving of her life."

Rod dropped to one knee.

"I am indeed fortunate," Catharine went on, "to be so loyally served. You have given me my life; and I think that few soldiers would have given me safe deliverance, as you have done."

Rod flinched.

She smiled, her eyes glittering malice and satisfaction for just a moment.

Then her eyes dropped to her hands. "Leave me now, for I shall have a trying day tomorrow, and must make good use of the night, for sleeping."

"As the Queen wishes," Rod answered, poker-faced. He rose and turned away, his belly boiling with anger—at himself. It wasn't her fault he was a fool.

He closed the door behind him, then spun and slammed his fist against the rough stone of the entryway wall. The nerves in his fist screamed agony.

He turned back to the hall, forearm laced with pain—and there stood Brom O'Berin, face beet-red, trembling.

"Well, shall I kneel to thee? Art thou our next king?"

The anger in Rod's belly shot up, heading for Brom O'Berin. Rod clamped his jaws shut to hold it back. He glared at Brom, eyes narrowing. "I have better use for my time, Brom O'Berin, than to rob the royal cradle."

Brom stared at him, the blood and fury draining out of his

face. " 'Tis true," he murmured, nodding. "By all the saints, I do believe 'tis true! For I can see in thy face that thou art filled with Furies, screaming madness at thy manhood!"

Rod squeezed his eyes shut. His jaw tightened till it felt as if a molar must break.

Something had to break. Something had to give, somewhere.

Somewhere, far away, he heard Brom O'Berin saying, "This one hath a message for thee, from the witches in the tower. . . ."

Rod forced his eyes open, stared down at Brom.

Brom was looking down and to his left. Following his gaze, Rod saw an elf sitting tailor-fashion by Brom's foot. Puck.

Rod straightened his shoulders. Smother the anger; vent it later. If the witches had sent word, it was probably vital.

"Well, spill it," he said. "What word from the witches?"

But Puck only shook his head and murmured, "Lord, what fools these mortals be!"

He skipped aside a split second before Rod's fist slammed into the wall where he'd been sitting.

Rod howled with pain, and spun. He saw Puck and lunged again.

But "Softly" said Puck, and a huge chartreuse-and-shock-pink filled the hall, a full-size, regulation, fire-breathing dragon, rearing back on its hind feet and bellowing flame at Rod.

Rod goggled. Then he grinned, baring his teeth in savage joy.

The dragon belched fire as it struck. Rod ducked under the flames and came up under the monster's head. His fingers closed on the scaly neck, thumbs probing for the carotid arteries.

The dragon flung its head up and snapped its neck like a whip. Rod held on grimly, held on and held on while the dragon battered him against the granite walls. His head slapped stone and he yelled with pain, stars and darkness before his eyes, but he tightened his grip.

The great neck bowed, and the huge talons of the hind feet raked at Rod's belly, splitting him from collarbone to thigh. Blood fountained out, and Rod felt himself reeling into blackness; but he held on, determined to take the dragon with him into death.

Yeah, death, he thought, amazed, and was outraged that

he should die over a puny fit of anger, anger over a slip of a bitch of a girl.

Well, at least he'd have a mount in the land of the dead. As darkness sucked him down, he felt the great head drooping, bobbing lower and lower, following him down to death. . . .

His feet felt solid ground and, for a miracle, his legs held him up. Light misted through the dark around him, misted and gathered and grew, and he saw the beast lying dead at his feet.

The darkness ebbed away from the dragon; light showed Rod granite walls and brocade hangings; and the castle hall swam about him, reeled, and steadied.

At his feet, the dragon's colors faded. Its outlines blurred and shimmered, and the beast was gone; there was only clean gray stone beneath Rod's feet.

He looked down at his chest and belly; his doublet was whole, not even wrinkled. Not a trace of blood, not a scratch on him.

He squeezed an elbow, expecting the pain of bruises; there was none.

His head was clear, without the ghost of even an ache. Slowly, he raised his eyes to Puck.

The elf looked back, eyes wide and mournful. Amazingly, he wasn't smiling.

Rod covered his face with his hands, then looked up again. "Enchantment?"

Puck nodded.

Rod looked away. "Thanks."

"Thou hadst need of it," Puck answered.

Rod squared his shoulders and breathed deeply. "You had a message for me?"

Puck nodded again. "Thou art summoned to a meeting of the Coven."

Rod frowned, shaking his head. "But I'm not a member."

Brom O'Berin chuckled like a diesel turning over. "Nay, thou art of them, for thou art a warlock."

Rod opened his mouth to answer, thought better of it, and closed his jaws with a snap. He threw up his hands in resignation. "Okay, have it your own way. I'm a warlock. Just don't expect me to believe it."

"Well, thou wilt, at least, no longer deny it." Toby filled Rod's mug with the hot, mulled wine. "We ha' known thou wert a warlock even before we had set eyes on thee."

Rod sipped at the wine and looked about him. If he'd thought it was a party last night, his naïveté had been showing. That had just been a *kaffeeklatsch*. This time the kids were really whooping it up.

He turned back to Toby, bellowing to hear his own voice. "Don't get me wrong; I don't mean to be a cold blanket, but what's the occasion? How come all the celebrating?"

"Why, our Queen lives!" yelled Toby. "And thou art hero of the night! Thou hast banished the banshee!"

"Hero . . ." Rod echoed, a wry smile twisting his face. He lifted his mug and took a long, long draft.

Suddenly he swung the mug down, spluttering and coughing.

"What ails thee?" Toby asked, concerned. He pounded Rod on the back till the older man wheezed, gasping.

"Leave off," he said, holding up a hand, "I'm okay. I just thought of something, that's all?"

"What is thy thought?"

"That banshee ain't real."

Toby stared. "What dost thou say?"

Rod clamped a hand on the back of Toby's neck and pulled the boy's ear down to his own level.

"Look," he yelled, "the banshee only appears before someone dies, right?"

"Aye," said Toby, puzzled.

"Before someone *dies*," Rod repeated, "not every time someone's just in *danger* of death. And the Queen's still alive!"

Toby pulled back, staring at Rod.

Rod smiled, eyes dancing. "It's only supposed to show up when death's inevitable."

He turned, looked out over the great tower room. The witches were dancing on the walls, the ceiling, occasionally the floor, and in mid-air, with a fine disregard for gravity. They were twisting through gyrations that would have given a snake triple lumbago.

Rod looked back at Toby, lifted an eyebrow. "Doesn't look much like a funeral."

Toby frowned; then his face split into a grin. "I think thou hast not seen a Gramarye wake," he yelled. "Still, thou art aright; we dance this night for Life, not Death."

Rod grinned savagely, took another pull from his mug, and wiped his lips with the back of his hand. "Now. If it's a fake, and it is, the next question is, who put it there?"

121

Toby's jaw dropped open. He stared.

"Get me Aldis," Rod shouted.

Toby closed his mouth, gulped, and nodded. He closed his eyes; a moment later, Aldis swooped down and brought her broomstick in for a two-point landing.

"What dost thou wish?" she panted. She was blushing, face lit with excitement and joy. The sight of her gave Rod a sudden pang of mourning for his own lost youth.

He leaned forward. "See if you can tune in on Durer, Loguire's chief councillor."

She nodded, closed her eyes. After a few moments she opened them again, staring at Rod in fear.

"They are much wroth," she reported, "that the Queen did not die. But they are more wroth in that they know not who put the banshee on the roof of the castle this night."

Rod nodded, lips pressed into a tight, thin line. He took a last draft from his mug and rose, turning away toward the stairwell.

Toby reached up, catching his sleeve. "Where dost thou go?"

"To the battlements," Rod called back. "Where else would you look for a banshee?"

The night breeze cut chill through his clothes as he stepped out onto the battlements. The moon, over his shoulder, sent his shadow pacing before him.

The battlements stretched out before him like a great gap-toothed row of incisors.

"Fess," Rod called softly.

"Here, Rod," murmured the voice back of his ear.

"Does this banshee seem to be fonder of one stretch of battlements than another?"

"Yes, Rod. During the period in which we have been in Gramarye, the banshee has appeared under the east tower."

"Always?"

"To judge by an inadequate sample, yes."

Rod turned to his left, strolling east. "Well, you go on collecting an adequate sample while I do something about it."

"Yes, Rod," said the robot, somehow managing a tone of martyred patience.

Rod looked out over the battlements at the town, nestled below them at the foot of the great hill that served as the foundation for the castle. A long, white road wound up from the town to the drawbridge, with here and there the outpost of a low, rambling inn.

And down there below, in the rotting heart of the town, like some great basalt gravestone, stood the House of Clovis.

A stumbling, a scrabbling behind him. Rod snapped about into a wrestler's crouch, dagger a bite of moonlight in his hand.

Big Tom stumbled out of the winding stairway, with something draped across his arm. He stood, looking about him with wide, white-rimmed eyes, heaving hoarse gusts of air into his lungs.

He turned, saw Rod, and came running, his face flooded with relief. "Eh, master, thou'rt still whole!"

Rod relaxed and straightened up, sliding the dagger back into its sheath. "Of course I'm whole! What're *you* doing here, Big Tom?"

The big man stopped, the grin wavering on his face. He looked down at the cold stones, shuffling his feet. " 'Ell, master, I had heard . . . I . . . well . . ." He looked up; the words came in a rush: "Tha must not go again' the banshee; but if thou'lt go, thou'lt not go alone."

Rod studied the big man's face for a long moment, wondering where this deep devotion had come from.

Then he smiled gently. "Your knees have turned to jelly at the mere thought of the monster, but you still won't let me go alone."

He clapped Tom on the shoulder, grinning. "Well, then, come along, Big Tom; and I'm downright glad of your company, I don't mind telling you."

Tom grinned and looked down at the stones again. It was hard to be sure in the moonlight, but Rod thought there was a faint blush creeping up from the big man's collar.

He turned and set out toward the tower. Tom plodded along by his side. " 'Ere now, master, thou'lt grow a-cold," and Tom flung the cloak he had been carrying over his arm around Rod's shoulder.

A warm, friendly gesture, Rod thought as he thanked Big Tom. He was touched that the clumsy ape should be worried about him—but he was also aware that the cloak hampered his knife hand, and was pretty sure Big Tom was aware of it, too.

"Art not afraid, master?"

Rod frowned, considering the question. "Well, no, not really. After all, the banshee's never been known to hurt anybody. It's just, well, a forecast, you know? Herald of Death and all that."

"Still, 'tis a marvel thou'rt not afeard. Wilt thou not even walk in the shadows by the wall, master?"

Rod frowned and looked at the shadows along the battlements. "No, I'll take the center of the way when I can. I'd always rather walk tall in the sunlight than skulk in the shadows at the side of the road."

Big Tom was silent a moment, his eyes on the shadows.

"Yet," he said, "of necessity, a man must go through the shadows at one time or other, master."

With a shock, Rod realized Tom had picked up the allegory. Illiterate peasant, *sure!*

He nodded, looking so serious it was almost comic. "Yes, Big Tom. There's times when he has to choose one side of the road or the other. But for myself, I only stay on the sidelines as long as I have to. I prefer the light." He grinned. "Good protection against spirits."

"Spirits!" Tom snorted. He quickly threw Rod a half-hearted grin.

He turned away, frowning. "Still, master, I do much marvel that you will take the middle road; for there may a man be attacked from both sides. And, more to the point, he cannot say that he has chosen either the right or the left."

"No," Rod agreed, "but he can say that he has chosen the middle. And as to attack, well, if the road is well-built, the center is highest; the pavement slopes away to right and left, and the shoulder is soft and may give way beneath you. A man in the middle can see where his enemies are coming from; and it's firm footing. The sides of the road are teacherous. Sure it's an exposed position. That's why not too many have the courage to walk it."

They walked a moment in silence; then Rod said, "Did you ever hear of dialectical materialism, Tom?"

"How . . . ?" The big man's head jerked up in surprise, almost shock. He recovered, scowling and shaking his head fervently, and muttering, "No, no, master, no, never, never!"

Sure, Big Tom, Rod thought. Aloud, he said, "It's a Terran philsophy, Big Tom. Its origins are lost in the Dark Ages, but some men still hold by it."

"What is Terran?" the big man growled.

"A dream," Rod sighed, "and a myth."

"Are you one man who lives by it, master?"

Rod looked up, startled. "What? The dream of Terra?"

"No, this dialec—what magic didst thou term it?"

"What, dialectical materialism?" Rod grinned. "No, but I find some of its concepts very handy, like the idea of a synthesis. Do you know what a synthesis is, Tom?"

"Nay, master." Tom shook his head, eyes round in wonder.

The wonder, at least, was probably real. The last thing Big Tom could have looked for was Rod to start quoting a totalitarian philosphy.

"It's the middle way," Rod said. "The right-hand side of the road is the thesis, and the left-hand side is the antithesis. Combine them, and you get a synthesis."

"Aye," Big Tom nodded.

Pretty quick thinking for a dumb peasant, Rod noted. He went on, "The thesis and antithesis are both partly false; so you throw away the false parts, combine the true parts—take the best of both of them—call the result a synthesis, and you've got the truth. See?"

Tom's eyes took on a guarded look. He began to see where Rod was going.

"And the synthesis is the middle of the road. And, being true, it's naturally uncomfortable."

He looked up; the east tower loomed over them. They stood in its shadow. "Well, enough philosophizing. Let's get to work."

"Pray Heaven the banshee come not upon us!" Big Tom moaned.

"Don't worry; it only shows up once a day, in the evening, to predict death within twenty-four hours," Rod said. "It's not due again till tomorrow evening."

There was a sudden scrabbling in the shadows. Big Tom leaped back, a knife suddenly in his hand. "The banshee!"

Rod's blade was out too, his eyes probing the shadows. They locked with two fiery dots at the base of the tower wall.

Rod stepped out in a crouch, knife flickering back and forth from left hand to right. "Declare yourself," he chanted, "or die."

A squeal and a skitter, and a huge rat dashed away past him, to lose itself in the shadows near the inner wall.

Big Tom almost collapsed with a sigh. "Saints preserve us! 'Twas only a rat."

"Yes." Rod tried to hide the trembling of his own hands as his knife went back to its sheath. "There seem to be a lot of rats in the walls of this castle."

Big Tom straightened again, wary and on his guard.

"But I saw something as that rat ran by me . . ." Rod's voice trailed away as he knelt by the outer wall, running his hands lightly over the stone. "There!"

"What is it, master?" Big Tom's garlic breath fanned Rod's cheek.

Rod took the big man's hand and set it against his find. Tom drew in a shuddering breath and yanked his hand away.

" 'Tis cold," his voice quavered, "cold and square, and—it bit me!"

"Bit you?" Rod frowned and ran his fingers over the metal box. He felt the stab of a mild electric shock and jerked his fingers away. Whoever had wired this gadget must have been the rankest of amateurs. It wasn't even grounded properly.

The box was easy to see once you knew where to look for it. It was white metal, about eight inches on a side, two inches deep, recessed so that its front and top were flush with the stone, halfway between two of the crennelations.

But come to think of it, that faulty grounding might have been intentional, to keep people from tampering.

Rod drew his dagger, glad of the insulation provided by the leather hilt. Carefully, he pried open the front of the box.

He could make out the silvery worm-trails of the printed circuit and the flat, square pillbox of the solid-state components—but the whole layout couldn't have been larger than his thumbnail!

His scalp prickled uneasily. Whoever had built this rig knew a little more about molecular circuitry than the engineers back home.

But why such a big box for such a small unit?

Well, the rest of the box was filled with some beautifully-machined apparatus with which Rod was totally unfamiliar.

He looked at the top of the box; there was a round, transparent circle set in the center. Rod frowned. He'd never run into anything quite like this before. At a guess, the circuitry was part of a remote-control system, and the machined parts were—what?

"Master, what is it?"

"I don't know," Rod muttered, "but I have a sneaking suspicion it's got something to do with the banshee."

He probed the mechanism with his dagger, trying to find

126

a moving part. He felt sublimely reckless; the gadget could very easily have a destruct circuit capable of blowing this whole section of the battlements halfway back to Sol.

The probing point found something; the machine clicked and began to hum, almost subsonic.

"Away, master!" Big Tom shouted. " 'Tis accursed!"

But Rod stayed where he was, hand frozen for fear the knife-point would lose whatever contact it had closed.

Smoke billowed out of the transparent circle, shooting ten feet into the air, then falling back. In less than a minute, a small localized cloud had formed.

A second machine clicked, somewhere in front of Rod, and a shaft of light stabbed upward from the outer wall, toward Rod but over his head, shooting into the smoke-cloud. The shaft of light spread into a fan.

Big Tom wailed in terror. "The banshee! Flee, master, for your life!"

Looking up, Rod saw the banshee towering ten feet above him. It seemed he could almost smell the rotting, tattered shrouds that covered the voluptuous woman's body.

The rabbit mouth opened, showing long, pointed teeth. A hidden loudspeaker hummed into life; the apparition was about to start its wailing.

Rod lifted his dagger a quarter of an inch; the fan of light blacked out, the hiss of the mechanical smoke-pot died.

The wind murmured over the battlements, dispelling the last of the smoke-cloud.

Rod knelt immobile, still staring upward; then, shaking himself, he picked up the front of the box and forced it back into place.

"Master," whispered Big Tom, "what was it?"

"A spell," Rod answered, "and the banshee it called up was a sham."

He stood, drumming his fingers on the stone.

He struck his fist against the wall. "No help for it. Come on, Big Tom, hold my ankles."

He lay face-downward between the two great granite blocks, his knees above the smoke-pot machine.

"What, master?"

"Hold my ankles," Rod snapped. "I've got to take a look at the outside of the wall. And you've got to keep me from falling into the moat."

Tom didn't answer.

"Come on, come on!" Rod looked back over his shoulder. "We haven't got all night."

Big Tom came forward slowly, a huge, hulking shape in the shadow. His great hands clamped on Rod's ankles.

Rod inched forward until his head was clear of the stone.

There, just under his chin, was a small, square box with a short snout: a miniaturized projecter, shooting a prerecorded banshee into the cloud of smoke, giving the illusion of three dimensions—a very compact projector and removable screen, all susceptible to remote control.

From where?

Rod craned his neck. All he could see was gray stone.

"Hold tight, Big Tom." He inched forward, hoping he'd guessed right about the big peasant.

He stopped crawling when he felt the granite lip of the battlements pressing his belt buckle. His upper body jutted free beyond the castle wall, with nothing underneath but air, and, a long way down, the moat.

He looked down.

Mm, yes, that *was* a long way, wasn't it? Now, just what would happen if he'd judged Big Tom wrong? If, contrary to expectation, the big lug let go of Rod's ankles?

Well, if that happened, Fess would send a report back to SCENT headquarters, and they'd send out another agent. No need to worry.

Tom's hoarse, labored breathing sounded very loud behind him.

Get it over with quick, boy. Rod scanned the wall under him.

There it was, just under the projector, a deep, silver-lined cup recessed into the wall—a hyperbolic antenna.

Why a hyperbolic? he wondered.

So that the radio impulse that turned the projection machines on could be very, very small, impossible to detect outside the straight line between the transmitting and receiving antennas.

So, if you want to find the transmitting antenna, just sight along the axis of the receiving dish.

And, looking along that line and allowing for parallax, he found himself staring straight at the rotting basalt pile of the House of Clovis.

For a moment, he just stared, dumbfounded. So it hadn't been the councillors after all.

Then he remembered Durer's poison attempt at breakfast,

128

have hurt us. And even as it was, I knew the spell that got rid of it."

"I was not speaking of the banshee, master."

"I know." Rod looked straight into Tom's eyes.

Then he turned and started down the stairs.

He'd gone six steps before he realized Big Tom hadn't followed.

He looked back over his shoulder. Tom was staring at him, mouth slack with shock.

Then the mouth closed, the face froze. "Thou didst know thy danger, master?"

"I did."

Tom nodded, very slowly. Then he looked down to the stairs and came down.

"Master," he said after the first landing, "thou'rt either the bravest man or the greatest fool that ever I met."

"Probably both," said Rod, keeping his eyes on the torchlit steps.

"Thou shouldst have slain me when first thou guessed." Tom's voice had an edge.

Rod shook his head, wordless.

"Why not?" Tom barked.

Rod let his head loll back. He sighed. "Long ago, Tom, and far away—Lord, how far away!"

" 'Tis no time for fairy tales!"

"This isn't a fairy tale. It's a legend—who knows? Maybe true. A king named Hideyoshi ruled a land called Japan; and the greatest duke in the land was named Ieyayasu."

"And the duke wished to be king."

"I see you know the basic techniques. But Hideyoshi did *not* want to kill Ieyayasu."

"He was a fool," Tom growled.

"No, he needed Ieyayasu's support. So he invited Ieyayasu to take a walk in the garden with him, just the two of them, alone."

Tom stopped, turned to look down at Rod. His eyes glittered in the torchlight. "And they fought."

Rod shook his head. "Hideyoshi said he was getting old and weak, and asked Ieyayasu to carry his sword for him."

Tom stared.

Then his tongue flicked out over his lips. He swallowed and nodded. "Aye. What happened?"

"Nothing. They talked a while, and then Ieyayasu gave

Hideyoshi his sword again, and they went back to the castle."

"And?"

"And Ieyayasu was loyal until the old man died."

Big Tom's eyes were hooded; he could have been carved from wood.

He nodded, mouth tightening. "A calculated risk."

"Pretty high-falutin' language for a peasant."

Tom snarled and turned away. Rod stood a moment, looking after him. Then he smiled and followed.

They were almost back to the guard room when Tom laid a hand on Rod's shoulder. Rod turned to face him.

"What are you?" Tom growled.

Rod smiled with one side of his mouth. "You mean who do I work for? Only myself, Big Tom."

"Nay." Tom shook his head. "I'll not believe that. But 'twas not what I asked."

Rod raised an eyebrow. "Oh?"

"Oh. I mean what are you, you, yourself, what manner of man?"

Rod frowned. "Nothing so strange about me."

"Aye, there is. Thou wilt not kill a peasant out of hand."

Rod stared. "Oh?" He pursed his lips. "That's out of the ordinary?"

"Most surely. And thou'lt fight for a manservant. And trust him. And speak with him, more than commands. What art thou, Rod Gallowglass?"

Rod shook his head and spread his hands in bewilderment. He laughed once, hollow. "A man. Just a man."

Tom eyed him for a long moment.

"Thou art," he said. "I am answered."

He turned away to the guard room door, flung it open.

"Master Gallowglass," said the page, "the Queen summons you."

One of life's greatest and least expensive treasures is false dawn. The world lies waiting for the sun, lit by a glowing sky, chill and fresh, filled with rippling bird song.

Big Tom took one long, deep breath of the morning air, filling his lungs with the innocence he had never known. "Eh, master!" he called back over his shoulder, "this is the world for a man!"

Rod answered with a feeble smile as Tom turned away,

to ride on ahead of Rod, singing jubilantly and with gusto, though somewhat off-key.

Rod, unfortunately, was in no condition to appreciate the aesthetic qualities of the dawn, having had about three hours of sleep in the last forty-eight hours.

Then, too, there was Catharine.

The interview had been short and sour. She'd received him in her audience chamber, and had kept her eyes on the fire, not once looking at him. Her face had been cold, lips drawn tight against her teeth.

"I fear for my Uncle Loguire," she had said. "There are men about him who would rejoice to see his eldest son become the Duke."

Rod had answered in the same stiff, formal tone. "If he dies, you lose your strongest friend among the lords."

"I lose one who is dear to me," she snapped. "I care not for friendship among the lords; but I care greatly for my uncle."

And that, Rod reflected, was probably true—to her credit as a woman, and her detriment as a ruler.

"Do you," she resumed, "ride south this day to Loguire's demesne; and do you see that none bring harm to him."

And that, aside from a very formal leavetaking, had been that. Hell hath no stupidity like a woman scorned, Rod thought; she was sending her most competent bodyguard as far away as she could.

"Fess?"

"Yes, Rod?" The horse turned its head to look back at its rider.

"Fess, I am without a doubt the prize booby ever hatched."

"You are a great man, Rod, from a line of great men."

"Oh yeah, I'm *so* great! Here I am, supposed to be turning this kingdom into a constitutional monarchy; and while I'm jauntily wandering southward, the councillors are tearing apart any possibility of a constitution, while the House of Clovis is on the verge of killing off the monarch!

"And here I ride south, with a manservant who would probably gleefully slip a knife between my ribs if his sense of duty got the upper hand over his conscience for half a minute.

"And what have I accomplished? I've established that the place is filled with ghosts, elves, witches, and a lot of other monsters that can't possibly exist; I've given you five or six seizures; and to top it all off, a beautiful woman propositioned me, and I refused! Oh, I'm so great it's unbelievable! If I were just a little bit more efficient, I'd have manged to botch the whole thing by now! Fess, wouldn't I be better off if I just gave up?"

The robot began to sing softly.

*"I am a man of constant sorrow,
I've seen trouble all my days. . . ."*

"Oh, shut up."

PART TWO

THE WITCH OF LOW ESTATE

DAWN FOUND THEM in the midst of hayfields, half-mown and dew-laden. Rod looked about him from the top of the rise, looking down on rolling farmland and tidy hedges, with here and there a clump of trees, dark against the rising sun.

"Big Tom!"

Tom turned in the saddle and looked back, then reined in his horse when he saw Rod had halted.

"Breakfast!" Rod called, dismounting. He led Fess off the road to a rock outcrop beneath a thicket of gorse. Tom shrugged and turned his mount.

Rod had the fire laid and kindled by the time Big Tom had hobbled his pony and turned it to graze. The big man stared in amazement as Rod unlimbered a frying pan and coffeepot, then turned away, shaking his head in wonder, and dried a place to sit on a log further down the slope. He sniffed at the scent of frying ham, sighed, and took out a pack of hardtack.

Rod looked up, frowning, and saw Big Tom sitting in wet grass with a biscuit and a skin of ale. He scowled and shouted.

"Hey!"

The shout caught Big Tom in mid-swig; he choked, spluttered, and looked up.

"Eh, master?"

"My food not good enough for you?"

Big Tom stared, open-mouthed.

"Come, on, come on!" Rod waved an arm impatiently. "And bring those biscuits with you; they'll go good fried in hamfat."

Big Tom opened and closed his mouth a few times, then nodded vaguely and stood up.

The water was boiling; Rod pried the lid off the coffeepot and threw in a handful of grounds. He looked up as Big Tom came to the fire, brow furrowed, staring.

Rod's mouth turned down at the corners. "Well, what're you looking at? Never saw a campfire before?"

"Thou bid me eat with my master!"

Rod scowled. "Is that some major miracle? Here, give a drag of that ale-skin, will you? That road gets dusty."

Tom nodded, eyes still fixed on Rod's, and held out the skin. Rod took a swig, looked up, and frowned. "What's the matter? Never saw a man take a drink? What am I, some alien monster?"

Tom's mouth closed; his eyes turned dark and brooding. Then he grinned, laughed, and sat down on a rock. "Nay, master, nay. Thou'rt a rare good man, and that only. Nay, only that!"

Rod frowned. "Why, what's so rare about me?"

Tom threw two cakes of hardtack into the frying pan and looked up, grinning. "In this country, master, a gentleman does not take food with his servant."

"Oh, that!" Rod waved the objection away. "It's just you and me out here on the road, Big Tom. I don't have to put up with that nonsense."

"Aye," Big Tom chuckled. "A most wonderous rare man, as I said."

"And a fool, eh?" Rod served up two slices of ham on wooden saucers. "Guess we eat with our knives, Tom. Dig in."

They ate in silence, Rod scowling at his plate, Tom leaning back and looking out over the countryside.

They were at the head of a small valley, filled now with the morning mist, a trap for small sunbeams. The sun lurked over the hedges, and the mist was golden.

Tom grinned as he chewed and jerked his thumb toward the valley. " 'Tis the end of the rainbow, master."

"Hm?" Rod jerked his head up. He smiled sourly; it was, after all, more of a pot of gold than he'd had any right to expect.

Tom gave a rumbling belch and picked at his teeth with his dagger. "A golden mist, master, and mayhap golden girls within it."

Rod swallowed quickly and objected. "Oh, no! No tom-catting on the side of this trip, Big Tom! We've got to get down to the South and get down there fast!"

"Eh, master!" Tom wailed in shocked protest, "what harm another hour or four, eh? Besides"—he sat forward and poked Rod in the ribs, grinning—"I'll wager thou'lt outdo me. What lasses may not a warlock have, mm? . . . Eh, what's the matter?"

Rod wheezed and pounded his chest. "Just a piece of hard-tack having an argument with my gullet. Tom, for the ump-teenth penultimate unprintable time, I am *not* a warlock!"

"Oh, aye, master, to be sure!" Big Tom said with a broad-lipped grin. "And thou mayst be certain thou'rt as poor a liar as thou art an executioner."

Rod frowned. "I haven't killed a man the whole time I've been here!"

"Aye, and that is my meaning."

"Oh." Rod turned and looked out over the fields. "Well, you might as well add lover to that list of things I'm not good at, Tom."

The big man sat forward, frowning, searching Rod's face. "In truth, I think he doth mean it!"

"Be sure that I doth."

Tom sat back, studying his master and tossing his dagger, catching it alternately by the hilt and the point. "Aye, thou speakest aright of thy knowledge." He sat forward, looking into Rod's eyes. "And therefore shall I dare to advise thee."

Rod grinned and gave him a hollow laugh. "All right, advise me. Tell me how it's done."

"Nay." Tom held up a palm. "That much I am sure that you knowest. But it is these farm girls against which I must caution thee, master."

"Oh?"

"Aye. They are—" Tom's face broke into a grin. "Oh, they are excellent, master, though simple. But"—he frowned again—"never give them a trace of a hope."

Rod frowned too. "Why not?"

" 'Twill be thy undoing. Thou mayst love them well, mas-ter, once—but once only. Then must thou leave them, right quickly, and never look back."

"Why? I'll be turned into a pillar of salt?"

"Nay, thou'lt be turned into a husband. For once given the merest shred of hope, master, these farm girls will stick tighter than leeches, and thou'lt never be rid of them."

Rod snorted. "I should have a chance to worry about it! Come on, drink up your coffee and mount up."

They doused the fire and packed up, and rode down into the red-gold mist.

They had gone perhaps three hundred yards when a long-drawn alto voice hailed them.

Rod looked up, tensed and wary.

Two big peasant girls stood with pitchforks at the base of a haystack in one of the fields, laughing and waving.

Big Tom's eyes locked on them with an almost-audible click. "Eh, master! Pretty little mopsies, are they not?"

They were pretty, Rod had to admit—though certainly anything but little. They were both full-hipped and high-breasted, wearing loose low-cut blouses and full skirts, their hair tied in kerchiefs. Their skirts were girded up to their knees, to keep them from the dew on the hay.

They beckoned, their laughter a mocking challenge. One of them set her hands on her hips and executed a slow bump-and-grind.

Big Tom sucked his breath in, his eyes fairly bulging. "Eh, now, master," he pleaded, "are we in so much of a hurry as all that?"

Rod sighed, rolling his eyes up, and shook his head. "Well, I'd hate to see them suffering from neglect, Big Tom. Go ahead."

Tom kicked his horse with a yelp of joy, leaped the ditch, and galloped full tilt into the field. He was out of the saddle before the horse slowed past a trot, catching a girl in each arm, lifting them off the ground and whirling them about.

Rod shook his head slowly, saluted Big Tom and his playmates, and turned away to find a neighboring haystack where he could catnap in peace.

"Rod," said the quiet voice behind his ear.

"Yes, Fess?"

"Your conduct disturbs me, Rod. It's not natural for a healthy young male."

"It's not the first time someone's told me that, Fess. But I'm methodical; I can't keep two girls on my mind at once."

He found another haystack just over the next hedge. Rod parked in the shadow and unbridled Fess, who began to crop at the hay, to keep up appearances. Rod remounted and jumped from the horse's back to the top of the haystack and wallowed down into the soft, fragrant hay with a blissful sigh. The pungent smell of new-mown hay filled his head, taking him back to his boyhood in the fields of his father's manor, during haying time; a *real* Eden, without any soft, nubile problems to run around creating havoc. Just robots. . . .

He watched the gilt-edged clouds drifting across the turquoise sky, not realizing when he dozed off.

He came wide awake and stayed very still, wondering what had wakened him. He ran through the catalog of sensations that were apt to start the alarm clock ringing in his subconscious.

Somebody was near.

His eyes snapped open, every muscle in his body tensed to fight.

He was looking into a very low-cut bodice.

He raised his eyes from the pleasant pastoral view, a task which required no small amount of willpower, and saw two large sea-green eyes looking into his. They were long-lashed, moist, and looked worried.

Their surroundings came into focus: arched eyebrows, a snub nose sprinkled with freckles, a very wide mouth with full, red lips, all set in a roundish face framed in long, flowing red hair.

The full red lips were pouting, the eyes were troubled.

Rod smiled, yawned, and stretched. "Good morning."

The pouting lips relaxed into a half-smile. "Good morning, fine gentleman."

She was sitting beside him, propped on one hand, looking into his eyes.

"Why do you sleep here alone, sir, when nearby a woman awaits your call?"

It felt as though someone had just poured bitters into Rod's circulatory system; a thrill, and not completely a pleasant one, flooded through him.

He smiled, trying to make it warm. "I thank you, lass, but I'm not feeling gamesome today."

She smiled, but there was still a frown between her eyes. "I thank you for your gentleness, sir; but I scarce can credit your words."

"Why?" Rod frowned. "Is it so impossible that a man shouldn't want a frolic?"

The girl gave a forlorn half of a laugh. "Oh, it might be, milord, but scarce is it likely. Not even with a peasant, and even less with a lord."

"I'm not a lord."

"A gentleman, then. That, surely, thou art. And therefore, surely, thou wouldst never lack interest."

"Oh?" Rod raised an eyebrow. "Why?"

She smiled, sadly. "Why, milord, a peasant might fear forced marriage; but a lord, never."

Rod frowned again and studied the girl's face. He judged

her to be a little younger than himself, about twenty-nine or thirty.

And for a peasant girl in this kind of society to be unmarried at thirty . . .

He threw out an arm. "Come here to me, lass."

There was hope, for a moment, in the girl's eyes; but it faded quickly, was replaced by resignation. She fell into the hay beside him with a sigh, rolling onto her side to pillow her head on his shoulder.

Hope, Rod mused, very conscious of her breasts and hips against the side of his body. *Hope to be tumbled, and thrown away. . . .*

He shuddered; and the girl raised her head, concerned. "Art chilled, milord?"

He turned to her and smiled, a sudden wave of gratitude and tenderness surging up to clog his throat. He clasped her tight against him, closing his eyes to better savor the touch of her body against his own. An aroma filled his head, not rose-oil or lilac, but simply the salt-sweet scent of a woman.

A pain was ebbing away inside him, he realized, faintly surprised, a pain that he had not known was there till it began to leave him.

She clung to him, fists clenched in the cloth of his doublet, face pressed into the angle of his neck and shoulder.

Then, gradually, he began to relax again, his embrace loosening. He lay very still, letting the focus of his mind widen, open him again to the world around him; faint in the distance he heard birdsong, and the gossip of the wind through the hedges and trees. Somewhere near his head, a cricket chirped in the hay.

Her embrace had loosened with his; her arms and head lay leaden on him now.

He kept his eyes closed, the sun beating down on the lids; he lay in crimson light, "seeing" the world with his ears.

There was a rustle, and her body rose away from his; she had sat up now. She would be looking down at him, hurt aching in her eyes, lower lip trembling, a tear on her cheek.

Pity welled up in him, pity for her and, close behind it, anger at himself; it wasn't her fault that all he wanted just now was peace, not romance.

He opened his eyes, rolling onto his side and frowning up at her.

But there was no hurt in her eyes—only a grave, deep acceptance, and concern.

She raised her fingertips to his cheek, shyly, not quite touching the skin. He caught it, nestling the palm against the line of his jaw, and was amazed at how small her hand was in his own.

He closed his eyes, pressing her hand tighter.

A cow lowed far away; the wind chuckled in the grain.

Her voice was low, and very gentle. "Milord, use me as you will. I ask no more."

I ask no more. . . . Love, she must have love, if only for a minute, even if desertion came hard on its heels; even if looking back, she must know that it was lust, and not love. Even if it brought only sorrow and pain, she must have love.

He looked into her eyes; they held tears.

He closed his eyes again, and Catharine's face was before him, and Tuan's face next to hers. A part of him stood back, aloof, and contemplated the faces; it remarked on how well they looked together, the beautiful princess and the gallant young knight.

Then his own face came up next to Tuan's, and, *compare,* the aloof part of him murmured, *compare.*

Rod's hands tightened, and he heard the peasant girl give a little cry of startled pain.

He let go his grip, and looked up at her; and Catharine's face swam next to hers.

He looked on the two of them, the one bent on using him, the other bent on being used by him, and anger suddenly burned in a band across his chest, anger at Catharine for her self-righteousness and determination to bend her world to her will; and at the peasant girl for her mute acceptance and deep resignation, for the depth of her warmth and her gentleness. The band of anger across his chest tightened and tightened, anger at himself for the animal in him, as his fingers bit into her shoulders, and he drew her down in the hay. She gasped with the pain, crying out softly till his lips struck hers, crushing and biting and bruising, his fingers clamped on the points of her jaw, forcing her mouth open and his tongue stabbed hard under hers. His hand groped over her body, fingers jabbing deep into the flesh, lower and lower, gnawing and mauling.

Then her nails dug into his back as her whole body knotted

in one spasm of pain. Then she went loose, and her chest heaved under him in one great sob.

Half his anger sublimed into nothingness; the other half turned about and lanced into him, piercing something within him that loosed a tide of remorse.

He rolled to the side, taking his weight off her. His lips were suddenly gentle, warm and pleading; his hands were gentle, caressing slowly, soothingly.

She drew in breath, her body tensing again. *Fool*, the detached voice within him sneered, *Fool! You only hurt her the more!*

Ready to turn away from her in shame, he looked up into her eyes . . . and saw the longing burning naked there, craving and demanding, pulling him down into the maelstrom within her. Her lips parted, moist and full and warm, tugging and yielding, pulling him down and down, into blind, light-flooded depths where there was no sight nor hearing, but only touch upon touch.

Rod levered himself up on one elbow and looked down at the girl, lying naked beside him with only his cloak for a rather inadequate coverlet. It clung to her contours, and Rod let his eyes wander over them, drinking in the sight of her, fixing every feature of her body in his mind. It was a picture he did not want to lose.

He caressed her, gently, very tenderly. She smiled, murmured, closing her eyes and letting her head roll to the side.

Then her eyes opened again; she looked at him sidelong, her lips heavy and languid.

"You have emerald eyes," Rod whispered.

She stretched luxuriously, her smile a little smug, wrapped her arms around his neck, and hauled him down to her, her kisses slow, almost drowsy, and lasting.

Rod looked into her eyes, feeling enormously contented and very much at peace with the world. Hell, the world could go hang!

He raised himself up again, his eyes upon her; then, slowly, he looked away and about him. There was only the bowl of hay under and about them, and the blue of the sky arching overhead . . . and a mound of clothing to each side.

He looked down again; there was nothing in his world now except her, and he found, vaguely surprised, that he rather liked it that way. The peace within him was vast; he felt completely filled, completely satisfied with the world, with life, at one with them and with God—and with her most of all.

He let his hand linger over the cloaked curve of her breast. She closed her eyes, murmuring; then, as his hand stilled, she looked up at him again. Her smile faded to a ghost; concern stole into her eyes.

She started to say something, stopped, and said instead, almost warily, "Are you well, lord?"

He smiled, his eyes very sober; then he closed them and nodded, slowly.

"Yes. I am very well."

He bent to kiss her again—slowly, almost carefully—then lifted away. "Yes, I am well, most strangely well, more than I have ever been."

The smile lit her face again, briefly; then she turned her eyes away, looking down at her body, then up at him again, her eyes touched with fear.

He clasped her in his arms and rolled onto his back. Her body stiffened a moment, then relaxed; she gave a little cry, half sob and half sigh, and burrowed her head into the hollow of his shoulder and was still.

He looked down at the glory of her hair spread out over his chest. He smiled lazily and let his eyes drift shut.

"Rod." Fess's voice whispered behind his ear, and the world came flooding in again.

Rod tensed, and clicked his teeth once in acknowledgment.

"Big Tom is dressed again, and coming toward your haystack."

Rod sat bolt upright, squinted up at the sun; it was almost to the meridian. Time and distance nagged him again.

"Well, back to the world of the living," he growled, and reached out for his clothes.

"Milord?"

She was smiling regretfully, but her eyes were tight with hurt—a hurt which faded into the deep acceptance and resignation even as he watched.

"The memory of this time will be dear to me, lord," she whispered, clasping the cloak to her breast, her eyes widening.

It was a forlorn plea for reassurance, a reassurance he could not honestly give, for he would never see her again.

It came to him then that she was expecting refusal of any reassurance, expecting him to lash out at her for her temerity in implying that she had some worth, that she was worthy of thanks.

She knew her plea would bring hurt, yet she pled; for a woman lives on love, and this was a woman near thirty in a land where girls married at fifteen. She had already accepted that there was to be no lasting love in her life; she must subsist on the few crumbs she could gather.

His heart went out to her, somewhat impelled by the jab of self-reproach.

So, of course, he told her one of the lies that men tell women only to comfort them, and later realize to be very true.

He kissed her and said, "This was not Life, lass, it was what living is for."

And later, when he mounted his horse and turned back to look at her, with Big Tom beside him waving a cheery farewell to his wench, Rod looked into the girl's eyes again and saw the desperation, the touch of panic at his leaving, the silent, frantic plea for a shred of hope.

A shred, Tom had said, would be too much, but Rod would probably never see this girl again. Not even a spark of hope—just a glimmer. Could that do any hurt?

"Tell me your name, lass."

Only a spark, but it flared in her eyes to a bonfire. "Gwendylon am I called, lord."

And when they had rounded a turn in the road and the girls were lost to sight beyond the hill behind them, Tom sighed and said, "Thou hast done too much, master. Thou shalt never be rid of her now."

There was this to be said for a roll in the hay: it had sapped enough of Big Tom's vitality so that he wasn't singing any more. Probably still humming, to be sure; but he was riding far enough ahead so Rod couldn't hear him.

Rod rode in silence, unable to rid his mind of flaming hair and emerald eyes. So he cursed at the vision, under his breath; but it seemed to his aloof self that the cursing lacked something—vehemence, perhaps. Certainly sincerity. It was, his aloof self accused, a very halfhearted attempt at malediction.

Rod had to admit it was. He was still feeling very much at one with creation. At the moment, he couldn't have been angry with his executioner. . . . And that worried him.

"Fess."

"Yes, Rod?" The voice seemed a little more inside his head than usual.

"Fess, I don't feel right."

The robot paused; then, "How *do* you feel, Rod?"

There was something about the way Fess had said that . . . Rod glanced sharply at the pseudo-horse head. "Fess, are you laughing at me?"

"Laughing?"

"Yes, laughing. You heard me. Chuckling in your beard."

"This body is not equipped with a beard."

"Cut the comedy and answer the question."

With something like a sigh, the robot said, "Rod, I must remind you that I am only a machine. I am incapable of emotions. . . . I was merely noting discrepancies, Rod."

"Oh, *were* you!" Rod growled. "What discrepancies, may I ask?"

"In this instance, the discrepancy between what a man really is and what he wishes to believe of himself."

Rod's upper lip turned under and pressed against his teeth. "Just what do I wish to belive?"

"That you are not emotionally dependent upon this peasant woman."

"Her name is Gwendylon."

"With Gwendylon. With any woman, for that matter. You wish to believe that you are emotionally independent, that you no longer enjoy what you call 'being in love.' "

"I enjoy love very much, thank you!"

"That is a very different thing," the robot murmured, "than being in love."

"Damn it, I wasn't talking about *making* love!"

"Neither was I."

Rod's lips pressed into a thin white line. "You're talking about emotional intoxication. And if that's what you mean—no, I am not in love. I have no desire to be in love. And if I have any say in the matter, I will never be in love again!"

"Precisely what I said you wished to believe," mused the robot.

Rod ground his teeth and waited for the surge of anger to pass. "Now what's the truth about me?"

"That you are in love."

"Damn it, a man's either in love, or he's not, and he damn well knows which."

"Agreed; but he may not be willing to admit it."

145

"Look," Rod snapped, "I've been in love before, and I know what it's like. It's . . . well . . ."

"Go on," the robot prodded.

"Well, it's like"—Rod lifted his head and looked out at the countryside—"you know the world's there, and you know it's real; but you don't give a damn, 'cause you know for a certainty that you're the center of the world, the most important thing in it."

"Have you felt that way recently?" Fess murmured.

"Well . . . yes, damn it." Rod's mouth twisted.

"With Catharine?"

Rod stared, and glared at the back of the horse's head. "How the hell would *you* know?" His eyes narrowed.

"Logic, Rod." The robot's voice had a touch of smugness. "Only logic. And how did you feel while you were with Gwendylon?"

"Oh . . ." Rod threw his shoulders back, stretching. "Great, Fess. Better than I ever have. The world's clearer, and the day's younger. I feel so healthy and clearheaded I can't believe it. It's just the opposite to how I feel when I'm in love, but I like it."

Rod frowned at the back of Fess's head. "Well?"

The robot plodded on, not answering.

"Cat got your tongue?"

"I am not equipped with a tongue, Rod."

"Don't change the subject."

The horse was silent a moment longer; then, "I was mistaken, Rod. You love, and are loved—but you are not in love."

Rod frowned down at the roadway. "Why not, Fess?"

The robot made a sound like a sigh. "How do the two women differ, Rod?"

"Well . . ." Rod chewed at the inside of his cheek. "Gwendylon's human. I mean, she's just an ordinary, everyday woman, like I'm an ordinary man."

"But Catharine is more?"

"Oh, she's the kind of woman I tend to put on a pedestal . . . something to be worshiped, not courted . . ."

"And not loved?" the robot mused. "Rod, of the two women, which is the better human being?"

"Uh . . . Gwendylon."

"The prosecution," said the robot-horse, "rests."

The demesne of the Loguires was a great, broad plain between the mountains and the sea. The low, rolling mountains stood at the north and east; beach curved in a wide semicircle in the south; a sheer, hundred foot high cliff face towered in the northwest. The ocean battered at its seaward side; a waterfall poured over the other face into the valley. A long, old river twisted over the plain to the sea.

The plain itself was a patchwork of fields, with here and there a cluster of peasant huts—Loguire's people.

Tom and Rod stood at the verge of one of the mountain forests, where the road from the North fell away to the plain.

Rod turned his head slowly, surveying the demesne. "And where," he said, "is the castle?"

"Why, back of the waterfall, master."

Rod's head jerked around, staring at Tom; then he followed the road with his eyes.

It wound across the plain to the foot of the waterfall; there, where the cliff met the plain, a great gate was carved in the rock, complete with portcullis and a drawbridge over the natural moat formed by an oxbow of the river. The lords of Loguire had honeycombed the cliff for their home.

An exclamation point formed between Rod's eyebrows as they drew together. "Is that a dike to either side of the drawbridge, Big Tom?"

"Aye, master; and there are said to be charges of gunpowder within it."

Rod nodded, slowly. "And the land before the portcullis gate sinks down. So if unwelcome callers come knocking, you blow up the dike, and your front door gets covered with thirty feet of water. Very neat. Then you just sit and wait out the seige. The waterfall gives you plenty of fresh water, so your only worry is food."

"There are said to be gardens within the keep," Big Tom supplied helpfully.

Rod shook his head in silent respect. "So you're completely defended, and stocked for a ten years' siege. This place ever been taken, Tom?"

The big man shook his head. "Never, master." He grinned.

"Wonder if the old boy who built this place was maybe a little bit paranoid. . . . Don't suppose they'd have room in that place for a couple of weary travelers, do you?"

Big Tom pursed his lips. "Aye, master, if they were noblemen. The hospitality of the Loguires is famed. But for the likes of me, and even yourself, who are no more than a squire, master, that hospitality lies in the cottages."

The sun winked. Rod scowled and peered into the sky. "There's that damn bird again. Doesn't it know we're too big for lunch?" He unlimbered his crossbow and cranked it back to cocked.

"Nay, master." Big Tom put out a hand. "You've lost four bolts on it already."

"I just don't like anything airborne following me, Tom. They're not always what they seem." Tom's brow furrowed at the cryptic statement. Rod tucked the stock into his shoulder. "Besides, I've taken one shot a day at it for the last four days; it's getting to be a habit."

The bow hummed, and the quarrel leaped upward; but the bird sailed up faster. The bolt passed through the place where the bird had been, rose another fifty feet, hit the top of its arc, and began to fall. The bird, fifty feet higher, watched it sink.

Big Tom raised an eyebrow, his mouth quirked up on one side. "You'll never strike it, master. The fowl knows the meaning of a crossbow."

"You'd almost think it does." Rod slung the bow over his shoulder. "What kind of country is this, with elves under every tree and hawks in the sky shadowing you?"

" 'Tis not a hawk, master," Big Tom reproved. " 'Tis an osprey."

Rod shook his head. "It started following us the second day out. What would a fish hawk be doing that far inland?"

"Myself, I cannot say. Thou might ask it, though, master."

"And I wouldn't really be all that surprised if it answered," Rod mused. "Well, it isn't doing us any harm, I suppose, and we've got bigger problems at the moment. We came here to get into that castle. Do you sing, Big Tom?"

Tom did a double take. "Sing, master?"

"Yeah, sing. Or play the bagpipes, or something."

Tom tugged at his lip, frowning. "I can make some manner of noise on a shepherd's flute, and the half dead might put the word *music* to it. But what folly is this, master?"

"Fool's folly." Rod unstrapped a saddlebag and took out a small harp. "As of now, we're minstrels. Let's hope the cliff-dwellers are a little short on music at the moment." He pulled an alto recorder out of the saddlebag and gave it to Tom. "I hope that's enough like your shepherd's flute to do some good."

148

"Aye, master, very like it. But—"

"Oh, don't worry, they'll let us in. Folks this far away from the capital tend to be out of touch; they're hungry for news and new songs, and minstrels carry both. Do you know 'Eddystone Light'?"

"Nay, master."

"Too bad; that's one that always goes over well in a seaport town. Well, no matter, I can teach it to you as we go."

They set off down the road, singing in accidentals unknown to any human mode or scale. This fish hawk screamed and sheered off.

"Bring ye news from the North?" the sentry had asked eagerly; and Rod, recollecting that minstrels were the closest medieval equivalent to journalists, had replied in the affirmative.

Now he and Tom stood before a gathering of twenty-eight noblemen, their wives and attendants, ranging in age from pretty teenage serving maids to the ninety year old Earl of Vallenderie, all with the same eager, hungry glint in their eyes, and Rod without a scrap of news to tell them.

Well, no matter; he'd make it up as he went along. He wouldn't be the first journalist who'd done it.

The crusty old Duke of Loguire sat in a great oaken chair in the midst of the company; he didn't seem to recognize Rod. But Durer did; he stood hunched over Loguire's left shoulder, eyes twisting hate at Rod. But it would have done him no good to expose Rod, and he knew it; Loguire still loved his niece, though he was at odds with her. He would have honored Rod for saving Catharine's life.

It was Loguire who voiced the question for all his people; and Rod, reflecting that the Duke had very personal reasons for wanting news of the House of Clovis, had replied that as yet, all was quiet in the North. Oh, one heard talk and saw signs of the House; but that was talk, and talk only—so far.

Then he and Tom swung into a foot-stamping rendition of "Eddystone Light." The gathering stood in astounded silence a moment; then grins broke out, and hands started clapping the rhythm.

Encouraged, Big Tom picked up both the tempo and the volume; Rod struggled to match him while he scanned the faces of the audience.

The old Duke was trying to look sternly disapproving, and not succeeding too well. A tall young man of about Rod's age stood behind the old man's right shoulder, a grin coming to his lips and a gleam to his eye as he listened to the song, displacing a grimace of discontent, self-pity, and bitterness. The elder son, Rod guessed, with a host of weaknesses Durer could prey upon.

It was easy to pick out Loguire's vassal lords; all were richly dressed, and accompanied by an even more richly-dressed wire scarecrow of a man: the councillors, Durer's boys.

Rod felt strangely certain that anything Durer proposed would have the unanimous approval of all the Southern lords, with only Loguire dissenting.

And Loguire, of course, had one more vote than all the vassal lords put together Rod remembered Loguire's unsolicited promise to Catharine: "No harm shall come to the Queen while I live. . . ."

"While I live. . . ."

The performance was literally a howling success; Rod had managed to keep it on a ribald rather than a political level, walking the thin line between the risqué and the pornographic. The audience had loved it; Rod decided that the tin ear must be a genetic dominant in Gramarye He'd noticed, too, that the eyes of all the serving girls had been riveted to himself and Big Tom; he was still trying to understand why. It didn't seem to have done Big Tom's ego any harm, though.

But now and again, one of the councillors had asked a question that could not be put off; and when Rod had answered with rumors that the House of Clovis would rise against the Crown, a frantic, acid joy had burned in their eyes.

That, at least, he understood. The important thing about a revolution is that it begin; you can always take control of it later.

That he understood; but now, with the singing done, as he was going to the loft which had been temporarily assigned to Tom and himself, he was still pondering the look on the faces of the serving maids. When they had looked at Tom, he'd been quite sure what it was; he expected to find the loft fully occupied by the time he arrived, since Big Tom had gone on ahead.

But that look couldn't mean the same thing when applied

to himself—unless the occupation of minstrel carried a great deal more prestige than he'd thought.

So, all in all, he was even more confused but not too surprised when one of the servant girls intercepted him with a cup of wine.

"Salve for a parched throat, Master Minstrel," she murmured, her eyes shining as she held the cup out to him.

He looked at her out of the corner of his eye and reluctantly accepted the cup; no call for bad manners, was there?

"And," she murmured as she drank, "warmth for your bed, if you will."

Rod choked and spluttered, lowered the cup, glaring at her; then he looked her up and down quickly. She was full-bodied and high-breasted, with a wide, full-lipped mouth—very like Gwendylon, in some ways. . . .

Suddenly suspicious, Rod looked more sharply; but no, this girl's eyes were tilted upward at the outer corners, and her nose was long and straight, not snub. Besides, her hair and eyes were black.

He smiled wryly and drank off the rest of the cup and returned it to her. "Thank you, lass, right deeply."

It was indicative, he thought, that she had come to him instead of Big Tom. Tom was certainly the more appealing chunk of man; but Rod was obviously the one who had the status. A bitch like any of them, he thought: she doesn't give a damn for who the man is, just as long as *what* he is is a station higher than hers.

"I thank you," he said again, "but I have been long on the road, and am like to swoon from my weariness." A very pretty speech, he thought; and go ahead, let her think less of my manhood for it. At least she'll leave me alone.

The serving maid lowered her eyes, biting her lip. "As you will, good master." And she turned away, leaving Rod staring after her.

Well, that hadn't taken much refusing. Come to think of it, he was a little indignant . . . but had there been just a hint of triumph in her eyes, a shard of rejoicing?

Rod went on his way, wondering if perhaps he hadn't inadvertently stepped into the pages of a Machiavellian textbook.

The door to the loft was closed, as Rod had guessed; a muffled feminine squeal, followed by Tom's bass laugh, further confirmed his guess.

So he shrugged philosophically, settled his harp over his shoulder, and turned back down the long, winding staircase. He could put the time to good use, anyway. The castle had so obviously been built by a paranoid that he was certain there had to be secret passages.

He sauntered down the main corridor, whistling. The granite walls were painted ocher, ornamented with standing suits of armor and here and there a tapestry. Some of the tapestries were huge, reaching from floor to ceiling; Rod noted their locations carefully in his mind. They could very easily conceal the mouths of passageways.

Twelve sub-corridors intersected the main hall at right angles. As he came near the seventh, he noticed that his footsteps seemed to have acquired an echo—a very curious echo, that took two steps for each one of his. He stopped to look at a tapestry; the echo took two more steps and stopped. Looking out of the corner of his eye, Rod caught a glimpse of one of the wizened, richly-dressed scarecrows; he thought he recognized Durer, but it was hard to tell by peripheral vision.

He turned away and swaggered on down the hall, humming "Me and My Shadow." The echo started again.

Now, Rod was mildly gregarious; he didn't really mind company. But it was a safe bet that he wasn't going to learn very much with Durer on his tail with a saltshaker. Ergo, he had to figure some way to lose his emaciated companion. This would not be easy, since Durer almost surely knew the castle very thoroughly, while Rod knew it not at all.

But the ninth cross-corridor seemed as though it would do nicely for the purpose—it was unlit. Strange, Rod mused; the other halls had all had a torch every several paces. But this was as dark as Carlsbad before the tourists came; it also had a thick carpet of dust, with not a single footprint in evidence. Cobwebs hung thick from the ceiling; trickles of moisture ran down the walls, watering patches of moss.

But the darkness was the main feature. He would leave a nice trail in the dust, but the darkness offered a chance of ducking into a room or side-hall; also, Durer couldn't very well pretend he just happened to be going the same way.

Rod turned into the corridor, sneezing in the cloud of dust he kicked up, and heard a sudden scurrying behind him. A claw grabbed his shoulder; he turned to face the little man, ready to swing.

Yes, it was Durer, glaring at Rod with his usual look of

hate and suspicion. "What seek you in there?" he croaked.

Rod brushed the bony hand off his shoulder and leaned back against the wall. "Nothing in particular; just looking around. I don't have much of anything to do at the moment, unless you'd like a song?"

"Damn your caterwauling!" Durer snapped. "And you may leave off your pretense of minstrelsy; I know you for what you are."

"Oh?" Rod raised an eyebrow. "How'd you know I'm not really a minstrel?"

"I heard you sing. Now off to your chamber, if you've no business elsewhere!"

Rod scratched his nose. "Ah—about that chamber," he said delicately. "My companion seems to have found, uh, a better use for it than sleeping. So I'm, ah, sort of locked out, if you follow me."

"Corruption!" the councillor hissed.

"No, I suspect Big Tom goes about it in a very healthy manner. And since I have no place to stay at the moment, I thought none would mind my wandering about."

Durer glared at him, a look like a laser beam. Then, very reluctantly, he backed off a pace or two.

"True," he said. "There are no secrets here for you to pry out."

Rod managed to limit his laughter to a mild convulsion in the depths of his belly.

"But did you not know," the scarecrow continued, "that this is the haunted quarter?"

Rod's eyebrows shot up. "You don't say." He tugged at his lower lip, eyeing Durer judiciously. "You seem to know the castle pretty well."

Durer's eyes snapped like a high-voltage arc. "Any in this castle could tell you that. But I am Durer, councillor to the Duke of Loguire! It is my place to know the castle well— as it is *not* yours!"

But Rod had turned away, looking down the dark hallway. "You know," he mused, "I've never seen a ghost before. . . ."

"None have, and lived to tell of it! To enter there is the act of a fool!"

Rod turned, smiling cheerfully. "Well, I'm qualified. Besides, a meeting with a ghost would make a good ballad."

The little man stared; then a contemptuous smile twisted into his face. He began to chuckle, sounding strangely like

153

ball bearings rolling over corrugated iron. "Go then, fool! I should have seen 'twould be no matter whether you went there or not."

Rod grinned, shrugged, and stepped into the black corridor.

"A moment!" Durer called.

Rod sighed and turned. "What do you want now?"

"Before you go to your death," said Durer, his eyes feverishly bright, "tell me: what are you?"

A chill ran down Rod's back. The little man had seen through his cover.

He leaned against the wall, radiating boredom. "A minstrel, of course. What else would I be?"

"Nay, fool! Do you think me so blind? You are a spy!"

Rod's hand crept to his dagger-hilt. It was balanced for throwing.

"A spy from the House of Clovis!" Durer howled.

Rod's hand relaxed; he let out a breath that he hadn't known he'd been holding. "Guess again, little man."

Durer scowled. "Not from the House? But then . . . Nay, you are their spy! Even now you will not admit to it!"

A synapse spat in Rod's brain.

He leaned back against the wall, folding his arms, grinning. "Why, what interest have you in the House of Clovis, good councillor? And why would Clovis wish to know of your doings here?"

"Nay!" Durer hissed, his eyes widening. "Fool, do you think I would answer such . . . Aie! Curse my old mind, not to have thought it! You are a spy from the Queen!"

Rod stepped away from the wall, loosening the dagger in its sheath. He didn't particularly care if Durer knew Catharine had sent him; but he did want an answer. "I asked you a question," he said mildly.

Terror welled up in the little man's eyes. He leaped back against the far wall. "Hold! At my call a score of soldiers come!"

Rod gave him a look that was somewhere between a sneer and a smile. "That won't do you much good if you're dead by the time they get here." He gestured toward the dark corridor. "Also, I'd probably be gone by the time they arrive."

The little man stared, horrified, and began to tremble. But the little bastard had guts, Rod had to give him that. His voice broke like a cicada in autumn, but he kept talking.

"It might be . . . it just might be that it is even as you say, that you are not of Clovis! And if you come from the Queen, why, then, you are welcome among us!"

Rod half-turned his head, giving the little man a measuring, sidewise look.

"I will tell all that you wish to know!" The councillor's hands came up in pathetic eagerness. A strange light came into his eyes. "Aye, all will I tell you, even to the day that we march on the Queen's capital! Then you may tell her, and she can march south to meet us halfway! Even this will I tell you!"

He leaped forward, hands clawing. "Only come out from the hallway! If you come from the Queen, I would not have you die!"

Rod's face turned to stone. "No. You've got something hidden in there, and I've got a strange notion it might be more important than the date set for your rebellion. I think I'll just have a look." He turned back into the dusty hallway.

Durer ran after him a few steps, almost wailing. "No, no! You must carry word North! Come away, you fool!"

Rod kept walking.

Behind him, the little man screeched in anger. "Go, then, to your death! There is no need for you! I will take word to the North myself! Die, like the fool that you are!"

His shrill, hysterical laughter echoed and slapped from the walls, beating into Rod's ears as he strode into the moldering, lightless depths of the Castle Loguire.

He turned a corner, and the laugh died away. The faint torchlight from the main hall died with it; here the darkness was complete.

Rod walked through it, chewing at the inside of his cheek. Obviously, the little man really expected him to die . . . which was strange, since he had tried to keep Rod from going in. Which meant he'd really wanted Rod to carry word of the rebellion back to Catharine. But why did he want to double-cross the rebels?

Unless it was a triple-cross, somehow. . . .

Then, too, he obviously had something hidden back in these corridors, and might be afraid Rod would find it and somehow manage to come out alive.

However, he expected Rod to die, which meant automated defenses surrounding Durer's Big Secret. . . .

Unless, of course . . .

Rod stopped, suddenly realizing he didn't know the way out. He had a hazy recollection of having turned several corners while he'd been pondering; but he couldn't remember which corners, or how many, or which way he'd turned.

He noticed that his voice shook just a trifle when he murmured "Fess."

"Yes, Rod," the calm voice behind his ear answered instantly. It was vastly reassuring.

"Fess, I'm in the haunted part of the castle."

"Haunted?"

"It has that reputation, yes."

There was a pause; then the robot said, "Rod, an analysis of your voice patterns indicates mild fear. Surely you do not believe in ghosts."

"No, I don't. But I just remembered, Fess—I didn't believe in elves, either. Or banshees. Or—"

"Elves," Fess replied evenly, "are a myth."

"Uh, Fess . . ."

"Yes, Rod?"

"I've seen quite a few elves since we landed."

"A *fait accompli,*" the robot admitted reluctantly, "which I am constrained to acknowledge. I have not as yet sufficient data to explain the seeming conflict with known principles."

"You're as bad as a Catholic," Rod growled. "But at least it doesn't give you fits any more?"

"No-o-o." The robot was thoughtful. "The initial datum caused an overload; but that datum has since been assimilated."

"As long as you're sure there's a rational explanation."

"Precisely."

"So you're capable of handling the practical matters?"

"Quite capable."

"Because you're sure you'll be able to fit it into the Laws of Science eventually."

"Very perceptive, Rod."

"Sounds like a Jesuit," Rod growled. "But the practical matter at hand is that I *am* scared. And for a very good reason. Fess . . ."

"Yes, Rod?"

"If elves can exist on this crazy planet, why not ghosts?"

There was another pause; then Fess admitted, "There is no evidence that would directly contradict the hypothesis."

A moan, so deep that Rod could hardly hear it, and so loud that he winced in pain, shook the walls of the hallway.

Rod gasped. "What was *that?*"

"A complex wave-pattern of low frequency and high amplitude," Fess answered obligingly.

"Thank you, Dr. Slipcam. *What caused it?*"

"There is as yet insufficient data for—"

The moan came again, and a wraith of mist with hollow black eyes and a black circle of mouth swooped straight at Rod's head, starting as a pinpoint far down the hall and towering over him a second later.

Rod screamed and plastered himself against the wall. Fear knotted his belly, fear slackened his limbs, fear jellied his brain and squeezed at his heart.

Another moan sounded, a half-step above the first; Rod jerked his head to his right. Another ghost loomed over him.

A third moan, and Rod's eyes slapped up; a third specter towered before him.

Three ghosts, towering high about him, ringing him in against the stone wall. Their mouths formed great, lightless O's, cold bony fingers reaching out for him.

Through the moiling panic of his brain fought a single thought: *Fess didn't believe in ghosts.*

"Ghosts!" Rod screamed. "Ghosts, Fess, ghosts!"

"Ghosts," droned the robot, "are immaterial, even if they did exist. They are manifestations of neither energy nor matter, incapable of causing damage to a material being."

"Tell *them!* Tell *them!*" Rod shrieked.

The hand around his heart tightened. He gasped and coughed. Something was mashing his lungs, a steel band around his chest, tightening, tightening. . . . Fear was a physical thing, a looming presence, armed and hating. Fear could paralyze, fear could kill . . .

"Rod, cover your ears."

Rod tried to obey the robot's order, and couldn't. "Fess!" he screamed. "Fess, I can't *move!*"

A loud, raucous buzz shook his skull, blotting out the moans. It modulated into monotone words: "C-O-V-E-R Y-O-U-R E-A-R-S."

And the fear was gone, vanished—or almost gone, at least; reduced to the cold, familiar lump in the pit of the belly. Rod could move again, as easily as he ever had. He put his fingers in his ears. The buzz stopped, and he could hear the ghosts again, their moans dulled and distant through

157

his fingers. The fear rose into his throat again, but it was no longer paralyzing.

"Can you hear them, Rod?"

"Yeah, but it's not so bad now. What'd you do, Fess?"

"Nothing, Rod. Their moans have a harmonic frequency in the subsonic range, capable of inducing fear in members of your species."

"Oh."

"The fear-inducing tone is a beat frequency produced by the simultaneous emission of subsonic harmonics incorporated in the three moans."

"So it takes three of them to scare me?"

"Correct, Rod."

"And they're not really scaring me, just making me feel scared?"

"Again, correct."

"Well, that's a relief. For a minute there I was afraid I'd all of a sudden turned into a full-blown coward."

"All men fear, Rod."

"Yeah, but only a coward lets it stop him."

"That is a redundant statement, Rod."

"Oh, the hell with theory! Pardon me while I put it into practice."

Rod stepped away from the wall, forcing himself to move. He kept walking, right through the ghost in front of him. The moans suddenly ceased; then, with a howl of despair, the ghosts disappeared.

"They're gone," Rod croaked.

"Of course, Rod. Once you have demonstrated their inability to control you, they begin to fear you."

"Ye-e-es," Rod breathed. He set his feet wide apart, jammed his fists on his hips, flung his head back, and grinned. "Okay, spooks! Any doubts about who's boss?"

He stood, listening to the echoes of his voice die away among the empty corridors. A loud voice could be pretty impressive in here.

A mournful, sepulchral voice answered him out of thin air, moaning. "Leave us, mortal. Leave us to the peace of our graves. We harm no one here, in our cold, old halls."

"No one except the people who come in here," Rod snapped. "Them you kill, as you would have killed me, through weight of fear alone."

"Few," mourned the ghost. "Very, very few, mortal man. Only madmen, and fools."

"If you have killed one man here in your halls, you have killed one too many!" Rod rapped back.

"Would you not slay, Man, in defense of your home?" Rod snorted. "What right have you to these halls?"

Suddenly the ghost was there, towering over him. "I once was Horatio, first Duke Loguire!" it thundered in anger. "I it was built this keep! Have I no right to a poor, cold quarter of its halls?"

Fear lanced Rod's belly; he took a step back, then set his teeth and stepped forward again. "You got a point there," he admitted. "And possession *is* nine-tenths of the law. But how many did you have to kill to gain possession?"

"None." The ghost sounded very unhappy about it. "All fled in fear."

Rod nodded, revising his estimate of the ghost. Apparently Horatio didn't kill if he could help it. Probably delighted when it became necessary, though. . . .

"I mean you no harm, Horatio." He grinned suddenly, sardonically. "What harm could I do you, even if I wanted to?"

The ghost's head snapped up, empty eyes staring into Rod's. "You know not, mortal?"

"A ghost," Fess's voice said hurriedly behind Rod's ear, "like all supernatural creatures, can be hurt by cold iron or silver, or any medium of good conductivity, though gold is usually regarded as too expensive for such uses."

The ghost loomed larger over Rod, advancing on him. Rod stepped back, his dagger at the ready. "Hold it right there," he snapped. "Cold iron, remember?"

"Then, too," Fess murmured, "you do know the secret of their power. You could bring in an army with earplugs."

"Then, too," said Rod, "I *do* know the secret of your power. I could bring in an army with earplugs."

The ghost halted, the corners of its mouth turning down. "I had thought thou hadst said thou knew not."

"I do now. One step backward, if you please."

The ghost reluctantly retreated, groaning, "What phantom stands at your side to advise you?"

Rod's teeth bared in a grin. "A black horse, made of cold iron. It's in the castle stables, but it can talk to me from there."

"A pouka," Horatio growled, "a spirit horse, and one who is a traitor to the world of ghosts."

"No." Rod shook his head grimly. "It's not a spirit at all. I said it was made of cold iron, didn't I?"

The ghost shook its head decisively. "No such thing could exist."

Rod sighed. "There are more things in Heaven and Earth, Horatio, than are dreamt of in your philosophy. But that's beside the point. All that matters to you is that I don't mean any harm here. I'm just looking for something. I'll find it and go. Okay?"

"You are master. Why dost thou ask?" the ghost said bitterly.

"Courtesy," Rod explained. Then a vagrant and vague possibility crossed his mind. "Oh, by the way, I'm a minstrel. . . ."

The ghost's mouth dropped open; then it surged forward, hands grasping hungrily. "Music! Oh, sweet strains of melody! But play for us, Man, and we are thine to command!"

"Hold on a second." Rod held up a hand. "You built these halls, Horatio Loguire, and therefore do I ask of you the boon that I may walk these halls in peace. Grant me this, and I will play for you."

"You may walk, you may walk where you will!" the ghost quavered. "Only play for us, Man!"

Very neat, Rod thought. As good a job of face-saving as he'd ever done. After all, no sense making enemies if you can help it.

He looked up, started, and stared in shock. He was ringed by a solid wall of ghosts, three deep at least, all staring like a starving man in a spaghetti factory.

He swallowed hard and swung his harp around with a silent prayer of thanks that he hadn't been able to leave it in the sleeping-loft.

He touched the strings, and a groan of ecstasy swept through the ghost like the murmur of distant funeral bells on the midnight wind.

It then occurred to Rod that he was an excellent bargaining position. "Uh, Lord Horation, for *two* songs, will you tell me where the secret passages are?"

"Aye, aye!" the ghost fairly shrieked. "The castle is thine, my demesne, all that I have! The kingdom, if thou wish it! Only play for us, Man! For ten hundreds of years we have heard not a strain of Man's music! But play, and the whole world is thine!"

His fingers started plucking then, and the ghosts shivered like a schoolgirl getting her first kiss.

He gave them "Greensleeves," and "The Drunken Sailor," they being the oldest songs he knew. From there he went on to "The Ghost's High Noon," and "The Unfortunate Miss Bailey." He was about to swing into "Ghost Riders in the Sky" when it occurred to him that ghosts might not particularly like songs about ghosts. After all, mortals told spook stories for escapism; and by that yardstick, specters should want songs about humdrum, ordinary, everyday life, something peaceful and comforting, memories of green pastures and babbling brooks, and the lowing herd winding slowly o'er the lee.

So he went through as much of Beethoven's Sixth as he could remember, which was not easy on an Irish harp.

The last strains died away among the hollow halls. The ghosts were silent a moment; then a satiated, regretful sigh passed through them.

Horatio Loguire's great voice spoke quietly at Rod's elbow. "In truth, a most fair roundelay." Then, very carefully: "Let us have another, Man."

Rod shook his head with a sorrowful smile. "The hours of the night crowd down upon us, my lord, and I have much that I must do ere daybreak. Another night I shall return and play for you again; but for this night, I must away."

"Indeed," Horatio nodded, with another mournful sigh. "Well, you have dealt fairly with us, Man, and shown us courtesy without constraint to it. And shall we, for hospitality, be beholden to a guest? Nay; but come within, and I will show you doors to the pathways within the walls of this keep, and tell you of their twists and turnings."

All the ghosts but Horatio disappeared, with the sound of mouse feet running through the autumn leaves. Horatio turned abruptly and fled away before Rod, who dashed after him.

Rod counted his running steps; after fifty, the ghost made a right-angle turn with a fine disregard for inertia and passed through a doorway. Rod made a manful attempt at the inertialess turn, and got away with only a slight skid.

The ghost's voice took on the booming echo of the cavern-like room. "This was a cavern indeed, ready-made by God, lo, many centuries before I came. Loath to begrudge His gifts, I took it for my great banquet hall." The room seethed with the voices of a thousand serpent-echos as the patriarch ghost heaved a vast sigh. "Boisterous and many were the feastings held within this great hall, Man. Beauteous the maidens and valiant the knights." His voice lifted, exulting. "Brilliant with light and music was my banquet hall in that lost day, the tales and sagas older and more vital than the singing of this latter world. Wine flushed the faces of my court, and life beat high through the veins of their temples, filling their ears with its drumming call!

"The call of life . . ." The spirit's voice faded; its echoes died away among the cold cavern stones, till the great hall stood silent in its enduring midnight.

Somewhere a drop of water fell, shattering the silence into a hundred echoes.

"Gone now, o Man," mourned the ghost. "Gone and dead, while threescore of the sons of my blood have ruled these marches in my stead, and come home to me here in my halls. Gone, all my bold comrades, all my willing maidens—gone, and dust beneath our feet."

Rod's shoulders tightened as though a chill wind had touched him between the shoulder blades. He tried to stand a little more lightly in the dust carpet of the old banquet hall.

"And now!" The ghost's voice hardened in sullen anger. "Now others rule these halls, a race of jackals, hyenas who blaspheme my old comrades by walking in the forms of men."

Rod's ears pricked up. "Uh, how's that again, my lord? Somebody's stolen this hall from you?"

"Twisted, stunted men!" grated the wraith. "A race of base, ignoble cowards—and the lord of them all stands as councillor to a scion of my line, the Lord Duke Loguire!"

"Durer," Rod breathed.

"Calls he himself by that name" growled the ghost. "Then well is he named, for his heart is hard, and his soul is brittle.

"But mark you, Man," and the ghost turned his cavern eyes on Rod, and the base of Rod's scalp seemed to lift a little away from his skull, for embers burned at the backs of the specter's eyes.

"Mark you well," it intoned, stretching forth a hand, forefinger spearing at Rod, "that the hard and brittle steel will break at one strong blow of iron forged. And so may these evil parodies of humankind be broken by a man that you may call a man!"

The ghost's hand dropped. His shoulders sagged, his head bowed forward. "If," he mourned, "if any live in this dark day who may call themselves men in truth. . . ."

Rod's eyes broke away from the ghost and wandered

slowly about the great chamber. There was only blackness, close and thick. He blinked and shook his head, trying to rid himself of the feeling that the darkness was pressing against his eyeballs.

"My Lord Loguire," he began, stopped, and said again, "My Lord Loguire, I may be your lump of iron—I've been called things like that before, anyway. But if I am to break the councillors, I must know as much about them as I can. Therefore tell me: what work do they do within these halls?"

"Witchcraft," growled the ghost, "black witchcraft! Though the manner of it I scarce could tell . . ."

"Well, tell me what you can," Rod prodded. "Anything you can spare will be gratefully appreciated."

"Thou speakest like the parish priest a-tithing," the ghost snorted. "Naetheless, I will tell thee what I can. Know, then, Man, that these twisted men have builded themselves a great altar here, of a shining metal, it is not steel, nor silver or gold, nor any metal that I wot of—here in the center of my hall, where once my courtiers danced!"

"Oh." Rod pursed his lips. "Uh, what worship do they make before this altar?"

"What worship?" The ghost's head lifted. "Why, I would warrant, 'tis a sacrifice of themselves; for they step within that evil artifice, and then are gone; then lo! there they are again, and come forth whole! I can only think they must have given of their life's blood to the dark demon within that shining altar, for they come forth gaunt and shaken, Indeed," he mused, "why otherwise would they be shriveled, little men?"

An uneasy prickle began at the base of Rod's skull and worked its way down his neck to spread out across his shoulders. "I must see this artifice, my lord." He fumbled at his dagger. "Let us have some light!"

"Nay!" The shriek tore at Rod's eardrums. The ghost pulsed, shrinking and growing, its outline wavering, like a candle-flame.

"Would you destroy me, Man, and send me screaming to a darker realm than this?"

Rod massaged the back of his neck, trying to loosen the muscles that had cramped themselves together at the ghost's shriek. "Forgive me, Lord Loguire; I had forgotten, My torch will rest darkened; but you must, then, lead me to this strange altar, that I may see it with my hands."

"Would you worship there, then?" The hollow eyes deepen ominously.

"No, my lord; but I would know this thing, that I may bring it down in the fullness of time."

The ghost was silent a moment; then it nodded gravely, and glided ahead. "Come."

Rod stumbled forward, hands outstretched, in the ghost's wake, till his palms came up against something hard and cold.

"Beware, Man," rumbled the ghost, "for here lie dark powers."

Hand over hand, Rod felt his way slowly along the metal, glinting softly in the ghost's faint luminescence. Then his right hand fell on nothingness. He groped, found it was a corner, wished the ghost gave off just a little more light, and groped until he had located the outline of a door, or rather a doorway, seven feet high by three wide.

"What lies within, my lord?" he whispered.

"It is a coffin," the ghost moaned; "a metal coffin without a lid, standing on end, and you have found its open side."

Rod wondered what would happen if he stepped into the cubicle; but for some strange reason, he lacked the experimental urge of the true scientist.

He groped across the doorway. A circle pressed into his palm, a circle protruding slightly from the face of the metal block.

Running his fingers over the area to the right of the doorway, he discovered a full array of circles, oblongs, and buttons. The area within their outlines was smoother and less cold than the metal around them—glass, he decided, or plastic. He had found a control panel.

"My Lord Loguire," he called softly, "come here to me now, I beg of you, for I must have light."

The ghost drifted up beside him; and, by the light of its cold radiance, Rod made out a set of meters, a vernier dial, and a set of color-coded buttons.

The ghost's voice was gentle, almost sympathetic. "Why do you tremble, Man?"

"It's cold," Rod snapped. "Milord Loguire, I'm afraid I have to agree with your opinion of this monstrosity. I don't know what it is, but it ain't pretty."

The ghost rumbled agreement. "And that which is evil to look upon must be doubly so in its action."

"Well, I'm not so sure about that as a basic principle," Rod demurred, "but it might apply in this case. Milord, pay no heed to my mumblings in the next small while; I must, ah, recite an incantation against the malice of this, ah, engine."

He switched to the patois of the galactic deckhand while the ghost scowled in perplexity. "Fess, you there?"

"Yes, Rod."

"Have you been listening in?"

"Certainly, Rod."

"Um. Well, then, uh, this thing's a hunk of metal, rectangular, about, uh, twenty feet long by, say, ten high, and maybe ten wide. Got a little cubicle cut into the front, just about the size of a coffin."

"Appropriate," the robot murmured.

"No kibitzing on the job, please. It's white metal with a dull finish, and colder than hell, right now, anyway. Set of controls next to the cubicle—a long strip-meter with a scale and a slider."

"How is the scale calibrated, Rod?"

"Looks like logarithms, Fess. Arabic numerals. The zero's about three-quarters of the way from left end. Left side of the scale is marked to ten thousand. The right-hand side goes up to, uh, 2,385. Sound like anything you've heard of?"

There was a pause; then the robot answered, "Filed for analysis. Proceed with the description."

Rod ground his teeth; apparently the huge gizmo was as much of an unknown to Fess as it was to himself.

"There's a dial with a knob in the middle of it, just to the right of the strip-meter. Reference point at the top, twelve o'clock, negative numbers to the left, positive to the right. At least, I assume they're numbers. The thing just to the right of the reference point looks something like a French curve, or maybe a paranoid sine wave. Then there's a shape like an upside-down pear. Then there's a pair of circles with a line lying across them. The last one is a question mark lying on its side; then there's infinity in the six o'clock position. Left-hand side is the same way, only all the symbols are marked with a negative sign."

The robot hummed for a moment; Rod recognized the tune: "Sempre Libera" from *La Traviata*. Fess was enjoying himself.

"Filed for anaylsis and reference, Rod. Proceed with description."

"You don't recognize 'em either, huh?"

"They are totally without precedence in the discipline of

mathematics, Rod. But if there is any logic to their derivation, I will decipher them. Proceed."

"Well, there're seven buttons set flush with the surface, in a row just under the strip-meter, color-coded. Colors are—uh—hey, it's the spectrum!"

"So I feared," the robot murmured. "Use of the spectrum in color-coding would indicate arbitrary assignation of values. There is no anomaly in the color sequence?"

"Well, the paint's iridescent . . ."

"Not quite what I meant by anomaly. Well, it is filed. Proceed."

"Nothing. That's all."

"All? Only three controls?"

"That's all."

The robot was silent a moment.

"What do you make of it, Fess?"

"Well . . ." the robot's voice was hesitant. "The control system appears to be designed for the layman, Rod. . . ."

"Why? Because it's so simple?"

"Precisely. Beyond that, there is insufficient data for—"

"Oh, make a guess, damn it! Make a wild guess!"

"Rod, guesswork is not within the capabilities of a cybernetic mechanism, involving as it does an exercise of the intuitive—"

"So extrapolate from available data, already!"

He heard *La Traviata*, as it might have been sung by a wistful audio generator; then Fess said, "The irregularity of the figure 2,385 would seem to indicate the number of a year, Rod, due to its juxtaposition with the figure ten thousand."

"Uh, how's that again?"

"The figure ten thousand," Fess lectured, "has many probable referents, one of which is the period of recorded human history."

"Now, wait a minute, Fess. Written history doesn't go back beyond 2000 B.C.; even I know that."

"And a miracle it is, Rod, considering your resistance to instruction from your earliest ages."

"All right, all right! I was a bad little boy who didn't do his homework! I'm sorry! I repent! Just get on with the extrapolation, will ya?"

He heard the burring of serially closing relays that always reminded him of a chuckle; then Fess said, "Human history prior to the development of written language may be said

166

to have been recorded in the legends and mythology of the vocal tradition, in works such as *The Epic of Gilgamesh*. The period included by such works may be estimated as having begun nearly four thousand years B.C. This figure, added to the present date, gives us the figure 9,432, which is a sufficiently close approximation to the figure ten thousand to be included as a referent."

"Hmm." Rod gnawed his upper lip. "Well, when you look at it that way, I suppose 2,385 could be a date. But what does that mean?"

"Why, the inference is obvious, Rod."

"So I'm a microcephalic idiot. Spell it out."

The robot hesitated. "The accuracy of the inference has a very low probability rating. . . ."

"I asked for guesswork, didn't I? Come on, out with it."

"The artifact, Rod, would by this theory be a vehicle for chronical travel."

Rod stared at the strip-meter. "You mean it's a time machine?"

The slider was shoved all the way to the right, resting over the figure 2,385.

"Rod, you must bear in mind that the theory's probability index—"

"A time machine!" Rod's brain whirled. "Then the little bastards came out of the future!"

"Rod, I have cautioned you before about your tendency to accord an unproved hypothesis the weight of a conviction."

Rod gave his head a quick shake. "Oh, don't worry, Fess. It's just a guess, probably wrong. I'm keeping that in mind."

He turned away from the control panel, eyes glowing. "A time machine! Whaddaya know!"

He became aware of the faint glow to his left again. Horatio Loguire towered over him, brooding.

"What witchcraft is it, Man?"

Rod frowned, turning back toward the machine. "Strange, my lord, both dark and strange. I have some knowledge of the various, ah, magics; but this is one with which I have no acquaintance."

"What then will you do?"

Rod scowled at the floor, looked up with a bleak smile. "Sleep. And ponder what I have seen."

"And when will you destroy this plaything of Satan?"

"When I am sure," murmured Rod, turning back to look

at the machine again; "sure that this is the plague, and not the cure, of this benighted world."

Loguire's eyebrows drew together as his scowl deepened. He seemed almost to swell, looming taller and wider, dwarfing the man before him. Rod had the insane feeling that an ancient locomotive was roaring down on him.

The voice was distant thunder. "I charge you, then, with the exorcising of this demon altar and the rending of its ragtag priests."

The old boy, Rod decided, had definitely slipped a cog.

The ghost's sword flashed out of its scabbard; involuntarily, Rod fell back into defense stance. Then he straightened, cursing himself; a spectral sword could scarcely hurt him.

The sword floated before him, point downward, a glittering cruciform ghost-light.

"Swear now upon the hilt of this my sword, that you shall not rest until you have purged this land of corruption in the seats of power, that you shall exorcise this dark altar and all its minions, and more: that you shall never till you die desert this Isle of Gramarye in the hour of its peril."

Awe slacked Rod's jaw; he stared wide-eyed at the sudden power and majesty of the ghost. An alien, formless dread crept into his belly. The hairs at the nape of his neck lifted with a chill of nameless apprehension.

He shrank back. "My lord, this scarce is necessary. I love the Isle of Gramarye; I would never—"

"Lay your hand upon this hilt and swear!" The words were terse and stern.

Rod fairly cowered, well aware that the oath would bind him to the planet for life. "My lord, are you asking me to take a loyalty oath? I am insulted that you should doubt my—"

"Swear!" the ghost thundered. "Swear! Swear!"

"Art there, old mole?" Rod muttered under his breath, but it didn't work; he had never felt less funny.

He stared at the glowing hilt and the stern face beyond it, fascinated. Almost against his will, he took one step forward, then another; he watched his hand as it closed itself around the hilt. His palm felt nothing within it, no pressure of solid metal; but the air within his fist was so cold it paralyzed the knuckles.

"Now swear to me and mine!" Horatio rumbled.

Oh, well, Rod thought, *it's only words. Besides, I'm an agnostic, aren't I?*

"I . . . swear," he said reluctantly, fairly forcing out the words. Then inspiration glimmered in his brain, and he added easily, "And I further swear that I will not rest until the Queen and all her subjects with one voice shall rule again."

He took his hand from the sword, rather pleased with himself. That additional clause gave him a clear track to the goal of his mission, whether or not Horatio counted democracy among the perils of Gramarye.

The ghost frowned. "Strange," he grumbled, "a most strange oath. Yet from the heart, I cannot doubt, and binding to you."

Of course, Rod admitted to himself, the oath still bound him to Gramarye; but he would bridge that gulf when he came to it.

The sword glided back to its scabbard. The ghost turned away, his voice trailing over his shoulder. "Follow now, and I shall show you to the halls within these halls."

Rod followed until they came to the wall. The ghost pointed a long, bony finger. "Grope until you find a stone that yields to your hand."

Rod reached for the stone the ghost pointed to, and pushed, leaning all his weight against it. The stone groaned and grudgingly gave way, sliding back into the wall. As it fell back, a door ground open with the protest of hinges that were long overdue for an oil break. Cold, dank air fanned Rod's cheek.

"Leave me now," said the ghost, tall and regal beside him, "and go to your duty. Yet remember, Man, your oath; and be assured that if ever you should lay it aside, the first Duke Loguire shall ever stand beside your bed until at last you yield to fear."

"Definitely a comforting thought," Rod mused. He groped his way down the moss-grown steps, humming "You'll Never Walk Alone."

This time, the door to the loft was open, and Tom's deep earthquake snores echoed in the rocky chamber.

Rod paused in the doorway, chewing at his lip. He went back into the hall, pulled a torch from its bracket, and thrust it ahead of him into the room, peering in cautiously, just to be sure there was no one trying to rearouse Tom with a paternity suit in mind.

The wavering light of the torch disclosed the stocky peasant's slumbering form, his cape thrown over his body from the rib cage down. One ursine arm was curled comfortably about the soft, rounded body of a blonde, covered (or uncovered) to the same degree by the cape. Her small, firm breasts were pressed against Tom's side; her head rested on his shoulder, long hair flung in a glorious disarray over her shoulders. One sun-browned arm was flung possessively across the big man's beer-keg chest.

Rod frowned, and stepped over for a closer look. The face was slender, the nose tilted, mouth small, with a smug little smile of content.

It was obviously not the brunette who had accosted Rod in the hallway earlier. He grunted in surprise; so the wench hadn't gone after the servant when she was refused by the master.

Of course, it might be just that she hadn't moved fast enough. . . . But no, Big Tom would've been glad to accommodate both.

He replaced the torch, came back to the loft with a nod of grudging admiration at Big Tom, and without bothering to pull off his doublet, dropped into the heap of hay that served for a bed. It brought back fond memories. He yawned, cushioned his head on his forearm, and drifted slowly toward sleep.

"Man Gallowglass!"

The voice boomed in the little room. Rod jerked bolt upright; the girl screamed, and Big Tom swore.

A ghost towered before them, glowing cold in the dark.

Rod came to his feet, flicking a glance at Tom and the girl. She cowered in abject terror against the bear-hide of his chest. Tom's face had already settled into surly (and probably frightened) defiance.

Rod switched his eyes to the ghost, standing tall above him in plate armor, its face incredibly long and thin. The sword at its hip was a rapier; it was not Horatio Loguire.

Rod reminded himself that he was boss, a fact he had almost forgotten. He repaid the hollow gaze with the haughtiest look he could manage. "What sty were you raised in," he snapped, "that you come before a gentleman with such ill ceremony?"

The cavern eyes widened, the ghost's jaw dropping down inside its mouth. It stared at Rod, taken aback.

The mortal pressed his advantage. "Speak, and with courtesy, or I'll dance on your bones!"

The ghost fairly cringed; Rod had struck pay dirt. Apparently there was some sort of ectoplasmic link between a ghost and its mortal remains. He made a mental note to track down the graves of all relevant ghosts.

"Your pardon, milord," the ghost stammered. "I meant no offense; I only—"

Rod cut him off. "Now that you have disturbed my rest, you may as well speak. What brings you to me?"

"You are summoned—"

Rod interrupted him off again. "None summon me."

"Your pardon, lord." The ghost bowed. "Milord Loguire requests your presence."

Rod glared a moment longer, then caught up his harp with a sigh. "Well, he who deals with spirits must deal at odd hours." He cocked his head. "*Horatio* Loguire?"

"The same, my lord."

The servant girl gasped.

Rod winced; he had forgotten his audience. His reputation would be all over the castle by noon.

"Well," he said, shouldering his harp, "lead on."

The ghost bowed once more, then turned toward the wall, stretching out a hand.

"Hold it," Rod snapped. Better to leave the secret passages secret. "Go ye to Milord Loguire and tell him I shall come to him presently. You forget that I cannot walk through walls, like yourself."

The ghost turned, frowning. "But, my lord . . ."

"Go to Milord Loguire!" Rod stormed.

The ghost shrank away. "As you will, my lord," it mumbled hastily, and winked out.

In the sudden darkness, the girl let out her breath in a long, sobbing sigh; and, "How now, master," said Big Tom, his voice very calm, with only a trace of wonder, "do you traffic with spirits now?"

"I do," said Rod, and flung the door open, wondering where Tom had picked up a word like "traffic."

He turned to look at the couple in the light from the doorway, his eyes narrowed and piercing. "If word of this passes beyond this room, there shall be uneasy beds and midnight guest for the both of you."

Big Tom's eyes narrowed, but the girl's widened in alarm. *Good,* thought Rod, *I've threatened her income. Now I can be sure she'll keep quiet.*

He spun on his heel, pulling the door shut behind him. Big Tom would console her, of course, and his master's control over ghosts wouldn't exactly hurt his standing with her.

And, of course, she'd keep her mouth shut.

Which was just as well. For a man who didn't believe in magic, Rod already had altogether too much of a name as a warlock.

He prowled along the hall till he found an empty chamber with access to the hidden tunnel. The granite blocks of one wall had been carved into a bas-relief of an orange flute being burned at the stake; apparently the Loguires took their adopted Irish name rather seriously. Rod found the one coal in the pile of faggots that was cut a little deeper than the rest, and threw all his weight against it, pushing it to his right. The ancient machinery gave a deep-throated grumble, and a trapdoor pivoted up from the stone flags of the floor.

Rod felt for the steps with his toes, reached up for the great iron ring set in the underside of the trapdoor, and pulled it shut as he went down the stairs.

He emerged from the massive door in the great hall with the dark altar. His phantom guide was there before him, waiting.

The ghost bowed. "If you would be so good as to follow me, master . . ." It turned away, drifting toward the archway into the corridor.

Rod followed, muttering, "A little lighter on the sarcasm there."

They came out into the corridor; and, off to his right, Rod saw the fox-firelight of a cluster of ghosts. They were motionless, their heads bent, looking at something on the floor in the center of their circle. Rod heard a very mortal, and very terrified, whimper.

Horatio looked up at Rod's approach. He glided apart from the knot of ghosts, his cadaverous face knotted with anger.

"My Lord Loguire!" Rod bowed his most courtly, straightend. "Why do you summon me?"

The ghost's brow smoothed a little, somewhat mollified. "Man Gallowglass," it growled, "wherefore did you not tell me you had come accompanied into our halls?"

"Accompanied?" Rod's eyebrows lifted. "Oh, was I, now?"

Loguire's frown deepened again, puzzled. "In truth, there was one who followed after you, as I found upon my outgoing from the chamber with the strange device."

"Excelsior," Rod murmured.

"*Gesundheit*," said Loguire. "If we are to have a continual passage of mortals here, I shall have to see to the heating of these halls. But anon: I found your servant, as I have said, directly without the chamber."

"Servant?" Rod frowned. "How do you know it was a servant?"

"It was listening at the door. And we may know that it is yours, for when we advanced upon it, it cried your name."

"Oh." Rod scratched at the base of his skull, frowning. "It did, did it?"

"Aye; else would we have slain it. And therefore did I send to you to claim it."

Loguire stepped aside; the circle of ghosts parted, and Rod stepped up. By the cold light of the ghosts, he saw a huddle of misery trying to push itself into the wall. The face was turned away from him. Long black hair flowed down over the shoulders. It wore white blouse, full skirt, and black bodice. The last was very well filled.

"My Lord Loguire," Rod began; his voice cracked; he tried again. "My Lord Loguire, this is scarcely an 'it.' " Then, in the gentlest voice he could manage, "Look at me, wench."

The girl's head jerked up staring, lips parted. Joy and relief flooded her face. "My lord!"

Then her arms were about his neck, so tight he had to fight for breath; and her body was pressed tight against him, head burrowing into his shoulder, her whole frame trembling with sobs. "My lord, O my lord!"

"My Lord!" Rod echoed, prying at her shoulder to get clearance for his larynx.

He recognized her, of course. It was the servant girl who had propositioned him earlier in the evening.

"There, there, now, lass, it's all right," he murmured, rubbing her back. The room seemed to reel about him; he picked out a fixed point of light and stared at it.

It turned out to be Horatio Loguire, face contorted by a touch of disgust. "Take her out from my halls, Man. They are damp enough of their own."

Rod was just noticing how nicely the peasant girl fitted in his arms. He closed his eyes, savoring the warmth and closeness of her. He nodded. "Aye, my lord, that I shall. There, there, now, lass, you mustn't cry." He pulled a handkerchief from his cuff and dabbed at her cheeks with it. "No more tears, there's a darling, you're raising the humidity, and Horatio's got arthritis, if he can just remember where he put his bones—there, that's right."

Her head lay against his chest, sniffling. Her eyes closed, her face relaxed; it almost seemed she was asleep. Rod was swept with a sudden wave of tenderness, aided and abetted by a feeling of towering strength contributed by his protective instinct, and silently cursed the adhesive effect of a damsel in distress.

He looked up into the brooding, empty eyes of the Loguire.

"Thou'rt ensnared, Man."

"Who, me?" Rod scowled and thumped his throat in the carotid region. "Fire seven times tried this."

"And found it wanting," Loguire agreed, "and seven times tried *that* judgment is. Take her from my halls, Man."

Rod threw him one last look of defiance and turned to the girl. "Come, lass," he murmured, "we must go out from this place now."

He swung her up into his arms. She stirred, murmured petulantly, and burrowed her head tight into his shoulder again, her arms tight about his neck.

Babies and women, Rod thought, exasperated; *they're worse than quicksand.*

"My lord," he said to Loguire, "will you lead me? You may understand that I am somewhat turned about. . . ."

"Aye," said the ghost, and turned away down the hall; but not before Rod had glimpsed a faint, phantom smile on the ghost's face. . . .

He came out into the torchlit corridor, where he had met Durer earlier. The little man was gone; apparently he had assumed the worst and gleefully gone his way.

Rod lowered the girl's feet to the floor. She murmured another little inarticulate protest, and pressed her head tighter against him.

Rod tightened his arms about her and brushed his cheek against her hair, drawing out the moment as long as he could.

Then he smiled sadly and lifted his hand to stroke along her jaw, tilting her chin up. The long-lashed eyes were still closed; the full red lips pursed and parted, just a little . . .

Rod steeled himself and said gently, "You must tell me now, lass. Why did you follow me?"

Her eyes flew open, widened in alarm. Then she bit her

lip, bowing her head, and stood away from him, clenching her hands in the cloth of his doublet.

"You must tell me, lass," he repeated softly. "Who sent you to spy on me?"

Her head flew up, eyes wide in dismay. She shook her head. "None, my lord. None, only myself."

"Oh?" Rod smiled sadly. "Of your own doing, you followed me into the haunted quarter?"

She looked down again. "I did not fear the spirits, lord."

Rod pursed his lips in surprise. If it was so, she had uncommon courage for a serving maid. Her nerve hadn't broken till she actually saw the ghosts—and having experienced their moans himself, Rod could understand her breaking then.

Too, she might have followed him in hopes that he might reconsider his decision to sleep alone. Or maybe she'd thought she could help if he got into trouble. Rod smiled at that last thought. But he had to make sure.

"Still, you have not yet told me: why did you follow me?"

She bit her lip again, her face twisting. Rod waited, quietly.

Grudging every word, she said, "I—I feared for you, my lord."

Rod stared; then his mouth twisted into a wry smile. He shook his head, slowly. "You *feared* for me!"

"Aye!" Her head snapped up, eyes flashing. "I had no knowing you were a warlock, and . . . a man alone, in those halls . . ."

Her voice trailed off; her eyes dropped again.

Rod heaved a sigh and clasped her to him. She resisted a moment, then yielded.

"Lass, lass!" he murmured. "What could you have done to help me?"

"I—I have some small way with some spirits, lord." Her voice was muffled by the cloth of his tunic. "I had thought . . ."

Rod scowled. Was communication with the spirit world the norm on this kooky planet?

He rubbed her back gently, pressed his cheek against her hair. She could be lying, of course; but that would imply she was an excellent actress, and she seemed a little too ingenuous for that.

He sighed and tightened his arms about her. She murmured sulkily and pushed her hips against him.

Rod closed his eyes and wiped his mind of all but the touch of her body. She felt good, very good. Almost like that farm wench, Gwendylon . . .

His eyes snapped open. He stared into the torchlit dusk of the hall, picturing the two faces before him, side by side. Dye the hair black, tilt the eyes a little, straighten the nose . . .

She had felt him tense; she looked up at him. "What is it, my lord?"

The voice was a little higher-pitched, yes; but it had that same quality.

He looked down at her. The complexion was flawless, not a single freckle; but it didn't take that much technology to concoct a makeup base.

He pointed his forefinger between her eyes. "You," he said, "have been deceiving me." His finger came to rest on the tip of her nose.

There was a flicker of disappointment in her eyes; then she was all innocence. "Deceiving you, my lord? I—I know not . . ."

Rod flicked his finger; the tip of her nose came off. He smiled grimly, nodding. "Cornstarch and water. But you were wrong to straighten it; I like it much better with that little tilt at the end."

He rubbed his fingertip across the corner of her eye; the eye was no longer slanted, and there was a dark smudge on his finger. "Cornstarch and water, and black paint at the eye-fold. Flour mixed with a little burnt umber on the face, and henna in the hair."

The corners of her mouth tightened. Her face flushed with the heat of anger under the paint.

He shook his head, brow puckered. "But why, lass? Your face is so much more beautiful."

He allowed himself a shot of self-satisfaction as the anger in her face melted into tenderness and longing.

She lowered her eyes. "I—I could not leave you, lord."

He closed his eyes, grinding his teeth, and only by main force of will kept himself from squeezing her.

"But . . ." He stopped, and drew a long hissing braath. "But how did you follow me, lass?"

She looked up, eyes wide in innocence. "In the guise of an osprey, lord."

His eyes snapped open with a near-audible click. He stared. "A witch? You? But . . ."

"You will not despise me for it, lord?" she said anxiously. "You, who are a warlock?"

His eyes had lost focus. "Huh? Uh—warlock? He shook his head, trying to clear it. "Uh, I mean . . . No, of course I don't. I mean . . . well, some of my best friends are . . ; uh . . ."

"My lord?" She peered into his face. "Art thou well?"

"Who, me? Of course not! No, wait a minute . . ." He stopped and drew a very, very deep breath. "Now, look. You're a witch. So. Big deal. I'm far more interested in your beauty than your talents."

Embers there, in her eyes, ready to flame if he breathed upon them.

He took another deep breath and called his hormones to order. "Now. Let's get one thing straight."

She brushed up against him, breathing, "Aye, my lord."

"No, no! I didn't mean *that!*" He took a step back, hands coming up to hold her off. "Look. The only reason you followed me here was because you were afraid I'd get into trouble I couldn't handle, right?"

She paused, the glow dying in her eyes under a chill flow of disappointment. She lowered her eyes. "Aye, my lord."

The way she said it made him think she was leaving an awful lot to implication; but he hurried on to the next point.

"But now you know I'm a warlock. Right?"

"Aye, my lord." He could scarcely hear her.

"So you know I don't have to be afraid of anything, right? So there's no reason to follow me any more, right?"

"Nay, my lord!" Her face whipped up to him, glaring; then her chin lifted a little higher, proud and haughty and stubborn. "Still will I follow you, Rod Gallowglass. There be spells in this world that you wot not of."

And one of the most galling things about her, he decided, was that she was always so damned *right*. In this crazy, topsy-turvy world, there probably were quite a few "spells" he couldn't even imagine.

But, on the other hand, there seemed to be a few that she didn't know, either. An amateur witch, most likely, and too old to join the union—she must be almost as old as Rod was. In fact, her "witchcraft" seemed to consist of cosmetic skill, the ability to go birdie (he hadn't quite figured that one out yet), and a degree of courage that was totally unexpected in a woman.

So she was right, she had good cause to worry about him, he would still be in danger—but so would she.

No. It wouldn't do any good to tell her she couldn't follow him—she would anyway. And he'd come out of it alive, like he always did, but she'd get murdered in a ditch somewhere along the way. Or maybe she'd handicap him enough so they'd both wind up dead.

His head moved from side to side, tightening into a quick shake. He couldn't let her get killed. He had to shake her somehow—and he knew just how.

His mouth quirked into a sour smile. "It's true, what they say about farm girls: give them a moment of kindness, and you'll never be rid of them. My dear, you have an excellent nuisance rating."

She gasped, stepping away from him, her face twisting into a grimace of pain, the back of her hand coming up to her lips. Her eyes flooded with tears; she bit on her hand, turned, and fled.

He stared at the floor, listening to her sobs fading, feeling the hollowness grow within him.

A fist thundered on the heavy oaken door. Rod struggled up out of the dpeths of sleep, floundering to sit up in the hay.

Big Tom and his wench lay still, eyes fixed on the door.

Rod grunted and levered himself to his feet. "Don't worry," he growled. "Ghosts don't knock."

"Ho, minstrel!" a gruff beery voice bellowed. "Come forth to my master!"

Rod struggled into his doublet and caught up his harp. He swung open the great oak door, shaking his head to clear the traces of his meager sleep. "You might at least try to be civil at this hour of the damn morning," he growled. "And just who the hell is your master?"

The heavy fist caught him under the ear, sent him sprawling against the wall. He fought down the instant impulse to break the man's neck.

Through a ringing, blurred haze he heard a deep, sadistic chuckle. "Mind how you speak to your betters, gleeman. 'Tis a good rule for a peasant."

Rod gathered himself, hands braced against the wall, and sized up his persecutor. It was a common foot soldier in leather and mail, both of which needed cleaning, as did the soldier himself. He might have been a commoner, but he had an uncommon case of B.O., and halitosis on top if it, possibly due to the rotting teeth he was exhibiting in a self-satisfied grin.

Rod sighed and straightened, deciding it might be better to play his part; in fact, he'd deserved the blow, for having dropped out of character. The jester in medieval society served as an emotional release, not only through entertainment, but also through providing an outlet for aggressions by becoming their object.

"All right," he said, "I'm schooled. Let's go."

The fist caught him beneath the jaw this time. As he rolled with the blow, he heard the gleeful voice growl, "Thou'rt not schooled enough. To address your betters with *master* is the rule."

Rod fought the anger down into a cold, calm, calculating rage and lunged, his hands chopping out in three quick blows.

"I've got a better rule for a soldier," he informed the crumpled heap at his feet. "First be sure who your betters are. Now take me to your master."

The master, as it turned out, was Loguire. Rod was ushered into a medium-sized room, high-ceilinged and hung with tapestries. Three tall, narrow windows, through which Rod saw sunlight, dawn-colored, broken by the shifting prism of the waterfall. The room was filled with its roaring. But the sound was muted; looking closer, Rod saw the windows were double-paned, and three feet deep. Somebody had remembered some of the old technology.

The walls were hung with tapestries; there was a heavy carpet underfoot. A great oval table took up the center of the chamber. At its head sat Loguire; at his right, his eldest son. Durer sat at his left. The other places were taken up by eight men who had a familiar look. Rod's eyes widened as he recognized them: the Duke Di Medici, the Earl of Romanoff, the Duke Bourbon, and the Prince Hapsburg, and their councillors.

After Loguire, they were the four most powerful of the Great Lords. And if these five were gathered together, might not the other seven be close by?

All were at breakfast, but none of them really seemed to realize they were eating. Take Anselm, there, Loguire's son—he ate like a machine, glaring at his plate, face set like a sculpture of cold fury.

His father sat with head bowed, hands pressed tight to the table before him.

At a guess, Rod decided, there had been a bit of a quarrel here, between father and son, and Loguire had won—but only by ordering his son to shut up.

And Rod had been called in to heal the breach. Oy! The things people expect of performers!

Durer's face was lit with a subterranean glow of vindictive joy; the other councillors had milder versions of the same look. Whatever had happened here had gone the way Durer wanted; in fact, he'd probably instigated it. The man was the perfect catalyst, Rod decided: he never got involved in the reactions he caused.

Loguire looked up at his son, mute appeal in the old, red-rimmed eyes. But Anselm gave him not so much as a glance, and Loguire's face firmed into flint.

Turning, the old man saw Rod. "Minstrel!" he barked. "Why stand you there idle? Give us merriment!"

Durer's head snapped around, his eyes locked on Rod. Alarm chased shock across his face, to be followed by distilled, murderous hate.

Rod smiled cheerfully, bowed, and touched his forelock in salute. Inwardly, he wondered what song could possibly burn away the tensions in this room. He strongly suspected the custom was to clear the air by beating the minstrel for failing to fulfill his assignment.

He began to play "Matty Groves," figuring his only chance lay in giving them something more gruesome than anything that could possibly have just taken place.

He held off on the words for a few minutes, though, to give him time to study the faces of the four lords. Their looks ranged from ruminative speculation to outright (though veiled) contempt, the last apparently directed at the old Duke. It would seem that Loguire had no virulent supporters here; the balance of opinion seemed to rest with his son.

"Minstrel!"

Rod looked up; it was Anselm who had spoken.

The young man's face seemed to have soured so much it had curdled. "Have you a song for a lad made a fool by a woman, yet doubly a fool, still, to love her?"

"Ha' done!" Loguire snapped; but before Anselm could reply, Rod said, "Many, my lord, of a man still loving a woman who scorned him; and in all of them, the lady comes back to him."

"Comes back!" Anselm spat. "Aye, she'd take him back—to hang him in shame at her castle gate!"

The old Duke drew himself to his feet, roaring, "Enough of your slander!"

"Slander!" Anselm's chair crashed over as he rose to meet his father. "And is it slander to say she has spit on the proud name of Loguire, aye, and not once but twice, and will do so again?

"Nay!" He slammed his fist on the board, turning to rake the lords with his glare. "This vile wench shall learn that she dare not trample the honor of her peers! We must tear her from the seat of power and break her beneath us for ever and aye!"

Loguire's face reddened, his throat swelled with a rebuke; but before he could speak it, Rod murmured, "Nay, my lord, not so harsh. Not a defeat, but a discipline."

He was caught in a crossfire of laser-beam glares from Anselm and Durer; but Loguire boomed "Aye!" with a giant's joy and relief. "He speaks out of place, but his speaking is true! Our young Queen is headstrong; but so is a filly before it is bridled. She must learn her authority is not absolute, that there are checks upon her power; but she is the sovereign, and must not be torn down!"

Anselm made a gurgling sound, his face swollen red and his eyes starting forth from their sockets, choking with rage; then he managed to speak, fairly stuttering in his wrath.

"Nay, now! Now I say nay! A woman for a sovereign? 'Tis a mockery! And a whoring, arrogant bitch of a—"

"Be still!" Loguire thundered, and even the four great lords shrank away from the savage power of his voice.

As for Anselm, he fairly cowered, staring appalled at the white-bearded giant before him, who almost seemed to swell and tower higher as they watched.

Then, slowly, and with greater dignity than Rod had ever seen in a man, the true regal dignity that only comes unaware, Loguire resumed his seat, never taking his eyes from his son. "Retire to your chambers," he said in a cold, still voice. "We shall speak no more of this till the conclave at sunset."

Anselm somehow managed to summon the strength to lift his chin again, a gesture that somehow seemed pompous and ridiculous, and turned on his heel. As he stalked to the door, his eyes fell on Rod. Rage and humiliation boiled up in him, and he swung up his arm to favor the minstrel with a back-handed slap.

"Nay!" barked Loguire, and Anselm froze.

"This man," said the Duke, speaking in centimeters, "has spoken truth. I will not have him maltreated."

Anselm locked glares with his father; then his look faltered, and dropped. He turned away; the door slammed behind him.

"Minstrel," rumbled Loguire, "play!"

Rod let his fingers ramble through "The Old Man of Tor Tappan" while he reflected.

So there would be a council of war tonight, eh? And the main issue would apparently be constitutional monarchy versus warlordism, though only he and Durer might know it. Well, he knew which side he was on.

He looked again at the straight-backed old Duke, eating token bits of food, lips pressed tight under his flowing white beard, brow locked in a slight scowl, only the slightest hint of his grief showing in the deep, shadowed eyes.

Yes, Rod knew which side he was on.

They met in the great hall, large enough to act as a hangar for a good-sized spaceship, if the Gramarians had known what a spaceship was.

The stone floor was inlaid with Loguire's coat of arms. Great silver sconces supported torches every yard or so along the walls. The ceiling was concave and gilded, with an im- immense silver chandelier suspended from its center. There were no windows; but that made little difference, since night had fallen.

Loguire sat in a great carved chair at one end of the hall, bunting of his family's colors draped on the wall behind him. His chair was raised on a four foot dais, so that the standing lords must look up at him.

There were a good many of them, not only the twelve greats, but with them a host of counts, barons, and knights, their vassals.

And at each one's elbow stood, or rather hunched, a thin-faced, bony little man, with scant light hair lying close against his scalp.

Rod surveyed the hall; his lips pursed into a soundless whistle. He hadn't realized the councillors were so numerous. There were at least fifty, maybe seventy.

And there might be more outside his field of view. At the moment, he had literal tunnel-vision, and one-eyed at that. The torches that illuminated the hall sat in sconces that were held to the wall with three rough bolts.

But one of the sconces behind Loguire's throne was missing a bolt, and the stone behind it was bored through for an inch, then hollowed out to the depth and width of a man's head. The head, at the moment, was Rod's, where he stood in the clammy darkness of a narrow passage behind the wall.

His peephole afford him an excellent view of the back of Loguire's head, and some nice over-the-shoulder shots of anyone addressing him.

His right hand rested on a lever; if he pushed it down—if it wasn't rusted tight—the stone before him *should* swing wide to make a handy door. From the looks on the faces of the lords confronting the Duke, it might be very handy.

The man immediately in front of the Duke was Anselm. Bourbon and Di Medici stood at either side of the young man. Durer, of course, stood at Loguire's left hand.

Loguire rose heavily. "We are met," he rumbled. "Here in this room is gathered all the noble blood of Gramarye, the true power of the land." He scanned the faces before him slowly, looking each of his brother Great Lords directly in the eye.

"We are met," he said again, "to decide on a fitting rebuke for Catharine the Queen."

The Duke of Bourbon stirred, unfolding his arms and setting his feet a little further apart. He was a great black bear of a man, with shaggy brows and a heap of beard on his chest.

His fists clenched, his mouth tightened. There was something furtive, sheepish, in his stance.

He glared at Loguire. "Nay, good Uncle, you have the wrong of it. We are met to say how we may pull her down, she who would trample upon the honor and the power of our nobles Houses."

Loguire stiffened, his eyes widening in outrage. "Nay!" he choked, "there is not cause enough . . ."

"Cause!" Bourbon straightened, his black beard jumping with his jaw. "She hath taxed our lands more heavily than ever in the traditions of our lore, and wasted the substance upon the filth and dirt of peasants; she sends her judge amongst us every month to hear complaints from all the manor; and now she will appoint her priests within our lands

—and we have no cause? She robs us of our rightful rule within our own demesnes, and then upon this all insults us to our faces by hearing the petitions of besotted beggars ere she will bend her ear to ours!"

Di Medici had bent to listen to the slight man at his elbow; now he straightened, smiling faintly, and murmured, "And was it custom, ever, for a monarch to receive petitions from his peasants within his own Great Hall?"

"Never!" thundered Bourbon. "But now our gentle monarch will place the rabble thus before us! And these, my *reverend* Duke, be but the greatest of her enormities, and the atrocities she hath wreaked upon the custom of the land. And this while she is but a child! What will she do, my lord, when she is grown!"

He paused for breath, then shook his head and growled, "Nay, good coz! We must needs pull her down!"

"Aye," murmured Di Medici, and,

"Aye," declared the other lords, and

"Aye" rolled through the hall and swelled, till the word came full, clamoring from every throat, again and yet again.

"Aye!" and "Aye!" and "Aye!"

"Now I say *nay!*" Loguire roared above them all.

The hall fell still. Loguire drew himself up to his full height and breadth, looking more a king than duke.

His voice was only a little calmer, falling like the toll of a battle tocsin. "She is the sovereign. Capricious, aye, and arbitrary, hot and headstrong, aye. But these are faults of youth, of a child who must be taught that there are limits to her power. We must now show her those limits that she has exceeded. That may we do, and nothing more. Our cause does not admit of further action."

"A woman cannot rule wisely," murmured Di Medici's councillor, and Di Medici took it up: "My good and gentle cousin, God did not make Woman wise in ruling."

Bourbon took his cue. "Aye, good Uncle. Why will she give us not a king? Let her marry, if she doth wish this land well-governed."

Rod wondered if Bourbon was a disappointed suitor. There was something vaguely lecherous about him, and nothing at all romantic.

"The rule is hers by right!" Loguire rumbled. "Hers is the blood Plantagenet, the Crown of this land since its birth! What, good nephew, have you so easily forgotten the oath you swore in fealty to that good name?"

"Dynasties grow corrupt," muttered Bourbon's councillor, eyes gleaming.

"Aye!" Bourbon bellowed. "The blood Plantagenet has thinned and soured, *good* my lord!"

Ah, so! Rod thought. *He's not an uncle any more. . . .*

"Weakened sore, my lord!" Bourbon ranted. "Weakened till it can no longer sire a man, but only a woman, a slip of a girl, with a woman's moods and whims, to reign! The bloodline of Plantagenet is worn and spent; we must have new blood now for our kings!"

"The blood of Bourbon?" Loguire lifted an eyebrow, his smile contemptuous.

Bourbon's face swelled red, eyes bulging. He had begun to splutter when Di Medici's voice interposed itself smoothly.

"Nay, good cousin, not the blood of Bourbon. What throne-blood should we have but the noblest in all the South?"

Loguire stared, the blood draining out of his face in shock and horror. "I will not!" he hissed.

"Nay, my lord, and this we knew." Di Medici went oily on. "Yet must we have good blood, and a man of courage and decision, a man of youth who knows what must be done and will not hesitate to do it."

His voice rose. "What king should we have but Anselm, Loguire's son?"

Loguire's head jerked as though he had been slapped. He stared, his face paling to a waxen texture, taking on a grayish hue.

He reached behind him with a palsied hand, groping for his chair, and age draped heavy on his shoulders.

He lowered himself to the edge of the seat, leaning heavily on the arm. His vacant eyes sought out his son, then turned slowly from side to side.

"Villains!" he whispered. "Bloody, bawdy villains! And thus you steal my son . . ."

Anselm's chin was lifted in defiance, but guilt and fear had hollowed his eyes. "Nay, my lord, I was with them from the first."

Loguire's empty eyes sought him out again. "But thou, even thou . . ."

His voice strengthened. "But it is, thou more than any. Above all, it is thou!"

Durer now stepped forward, away from Loguire, to take his place by Anselm's side, his smile split into a grin of triumph.

Loguire's eyes gradually focused on him. Their eyes met, and held.

A slight rustle passed through the hall as all the councillors craned for a better view.

"Nay," Loguire whispered, "it was *thou. . . .*"

He straightened slowly. Then, deliberately and slowly, he looked each Great Lord in the eyes once more. His eyes turned back to Durer.

"You are all of one mind." His voice had gained strength; but it was the strength of bitterness and contempt. "The debate has been before this, has it not? For you are all agreed; each man among you has quarreled with his conscience and won over it."

His voice hardened even more. "What wasp has flown among you, to sting your souls to such accord?"

Durer's eyes snapped fire. His mouth broke open for retort; but Loguire cut him off.

"Thou! Thou from the start! Thou camest to me five years ago, and I, aged fool, thought 'Well and good'; and as thy bastard, cringing servants crept one by one into our households, still I rejoiced—poor, aged, doddering fool!"

He lifted his eyes to seek out Anselm's. "Anselm, who once I called my son, awake and hear! Beware the man who tastes thy meat, for he it is who best may poison it."

Rod suddenly realized how the meeting would end. The councillors couldn't risk leaving Loguire alive; the old man was still strong and vital, still indomitable. He just might be able to sway the lords to loyalty again. The chance was slight, but definite, and Durer couldn't afford it.

Anselm straightened his shoulders, his face set with rebellion. He clapped a hand to Durer's shoulder, not noticing that the little man's teeth grated as his jaws clamped shut.

"This man I trust," he stated in what might have been intended to be ringing tones. "He was with me from the first, and I welcome his wisdom—as I will welcome yours, if you are with us."

Loguire's eyes narrowed. "Nay," he spat. "Away with you, false child, and your tongue of treachery! I had sooner die than join you."

"You shall have your preference," Durer shapped. "Name the manner of your dying."

Loguire glared, then threw himself to his full height in one lurching motion.

Anselm stared, then reddened. "Be—be still, Durer! He

is—is a fool, aye, and a traitor to the land. But he is my father, and none shall touch him!"

Durer's eyebrow shot up. "You would harbor snakes within your bed, my lord? Naetheless, it is the wish of all the nobles, not yours alone, that must be done."

He raised his voice, shouting, "What say you, lords? Shall this man die?"

There was a moment's pause. Rod rested his hand on the door-lever; he had to get Loguire out of there. He could open the door and pull Loguire into the passage before anybody realized what was happening . . .

But could he close it before they came running? Probably not; there were just too many too close. And Durer, at least, would react very quickly.

If only the hinges and springs were in decent shape! But he had a notion they hadn't been too well maintained in the last few centuries.

A chorus of reluctant "Ayes" rolled through the great hall.

Durer turned to Loguire, bowing his head politely. "The verdict, my lord, is death."

He drew his poniard and started forward.

And the lights went out.

Rod stood a moment in the total blackness, stunned. How . . . ?

Then he threw his weight on the lever. He jerked out his dagger as the stone slab groaned open. Act now, understand later.

The grating of the stone door broke the instant of shocked silence. Pandemonium struck as every voice in the hall started shouting—some in anger, some in distress, some calling for a porter to bring a torch.

The noise would be a good cover. Rod lunged out of the passage, groping blindly till he slammed into somebody's rib cage. The Somebody roared and lashed out at him. Rod ducked on general principles, felt the blow skim his hair. He flicked the button on the handle of his dagger and identified Somebody as the Duke Loguire in the flicker of light that stabbed up from the hilt.

A kindling-wood, twisting body struck into Rod with a howl of rage. Rod gasped and stumbled as steel bit into his shoulder. Apparently Durer had seen the flicker of light, too.

The dagger wrenched itself out of Rod's shoulder; he felt the warm welling flow out of the blood, and rolled away.

But the scarecrow was on him again. Rod groped, and by great good luck caught the man's knife-wrist.

But the little man was unbelievably strong. He forced Rod's arm down, down, and Rod felt the dagger's point prick his throat.

He tried to force his other hand up to help push the needle-point away. His shoulder screamed pain, but the hand wouldn't budge.

The dagger pricked a fraction of an inch deeper. Rod felt blood rise on his throat, and fear clawed its way up from his guts.

Total, numbing, paralyzing fear—and Rod heard a booming moan.

Durer gasped; the poniard clattered to the floor, and the weight rose off Rod's body.

The whole hall rang with a triple, very low moan, counterpointed with shrieks of terror.

Three huge white forms towered high in the blackness. At the tops were skeletal faces, their mouths rounded into O's: Horatio and two other erstwhile Lords Loguire, having the time of their afterlives.

Rod forced a shout out of his terror. "Fess! Sixty cycles!"

His head clamored with the raucous buzzing, and the fear evaporated. His light flicked again, found Loguire. Rod sprang, struck him in the midriff. The breath went out of the old lord in a *whoof!* and he doubled over Rod's shoulder —the good one, fortunately.

Rod turned and ran, stumbling, hoping he was headed in the right direction.

Behind him, Durer was shrieking, "Clap your hands to your ears, fools! Fools! Fools!"

Rod blundered about in the dark, Loguire's weight dragging heavier on his shoulder. He couldn't find the door! And now he heard staccato steps in short, quick bursts—Durer, trying to find Rod by blind chance. And now that he had his earplugs in, Durer would once again be a formidable enemy. Also, Rod couldn't fight with one shoulder shot and the other under Loguire.

Cold air fanned his cheek, and a dim white form brushed past him. "Follow!" boomed Horatio Loguire.

Rod followed.

He ran after Horatio, his good arm out like a broken-field runner. It didn't help; his wounded shoulder slammed against the stone of the doorway and spun him around with a wrench of pain. He gasped, almost dropping Loguire, and stumbled back against the wall of the narrow passage.

He leaned against the wall, breathing horsely.

"Quickly, Man!" boomed Horatio. "The slab! You must close it!"

Rod nodded, gasping, and groped for the lever, hoping Loguire would stay balanced on his shoulder. His hand found rusty metal. He hauled upward; the door grated shut.

He stood hunched over, just breathing.

After a small eternity, Loguire began to struggle. Rod called up the energy to lower him to the floor. Then, still panting, he looked up at Horatio.

"Many thanks," he wheezed, "for this timely rescue."

Horatio waved away the thanks, coming dangerously close to a smile. "Why, Man, how could you fulfill your oath to me dead?"

"Oh, I dunno." Rod sagged against the wall. "You seem to manage all right. I'd love to know how you pulled the fuse on those torches."

"Pulled . . . the fuse?" Horatio frowned.

"You know, the trick with the lights."

The ghost's frown deepened. "Was that not your doing?"

Rod stared. Then he raised a hand, palm out. "Now, wait a minute. Wait a minute. Now. You thought I did it . . . and I thought you did it."

"Aye."

"But, you didn't do it?"

"Nay."

"And I didn't do it."

"It would seem not."

"Then"—Rod gulped—"who . . . ?"

"Who is this?" Loguire rumbled at Rod's elbow.

A beam of light stabbed through the peephole.

Horatio gave one moan of fear, and winked out.

Rod put his eye to the peephole. The torches were lit again. Durer was on the dais, stabbing the air about him with his dagger and screaming, "Where? Where?"

Rod lifted his head away from the peephole and smiled up at Loguire thinly. "I don't think we ought to stay to find out, my lord. Shall we go?"

He turned to go; but Loguire's fingers dug into his shoulder. Rod gasped. "Please, milord—would you mind—the other shoulder, please. . . ."

"What man was that?" Loguire growled.

"Man?" Rod looked about him. "What man?"

"Why, he who stood before us in white!"

"Oh." Rod scanned the old man's face. Apparently Loguire was still in shock, not quite yet ready to face reality, such as it was. "Uh, just a relative, milord."

"Your relative? Here?"

"No, milord. Yours." He turned away, groping down the passage.

After a moment, Loguire followed.

The light from the peephole fell off after a few yards. Rod groped his way, cursing; it would be pitch dark when they turned the corner to go down the narrow steps.

He turned the corner, fumbling out his dagger—and saw a ball of fox-fire before him. He stared, an eerie tingling nesting at the base of his neck; then, as his eyes adjusted to the dim glow, he made out a face and a body (it was impossible to see them as a unit, since each was worthy of independent study), one arm extended, with the fox-fire sitting on her palm. Her face was tense with worry.

"Gwendylon," he stated.

Her face flooded with relief and joy, but only for a moment; then the light of mischief was in her eyes.

She bobbed in a mock courtsy. "My lord."

"My Aunt Nanny!" he growled. "What the hell are you doing here?"

Her eyes widened in offended innocence. "I followed you, lord."

"No, no, no!" Rod squeezed his eyes shut. "That's not in the script. You were supposed to hate me now. You were supposed to quit following me."

"Never, lord." Her voice was very low.

He looked up to see if she was joking. No luck. Tom's line about farm girls ran through his mind.

"What," he said, nodding at the ball of fox-fire, "have you got there?"

"This?" She glanced at the ball of light. "Only a little spell my mother taught me. 'Twill light us through this maze, lord."

"Light," Rod agreed. "And may I ask how you killed the torches in the great hall?"

She started to answer, then frowned. " 'Tis not quickly said, lord. Have we time?"

Rod studied her face with his lips pursed. "But it was you who did it?"

190

"Aye, lord."

"Just another little spell that . . ."

". . . my mother taught me, yes." She nodded brightly

"Oka-a-a-y!" He shrugged. "Why not? Let's go, babe."

He started groping his way down the narrow stairs, wincing as his shoulder brushed the wall.

"My lord!" Gwendylon gasped, her hand darting out to touch his shoulder. "You're hurt!"

He half-turned toward her, lurching against the wall, still groping for the stone; but the full, firm mound that his hand found was anything but granite.

He jerked his hand away. She stared at him a moment, surprised; then her lids drooped, she smiled lazily, and caught up his hand, pulling it toward her. "Milord, you need not—"

"Yegad!" He pulled his hand away, shrinking back against the wall. She swayed toward him, lips parting.

"My dear lady . . . !"

"I ha' ne'er claimed that title," she murmured, her voice warm, rich, and husky. Her body pressed softly against him.

"Woman, please!" Rod made a valiant attempt to push his way into the stone. "I can't imagine a less aesthetic atmosphere."

"Neither time nor place matter to me, lord, when you are near," she breathed into his ear, and nibbled.

And I thought I had some lines, Rod told himself. "Look," he said, wriggling, "we don't have time, we don't have room . . ." He gasped and shivered as she caught just exactly the right spot. "Look, baby, just get us out of here, and I'm yours to command!"

She caught her breath and stood just far enough back to look up at him. "Truly, lord?"

"Well, uh . . ." Rod backpedaled furiously. "For twenty-four hours, anyway."

"That will do," she murmured smugly, with a similar quality in her smile.

He glowered down at her for a moment; then, "Take those canary feathers out of your mouth," he growled, "and get us out here!"

"Aye, lord!" She turned in a swirl of skirts and ran lightly down the mossy steps.

He watched her run for a moment, a gleam coming into his eye.

He caught up to her in three bounds and swung her around to face him.

She looked up in surprise, then turned on the sultry look again. "My lord, we must not delay. . . ."

"This won't take long," he answered, and pulled her hard against him. Her lips were moist and warm, and parted . . .

She gave a happy little sigh and pushed him away. "Well! And what was that for?"

"Promissory note." He grinned.

She giggled, then spun away, tugging him down the hall. "We must hurry!"

He freed his arm and watched her run.

A deep, warm chuckle sounded behind him.

Rod threw Loguire a look of disgust. "Dirty old man," he growled, and ran after Gwen.

The slimy stones of the passage slid by on either side, scarcely three inches from each shoulder. Up a flight of steps, turn, up another flight, the stones greasy and slippery with dripping water, seepage from the lake overhead. Patches of pale moss grew like sores on the walls. Old spiderwebs festooned the low ceiling.

At the top of the twelfth staircase, Rod heard water chuckling somewhere in the distance.

"The inlet to the lake," Gwendylon informed him. "We shall come out along its border." She glanced back over her shoulder. "Your shoulder, Lord Rod?"

"Oh, it'll wait," he growled.

"Doth it yet bleed?"

"No; the doublet seems to have stanched it. Be a hell of a cleaning bill though."

"Hmm." She turned away, hurrying. " 'Twill hold till we come to the riverbank, then. Hurry, lords; we must be away ere they think to search in the stables."

Rod frowned. "Why? Are we coming out in the stable-yard?"

"Nay, by the river; but when they look in the stables, they shall see that your black and the Duke's dun stallion have fled."

"You don't say!" He cleared his throat and spoke a little louder than necessary. "And where would my horse be?"

"By the riverbank, Rod," Fess's voice murmured, "with Big Tom and two real nags."

Gwendylon had started to answer, but Rod cut her off. "Yes, yes, they're by the riverbank, I know."

Gwen looked faintly surprised.

"But how," Rod went on, "did Big Tom know we'd be needing horses?"

She frowned at him a moment, then turned away. " 'Twas at my urging, lord. 'Twas but a thought, and could do little harm. I had a seeming they might be needed."

"A seeming," Rod echoed. Was she clairvoyant, too?

"Aye, lord, a seeming." She slowed suddenly. "Walk wary, lords." She stepped carefully over something lying in the passage.

Rod stopped and stared at it.

It was a miniature human skeleton, perhaps eighteen inches long; but the proportions were those of an adult, not a baby. It was green with mold.

He looked up at Gwendylon. "This has not been here so very long," he said. "What is it?"

"One of the Wee Folk, lord." Her mouth hardened. "There ha' been evil spells in this keep of late."

Rod looked up, surprised at the tone of her voice, ignoring Loguire's startled exclamation.

Her face was flint, set in a mold of bitterness. "Poor wee fellow," she murmured. "And we dare not stop to give him burial." She spun about and hurried on.

Rod stepped carefully over the tiny skeleton and followed.

"What manner of spell?" he asked as he caught up to her.

" 'Twas a sort of . . . singing . . . in the air, lord, though not for the ear, but the mind. If you or I tried to move against it, 'twould but stop us, like a wall. But it slew the Wee Folk."

Rod frowned. "A *singing*, you say?"

"Aye, lord. Yet not of the ear, as I told you."

A force field! But that was impossible. Ask any physicist, he'd tell you . . .

"How long ago?"

"It was cast five years agone, milord. It lasted no more than a month, for its master took no note of my stopping it, nor did he cast it again."

Rod stopped so fast Loguire stumbled into him. He stared at the gentle, very feminine form hurrying down the passage before him. Then he closed his mouth, swallowed, and followed.

A force field! And five years ago, that was when Durer had shown up. . . .

Rod thought again of the dial on the supposed time machine. Then he stared at Gwen's long, red hair, swinging with her steps.

And she had stopped it? A machine out of the future, and *she* had stopped it?

He looked at his farm girl with new respect.

"Uh, Gwen, dear . . ."

"Aye, my lord?" She looked back at him, with a look of pleased surprise and a faint blush.

He frowned. *What . . . ?* Oh. He'd called her "Gwen." Also "dear."

"Aye, my lord, exorcized it. But the Wee Folk would not come here more, and I too thought it wise."

Yes, Rod mused, *very wise.* Durer & Co. would not have taken kindly to diminutive spies, and could probably have devised some very unpleasant preventatives. He fastened his eyes on Gwendylon's retreating back, watching her absently; she was just full of surprises, this one. . . .

"We come near, lords!"

Rod jerked his head up and saw a point of dim light ahead. The ball of light in Gwen's hand flickered out.

A moment later, they stepped through the weathered, weed-grown mouth of the tunnel into the moonlit night. The river flowed by a few dozen yards away, bordered with willow and cypress. The breeze was chill after the dampness of the tunnel. Loguire shivered.

"Master!" came a soft, low cry, and Big Tom stepped out of the riverbank shadows, leading three horses.

Rod grabbed Gwendylon's hand and ran for the horses . . . and was brought up sharp by a most unfeminine jerk on his arm—fortunately, the good one.

"Nay, my lord," she said firmly. "First we must see to your arm."

"Which one," Rod grumped, swiveling his good shoulder; it had developed a sudden ache. "Look, we don't have time . . ."

"It will slow us in our ride soon or late," she said sternly. "Better to tend it now, when it will take but a moment."

Rod sighed and capitulated. He watched her run to the riverbank with a connoisseur's interest and wondered what the strange, pleasant feeling inside him was.

"She hath the right of it," growled Loguire, swinging Rod about to face him. "Clamp your teeth."

He unbuttoned Rod's doublet. Rod's nascent protest was

cut off by a gasp of agony as Loguire snapped the doublet open, tearing the scab off in the process.

"Let it bleed freely a moment," Loguire growled, jerking the doublet off the injured shoulder.

Then Gwendylon came up with a handful of some sort of herb and a small wineskin—*trust Big Tom to have one on him,* Rod thought—and perhaps five minutes later, Rod swung her onto Fess's saddle and leaped up behind her. He dug his heels into Fess's sides. Gwendylon started at the muted clang, and, as Fess sprang out into a gallop, she twisted about to frown, puzzled, at Rod.

"That's why I call him Old Ironsides," Rod explained. "Just relax and lean back against me. It's going to be a long ride."

"But, my lord, I have no need to—"

"There're only three horses, Gwen. Somebody has to ride double. Don't worry, Fess won't even notice the difference."

"But my lord, I—"

"Hush. My Lord Loguire!" he called back over his shoulder. "Lead us, my lord; you know this land best."

Loguire nodded mutely and spurred the big bay; it speeded a little, and passed Rod. Rod followed him, listening to the drum of hooves from Tom's mount behind him.

"Believe me, my lord, there is no need for—"

"Time enough to talk later," Rod growled. "We're leaving a trail as clear as Polaris. We've got to get far enough away fast enough so it won't matter if they follow us."

Gwendylon sighed. "Look behind you, my lord."

Rod turned, and saw a crowd of at least a hundred elves lined along their trail with miniature brooms, sweeping away every trace of their passing—even straightening the grass the horses' hooves had flattened.

Rod squeezed his eyes shut. "No. Oh, no. Why me, Lord? Why me?"

He turned back to Gwendylon. "Gwen, did you call out these . . . Gwen!"

The saddle was empty. She was gone.

"Gwen!" he shouted, and sawed back on the reins.

"Really, Rod," protested the murmur in his mastoid, "I must ask that you attempt to control—"

"*Gwendylon!*" Rod yelled.

A cry like the mew of a seagull drifted down from the sky.

Rod looked up.

The osprey. The same one. He was willing to swear to it. Anyway, he was willing to swear.

The bird plummeted low and circled Rod's head, mewing urgently.

How the hell could she make a fish hawk sound so feminine?

The osprey shot away in front of him, skimming low over the ground after Loguire's horse.

Then it wheeled back, circled his head again, then lit out on the straightaway again.

"Yeah, yeah," Rod growled, "I get the message. I should quit holding up the party. Fess, follow that bird! Fess? Fess!"

The horse stood stiff-legged, head swinging between the fetlocks.

Oh, well, it had been a strain on Rod's neurology, too. He slapped at the reset button.

They rode the moon down, slowing to a trot after the first half-hour. Loguire was slumped in his saddle, almost too exhausted to stay on his horse, by the time the air freshened with dawn.

Rod, frankly, wasn't in much better shape. He reined in beside the Duke. "There're haystacks in that field over there, my lord. We must pause to rest. It will be dawn soon, and we dare not travel by day."

Loguire lifted his head, blinking. "Aye. Aye, most certain." He reined in his horse. Rod and Tom followed suit.

They broke through the hedge at the roadside and trotted for the nearest haystack. Rod dismounted and caught Loguire as he all but fell from his saddle. Big Tom unsaddled the horses and turned them out to the field with a slap on the rump as Rod half-led, half carried the old nobleman to the top of the haystack.

He lowered Loguire into the hay, stepped back, and murmured, "Fess."

"Yes, Rod."

"Get those nags far away from here, someplace where it's not too likely they'll be noticed, will you? And bring them back at sundown."

"I will, Rod."

Rod stood a moment, listening to the fading drum of hooves.

He looked down at Loguire; the old man was out cold: the strain, and the long night ride, to say nothing of how long it had been since he'd slept.

Rod pulled hay over the sleeping lord to hide him. Looking for Big Tom, he saw shins and feet disappearing into the side of the haystack. The saddles and bridles had already disappeared into the hay.

The feet were likewise removed from sight; then there was a protracted rustling, and Tom's ruddy face popped out of his burrow-hole. "Thou must take tha'self from sight right quickly, master. 'Twill be sunrise ere long, and the peasants mustn't see us."

"They won't come near this stack?"

"Nay. This field is far from the keep, so 'twill be some days yet ere they take in this hay."

Rod nodded. He threw up his hands and jumped, sliding down the side of the stack. He turned to see Tom's burrow fast closing. He grinned. "Good night, Big Tom."

"Good morn, master," answered the muffled voice within.

Rod chuckled, shaking his head, as he went to the nearest other haystack. He climbed to the top, mashed the hay down into a bowl, and stretched out with a blissful sigh.

There was a soft mew, and the osprey dropped down beside him into the hay. It fell onto its side, its form fluxed and stretched, and Gwendylon was lying beside him.

She smiled mischievously and began to untie the strings of her bodice. "Twenty-four hours, my lord. Sunrise to sunrise. You ha' said you would obey my commands for so long."

"But—but—but . . ." Rod stared and swallowed as the bodice fell open and was thrown away. The blouse began to inch upward.

He swallowed again and stammered, "Bu-but somebody's got to keep watch!"

"Never fear," she murmured. The blouse went flying. "My friends shall do that."

"Your friends?" In a detached sort of way, Rod noted that in this culture the concept of the brassiere was not yet developed.

Gwendylon was, though.

"Aye, the Wee Folk." Skirt and slippers joined the discard pile with one smooth, sinuous motion.

The setting sun turned the straw blood-gold as Rod's head poked up out of the hay.

He looked around, sniffed the cool, fresh evening breeze, and expelled a sign of great satisfaction.

He felt immensely well.

He thrust the covering of hay aside with one sweep of his arm and reflected that it had been a busy day, as his eyes traveled slowly and lovingly over Gwen's curves.

He leaned forward and touched his lips to hers for a long, deep kiss. He felt her come awake beneath him.

He drew back; her eyes opened halfway. Her lips curved in a slow, sultry smile.

She stretched, slow and feline. Rod was surprised to feel his pulse quicken. His opinion of himself went up a notch.

His opinion of her was altogether too high already. With a twinge of alarm, Rod realized he was regretting that he was a traveling man. He also realized something was gnawing at the base of his conscience. She looked into his eyes and sobered. "What saddens you, lord?"

"Don't you ever worry about being used, Gwen?"

She smiled lazily. "Do you, lord?"

"Well, no . . ." Rod frowned at his palms. "But that's different. I mean, I'm a man."

"I would never ha' guessed," she murmured, biting his ear lobe in the process.

He grinned and twisted, trying to retaliate; but she wasn't done with his ear yet.

"Men are fools," she murmured between bites. "You are forever saying what is not instead of what is. Be done with the night, and live in the evening while you are in it."

She eyed him then through heavy lids with a somewhat proprietary joy, looking him up and down slowly.

Oh, well, Rod thought, *so much for my one attempt to be honorable* . . . "Kamere!" After all, there was only one way to wipe that smug smile off her face.

Big Tom chose just that moment to call, "Master! The sun has set, and we must away."

Rod let go of Gwen with a disgusted growl. "That boy has definitely the greatest sense of timing . . ." He started pulling on his hose. "Up and away, my dear!"

"Must we, lord?" she said, pouting.

"We must," he answered. "Duty calls—or at least Big Tom. Onward for the glory of France! or something like that. . . ."

Two nights of pushing the pace, alternating canter and walk, brought them back to the capital.

As they came to the bridge over the river that curved around the town, Rod was surprised to see two foot soldiers armed with pikes, torches flaring by their sides in the darkness of the seventh hour of night.

"I shall clear the way," Tom muttered, and spurred his horse ahead of Rod and Loguire. "Stand aside," he called to the guards, "for my masters wish to enter."

The pikes clashed as they crossed, barring the bridge. "Who are your masters?" retorted the one of them. "Be they rebels? Or Queen's men?"

"Rebels?" Tom frowned. "What ha' passed in the Queen's Tow while we ha' been to the South?"

"The South?" The guard's eyes narrowed. " 'Tis the lords of the South that rebel."

"Aye, aye!" Big Tom waved the objection away impatiently. "We ha' been there on the Queen's affairs—spies, i' truth. We bear word that the lords of the South rise in revolt, and the name of the day that they march; but how has this news come here afore us?"

"What is this badinage?" snapped Loguire, riding up with Rod at his side. "Stand aside, sirrahs, that a man of noble blood may enter!"

The guards' heads swiveled to stare up at Loguire; then both pikes jumped forward, their points scarce an inch from his chest. "Dismount and stand, Milord Duke of Loguire!" The first guard's voice was firm, but deferential. "We must hold you in arrest, on command of her Majesty the Queen."

And the other guard bawled, "Captain! Captain of the Guard!"

Loguire stared in disbelief. Rod nudged his way past the lord and glared at the guard. "Name the crime for which the Queen holds Milord Loguire in arrest!"

The guard's eyes flicked from Loguire's face to Rod's, and back; then, dubiously, he answered, "Most high treason to the body and person of her Majesty the Queen."

Loguire's jaw sagged. Then his lips pressed thin and his brows beetled down, hiding his eyes in caves of shadow. His face seemed bloody in the torchlight.

"I am most sternly loyal to her Majesty the Queen!" he exploded. "Be done with your impertinence and stand aside!"

The sentry swallowed and stood his ground. "It is said Loguire leads the rebels, milord."

"Soldier." Rod spoke quietly, but with the tone of an old field sergeant.

The sentry's eyes jumped to him, but the pike didn't waver.

"You know me," and Rod's voice held the veiled threat of non-com authority.

It had more effect than all Loguire's lofty phrases. The soldier licked his lips and agreed, "Aye, master."

"Who am I?"

"You are Master Gallowglass, late of the Queen's Guard."

"*Still* of the Queen's Guard," Rod corrected, still softly. "Sent to the South a week agone, to guard Milord Loguire."

Loguire's head jerked up; his eyes blazed at Rod.

"We ha' known that you were gone," the soldier mumbled.

"And now you know why." Rod kept his voice under careful control, managing to imply that the Queen's Own Wrath would fall on the guard's miserable head if he disobeyed. "My Lord Loguire cries sanctuary from his kinswoman 'and suzerain, her Majesty the Queen. She would be wroth to hear him detained. Let us pass."

The guard took a firmer hold on his pike, gulped, and thrust out his jaw stubbornly. "The order ha' gone forth that Milord Loguire be held in arrest in the Queen's dungeon, good master. More than that I know not."

"Dungeon!" Loguire thundered, beet-red. "Am I a tuppenny footpad, to be crooked from a hedgerow to a dungeon cell? Is it thus that the Queen would acknowledge her vassal? Nay, nay! The blood Plantagenet hath not ebbed so low! Knave, I'll hale thy lying tongue from thy head!"

His hand went to his dagger, and the soldier cowered back; but Rod's hand stayed the nobleman's.

"Calm yourself, milord," he murmured, " 'Tis Durer hath sent this word here before us. The Queen could not know of your loyalty."

Loguire checked his temper with vast effort, subsiding into a sort of gurgling fury. Rod leaned over and whispered to Tom.

"Tom, can you find someplace to hide the old man where he'll be safe?"

"Aye, master," Tom frowned down at him. "With his son. But why . . . ?"

"At the House of Clovis?"

"Aye, master. 'Twould take all the Queen's men, and great bombards, to hale them forth from the House."

"I would have said a good strong wind would've done it," Rod muttered, "but I guess it's the best we can do. So . . ."

"Speak so that all may hear!" shouted a new voice.

"That had a familiar ring," Rod muttered, looking up.

Sir Maris strode forth between the two vastly relieved guardsmen. "Well done, Rod Gallowglass! Thou hast brought a most pernicious rebel to the safekeeping of our stronghold!"

Loguire's narrowed eyes stabbed hate at Rod.

"Do not speak among yourselves," Sir Maris went on; "I forbid it. And hearken well to my orders, for there are twelve good crossbowmen with their quarrels aimed at your hearts."

Loguire sat back in his saddle, tall and proud, his face composed in the granite of fatalism.

"Twelve?" Rod gave Sir Maris a one-sided mocking smile. "Only twelve quarrels, to kill the Loguire? Good Sir Maris, I must think you grow rash in your old age."

The granite mask cracked; Loguire darted a puzzled glance at Rod.

Rod dismounted and stepped out toward the bridge, away from the horses. He shook his head woefully. "Sir Maris, Sir Maris! My good Sir Maris, to think that—"

Suddenly he whirled, with a high, piercing cray, slapping at the horses' chests. "Turn and ride!" he shrieked. "Ride!"

Sir Maris and his men stood frozen with surprise as the horses reared, wheeled about, and sprang away. An instant later, twelve crossbow bolts bit the ground where they had been.

One archer had been a little quicker than his fellows; his bolt struck Fess's metal hindquarters with a clang and ricocheted off into the river.

There was an instant's shocked silence; then the whisper ran through the ranks, swelling with fear: "Witch horse! Witch horse!"

"Cloud the trail, Fess," Rod murmured, and the great black horse reared, pawing the air and screaming combat; then it wheeled away and was gone, lost in the night, hoofbeats drumming away.

Rod smiled grimly, sure that Fess's trail would cross and recross Tom and Loguire's till an Italian spaghetti cook wouldn't be able to unsnarl it.

He peered up into the sky. He couldn't see beyond the circle of torchlight, but he thought he heard a faint mewing.

He smiled, again, a little more sincerely this time. *Let Catharine try to imprison. Let her try.*

Then his smile settled and soured as he turned to face Sir Maris.

The old knight was struggling manfully to look angry; but the fear in his eyes blared as loud as a TV commercial. His voice quavered. "Rod Gallowglass, you have abetted the escape of a rebel."

Rod stood mute, eyes glittering.

Sir Maris swallowed hard and went on. "For high treason to the body and person of her Majesty Queen of all Gramarye, Rod Gallowglass, in arrest I must hold thee."

Rod inclined his head politely. "You may try."

The soldiers muttered fearfully and drew back. None wished to match arms with the warlock.

Sir Maris' eyes widened in alarm; then he spun and grabbed one of his soldiers by the arm. "You there! Soldier! Soldier!" he hissed. "Run ahead and bear word to the Queen. Say what transpires here."

The soldier bolted, overwhelmingly glad to lose out on the action.

Sir Maris turned back to Rod. "Thou must now come to judgment before the Queen, Master Gallowglass."

Oho! thought Rod. *I'm a master now, am I?*

"Wilt thou go to her freely?" said Sir Maris apprehensively, "Or must I compel thee?"

Rod fought to keep his shoulders from shaking with laughter at the dread in the old knight's voice. His reputation had decided advantages.

"I will come freely, Sir Maris," he said, stepping forward. "Shall we go?"

Sir Maris' eyes fairly glowed with gratitude.

Abruptly, he sobered. "I would not be in thy place for a castle and dukedom, Rod Gallowglass. Thou must needs now stand alone before our Queen's tongue."

"Well, yes," Rod agreed. "But then, I've got a few things to say to her too, now haven't I? Let us go then, Sir Maris."

Unfortunately, the march to the castle gave Rod time to mull over Catharine's latest churlish tricks; so by the time they came to the door to her chambers, Rod's jaw was clenched and shivering with rage.

And, equally unfortunately, there was a reception committee, consisting of two sentries, the soldier who had been sent ahead as messenger, and two pikes pointed right at Rod's midriff.

The procession halted. "And what," said Rod, with icy control, "is *this* supposed to mean?"

The messenger stammered an answer. "Th-the Queen forbids that the w-warlock be brought before her unch-chained."

"Oh." Rod pursed his lips for a moment, then gave the messenger a polite lift of the eybrow. "I am to be chained?"

The messenger nodded, on the verge of panic.

The pikes crashed as Rod knocked them away to each side. He grabbed the messenger by the scruff of the neck and threw him into the pack of Guardsmen as they surged forward. Then he lashed out with a kick that wrenched the crude metal hinges from their bolts.

The door crashed down, and he strode in over it, stepping hard.

Catharine, the Mayor of the Queen's Town, and Brom O'Berin shot to their feet from their chairs around a map-laden table.

Brom sprang to bar Rod's path. "What devil possesses you, Rod Gallowglass, that you . . ."

But Rod was already past him and still moving.

He swung to a stop before the table, glaring across at her, his eyes chips of dry ice.

Catharine stepped back, one hand coming to her throat, disconcerted and afraid.

Brom leaped to the tabletop, thundering, "What means this unseemly intrusion, Rod Gallowglass? Get thee hence, till the Queen shall summon thee!"

"I would prefer not to come before her Majesty in chain—" his words cold and clipped. "And I will not allow that a nobleman of the highest rank be clapped in a common, noisome dungeon with rats and thieves."

"*Thou* wilt not allow!" Catharine gasped, outraged; and, "Who art thou to allow or not allow?" roared Brom. "Thou hast not even gentle blood!"

"Then I must think that blood is opposed to action," Rod snapped.

He flung the table out of his way and advanced on the Queen. "I had thought you noble." The word was a sneer. "But now I see that you will turn against your very family, even to one near as nigh you as a father! Certes, if you would fight any of your nobles, you must needs fight a kinsman; but your very uncle? Fie, woman! Were he the foulest

203

murderer, you had ought to receive him with courtesy and the honor due his station. Your finest chamber you should appoint his cell; 'tis but your duty to blood!"

He backed her up against the fireplace, glowering deep into her eyes. "Nay, were he but a murderer, no doubt you would receive him with all honor! But no, he has committed the heinous crime of objecting to your high-handed, arbitrary laws, and the further calumny of maintaining his honor against your calculated insults. He will insist on being accorded the respect due a man during the reign of a vindictive, childish, churlish chit of a girl who hath the title of a Queen but none of the graces, and for this he must needs be damned!"

"Fie, sirrah," she quavered, waxen pale, "that you would speak so to a lady!"

"Lady!" he snorted.

"A lady born!" It was a forlorn, desperate cry. "Will you, too, desert me? Will you speak with the tongue of Clovis?"

"I may speak like a peasant, but you act like one! And now I see why all desert you; for you would whip to scorn Loguire, who alone of all your lords is loyal!"

"Loyal!" she gasped. "He, who leads the rebels?"

"*Anselm* Loguire leads the rebels! For keeping faith with you, the old Duke is now deposed in favor of his son!"

He smiled bitterly as the horror and guilt dawned in her, then turned his back upon her and stepped away, giving her time to realize the breadth of her betrayal. He heard a long-drawn, shuddering breath behind him; Brom rushed past him to aid his Queen. He heard a chair creak as Brom made her sit.

Looking up, he saw the Lord Mayor staring past him wide-eyed. Rod cleared his throat; the burgher's eyes shifted to him. Rod jerked his head toward the door. The Mayor glanced back at the Queen, hesitating. Rod toyed with the hilt of his dagger. The Mayor saw, blanched, and fled.

Rod turned back to the stricken girl.

Brom, at her elbow, threw Rod a glance of withering hatred and growled, "Ha' done! Have you not cut deep enough?"

"Not yet." Rod's lips thinned. He stepped up to the Queen again, his voice cold. "This good nobleman, the Duke Loguire, your own uncle, out of love for you stood against the whole of your nobility, *even his own son!*" His voice crackled. Her eyes jerked up to him, filling with dread. "And it is your doing, by your high-handed lawmaking and utter lack of diplomacy, that Anselm turned against his father. He had two sons, and you have robbed him of both!"

She shook her head, faster and faster, lips shaping silent denials.

"Yet still he is loyal!" Rod murmured. "Still he is loyal, though they would have slain him for it—and damn near did!"

She stared in horror.

Rod tapped his shoulder. "This took the dagger that would have pierced his heart. And even at that, 'twas only by a miracle, and the help of one of the witches whom you scarce acknowledge, that I managed to bring him out alive!"

Brom's head snapped up, searching Rod's face for something. Rod frowned, and went on.

"But bring him out I did, at peril of my life, and brought him safely back. And what do I find? He is to be held a prisoner! And not even as befits a royal prisoner! No, not to be treated with due courtesy and deference, but as a common cutpurse, in a lightless, damp, dank dungeon!"

He paused for effect, rather proud of the last bit of alliteration.

But he had overdone it a bit; she rallied. Her chin came up, and she sniffled back some tears. "Before my laws, sirrah, all are equal!"

"Yes," Rod agreed, "but that should mean you treat a peasant like a lord, not that you treat a lord like a peasant!"

He leaned over her, his face an inch from hers. "Tell me, Queen: why is it that Catharine must treat all with contempt?"

It was a lie; she didn't treat all with contempt, just the noblemen; but anguish and sudden self-doubt showed in her eyes.

Still she tilted her chin a fraction of an inch higher, and declaimed, "I am the Queen, and all must bow to my power!"

"Oh, they bow, they bow! Until you slap them in the face; then they slap back!"

He turned away, glowering at the hearth. "And I can't say I blame them, when you deprive them of liberty."

Catharine stared. "Liberty? What talk is this, sirrah? I seek to give the serfs greater liberty!"

"Aye, so you seek." Rod smiled sourly. "But how do you go about giving it? You gather all ever more tightly unto you.

You deprive them today, that you may give them more later!"

He slammed his fist onto the arm of her chair. "But later will never come, don't you see that? There is too much ill in the land, there will always be another evil to fight, and the Queen's word must be law unquestioned to command the army against the evil."

He drew his hand back slowly, eyes burning. "And so it will never come, the day that you set them free; in your land, none will have liberty, save the Queen."

He locked his hands behind his back and paced the room. "There is only just so much of it to go around, you know—this liberty. If one man is to have more, another must needs have less; for if one is to command, another must obey."

He held his hand before her, slowly tightening it into a fist. "So little by little, you steal it away, till your slightest whim is obeyed. You will have complete freedom, to do whatever you wish, but you alone will be free. There will be none of this liberty left over for your people. All, all, will be gathered unto Catharine."

His hand loosened and clasped her throat lightly. She stared and swallowed, pressing against the back of the chair.

"But a man cannot live without at least a little liberty," he said softly. "They must have it, or die." His hand tightened slowly. "They will rise up against you, made one by their common enemy—you. And then will squeeze their liberties out of you again, slowly, slowly."

Catharine tore at his hand, fighting for breath. Brom leaped to free her, But Rod loosed her first.

"They will hang you from your castle gates," he murmured, "and the nobles will rule in your stead; your work will all be undone. And of this you may be certain, for thus was it ever with tyrants."

Her head jerked up, hurt deep in her eyes. She gasped for breath to speak, shaking her head in ever harder denial.

"No, not I," she finally rasped. "Not that, no! Never a tyrant!"

"Always a tyrant," Rod corrected gently, "from your birth. Always a tyrant to those about you, though you never knew it till now."

He turned away, hands locked behind his back. "But now you know, and know also that you have none to blame but yourself for rebellion. You pushed them and pushed them, harder and harder, your nobles—for the good of your people, you said."

He looked back over his shoulder. "But was it not also to see which among them would dare say you nay? To see which among them were men?"

Contempt curdled her face. "Men!" The word was obscenity. "There are no men in Gramarye any more, only boys, content to be a woman's playpretties!"

He smiled, one-sided. "Oh, there be men still. Men in the South, and men in the House of Clovis—or one, at least, there. Men, my Queen, but gentle men, loving their Queen, and loath to strike at her."

Her lids lowered, the contempt playing over her lips in a smile. "It is as I have said: there are no men in Gramarye more."

"They are men," Rod answered, very quietly, "and they march north to prove it."

She stared.

Then slowly sat back. "Well, then, they march north, and I shall meet them on Breden Plain. Yet still there is none among them I would call man. Beasts, every one."

"Oh, you shall meet them." Rod gave her a syrupy, mocking smile. "And what shall you use for an army? And who will command it?"

"I will command," she replied hautily, "I and Brom. And there be five hundred of the Queen's Guard, and seven hundred of the Queen's Army, and threescore knights at my manors."

"Sixty knights!" Rod's lips tightened, pulling down at the corners. "Not even enough to give the Southern knights entertainment for one full charge! Sixty knights out of how many hundreds in your kingdom? And all the rest arrayed there against you! And twelve hundred footmen against the rebels' thousands!"

Her hands seized the arms of the chair in a spasm, to hide their trembling; fear drained her face of its color. "We shall win, for the honor of Plantagenet or Gramarye, or die nobly."

"I have yet," Rod said tightly, "to see a noble death in battle. They're all just a little on the messy side."

"Be still!" she snapped, then closed her eyes and bowed her head, knuckles whitening on the chair arms.

She rose, proud and calm again, and Rod couldn't help a brief, admiring thought for her spunk.

She sat at the table, drew up parchment and quill, scribbled a moment, then folded the parchment and held it out to Rod. "Bear this to my Uncle Loguire," she said. " 'Tis a command that he appear here before me, and a warrant of safe-conduct; for I bethink me that I shall need all loyal to me by my side ere greatly long."

Rod took the parchment and crumpled it slowly in his fist.

He flung it into the fire without taking his eyes from Catharine. "You shall write a letter to the Duke, and I shall bear it," he said in an antarctic voice; "but in it you shall beg of him the courtesy of an audience."

Her back stiffened and her chin came up. Rod warmed his voice hastily, smiling. "Come, come, my Queen! You already have all the liberty; can you not expend a little in courtesy?"

His eyes darkened, the smile faded. "Or will you be swept by the sin of pride, and allow your liberty to become license?"

He stepped a little closer, towering over her. "Will your people pay the price of your pride, my Queen? Or will you?"

She glared back at him a moment, but something inside her was clamoring for attention. She dropped her eyes and sat quiet a moment, then turned to the table again and wrote.

She folded the letter, sealed it, and held it out to him. He took it, bowed a little too deeply, with a click of the heels, and turned for the door.

He caught a quick scurry of movement along the baseboard out of the corner of his eye. He turned, saw a mouse duck under the tapestry, where it stayed very still.

Rod's jaw tightened. He crossed the room in two strides, lifted the tapestry.

The mouse looked up at him, its eyes very wide, very green, and very intelligent.

"I do not appreciate eavesdroppers," Rod said coldly.

The mouse flinched, but stared back defiantly.

Rod frowned at a sudden thought. Then his stern look melted. He picked the mouse up, gently, held it level with his eyes, with a tender look that did a very nice job of negating any image of dignity he might have built up.

He shook his head slowly. "You didn't really think I'd need help in here, did you?"

The mouse lowered its eyes, whiskers twitching a little.

"Certes," murmured Catharine, "methinks the man is possessed."

"Your Majesty," Brom said with a musing tone and a gleam in his eye, "may speak more truth than she knows."

The drawbridge echoed hollowly under Rod's striding feet. He ran lightly down the slope, away from the castle, and slipped into a copse of spruce.

"Fess," he called softly.

"Here, Rod." The great black steel horse came through the trees.

Rod smiled, slapped the metal side affectionately. "How the hell'd you know I'd come here?"

"Quite simply, Rod. An analysis of your behavior patterns, coupled with the fact that this grove is the closest to—"

"Skip it," Rod growled. "Big Tom took Loguire to the House of Clovis?"

"Affirmative, Rod."

Rod nodded. "Under the circumstances, it's probably the safest place for the Duke. What a comedown for a nobleman."

He swung into the saddle, then fumbled in his doublet and brought out the little mouse. It looked up at him apprehensively.

"Well," he sighed, "it doesn't seem to make any difference what I tell you to do; you're going to go right ahead and do whatever you want anyway."

The mouse lowered its eyes, trying to look guilty and ashamed; but its whiskers quivered with delight.

It rubbed its cheek against the skin of his palm.

"Affection will get you nowhere," Rod growled. "Now, listen. You go to the House of Clovis; that's where I'm bound. That's an order."

The mouse looked up at him with wide, innocent eyes.

"And it's one order I can be sure you'll obey," Rod went on, "since it's what you were going to do anyway. But, look!" A note of anxiety crept into his voice. "Be careful, will ya?"

He brought his hand forward and kissed the mouse's nose, very gently.

The mouse leaped, wriggled with delight, dancing gleeful on his hand; as it danced, it reared up, its front paws stretching and broadening into wings. Its tail fanned out; feathers sprouted on its body; its nose blurred and became a beak, and a wren was dancing on Rod's hand.

Rod caught his breath. "Uh . . . yeah," he said after a while. "That's just a little hard to take the first time I watch it happen. But don't worry, I'll get used to it."

The bird hopped from his hand, flew once around his head, hovered in front of him, then sprang arrowing into the sky.

Rod looked after the wren, murmured, "Do you think she'll do what I tell her this time, Fess?"

"She will." There was a strange quality to the robot's voice.

Rod looked sidewise at the great black head. "Thought robots couldn't laugh."

"A misconception," Fess replied.

"Git." Rod knocked his heels against the steel sides. Fess leaped into his long, steel canter.

"What else could I do?" Rod growled.

"With that lady," Fess answered, "nothing. But have no regrets, Rod. It's excellent policy. Many kings have used it."

"Yes," Rod mused. "And after all, being obeyed is the important thing, isn't it?"

Fess galloped silently into the moonlit courtyard on rubber-padded hooves and stopped abruptly. Rod's chest slammed against the horse's neck.

"Whuff!" He slammed back into the saddle. "Ohhhh! My tailbone! Look, Fess, warn me before you pull a stunt like that, will ya? Inertia may be just a nuisance to you, but it hits me right where I live."

"Where is that, Rod?"

"Never mind," Rod growled, dismounting. "Suffice to say that I just learned why the cavalry used split saddles."

He crossed the courtyard, glancing at the moon as he went. It was low in the sky; dawn was not far off.

He pounded on the door. There was a rustle of movement inside, then the door opened. The gnarled, bent figure of the Mocker stood before him.

"Aye, milord?" he said with a snaggle-toothed grin.

Wouldn't do to let him know that Rod knew he was the power behind the throne. Rod stepped in through the door, scarcely noticing the little man's presence. "Take me to the Lord Loguire, fellow."

"Certes, milord." The Mocker scurried around Rod and opened the inner door. Rod passed through it, pulling off his gauntlets . . . and stepped into the middle of a semicircle

210

of beggars and thieves, standing three deep and armed with truncheons and knives.

They grinned, their eyes hungry; here and there one licked his lips.

Their faces were dirty and scarred, mutilated and festering with sores; their clothes were threadbare, patched, torn; but their knives were remarkably well-kept.

Rod tucked his gloves into his belt, hands stiffening into karate swords, and turned to the Mocker. That worthy was now flanked by five or six prime samples of the lees of society.

"I come here in friendship." Rod's face was immobile.

"Do ye, now?" The Mocker grinned, exposing bleeding gums, and cackled. Suddenly his eyes gleamed with hate. "Declare yourself, lordling!"

Rod frowned. "Declare myself how?"

"For the noblemen, for the Queen, or for the House of Clovis!"

"Be done with your blathering!" Rod snapped. "I have small stomach for nonsense, and I'm beginning to feel very full. Take me to Loguire, *now!*"

"Oh, aye, that we shall. Yes, milord, at once, milord, straightaway." He rubbed his hands, chortling with glee. Then his glance darted over Rod's shoulder, and he nodded.

Rod started to turn, but something exploded on the back of his head. Stars reeled about him, then blackness.

Slowly, Rod became aware of pink light, pain, and a thousand discordant bass fiddles tuning up inside his head.

Slower yet, he became aware of something cold and slimy against his cheek. The pink light, he realized, was sunlight filtered through closed eyelids.

The pain pulled itself in and concentrated in his head. He winced, then by heroic measures managed to open his eyes, and winced again.

Everything was blurred, out of focus, sunlight and blobs of color.

The slime under his cheek was moss, and the coldness beneath it was stone.

He shoved hard with his hands; the slimy surface swung away, left him reeling, leaning on his hands heavily, stomach churning.

He shook his head, flinched at the pain, and blinked several times. His lids rasped over gummy eyeballs, but slowly his vision cleared. He forced his eyes to focus on . . . the face of Tuan Loguire.

Tuan sat with his back against black, old stone. There were huge iron staples in the stone, and the chains that hung from them ran to manacles on Tuan's wrists and ankles. He sat in a heap of dirty, moldering straw, in the watery light of a weak sunbeam.

Tuan smiled with irony as heavy as the rusty chains on his body, and lifted a hand in greeting, chain jangling with the movement. "Welcome."

Rod turned his eyes away, looking about him. The old Duke sat against the next wall, chained beside his son. "Cold welcome, Rod Gallowglass," the old lord mumbled, face heavy and brooding. "It is scant safety your serving-man has brought me to."

Treachery! Rod should have known better than to trust Tom. "Big Tom, you . . . !"

"Here, master."

Rod looked, turning; Big Tom sat against the far wall, chained like the rest of them.

Tom smiled sadly, bent a reproachful, bloodhound-eyed look on his master. "I had thought you would free us, master. Yet here art thou, chained one amongst us."

Rod scowled, looked down at his wrist, A rusty, thick iron band circled it. It had mates on his ankle and other wrist.

He looked up at Tom, smiled, and raised his hand, giving the chain a shake. "Ever hear tell that stone walls don't make a prison?"

"Who spoke those words was a fool," said Tom bitterly, from the shadows.

Rod lifted his eyes to the small, barred window set high in the wall. It was the only light in the room, a chamber perhaps ten feet wide by fifteen long, with a ten foot high ceiling, all moss-grown, rotting stone, floored with moldering straw.

The only decoration was a skeleton, held together by mummified ligament, chained to the wall like themselves.

Rod eyed the silent partner warily. "Not such great house-keepers, are they? They could at least have lugged the bones into the nether room."

He turned to the window again. "Fess," he mumbled, low enough so the others couldn't make out the words. "Fess, where are you?"

"In the most filthy, broken-down stable I've ever seen," the robot answered, "along with five of the sorriest nags outside of a glue factory. I think we're supposed to be the cavalry of the House of Clovis, Rod."

Rod chuckled softly. "Any mice with large green eyes running around, Fess?"

"No, Rod, but there is a wren perched on my head."

Rod grinned. "Ask her if she has any power over cold iron."

"How am I to speak with her, Rod?"

"Broadcast on human thought-wave frequency, of course! She's a telepath, you idiot savant!"

"Rod, I strongly resent the derogatory connotions of references to my abilities in areas in which I am not programmed to—"

"All right, all right, I'm sorry, I repent! You're a genius, a prodigy, an Einstein, an Urth! Just ask her, will you?"

There was a pause; then Rod heard a faint series of chirpings in the background.

"What's the chirping, Fess?"

"Gwendylon, Rod. She reacted significantly to the novel experience of telepathy with a horse."

"You mean she almost fell off her perch. But did she say anything?"

"Of course, Rod. She says that now she is certain you're a warlock."

Rod groaned and rolled his eyes up to the ceiling. "Look, get her back to business, will you? Can she get us out of these chains and cut the bars on our window?"

There was another pause; then Fess answered, "She says she has no power over cold iron, Rod, nor has any witch or elf that she knows. She suggests a blacksmith, but fears it is impractical."

"Genesis, Exodus, Leviticus . . . Well, tell her I'm glad she hasn't lost her sense of humor. And ask her how the hell she's going to get us out of here!"

"She says there is no need for hard language, Rod."

"You didn't have to transmit me literally, you bumblebrain!"

"And she thinks that the Prince of the Elves may be able to free you. She thinks he will come, but he is some short distance away, so it may be a while."

"I thought she said elves couldn't handle cold iron!"

There was another pause; then Fess said, "She says that the Prince of the Elves is not quite an elf, Rod, being but half of the Old Blood."

"Only half . . . Wait a minute!" Rod scowled. "You mean he's a half-breed between elf and mortal?"

"Precisely, Rod."

Rod tried to imagine how an eighteen-inch elf and a six-foot mortal could have a child; his brain reeled.

"She departs now, Rod, to summon him, and will return as quickly as she may, but will be a while. She bids you be of stout heart."

"If my heart were any stouter, it'd be positively obese! Give her my . . . No, just tell her I thank her, Fess."

He seemed to hear a faint sigh behind his ear, and the robot said, with a touch of resignation, "I'll tell her, Rod."

"Thanks, Fess. Stay lively."

Rod turned back to his prison. The Loguires were both plastered against the wall, looking at him strangely.

"He speaks to thin air," murmured Tuan. "Certes, the man is possessed!"

"Seems to me I've heard that before," Rod mused, "and the air in here is anything but thin."

"Still," muttered Loguire, " 'tis the act of one crazed!"

Big Tom rumbled a laugh. "Not so, my lords. This man speaks with spirits."

Rod smiled bleakly. "How come so cheerful all of a sudden, Big Tom?"

The big man stretched, chains clashing. "I had thought for a moment they had beaten you, master. Now I know 'twas fool thinking."

"Don't be so sure, Tom. Cold iron is a tough spell to break."

"Nay, master." Tom's eyelids drooped lazily. "Thou'lt find a way to it, I warrant."

He clasped his hands over his belly, leaned his head back against the wall.

Rod smiled as Tom began snoring. He looked at the Loguires and jerked his head toward Tom. "There's confidence for you. While I work things out, he takes a nap."

"Let us hope 'tis a faith warranted," said Tuan. He eyed Rod dubiously.

"Let's," Rod echoed grimly.

He nodded at the Duke. "Been renewing acquaintance?"

Loguire smiled. "I rejoice to see my son again, though I had lief it were more open welcome."

Tuan frowned at his hands. "It is sad news he hath brought me, Rod Gallowglass, most sad and sorrowful." He looked

214

at Rod, bright anger in his face. "I had known my brother hateful and ambitious, but I had not thought he would sink into treason."

"Oh, don't be too hard on the poor boy." Rod leaned back against the wall, closing his eyes wearily. "Durer's got him spellbound. And if his magic came so close on the father, how could it fail on the son?"

"Aye," Tuan agreed darkly. "Myself had fallen like prey to the Mocker."

"Oh?" Rod opened one eye. "You've realized that, have you?"

"Oh, aye! A most excellent villain is that! He will bow him most humbly before you, while his henchman is slitting your purse—and thus hath he served me!"

Rod pursed his lips. "He's the one who gave you the idea for organizing the beggars?"

"Aye." Tuan nodded heavily. "I had first thought only to provide them relief from hunger and chill; but his word in my ear made me think of an army, for defense of the Queen. And I had seen and heard in the South that which led me to think such an army might well be needed."

The old Duke made a choking sound.

"Pardon, my father," said Tuan, bowing his head, "but I knew even thou couldst not check them forever. But I had not thought"—and his voice hardened—" 'twould be trea-son from Anselm."

Rod twisted, feeling decidedly uncomfortable. "Well, as I said, you shouldn't blame him too much. After all, he did try to keep Durer from killing your father."

He stretched his legs and crossed them. "So when the Mocker learned that the South was up in arms, he decided it was time to assert his rightful authority and overthrow the Queen. Right?"

"Aye." Tuan's lips tightened as though he had his first taste of straight vermouth. "When I spoke against, saying that 'twas our time to defend the Queen, he called me traitor, and"—he frowned, words coming very hard—"one of the beggars would ha' slain me. But the Mocker would not hear of it; no, he threw me here without food or fire."

He looked up at Rod, frowning. "Which is most truly strange, Rod Gallowglass. Would not you ha' thought he would ha' killed me himself?"

"No." Rod closed his eyes, shaking his head. "He needs

somebody to be figurehead king after they've pulled down Catharine."

"Nay, not a king," Tuan said, brooding. "He cries that we shall ne'er have a king more, but only a sort of chieftain, raised by acclaim of the people."

" 'A sort of chieftain.' " Rod scowled. "What name does he call this chieftain by?"

"Dictator." Tuan chewed at the inside of his cheek. "A most strange title. There shall be no nobles or king, only the dictator. In all truth, most strange."

Rod's mouth tightened with sourness. "Not so strange as all that. But you don't mean to say the beggars think they can take the castle?"

"Nay, but it is known that the South is in arms, and Catharine was never one to be waiting till the battle was brought to her."

"Oh." Rod chewed that one over. "You mean the Mocker's pretty sure she'll march south to meet them?"

"Most assuredly. And the Mocker will march south behind her."

Rod nodded. "So when the armies join battle, the beggars will attack the royal forces from the rear."

"Ever their way," rumbled Loguire.

Tuan nodded agreement. "And caught between two forces, her armies will last scarce half an hour."

"And what does the Mocker propose to do about the councillors and noblemen after the battle's over? Durer means to make your brother king."

"So it would seem," Tuan agreed, "but the Mocker hath an answer to that, and to all the noblemen."

"Oh?" Rod raised an eyebrow.

"Aye, 'Tis a tube of metal fitted into a crossbow stock, nothing more; but it throws a ball of lead which can pierce the stoutest armor."

"And he means to put one of these into the hands of every man in the army?"

"Oh, nay." Tuan frowned. "He hath but the five of them, one for himself, one for each of his three lieutenants, and one for his fourth lieutenant." Tuan jerked his head toward Tom's recumbent mountain form. "But that one hath lately fallen into disfavor. He assures us the five tubes shall answer for the full force of noblemen and councillors."

But Rod was staring at Tom. "Big Tom?" He gulped. "A lieutenant?"

"Aye." Tuan frowned. "Did you not know he was of Clovis?"

Tom opened one hound's eye and looked back at Rod.

Rod looked away, cleared his throat, and pursed his lips. "Well, ah, that does explain a few things."

He switched his eyes back to Tom. "So you're part of the Inner Circle?"

Big Tom smiled sourly and held up one lumber forearm. The chain clashed and rattled. "Was," he said.

"He stood against them," rumbled Loguire, "stood against his fellows and this—how do you name him? The Mocker—stood against the Mocker and his three jackals when they commanded I be 'prisoned with my son. 'Nay,' quoth your man Tom, 'I must needs take him back to my master, where he will be aid to your plans.' 'The plans are changed,' quoth they, and would not hear of enlarging me; and then your man Tom, here, fought cheek by jowl at my side, and accounted for a most goodly number of them." This last was said in a tone of surprised respect.

Tom grinned, and Rod saw with a shock that one tooth was missing from the big man's smile. "Thou art braw brawler tha'self," Tom chuckled. "I ha' not thought gentlemen could fight so well without armor or sword."

Rod peered into the shadows at Tom's end of the room and saw that the big man's eye was swollen and purple; also, there was a slash with a new scab across one lumpy cheek.

He sat back, smiling on one side of his face. "How many heads did you bash in, Big Tom?"

"Scarce a round score," Tom replied with disgust. "I had but this one stalwart gentleman to guard my back, and there were too many for us."

Rod grinned, wondering if Loguire knew just how deeply he had been complimented.

He stretched, yawned. "Well, that pretty well brings us up to date. Anybody got a poker deck?"

The two Loguires frowned, puzzled; but a flicker of recognition passed in Big Tom's eyes.

Rod smiled sourly at the big peasant, and Tom's face turned wooden. He stared back at Rod.

"Oh, come on now, Tom!" Rod snapped. "Your secret's official knowledge now. No more point to playing games, is there?"

Tom glowered at him; then slowly, his face livened again, to a brooding, meditative look.

He leaned back against the wall, half closing his eyes. "Aye, tha hast the right of it, as when hast thou not?"

With a sinking feeling, Rod began to realize that Big Tom saw him as more than just an employer, or a piece in the game.

"My lot is cast with thee now," said Tom, "whether I would have it or no; so wherefore should I dissemble?"

"Dissemble?" Rod cocked an eyebrow at his serving-man. "Pretty high-falutin' vocabulary for a simple peasant, Big Tom."

Tom waved a hand impatiently. "Be done with your games! I am unmasked; do me the courtesy to take off your own."

Rod froze.

Then, slowly, he smiled. "You're quicker than the average ursine, Big Tom. How long have you known?"

The Loguires stared, totally lost.

Big Tom gave a short bark of laughter. "Why, master, since first you used judo on me!"

"Ah." Rod's eyebrows lifted. "From the first, then? So that's why you wangled the batman job."

Tom smiled lazily.

"Under orders?"

Tom nodded.

Rod lowered his eyes, studying the chain on his wrist. "What are you, master?"

"A warlock." Rod winced inside; but it was the best answer under the circumstances.

Big Tom spat. "Games, master, games! 'Twas yourself said to be done with 'em! You are not of the councillors, else you would not ha' stolen the Lord Loguire away from them; and you are not of the House, or I would ha' known you of old. What are you, then?"

"A warlock," Rod repeated. "A new player in the game, Big Tom, and one who stands squarely behind the Queen. X, the unknown factor in the councillors' and Clovis' equations, here by pure happenstance and coincidence."

"Warruh!" Big Tom spat again. "I ha' small faith in happenstance, master. I ha' known that you back the Queen; may I ask who stands behind you?"

"Strange manner of talk," growled Loguire, angering, "for a footman to his lord."

Rod smiled bleakly. "A most strange footman, my lord."

"Aye, and a most strange lord," Tom snarled. "Who backs you, Rod Gallowglass?"

Rod studied the big man, then shrugged. The word would mean nothing to the Loguires, and Tom was on his side now anyway.

"SCENT," he answered.

Tom stared; then, almost whispering, he said, "I ha' thought the last of them were dead." He swallowed, bit his lip. "Eh, but tha'rt alive. Tha might be a ghost, but nay; tha'rt alive, or the witch would scarce be so fond of thee. I ha' heard ye were dispersed, after ye won; but nay, I ought to ha' known. 'Twas secret, and secret from all, mayhap; but thou lived."

"Won?" Rod frowned.

And was answered by a frown of even deeper perplexity from Tom.

Then the big man's face cleared. He grinned, rocking back against the wall, and roared laughter.

The Loguires stared from him to Rod, who spread his hands, shaking his head. They looked back at Tom, wiping his eyes and eking the remains of his laugh into chuckles. "Eh, eh, now I see it, aye, now, and fool that I was not to see it before. What age art thou, master?"

"Age?" Rod scowled. "Thirty-two. Why?"

"Nay, nay!" Tom shook his head impatiently. "What age art thou *from?*"

Rod's mouth formed a round, silent O as the light dawned. "It *was* a time machine!"

Big Tom's face froze as he realized the implications of Rod's answer.

"And," Rod pressed, "there's another one hidden in this building, isn't there?"

"Enough!" Big Tom snapped, and his eyes were very cold. "You know too much already, Rod Gallowglass."

Fear gathered in Rod's belly and crawled up his spine as he saw chill, amoral murder come into the man's eyes.

"Big Tom." He cleared his throat, spoke in a swift, driving monotone. "Big Tom, your own kind have turned against you now. You owe them no allegiance; and the wrongs they said they'd fix, I can fix, too. Go back to them, and they'll kill you. I won't, you know that."

The annihilation ebbed from Tom's eyes, the huge body relaxed.

"Nay," Tom growled, "thou hast right again, though not in the way tha knowest. They ha' but bottled me up for now, till the great deeds are done; but they will hale me forth again, for I am too costly a man to discard so lightly. But tha'rt right they will slay me—in a year, two years, or five, when my office is done. And I do wish to live."

Rod raised an eyebrow skeptically. "They don't doubt your loyalty?"

Big Tom chuckled deeply. "They ha' no need to, master. I disagree only on means, not on goals. But I disagree, and for that, soon or late, they will slay me."

"Rod," said a quiet voice that only he could hear.

Rod held up a hand. "Hold it! Late news on the Rialto!"

"Rod, the Prince of the Elves has arrived. He is leading a squad of elves toward your cell." There was a touch of laughter to the robot's voice.

"All right, what's so funny?" Rod muttered.

"You have a surprise in store, Rod."

Two gnarled, bent, white-bearded figures scurried up to the window. Rod frowned.

"Fess, those are gnomes, not elves."

"Gnomes? Oh, yes, metal-working elves. Purely semantics, Rod. They are still incapable of dealing with iron."

The gnomes pulled out a hammer and cold chisel with a faint bronze sheen, then stepped back and handed them to a larger, darker figure that blocked out the sunlight.

The Loguires, chained under the window, craned their necks backward to try to see as the first blow sounded.

Big Tom frowned. "There be something that pricks at my memory about that form at the window. Ah, for light, to see his face!"

Rod frowned. "What's so great about his face? Probably pretty ugly."

Tom gave a toothy grin. " 'Twould be excellent fine to tell my children, good master, if I should live long enough to sire them. No mortal has yet looked upon the faces of the royalty of the Elves, though they are said to be aged past believing. They are . . . uh . . . ah . . . mmmmmm!"

Tom's head lolled forward; he began to snore.

Two other snores answered him. Turning, Rod saw the Loguires, chins on their chests, sleeping blissfully.

Rod stared.

A metal bar dropped from the window and bounced on the floor. The ends were sheered through.

Rod whistled. This Prince of the Elves might be old, but he certainly wasn't languishing—not if he could still cut through inch-thick iron with nothing but a cold chisel and a mallet.

The third bar fell down. There was a scrabbling sound, and the squat, broad form shot through the window and leaped to the floor.

Rod stared, squeezed his eyes shut, and shook his head. Then he looked again, and understood why Tom and the Loguires had suddenly dozed off.

He swallowed, fought for composure, and smiled. "Well met, Brom O'Berin."

"At your service." The little man bowed, smiling maliciously. "I owe you a rap on the head, Master Gallowglass, for the way that you spoke to the Queen: a rap on the head, or great thanks, I know not which."

He turned to the window and called softly in a strange, fluid tongue. The cold chisel arced through the air and fell to his feet. He reached up and caught the hammer as it dropped.

"Now, then." He dropped to his knees and pressed Rod's forearm flat against the floor. "Stir not, or thou'lt have a gouge out of thy wristbone." He set the chisel against the first link of chain and tapped lightly with the hammer. The link fell off, sheared through. Brom grunted and moved to Rod's other side.

"Thou'lt wear bracelets when I've done," he grumbled, "but no chains. The manacles must wait till we're at the castle smithy."

"Uh . . . that's pretty hard bronze you've got there," Rod ventured, watching the chisel slide through the iron.

"Most hard," Brom agreed, attacking the ankle chains. "An old recipe, known long in my family."

"Uh . . . in your family?"

"Aye." Brom looked up. "There were elves in lost Greece, too, Rod Gallowglass. Didst thou not know?"

Rod didst not; but he didn't figure this was the time to mention it.

He stood up, free of the chains at least, and watched Brom cutting the others loose. The Prince of the Elves bit explained a lot about Brom: his size and bulk, for one thing.

"Never knew you were royalty, Brom."

"Hm?" Brom looked back over his shoulder. "I would have thought thou'd have guessed it. Why else am I named as I am?"

He turned back to his work. Rod frowned. Name? What

221

did that have to do with anything? Brom? O'Berin? He couldn't see the connection.

"There, the last," said Brom, cutting through Big Tom's foot shackle. "Do thou now lend me aid of thine shoulder, Master Gallowglass."

He jumped back out through the window. Rod got a shoulder in Tom's midriff and, staggering, somehow manhandled him over to the window as a rope flew through.

Rod tied it under Tom's arms, threw the loose end out, and called "Heave!"

He heard Brom grunt, and marveled again at the little man's muscles as Big Tom moved jerkily up the wall, still snoring happily.

What with the beerbelly and the muscles, and the minimal size of the window, Big Tom was a tight fit.

"Why don't you just wake him and let him shove himself out?" Rod grunted as he shoved at Tom's ample rear.

"I have no wish for my office to be known among mortals," came Brom's muffled reply.

The window now framed only Tom's sizable posterior and sequoia shanks. Rod eyed the former, weighing the merits of a well-placed kick, and decided against it.

"So why'd you let me stay awake?" he grunted as he pushed.

"One amongst you must needs aid me with the others," answered Brom, but Rod had a notion that wasn't quite the whole story.

He left off the questions, however, until his cellmates were deposited on the ground outside the window. Tuan's shoulders had proved even more of an obstacle than Tom's belly; they had to back him up, feed his hands through in front of his head, while Rod wondered fleetingly about brachiator ancestry.

Then Brom hauled Rod out, muttering something about the fish being undersized these days. Rod snarled a return compliment as he gained his feet, then bowed double, putting his head on Brom's level.

"And what's that for?" Brom growled.

"For belting," Rod answered. "You owe me a rap on the head, remember?"

The dwarf chuckled, clapped him on the shoulder. "Nay, lad; you did only that which I should ha' done myself years ago; but I had never the heart. But come now, we must away."

Brom caught up Tuan's midsection. The gnomes took his shoulders and feet, and bore him away toward the ruined fountain in the center of the courtyard.

More gnomes materialized out of the stonework and tucked their shoulders under Big Tom.

Rod shook his head wonderingly, and stooped to sling Loguire over a shoulder.

Brom fumbled with a stone at the fountain's base and pulled it away to disclose the dark mouth of a small tunnel three feet in diameter.

Rod tapped Brom on the shoulder. "Wouldn't this be a little easier if we woke them first?"

Brom stared, scandalized; then his face darkened. "We go to Elfland, Master Gallowglass! And no mortal may journey there and remember it!"

"I have."

"Well, truth," Brom admitted, turning back to the Tuan problem, "but then thou'rt not so mortal as some. Thou'rt a warlock." He disappeared into the burrow.

Rod started to reply, then thought better of it. He contented himself with a few grunted remarks about discrimination and a report to the Human Rights Commission as he lugged Loguire into the tunnel.

Two gnomes started to swing the stone back into place, but Rod stopped them with an upraised hand.

"Fess," he murmured, looking at the stable, "we're on our way. Get out of that hole and meet me at the castle."

There was a moment's silence; then a crash and the sound of splintering wood came from the stables. The door crashed open, and the great black horse came trotting out into the morning sunlight, head held high, mane streaming.

Heads popped out of slit-windows in the inn as a bleary-eyed hostler came stumbling out of the stable in Fess's wake, screaming for the horse to stop.

"Come on, get moving!" Rod growled, but instead, Fess stopped and looked back over his shoulder at the hostler.

The youth came running up, shouting, one hand outstretched to grab Fess's bridle.

A great, blue electric spark crackled from Fess's hide to the youth's hand.

The hostler screamed and fell backward, nursing his hand and moaning as he rolled on the cobbles. Fess was off in a swirl and a clatter of hooves.

"Show-off," Rod growled as the horse disappeared.

"Not at all, Rod," came the horse's quiet answer. "Merely providing an instructive object lesson—at low amperage, it shook him up but didn't hurt him—and enhancing your reputation as a warlock."

Rod shook his head slowly. "As if it needed enhancing!"

"Why, Master Gallowglass," one of the gnomes chuckled in a voice strongly reminiscent of a rusty can opener, "wouldst thou have us believe thou'rt *not* a warlock?"

"Yes! Uh, that is, I, uh . . ." Rod glanced back at the tunnel. "Warlock? Of course I'm a warlock! Till we get through Elfland, anyway. Shall we go, boys?"

Not so very much later, they sat around the fire in the Queen's council chamber. Catharine had apologized profusely to Loguire, pointedly ignoring Tuan the while; and, the amenities over, reverted to type.

Tuan sat to the left of the fireplace, eyes fixed in brooding on the flames.

Catharine sat in the angle of the room, as far from Tuan as possible, with a heavy oak table and Brom O'Berin carefully interposed between.

". . . and that is full standing in the South, my Queen," said Loguire, gnarled hands twisting as he wound up his report, which had abounded in nuances of intrigue that Rod couldn't follow at all. "I am no longer duke; and the rebel lords march already."

Catharine stirred. "Thou shalt be Duke Loguire again," she stated coldly, "when we have beaten these traitors!"

Loguire smiled sadly. "They shall not be easily beaten, Catharine."

" 'Your Majesty'!" she snapped.

" 'Catharine'!" Rod barked.

She glared at him.

He glared back.

Catharine turned haughtily away. "What am I, Brom?"

" 'Your Majesty,' " Brom answered with the ghost of a smile. "But to your uncle, and to his son, your cousin, you must needs be Catharine."

Rod fought down a smile as Catharine sank back in her chair, staring aghast at Brom.

She composed herself, and gave Brom the best et tu, Brute? look in her repertoire. "I had thought you were for me, Brom O'Berin."

"Why, so I am," Brom smiled, "and so is this gyrfalcon,

here"—he jerked a thumb toward Rod—"if you would but see it."

Catharine favored Rod with a cold glance. "A gyrfalcon, aye." Her voice hardened. "And what of the poppinjay?"

Tuan's head shot up as though he'd been slapped. He stared at her, appalled, eyes wide with hurt.

Then his mouth tightened, and a crease appeared between his eyebrows.

Some day, Rod thought, *she will push him just a little too far, and that may be the luckiest day of her life—if she lives through it.*

"I am for you," Tuan breathed. "Even now, Catharine my Queen."

She smiled, smug and contemptuous. "Aye, I had known you would be."

Oh, bitch! Rod thought, his fist tightening. *Bitch!*

Catharine noticed the silent motions of his lips.

She smiled archly. "What words do you mumble there, sirrah?"

"Oh, ah, just running through a breath-exercise my old voice-and-diction coach taught me." Rod leaned back against the wall, folding his arms. "But about the rebels, Queenie dear, just what do you propose to do about them?"

"We shall march south," she snapped, "and meet them on Breden Plain!"

"Nay!" Loguire bolted from his chair. "Their force is ten to our one, if not more!"

Catharine glared at her uncle, the corners of her mouth curled into tight little hooks. "We shall not stay to be found like a rat in a crevice!"

"Then," said Rod, "you will lose."

She looked down her nose at him (no mean trick, when she was seated and he was standing). "There is naught of dishonor in that, Master Gallowglass."

Rod struck his forehead and rolled his eyes up.

"What else ought I do?" she sneered. "Prepare for a siege?"

"Well, now that you mention it," said Rod, "yes."

"There is this, too," Tuan put in, his voice flat. "Who shall guard your back 'gainst the House of Clovis?"

Her lip curled. "Beggars!"

"Beggars and cutthroats," Rod reminded her. "With very sharp knives."

"Shall the Queen fear a beggar?" she snapped. "Nay! They are dust at my feet!"

"That which crawls in the dust at your feet is a snake," Brom rumbled, "and its fangs are sharpened, and poisonous."

She caught her lip between her teeth and lowered her eyes, uncertain; then she lifted her chin again, and glared at Tuan.

"So you have armed them against me, and beaten them into an army, ruled and ordered and forged them into a dagger for my back! Most bravely well done, King of Vagabonds!"

Rod's head snapped up. He stared. He turned his head slowly toward Tuan, a strange light in his eyes.

"I will march," said Catharine. "Will you march at my side, my Lord Loguire?"

The old lord bent his head slowly in affirmation. "You play the fool, Catharine, and will die; but I will die with you."

Her composure wavered for a moment; her eyes moistened. She turned briskly to Brom. "And you, Brom O'Berin?"

The dwarf spread his hands. "Your father's watchdog, milady, and yours."

She smiled fondly.

Then her eyes snapped hard as she looked at Tuan. "Speak, Tuan Loguire."

The youth raised his eyes, very slowly, to the fires. "It is strange," he murmured, "at but twenty-two years of age, to look back over so very short a time, and see so much folly."

Rod heard a choked gasp from Catharine.

Tuan slapped his thigh. "Well, then, 'tis done; and if I have lived in folly, I might as well die in it."

He turned, his eyes gentle, brooding. "I shall die with you, Catharine."

Her face was ashen. "Folly . . ." she whispered.

"He knows not what wisdom he speaks," Brom growled. He looked over Tuan's shoulder at Rod. "What say you to folly, Rod Gallowglass?"

Rod's eyes slowly focused on Brom's. " 'Wise fool, brave fool,' " he murmured.

Brom frowned. "How say you?"

"I say that we may yet live through this!" Rod grinned, eyes kindling. "Ho, King of the Vagabonds!" He slapped Tuan's shoulder. "If the Mocker and his henchmen were gone, could you sway the beggars to fight for the Queen?"

Tuan's face came alive again. "Aye, assuredly, were they gone!"

Rod's lips pulled back in a savage grin. "They shall be."

The moon was riding high when Rod, Tuan, and Tom darted from the shadow of the tottering wall to the shadow of the ruined fountain in the courtyard of the House of Clovis.

"Thou wouldst make most excellent burglars, thou," growled Big Tom. "I might ha' heard thee a league or three away."

It hadn't been easy to persuade Tom to come along. Of course, Rod had started on the wrong tack; he'd assumed Tom's loyalties to the proletarian idea had died when he was clapped into irons. He'd clapped Tom on the back, saying, "How'd you like a chance to get back at your friends?"

Tom had scowled. "Get back at 'em?"

"Yeah. They booted you out, didn't they? Threw you in the calaboose, didn't they? After your blood now, ain't they?"

Tom chuckled, "Nay, master, not by half! Eh, no! They'd ha' freed me when the trouble was done!"

"Oh." Rod scowled. "I see. Trained men are hard to come by."

Tom's face darkened. "Thou seest too quick for my liking."

"Well, be that as it may . . ." Rod slung an arm around the big man's shoulder, almost dislocating his arm in the process. "Uh, in that case . . . what did they lock you up for?"

Tom shrugged. "Disagreement."

"Ways and means, eh?"

"Aye. They held for attacking Queen and nobles both at one time, though 'twould mean dividing of forces."

"Sounds risky. What did you want to do?"

"Why, to bring down the noblemen and their councillors first, under guise of loyalty to the throne. Then we might slowly woo all the land to the House of Clovis, and, secured by the people, pull down the Queen and Brom O'Berin with two blows of a knife."

Rod swallowed and tried to remember that the man was on his side now. "Very neat." He slapped Tom on the back. "Spoken like a good little Bolshevik. How much does that way of doing things mean to you, Tom?"

Big Tom gave him a long, calculating look. "What price were you minded of, master?"

Rod grinned. "Shall we throw your four colleagues in the cell they'd reserved for you?"

" 'Twould be pleasant," said Tom slowly. "What comes after, master?"

"Why, then," said Rod, "the House of Clovis fights on the

Queen's side, against the nobles. That gives you a better chance of beating the councillors and nobles; after afterward, you can follow through with your own plan."

Tom nodded, slowly. "But will the beggars fight for the Queen?"

"That, we leave to Tuan Loguire."

Tom's face stretched into a huge grin. He threw back his head and roared, slapping Rod on the back.

Rod picked himself up off the floor, hearing Big Tom gasp between spasms of laughter, "Eh, I should ha' thought of it, master! Aye, that boy will charm them! You know not the powers of that silver tongue, master. The lad could make a leopard believe it had no spots!"

Rod held his peace, trying to remember if he'd seen a leopard on Gramarye, while he tried to rub the sore spot between his shoulders.

"Thou'll twist thine arm loose that way." Tom grinned. He turned Rod around and began to massage his back. "Thou knowest, master, if together we bring down the councillors, 'twill be thy head, alongside Brom's and the Queen's, that I'll next be a-chasing."

Rod closed his eyes, savoring the massage. "It oughta be a great fight. A little further to the left, Big Tom."

So now they stood in the shadows of the fountain with Tuan between them, planning assault on the moldering heap of stone that stood across a moon-filled expanse of courtyard.

Rod counted his pulse beats, wondering if his heart had really slowed that much, until Tom whispered, "No alarm. They ha' not seen us, good masters. Ready thyselves, now."

Tom gathered himself, looking like a diesel semi that had decided to turn cat-burglar.

"Now!" he growled, and ran.

They charged lightly, quietly, through the seeming glare of the moonlight to the welcoming shadow of the walls, then flattened themselves against the stone, hearts thudding, breath held as they strained their ears for some sound of alarm.

After a small eternity of three minutes, Big Tom loosed his breath in a great, gusty sigh.

"Eh, then, lads!" he hissed. "Come along, now."

They crept around the corner of the great dank stone pile. Big Tom splayed his fingers out wide, set his elbow at the corner of the wall, and marked the spot where his second finger ended. He put his other elbow against the mark.

"Big Tom!" Rod called in an agonized whisper, "we don't have time for—"

"Hsst!" Tuan's fingers clamped on Rod's shoulder. "Silence, I pray thee! He measures in cubits!"

Rod shut up, feeling rather foolish.

Tom made a few more measurements, which apprently resulted in his finding what he was looking for. He pulled a pry from the pouch at his belt and began to lever at the base of a three-foot block.

Rod stared, uncomprehending. It would take all night and most of the next day to dig the block out. What was Tom trying to do?

Tom gave a last pry, and caught the sheet of stone as it fell outward. It was perhaps an inch thick.

He laid the slab on the ground and looked up at his companions. His grin flashed chill in the moonlight. "I had thought I might have need of a bolthole one day," he whispered. "Gently now, lads."

He ducked head and arms through the hole, kicked off with his feet, and slithered through.

Rod swallowed hard and followed Tom. Tuan came through at his heels.

"All in?" Tom whispered as Tuan's feet stood hard to the floor, and the moonlight was cut off as Tom fitted the stone plug back into place.

"Light," he whispered. Rod cupped his hand over the hilt of his dagger and turned it on, letting a ray of light escape between two fingers. It was enough to see Big Tom grope up a worm-eaten panel from the floor and fit it back into place in the bolthole.

Tom straightened, grinning. "Now let them wonder at our coming. To work, masters."

He turned away. Rod followed, looking quickly about him.

They were in a large stone room that had once been paneled. The panels were crumbled and fallen away for the most part. The room held only cobwebs, rusty iron utensils, and long trestle tables, spongy now with rot.

" 'Twas a kitchen, once," Tom murmured. "They cook at the hearth in the common room, now. None ha' used this place for threescore years or more."

Rod shuddered. "What's a good kid like you doing in a place like this, Tom?"

Big Tom snorted.

"No, I mean it," said Rod urgently. "You can judge a god, an ideal, by the people who worship it, Tom."

"Be still!" Tom snapped.

"It's true, though, isn't it? The councillors are all rotten, we know that. And the Mocker and his buddies are lice. You're the only good man in the bunch. Why don't you—"

"Be still!" Tom snarled, swinging about so suddenly that Rod blundered into him. Rod felt the huge, hamlike hand grabbing a fistful of his doublet, right at the throat, and smelled the beery, garlic reek of Tom's breath as the man thrust his face close to Rod's.

"And what of the Queen?" Tom hissed. "What says she for her gods, eh?"

He let Rod go, with a shove that threw him back against the wall, and turned away.

Rod collected himself and followed, but not before he had caught a glimpse of Tuan's eyes, narrowed and chill with hate, in the beam of the torch.

"We approach a corner," Tom muttered. "Dampen the light."

The torch winked out; a few moments later, Rod felt the stone wall fall away under his left hand. He turned, and saw a faint glow at the end of the blackened, short hallway ahead.

Big Tom stopped, " 'Tis a corner again, and a sentry beyond. Walk wary, lads."

He moved away again, stepping very carefully. Rod followed, feeling Tuan's breath hot on the back of his neck.

As they neared the corner, they heard a rhythm of faint snores to their right, from the new hallway.

Big Tom flattened himself against the wall with a wolfish grin. Rod followed suit . . . and drew away with a gasp and a convulsive shudder.

Tom scowled at him, motioning for silence.

Rod looked at the wall and saw a thick blob of grayish-white stuff fastened to the wall. It had brushed the back of his neck, and he could say with authority that the texture was flaccid, the touch cold and moist.

He looked at the obscene glop and shuddered gain.

" 'Tis but witch-moss, Rod Gallowglass," Tuan whispered in his ear.

Rod frowned. "Witch-moss?"

Tuan stared, incredulous. "Thou'rt a warlock, and knowest not witch-moss?"

Rod was saved from an answer by the cessation of the snores from around the corner.

The trio caught their collective breath and flattened themselves against the wall, Rod carefully avoiding the witchmoss. Tom glared at his sidekicks.

The moment of silence stretched out as thin as the content of a congressman's speech.

"Hold!" shouted a voice from around the corner.

Their muscles snapped tight in a spasm.

"Where do you go at this hour?" the sentry's voice snarled.

Dread clambered its way up Rod's spine.

A quaking, nasal voice answered the sentry. "Nay, I do but seek the jakes!"

The three men let their breath out in a long, silent sigh.

"*Sir*, when yer speak to a soldier!

"Sir," the whining voice echoed, surly.

"What was your reason for walking past curfew?" the sentry threatened in ominous tones.

"I do but seek the jakes, *sir*," the nasal voice whined.

The sentry chuckled, mollified. "And the jakes are near to the women's hall? Nay, I think not! Back to your pallet, scum! Your doxie's not for you this night!"

"But I—"

"Nay!" the guard snapped. "You do know the rule, fellow. Do you ask of the Mocker first." The voice became almost confidential. " 'Tain't so much as all that, chum. Like as not he'll give yer the paper says yer can do't, an' set yer a fit place an' time. He's free 'nough about it."

The nasal one hawked and spat.

"Come on, now," the guard growled. "Yer've but to ask of him."

"Aye," sneered the nasal voice, "and ask again every night that I'm wishin' to see her! Hell, 'twas the one thing in this world that came cheap!"

The guard's voice hardened again. "The Mocker's word is the law in this House, and my club'll remind you of it, if my word's not enough!"

There was a pause, then an angry, despairing snarl, and feet padded away.

There was silence again; after a while, the guard began to snore again.

Rod glanced at Tuan. The boy's face was dead white, lips pressed so tight the color'd gone out of them.

231

"I take it you didn't know anything about this?" Rod whispered.

"Nay," Tuan whispered back. "Once they'd set me by, they wasted no time. A guard at each hall, a writ ere two may share a bed—this is worse than the lords of the South!"

Tom's head jerked up. "Nay!" he snarled. " 'Tis but inconvenience. The gains to be got from it are well worth the price."

For his part, Rod agreed with Tuan. Police state, control over every facet of the people's lives—yes, the Mocker's Marxism was showing.

"What gains are worth *that* price?" Tuan snorted, raising his whisper a trifle.

"Why," growled Big Tom, at minimum bullfrog volume, "more food for all, more and better clothing, none poor and none starving."

"And all thanks to planned parenthood," Rod murmured, with an apprehensive glance at the corner.

"And how may this come?" asked Tuan, hiking his voice another notch and ignoring Rod's frantic signals. "From a writ of consent for a lovemaking? I cannot see how!"

Tom's lip twisted in scorn, and the bullfrog croaked louder. "Nay, you cannot! But the Mocker can!"

Tuan stared; then his jaw tightened, and his hand slipped to his dagger. "Do you place yourself and your kind above a nobleman, churl?"

"Uh, gentlemen," Rod whispered.

Big Tom tensed, grinning; his eyes danced mockery. "Blood will tell," he said, full voice.

Tuan's dagger leaped out as he sprang.

Tom lugged out his minor sword.

Rod threw out his hands, stiff-arming both of them at the collarbone. "Gentlemen, *gentle*men! I realize you both feel very strongly about the issues at hand; but it is my bounden duty to remind you that a sentry fully capable of bringing the wrath of the House down on our heads is dozing, and not too heavily either, just around the corner!"

"This is not to be borne, Rod Gallowglass!"

"Aye," chuckled Big Tom, "the truth was ever hard to bear."

Tuan lunged, trying to stab at Tom over Rod's head. Rod shoved back on the boy's collarbone and ducked as the knife arced past his head.

Tom chuckled softly. "There is a nobleman for you! A fool

could see the reach is too great! Ever will he overreach himself, when he knows he must fail."

Rod eyed Tom sideways. "You're slipping, Big Tom. That was almost a compliment."

"Nay!" Tom hissed, his eyes fire. "To attempt the impossible is the act of a fool! The nobles are fools, and the roads to their utopias are paved with the bones of the peasants!"

Tuan spat. "And what else are they—"

"Be still!" Rod gave them both a shake. "Could I possibly persuade you to overlook your obvious differences in favor of the common good for a moment?"

Tom straightened to his full height and looked down his nose at Tuan. "*Little* man," he crooned.

Rod let go of Tuan and swung on Big Tom, grabbing the big man's collar with both hands. Tom grinned and brought up a hamlike fist. "Aye, *master?*"

"What's the utopia right now, Big Tom?" Rod breathed.

Tom's grin faded to a frown. "Why, that the people of Gramarye should rule their land for themselves."

"Right!" Rod let go of Tom's collar, patting the man's cheek. "Bright boy! You get the silver star this week! And what do you have to do first?"

"Kill the councillors and noblemen!" Tom grinned.

"*Very* good! A gold star for the boy! You'll make valedictorian yet, Big Tom! Now, if you *really* want to be a good boy, tell teacher what you have to do before that!"

Tom sobered. "Jail the Mocker."

"A-plus! And what comes before that?"

Big Tom knit his brown, confused. "What?"

"*Be quiet!*" Rod roared in his face, in a stage whisper. He spun on Tuan. "Now! What do we do about that sentry?" And to himself, he mumbled, "Sheesh! I should maybe have brought a political convention in here!"

Tuan's chin jutted out stubbornly. "Ere we go further, this fellow must acknowledge me lord!"

Tom took a breath for a fresh blast.

"Down, boy!" Rod said hurriedly. "High blood pressure's bad for you! Is Tuan Loguire a nobleman born, Tom?"

"Aye," Tom grudged, "but that does not—"

"Is Loguire one of the greatest of the noble houses?"

"It is, but—"

"And your mother and father were peasants?"

"Yes, but that's not to say that—"

"And you have absolutely no wish to have been born a nobleman!"

"Never!" Tom hissed, eyes glowing. "May I be hanged from the highest gallows in Gramarye if ever I had wished that!"

"And you wouldn't want to be a nobleman if you could?"

"Master!" Big Tom pleaded, wounded to the core. "Hast so little regard for me that thou couldst think such of me?"

"No, I trust you, Big Tom," said Rod, patting his shoulder, "but Tuan has to be shown." He turned to the young nobleman. "You satisfied? He knows his place, doesn't he?"

"Aye." Tuan smiled like a fond father. "Fool I was to doubt him."

Understanding came into Tom's eyes as his mouth dropped open. His heavy hand closed on Rod's neck. "Why, thou lump of . . . !"

Rod reached up and squeezed Tom's elbow just at the funny bone. Tom let go, eyes starting from their sockets, mouth sagging in a cry of agony that he dared not voice.

"Now," said Rod briskly, "how do we get rid of that sentry?"

"Oh, thou scum!" Tom breathed. "Thou slimy patch of river-moss, thou mongrel son-of-a-democrat, thou!"

"Precisely," Rod agreed.

"Nay, but tell me," Tuan breathed in Rod's ear, eyes glowing. "What didst thou do to him? Thou didst but touch him and—"

"Uh . . . warlock trick," said Rod, falling back on the easiest, though most distasteful, excuse. He caught the back of Tuan's neck and jerked the youth's head down into the huddle with himself and Big Tom. "Now, how do we knock out that sentry?"

"There is but one way," murmured Tuan. "Wake him and fight him."

"And let him give the alarm?" Tom stared, horrified. "Nay, nay! Come catpaw behind him, and give him a blow o' the head!"

"That," said Tuan grimly, "lacks honor!"

Tom spat.

"Big Tom's plan is okay," said Rod, "except what happens if he wakes while we're sneaking up? And there's a very good chance of it; that lecherous beggar proved it for us!"

Tom shrugged. "Then a quick rush, and a hope. If we die, then we die."

"And the Queen dies with us," Rod growled. "No good."

Tom pulled out his short sword and balanced it on a finger. "I'll strike him in the throat with this blade at full fifty paces."

Tuan stared, appalled. "A man of your own men, sirrah!"

"One for the good of the cause." Tom shrugged. "What of it?"

Tuan's eyes froze. "That is worse than a stab in the back! We must needs give him lief to defend himself."

"Oh, aye!" Tom snorted. "Lief to defend himself, and to raise the whole House with his cries! Lief to . . ."

Rod clapped a hand over each mouth, glad that he hadn't brought three men with him. He hissed at Big Tom, "Be patient, will you? He's new to commando work!"

Tom sobered.

Tuan straightened, eyes icy.

Rod put his mouth next to Tom's ear and whispered, "Look, if you hadn't known he was an aristocrat, how would you have judged him?"

"A brave man, and a strong fighter," Tom admitted, "though foolish and young, with too many ideals."

Rod shook a finger at him. "Prejudice, Big Tom! Discrimination! I thought you believed in equality!"

"Well said," Tom growled reluctantly; "I'll bear him. But one more of his pious mouthings and . . ."

"If we get this job done fast, he won't have a chance to. Now, I've got an idea."

"Then why didst thou ask us?" growled Tom.

" 'Cause I didn't get my idea till you two started haggling. What we need is a compromise solution, right? Tuan won't stand for a knife in the back, or a knife while the guy's sleeping, or for killing a loyal retainer who might make good cannon fodder tomorrow. Right?"

"Aye," Tuan agreed.

"And Big Tom won't stand for him giving the alarm—and neither will I, for that matter: we're all good fighters, but just the three of us against the whole Houseful of cutthroats is straining the bonds of fantasy just a little bit far. So, Tom! If that sentry should come running around this corner all of a sudden, will you clobber him lightly?"

"Aye!" Tom grinned.

"*Lightly*, I said. Does that satisfy honor, Tuan?"

"Aye, since he faces us."

"Good! Now, if we could just get him to chase a mouse around this corner, we'd be all set."

"Aye," Tuan agreed, "but where's the mouse that would so nicely oblige us?"

"The master could make one," Tom growled.

"Make one?" Rod stared. "Sure if I had a machine shop and a . . ."

"Nay, nay!" Tuan grinned. "I know not those spells; but thou hast the witch-moss, and thou'rt a warlock! What more dost thou need?"

"Huh?" Rod swallowed. "Witches make things out of that stuff?"

"Aye, aye! Dost thou not know? Living things, small things—like mice!"

The missing piece in the puzzle of Gramarye clicked into place in Rod's mind. "Uh, say, how do they work that trick?"

"Why, they have but to look at a lump of the stuff, and it becomes what they wish it!"

Rod nodded slowly. "Very neat, ve-ry neat. The only hitch in the plan is, that's not my style of witchcraft."

Tuan sagged. "Thou craftest not witch-moss? Then how are we to . . . ? Still, 'tis most strange that thou shouldst not know of it."

"Not so," Tom dissented. "A very poor briefing bureau . . ."

"Oh, shut up!" Rod growled. "There are other ways to get a mouse." He cupped his hands around his mouth and called softly, "Gwen! Oh, Gwe-en!"

A spider dropped down on a thread right in front of his nose.

Rod jumped. "Ye cats! Don't *do* that, girl!"

"Vermin!" Tom hissed, and swung his hand back for a swat.

Rod poked him in the solar plexus. "Careful, there! Squash a spider, and you get bad luck, you know—namely, me!"

He cupped the spider in his hand and caressed it very gently with a finger. "Well, at least you didn't choose a black widow. Prettiest spider I ever saw, come to think of it."

The spider danced on his hand.

"Listen, sweetheart, I need a mouse to bring me that sentry. Can you handle it?"

The spider shape blurred, fluxed, and grew into a mouse. It jumped from his hand and dashed for the corner.

"Oh, no you don't!" Rod sprang, cupped a hand over it, then very carefully picked it up. "Sorry, sweetheart, you might get stepped on—and if anything like that happened to you, I'd be totally crushed."

He kissed its nose, and heard Tom gagging behind him. The mouse wriggled in ecstasy.

"No," said Rod, running a fingertip over its back and pinching the tail, "you've got to make me one instead, out of that blob of witch-moss. Think you can handle it, pet?"

The mouse nodded, turned, and stared at the witch-moss. Slowly, the blob pulled itself in, extruded a tendril into a tail, grew whiskers at the top end, changed color to brown, and a mouse crept down off the wall.

Tom gulped and crossed himself.

Rod frowned. "Thought you were an atheist."

"Not at times like this, master."

The witch-moss mouse scurried around the corner.

Big Tom lifted his dagger, holding it by the tip, the heavy, weighted handle raised like a club.

The snores around the corner stopped with a grunt.

"Gahhh! Nibble on me, will ya, y' crawlin' ferleigh?"

The sentry's stool clattered over. He stamped twice, missed both times; then the waiting men heard running footsteps approaching.

Tom tensed himself.

The mouse streaked around the corner.

The sentry came right behind it, cursing. His feet slipped on the turn. He looked up, saw Tom, and had just time enough to begin to look horrified before Tom's knife-hilt caught him at the base of the skull with a very solid thunk.

Rod let out a sigh of relief. "At last!"

The sentry folded nicely into Tuan's waiting arms. The young nobleman looked at Rod, grinning.

"Who fights by the side of a warlock," he said, "wins."

"Still, it was a pretty ratty trick," said Rod sheepishly.

Tom winced and pulled a length of black thread from his pouch.

"Nay, that will not hold him," Tuan protested.

Tom's only answer was a grin.

"Fishline?" Rod lifted an eyebrow.

"Better," said Big Tom, kneeling, beginning to wrap up the sentry. "Braided synthetic spider silk."

"And we owe it all to you," said Rod, petting the mouse in his hand.

It wriggled its nose, then dove between the buttons on his doublet.

Rod stifled a snicker, cupped a hand over the lump on his belly. "Hey, watch it! That tickles!"

Tom had the sentry nicely cocooned, with a rag jammed in his mouth and held in place by a few twists of thread. "Where shall we hide him?" Tuan whispered.

"There's nary a place close to hand," Tom muttered, tongue between his teeth as he tied a Gordion knot.

"Hey!" Rod clapped a cupped hand over a lump moving south of his belt buckle. "Cut that out!"

"There's a torch-sconce on this wall," said Tuan, pointing.

"The very thing," Tom growled. He heaved the inert sentry up, hooked one of the spider-thread loops over the sconce.

Rod shook his head. "Suppose someone comes by this way? We can't have him hanging around like that."

He reached in his doublet and hauled the mouse away from its exploratory tour of his thorax. "Listen, baby, you know what a dimensional warp is?"

The mouse rolled its eyes up and twitched its whiskers. Then it shook its head firmly.

"How about a, uh, time-pocket?"

The mouse nodded eagerly; then the little rodent face twisted up in concentration . . . and the sentry disappeared.

Tuan goggled, mouth gaping open.

Big Tom pursed his lips, then said briskly, "Ah . . . yes! Well, let's get on with it, then."

Rod grinned, put the mouse on the floor, turned it around, gave it a pat on the backside.

"Get lost, you bewitching beast. But stay close; I might need you."

The mouse scampered off with a last squeak over her shoulder.

"The Mocker will be sleeping in what was Tuan's chamber, I doubt not," Tom muttered, "and his lieutenants, we may hope, will not be far off."

"May not one of them be wakeful?" whispered Tuan. "Or might one be set Master of the Watch?"

Tom turned slowly, eyeing Tuan with a strange look on his face. He raised an eyebrow at Rod. "A good man," he admitted, "and a good guess." Then, "Follow," and he turned away.

They were able to bypass the only other sentry between themselves and the common room.

The room itself, cavernous and slipshod as ever, was lit

only by the smoky glow from the great fireplace, and a few smoldering torches. It was enough, however, to make out the great stone staircase that curved its way up the far wall with a grace that belied its worn treads and broken balustrade.

A gallery jutted out into the hall at the top of the stair. The doors opening off it gave onto private rooms.

A broad-shouldered, hatchet-faced man sat sprawled and snoring in a huge chair by the side of the vast fireplace. A sentry stood guard at the foot of the great staircase, blinking and yawning. Two more guards slouched at either side of the door in the center of the balcony.

"Here's a pretty mess," said Big Tom, ducking back into the hallway. "There's one more of them than there are of us, and they be so far between that two must surely take alarm as we disable two others."

"To say nothing of that wasteland of lighted floor that we have to cross to get to any of them," Rod added.

"We might creep up through the tables and stools," Tuan suggested, "and he at the foot of the stairs must surely nod himself asleep ere long."

"That takes care of the two on the ground floor," Rod agreed, "but how about the pair on the balcony?"

"To that," said Tuan, "I have some small skill at the shepherd's bow."

He drew out a patch of leather with two rawhide thongs wrapped about it.

"How didst thou learn the craft of that?" Tom growled as Tuan unwound the strings. " 'Tis a peasant's weapon, not a lordling's toy."

There was a touch of contempt in the glance Tuan threw Tom. "A knight must be schooled in all weapons, Big Tom."

Rod frowned. "I didn't know that was part of the standard code."

"It is not," Tuan admitted. "But 'tis my father's chivalry, and mine, as you shall see. Both yon knaves shall measure their length on cold stone ere they could know what has struck them."

"I don't doubt it," Rod agreed grimly. "Okay, let's go. I'll take the one by the fireplace."

"Thou'lt not," Big Tom corrected him. "Thou'lt take him by the stairway."

"Oh? Any particular reason?"

"Aye." Tom grinned wolfishly. "He in the great chair is

239

the lieutenant that Tuan foresaw—and one among those who ha' jailed me. 'Tis my meat, master."

Rod looked at Tom's eyes and felt an eerie chill wind blow up along his spine.

"All right, butcher," he muttered. "Just remember, the laddy's not for carving, yet."

" 'Let each man pile his dead according to his own taste and fashion,' " Tom quoted. "Go tend your corpses, master, and leave me to mine."

They dropped to their bellies and crawled, each to his own opponent.

To Rod, it was an eternity of table-legs and stool-feet, with plenty of dropped food scraps between, and the constant fear that one of the others might reach his station first and get bored.

There was a loud, echoing clunk.

Rod froze. One of the others had missed his footing.

There was a moment's silence; then a voice called, "What was that?" Then, "Eh, you there! Egbert! Rouse yourself, sot, and have a mind for the stairs you're guarding!"

"Eh? Wot? Wozzat?" muttered a bleary, nearer voice; and, "What fashes ye?" grumbled a deeper, petulant voice from the fireplace. "Must ye wake me for trifles?"

There was a pause; then the first voice said, with a note of obsequiousness, " 'Twas a noise, Captain, a sort of a knock 'mongst the tables."

"A knock, he says!" growled the captain. "A rat, mayhap, after the leavings, nowt more! Do ye wake me for that? Do it more, an' thou'lt hear a loud knock indeed, a blow on thy hollow head." Then the voice grumbled to itself, "A knock, i' faith! A damned knock!"

Then there was silence again, then a muted clang as one of the sentries shifted his weight uneasily.

Rod let out a sigh of relief, slow and silent.

He waited for the sentry to start snoring again.

Then he wormed his way forward again, till at last he lay quiet under the table nearest the stairway.

It seemed he lay there for a very long time.

There was a piercing whistle from the fireplace, and a clatter as Big Tom overturned a stool in his charge.

Rod sprang for his man.

Out of the corner of his eye, he saw Tuan leap upright, his sling a blurred arc; then Rod crashed into the sentry, fist slamming at the midriff, left hand squeezing the throat.

240

The man folded. Rod chopped at the base of the skull lightly, just under the iron cap, and the sentry went limp.

He looked up just in time to see a sentry on the balcony sag to the floor. The other lay writhing on the stones, hands clasped at his throat.

Rod was up the stairs in five leaps. He landed a haymaker on the man's jaw. The man's eyes closed as he went under.

His larynx was pushed out of line. It was not a pretty sight.

But at that, he'd been lucky. If it had been a direct blow, his trachea would have been crushed.

His companion hadn't been so lucky. The pebble had crushed his forehead. Blood welled over his face and puddled to the floor.

"Forgive me, man," whispered Tuan, as he contemplated his handiwork. Rod had never seen the boy's face so grim.

"Fortunes of war, Tuan," he whispered.

"Aye," Tuan agreed, "and had he been my peer, I could dismiss it at that. But a man of my blood is intended to protect the peasants, not slay them."

Rod looked at the boy's brooding face and decided it was men like the Loguires who had given aristocracy what little justification it had had.

Tom had glanced once and turned away to bind the remaining man, his face thunderous.

There had been only the one casualty; the captain and stair-guard lay securely trussed with Tom's black thread.

Tom came up, glowering at Tuan. " 'Twas well done," he growled. "You took two of them out, and were able to spare the one; tha'rt braw fighter. And for the other, do not mourn him; thou couldst scarce take the time for better aim."

Tuan's face was blank in confusion. He couldn't rightly object to Tom's manner; yet it was disquieting to have a peasant offer him fatherly advice, and forgiveness.

Rod gave him an out. "You used to sleep there?" He jerked a thumb over his shoulder at the door the sentries had guarded.

He broke through Tuan's abstraction; the youth turned, looked, and nodded.

"Well, that's where the Mocker'll be, then." Rod looked up at Tom. "That captain downstairs was one of the Mocker's cadre?"

"Aye."

"That leaves two lieutenants, then. How's chances for one

241

of them being in each of these rooms next to the Mocker's?" As Tom pulled at his lower lip and nodded, Rod went on: "One for each of us, then. You boys take the lieutenants. I'll take the Mocker."

He turned to the door. Big Tom's meaty hand fell on his shoulder.

"How now?" growled the big peasant. "How is the Mocker your meat, not mine?"

Rod grinned. "I'm the middleman, remember? Besides, what belt do you hold?"

"Brown," Tom admitted.

"And the Mocker?"

"Black," Tom answered reluctantly. "Fifth dan."

Rod nodded. "I'm black, eighth dan. You take the lieutenant."

Tuan frowned. "What is this talk of belts?"

"Just a jurisdictional dispute; don't worry about it." Rod turned to the center door.

Big Tom caught his arm again. "Master," and this time he sounded like he meant it. "When this is done, thou must teach me."

"Yeah, sure, anything. I'll get you a college degree, just let's get this over with, shall we?"

"I thank thee." Tom grinned. "But I've a doctorate already."

Rod did a double take, then stared at him. "In what?"

"Theology."

Rod nodded. "That figures. Say, you haven't come up with any new atheist theories, have you?"

"Master!" Tom protested, wounded. "How can one prove or disprove the existence of a non-material being by material data? 'Tis an innate contradiction of—"

"Gentlemen," said Tuan sarcastically, "I greatly dislike to interrupt so learned a discourse, but the Mocker awaits, and may shortly awake."

"Huh? Oh! Oh, yes!" Rod turned to the door. "See you in a few minutes, Big Tom."

"Aye, we must have further converse." Tom grinned and turned away to the right-hand door.

Rod eased his own door open, hands stiffened.

The door creaked. It groaned. It shrieked. It lodged formal protest.

Rod threw himself forward, having just time to realize that the Mocker had left his hinges carefully unoiled as a primitive but very effective burglar alarm, before the Mocker screamed "Bloody Murder!" and jumped from his bed, hands chopping.

Rod blocked an overhand blow and thrust for the solar plexus. His hand was skillfully rerouted, the Mocker's scream for help dinning in his ears.

Rod had just time to appreciate the humor of a black belt calling for help before he saw the kick smashing at his groin.

He leaped back, and the Mocker leaped after him. This time, the kick landed.

Rod rolled on the floor, curled around his agony.

He saw the foot aimed at his jaw and managed to turn his head aside just enough; the foot glanced off the side of his head.

He saw a shower of red asterisks, glowing against black, and shook his head frantically, trying to clear it.

Through the ringing in his ears, he heard another scream, suddenly cut off, then a thud; then Big Tom was bellowing, "Thy sling, Tuan! There'll be guards to answer that scream!"

Then the big man was bending over him, face close. "How bad art thou hurt, master?"

Rod had never known stale beer and onions could smell so good.

"I'm all right," he gasped. "The blow landed a little off-center, thank heaven!"

"Canst thou stand?"

"In a minute. Gwen may be in for a temporary disappointment, though. How'd you do it, Big Tom?"

"Caught his foot on the upswing," Tom grinned, "and threw him high. Then I got in an uppercut ere he landed."

Rod stared. "A what?"

"An uppercut. A haymaker."

Rod rolled over, got his knees under him, shook his head in amazement. " 'Uppercut takes out Black Belt.' Call the newspapers."

There was a cry outside, choked off suddenly.

Rod's head snapped up, listening. Then he stumbled to his feet, hands still pressed to his groin, and all but fell out the door, ignoring Big Tom's solicitous protests.

Three more bodies lay on the stone floor of the common room.

Tuan stood at the balcony rail, sling stretched tight between his hands, jaw clamped shut, bleak dismay in his eyes.

"First the one came," he said in a monotone, "then the other, then the third. The first two I dispatched ere they could cry; but on the third, I was tardy." Tuan turned back to the hall. After a moment, he said, slow and hard, "I do not like this killing."

Then his vision cleared.

"Huh." Rod nodded, gasping, as a brief spasm of nausea made him clutch at the railing. "No man worthy to be called a man does like it, Tuan. Don't let it worry you. It's war."

"Oh, I ha' slain before." Tuan's lips pressed thin. "But to slay men who three days agone drank my health . . . !"

Rod nodded, closing his eyes. "I know. But if you have any hope of being a king, Tuan, or even a good Duke, you've got to learn not to let it bother you."

He looked up at the boy. "Besides, remember—they'd have killed you if they could."

Tom came out on the balcony, carrying the trussed-up Mocker in his arms, like a baby.

He looked briefly at the common room; his face hardened. "More killing?"

He turned away, laying the Mocker carefully on the floor next to the prone bodies of his lieutenants, and sighed. "Ay de mi! But 'tis the times, and the fashion."

He bent to the work of binding up one of the lieutenants, a tall, emaciated skeleton of a man with a scar where he should have had an ear, a souvenir of royal justice.

Rod looked, and nodded; the Mocker had chosen his confederates well. They had cause for hating the monarch.

Rod slowly straightened, wincing at the pain.

Tuan glanced at him. "Thou ought to seat thyself and take rest, Rod Gallowglass."

Rod pulled in a sharp, quick breath and shook his head. "It's just pain. Hadn't we better cart these three down to the dungeon?"

A gleam sparked in Tuan's eye. "Nay. Bind them and keep them here; I have uses for them."

Rod frowned. "What do you mean, uses?"

Big Tom held up a hand. "Do not ask, master. If Tuan has need of them, let him have them. This lad knows his craft; I ha' ne'er seen, and but rarely heard, of any man who could so sway the mob."

He turned and leaped down the stairs, checked for heartbeats in the fallen men, bound up the one that still lived, and dragged them all under the balcony. Then he caught up the third lieutenant from the hearth, slung him over a shoulder.

"Tom!" Tuan called, and the big man looked up.

"Bring that horn that hangs o'er the mantle, and the drum beside it!" Tuan called.

Tom nodded and took down the battered, curled hunting horn from its nail and plucked one of the rude drums—nothing more than an empty cask with hide stretched over each end—from its place on the mantle.

Rod frowned, perplexed. "What do you want the drum and bugle for?"

Tuan grinned. "Canst play at the horn?"

"Well, I wouldn't exactly qualify for first chair in the Philharmonic, but . . ."

"Thou'lt do," said Tuan, eyes dancing.

Big Tom bounded back up the stairs with the Mocker's lieutenant over one shoulder and the trumpet and drum over the other.

He dropped the instruments and laid the bound man by his companions.

He straightened, fists on hips, grinning. "Halloa, my masters! What would you have us do with 'em, lordling?"

"Do thou take the drum," said Tuan, "and when I give the word, hang these four from the balcony rail, but not by their necks. 'Tis far more to our credit we've taken them living."

Rod cocked an eyebrow. "Not that old wheeze about being powerful enough to be merciful?"

He didn't hear the answer, because Tom started pounding the drum. The tenor throbbing filled the room.

Rod caught up the horn.

Tuan grinned, jumped up on the rail, stood with feet wide apart and arms folded. "Summon them, Master Gallowglass," he shouted.

Rod set the mouthpiece to his lips and blew "Reveille."

It sounded rather weird on a hunting horn, but it had its effect. Before he was halfway through with the second chorus, the hall had filled with beggars, muggers, lame, one-armed, thieves and cutpurses and murderers.

Their muttering, surf and wind before a storm, filled the hall as an undercurrent to the drum and horn. They were fresh-woken, bleary-eyed and fuzzy-brained, hurling a thousand incredulous questions at one another, shaken and cowed to see Tuan, whom they had jailed, standing tall and proud in the hall he'd been exiled from.

He should fear them; he should have feared to return; and if he had come back, it should have been as a thief in the night, skulking and secret.

Yet here he stood, free in their eyes, summoning them to him with bugle and drum—and where was the Mocker?

They were shaken, and more than a little afraid. Men who had never been taught how to think now faced the un-thinkable.

Rod ended with a flourish, and flipped the trumpet away from his lips, whirling it in a flashing circle to land bell-down at his hip.

Big Tom gave the drum a last final boom.

Tuan held his hand out to Tom and began clicking his fingers very softly.

The drum spoke again, throbbing, insistent, but very soft.

Rod looked up at Tuan, who was grinning, arms akimbo, a royal elf come into his kingdom. He looked down at the audience, shaken and fearful, staring, mouths agape, at the lordly, commanding figure above them.

Rod had to admit it was a great way to open a speech.

Tuan flung up his arms, and the hall stilled, except for the low-pitched throb of Tom's drum.

"You cast me out!" Tuan shouted.

The mob shrank back on itself, muttering, fearful.

"Cast out, thrown to exile!" Tuan called. "You had turned your eyes from me, turned away from me, thought never to look upon me!"

The muttering grew, began to take a surly, desperate quality.

"Was I not banished?" Tuan called, then, "Be still!" he snapped.

And, miraculously, the room stilled.

He leveled an accusing forefinger at the crowd and growled, "Was I not banished?"

This time there were a few muttered "Ayes."

"Was I not?"

The mutter of "Ayes" grew.

"Was I not?"

"Aye!" rolled across the heads of the crowd.

"Did you not call me traitor?"

"Aye," the crowd growled again.

"Yet here I stand," Tuan cried, "strong and free, and master again of the House of Clovis!"

Nobody disputed it.

"And where are the real traitors, who would ha' seen you all torn to bits in hopeless battle? The traitors, who ha' turned this House to a jail in my absence? Where are they now, to dispute my mastership?"

He rested his hands on his hips while the crowd took up the question in its own ranks, and Tom quickly lashed ten feet of thread to the Mocker's bonds, lashing the other end to a railing-pillar. As the mutters of "Where?" and "The Mocker!" began to grow, he served the three lieutenants likewise.

Tuan let the mutters swell and grow; then, just as they hit their peak, he gave Tom the signal.

Tom and Rod threw the bound men over, where they hung two on each side of Tuan. The Mocker had regained consciousness; he began writhing and kicking at the end of his rope.

A shocked silence filled the hall.

Tuan grinned and folded his arms.

The crowd roared, like one huge, savage beast, and pressed forward. The front ranks began to jump at the dangling feet. Obscene epithets, cursing the Mocker and his men, blasted from the packed floor.

"Behold!" Tuan shouted, throwing up his arms, and the crowd fell silent. "Behold them, the traitors who once you called masters! Behold them, the traitors, the thieves who took from you all the liberty I had gained for you!"

Big Tom was grinning, eyes glowing and fixed on the young lord, swaying to the rhythm of the boy's words. For, truly, the lad seemed twelve feet tall now.

"Were you not born without masters?" Tuan shouted.

"Aye!" the crowd roared at him.

"You were born to freedom!" Tuan bellowed. "The freedom of outlawry and poverty, aye, but born free!"

Then, "Were you not born wild?" he fairly shrieked; and: "Aye!" the crowd shrieked in response, "Aye, aye! *Aye!*"

"Did I steal your freedom from you?"

"Nay, nay!"

A twisted hunchback with a patch over his eye shouted, "Nay, Tuan! You gave us more!"

The crowd clamored.

Tuan crossed his arms again, grinning, letting the acclamation run its course.

When it had just passed his peak, he threw up his arms again, and shouted. "Did I tell you?"

Silence fell.

"Did I tell you that you must have my permission for a night's loving?"

"Nay!" they roared back, both sexes united for a change.

"And never I will!"

They cheered.

Tuan grinned, and bowed his head in thanks, almost shyly.

"And yet!" Tuan's voice dropped down low, surly, angry. He hunched forward, one fist clenched, shaking at the audience. "When I came back to your halls this dark eventide, what did I find?" His voice rose, building. "You had let these base knaves steal away all I had given you!"

The crowd roared.

Tuan flicked his left hand; Tom struck the drum with a boom that cut the crowd short.

"Nay, more!" Tuan cried. His forefinger jabbed out at the crowd, his eyes seeking hot individual faces. His voice was cold, now, and measured. "I found that in your base cowardice you had let them steal from you even that liberty you were born with!"

The crowd murmured, frightened, unsure. The front ranks shrank back.

"Even your birthright you had let them steal from you!"

The murmuring was a wave of fright at the contempt in the silver tongue.

"You would let them take from you even bed-freedom!"

He flicked his hand; the drum boomed.

"And you call yourselves men!" Tuan laughed, harsh and contemptuous.

The murmuring wave came back at him now, with sullen, protesting voices. "We are men!" someone cried, and the crowd took it up, "We are men! We are men! We are men!"

"Aye!" shrieked the eye-patched hunchback. "But give us these dangling knaves who ha' robbed us, Tuan, and we shall prove we are men! We shall rend them, shall flay them! We shall leave not an ounce of flesh to cling to their bones! We shall crack even their bones and hale out the marrow!"

The crowd howled in blood-lust.

Tuan straightened and folded his arms, smiling grimly. The crowd saw him; their roar subsided to a growl, with an undertone of guilt, then broke up into sullen lumps of murmurs, and stilled.

"Is this manhood?" said Tuan, almost quietly. "Nay!" His arm snapped out, pointing, accusing. "I ha' seen packs of dogs could do better!"

The muttering ran through the crowd, growing angrier, louder and louder.

"Careful, there!" Rod called to Tuan. "You'll have them tearing us apart next!"

"No fear," said Tuan, without taking his eyes from the crowd. "Yet let it work a while."

The muttering rose sharply. Here and there a man shouted, angry shouts, fists waved at Tuan where he stood on the balcony rail.

Tuan flung up his arms again, shouting, "But I say you are men!"

The crowd quieted, staring.

"There are others who slander you; but I call you men!" Then, looking from face to face: "And who will gainsay me?"

For a moment, they were quiet; then someone called, "None, Tuan!" and another answered, "None!"

"None!" called the several, and "None!" called the many, till "None!" roared the crowd.

"Will you prove you are men?" Tuan shouted.

"Aye!" the crowd bellowed.

"Will you fight?" Tuan howled, shaking a fist.

"Aye!" they cried, crowding closer with blood-thirst.

Tuan's hands shot out waist-high, palms down, fingers spread. The crowd stilled.

His voice was hushed, chanting. "You were born to filth and the scabs of disease!"

"Aye," they muttered.

"You were born to the sweat of your joints, and the ache of your back in hard labor!"

"Aye!"

"You were born to the slack, empty belly and the want of a home!"

"Aye!"

"Who filled your bellies? Who gave you a roof for your head in this very house?"

"You did!"

"Who gave you a fortress?"

"You did!"

"Who?"

"You!"

"Tell me the name!"

"Tuan Loguire!" they shrieked.

"Aye!" Tuan's hands went out again; he stood crouched, eye afire.

"This was the misery I took from you. But who gave it to you at birth? Who is it has beaten you down, century upon century, from father to son, age upon age to the time of your remotest grandfathers?"

The crowd muttered, uncertain.

"The peasants?"

"Nay," the crowd answered.

"Was it the soldiers?"

"Aye!" they shouted, come to life again.

"And who rules the soldiers?"

"The nobles!"

Rod winced at the hate they packed into the word.

"Aye! 'Twas the nobles!" Tuan shouted, thrusting upward with his fist, and the crowd howled.

He let pandemonium reign for a few moments, then threw up his arms again.

Then his hands dropped down to belt-level again; he fell into the crouch.

"Who!" he demanded, and the drum throbbed behind him. "Who! Who alone of all the high-born took your part? Who gave you food when you cried for it, heard your petitions? Who sent judges among you, to give you justice instead of a nobleman's whim?"

His fist thrust upward with his whole body behind it, "The Queen!"

"The Queen!" they echoed him.

"She shut her ears to the noblemen, that she might hear your cries!"

"Aye!"

"She hath shed tears for you!"

"Aye!"

"Yet," cried the hunchback, "she cast you out, our Tuan Loguire!"

Tuan smiled sourly. "Did she? Or did she send me among you!" He threw up his arms, and they roared like an avalanche.

"It is the Queen who has given you your birthright again!"

"Aye!"

"Are you men?" Tuan shouted.

"We are!"

"Will you fight?"

"We will fight! We will fight!"

"Will you fight the noblemen?"

"Aye!"

"Will you fight for your Queen?"

"Aye!"

"Will you fight the noblemen for Catharine your Queen?"

"Aye! Ayeayeaye*ayel*"

Then the noise of the crowd covered all. The people leaped and shouted; men caught women and swung them about.

"Have you weapons?" Tuan shouted.

"Aye!" A thousand daggers leaped upward, gleaming.

"Catch up your packs, fill them with journeybread! Burst out of this house, through the south gate of the city! The Queen will give you food, give you tents! So run you all to the South, south along the great highway to Breden Plain, there to wait for the noblemen!

"Go do it!" he shouted. "Go now! For the Queen!"

"For the Queen!"

Tuan flipped his hand; the drum boomed loud and fast. "Hunting call!" Tuan snapped in aside to Rod.

Rod flourished the trumpet to his lips and began the quick, bubbling notes.

"Go!" Tuan roared.

The people broke, to their rooms, to the armory. In ten minutes time they had caught up packs, staffs, and knives.

"It is done!" Tuan leaped down off the rail to the balcony floor. "They'll ha' run down to Breden Plain in two days!" He grinned, slapping Big Tom's shoulders. "We ha' done it, Tom!"

Tom roared his laughter and threw his arms about Tuan in a bear-hug.

"Whew!" Tuan gasped as Tom dropped him. He turned to Rod. "Do you, friend Gallowglass, tell the Queen, and see that the word of it goes out to her soldiers. Tell her to send meat, tents, and ale, and right quickly. And do you hurl these lackeys"—his thumb jerked at the Mocker and his lieutenants—"deep into the Queen's dungeon. Farewell!" And he was bounding and leaping down the stairs.

"Hey, wait a minute!" Rod shouted, running to the rail. "Where do you think you're going?"

"To Breden Plain!" Tuan shouted, stopping to look back up. "I must guard my people, or they'll strip the countryside worse than any plague of locusts could do, and kill themselves off in a fight o'er the spoils. Do you tell Catharine of my"—he paused; a shadow crossed his face—"loyalty."

Then he was gone, leading the mob that boiled out the great front doors of the house, running before them in a wild, madcap dance.

Rod and Tom exchanged one glance, then turned and ran for the stairs to the roof.

They watched from the rooftop as the chanting mob poured out the south gate. Somehow, by means of the chant, Tuan had gotten them moving in good order, almost marching.

"Do you think he needs any help?" Rod murmured.

Tom threw back his head and guffawed. "Him, master? Nay, nay! Rather, help those who come up against him, with that army at his back!"

"But only one man, Tom! To lead two thousand misfits!"

"Canst doubt it, master, when thou hast seen his power? Or didst thou not see?"

"Oh, I saw." Rod nodded, light-headed. "There's more witchcraft in this land than I thought, Big Tom. Yes, I saw."

"Waken the Queen, and beg of her that she join us here in her audience chamber!" Brom snapped at a hastily-wakened lady-in-waiting. "Go!"

He slammed the door and turned to the fireplace, where Rod sat with a bleary-eyed Toby, rudely awakened after only an hour of sleep; the nightly party in the Witches' Tower had run a little late tonight. He held a steaming mug in his hand and a throb in his head.

"Assuredly," he muttered thickly, "we wish to aid the Queen in any manner we may; but what aid would we be in a battle?"

"Leave that to me." Rod smiled. "I'll find something for you to do. You just get the Queen's Witches down to Breden Plain by . . . uh . . ."

"Three days hence." Brom smiled. "We march at down, and will be three days in our journey."

Toby nodded, hazily. "We shall be there, my masters. And now, with your leave . . ."

He started to rise, gasped, and sank back in his chair, hand pressed to his head.

"Easy there, boy!" Rod grasped an elbow, steadying him. "First hangover?"

"Oh, nay!" Toby looked up, blinking watery eyes. " 'Tis but the first time I've been wakeful when the drunk turned to the hangover. If you'll pardon me, masters . . ."

The air slammed at their eardrums as it rushed in to fill the space where Toby had been.

"Uh . . . yes," Rod said. He shook his head and eyed Brom. "Teleportative, too?"

Brom frowned. "Tele-what?"

"Uh . . ." Rod closed his eyes a moment, cursing the slip of the tongue. "I take it he's just gone back to bed."

"Aye."

"He can disappear from here and reappear there?"

"Quick as thought, aye."

Rod nodded. "That's what I thought. Well, it oughta come in handy."

"What wilt thou have them do, Rod Gallowglass?"

"Oh, I dunno." Rod waved his mug airily. "Conjure up feathers inside the Southern knights' armor, maybe. Or something like that, good for a joke. They'll just die laughing."

"Thou knowest not what thou'lt be having them do, yet thou would bring them?"

"Yeah, I'm beginning to think a little witchcraft can come in handy at times."

"Aye." Brom smiled covertly. "She hath saved your life twice over, hath she not?"

Rod swung about. "She? Who? She who, huh? What're you talking about?"

"Why, Gwendylon!" Brom's smile absorbed mischief.

"Oh, yes! Uh . . . you know of her?" Rod raised a cautious eyebrow; then he smiled, relaxing. "No, of course you'd know of her. I forget; she's on pretty good terms with the elves."

"Aye, I know of her." Brom's eyebrows pinched together. "Nay, but tell me," he said, almost anxiously, "didst thou love her?"

"Love her?" Rod stared. "What the hell business is that of yours?"

Brom waved a hand impatiently. " 'Tis of concern to me; let it pass at that. Dost thou love her?"

"I won't let it pass at that!" Rod drew himself up with a look of offended honor.

"I am Prince of the Elves!" Brom snapped. "Might I not have concern for the most powerful witch in all Gramarye?"

Rod stared, appalled. "The most . . . *what?*"

Brom smiled sourly. "Thou dist not know? Aye, Rod Gallowglass. 'Tis a most puissant wench thou hast grappled with. Therefore, do you tell me: dost thou love her?"

"Well, uh, I, uh . . . I don't know!" Rod sat, cradling his head in his hands. "I mean, uh, this is all so sudden, I, uh . . ."

"Nay, nay!" Brom growled impatiently. "Surely thou must know if thou lovest!"

"Well, I mean, uh . . . well, no, I don't know! I mean, that's a subject that it's a little hard to be objective about, isn't it?"

"Thou dost not know?" Thunderclouds gathered in Brom's face.

"No, damn it, I don't!"

"Why, thou fool of a puling babe, thou mock of a man! Dost thou not know thine own heart?"

"Well, uh, there's the aortic ventricle, and, uh . . ."

"Then how am I to know if thou lovest her?" Brom thundered.

"How the hell should *I* know?" Rod shouted. "Ask my horse!"

A quivering page thrust his head in, then came quivering into the room. "My lords, her Majesty the Queen!"

Brom and Rod swung about, bowed.

Catharine entered, in a dressing gown of the royal purple her loosened hair a pale, disordered cloud around her head. She looked very tired, and scarcely wakened.

"Well, milords," she snapped, seating herself by the fire, "what great news is it makes you waken me at so slight an hour?"

Rod inclined his head toward the page. The boy paled, bowed, and left.

"The House of Clovis is up, into arms, and away," Rod informed her.

She stared, lips parting.

"They have boiled out of the south gate, and this very night run south toward Breden Plain."

Catharine's eyes closed; she sank back in her chair with a sigh. "May Heaven be praised!"

"And Tuan Loguire," Rod murmured.

Her eyes opened, staring. "Aye. And Tuan Loguire," she said reluctantly.

Rod turned away, running his hand over the mantle. "They must be sent food and drink, so that they will not strip the countryside as they pass. And a courier must ride ahead to tell soldiers to let them pass."

"Aye," she said grudgingly, "surely."

Her eyes wandered to the fire. "And yet it is strange, that they who have ever raised their voices in clamor against me, now should fight for me," she murmured.

Rod looked at her, his smile tight and ironic.

"Tuan . . ." she murmured.

Brom cleared his throat and stumped forward, hands locked behind his back. "And this very night," he growled, "have I spoken with the King of the Elves; all his legions are ours."

She was her old self again, smiling sourly. "Legions of elves, Brom O'Berin?"

"Oh, don't underestimate them." Rod rubbed the back of his head, remembering a clout on the skull and a prisoned werewolf. "And to top it off, we've got your own personal coven of witches . . ."

". . . and the most powerful witch in all Gramarye," Brom interjected.

"Uh, yes, and her," Rod agreed, with a shish-kebab glance at Brom. "All ready and eager to serve the only ruler in history who has protected witches."

Catharine's eyes had slowly widened as she listened; now her eyes took on a distant look, and wandered to the fire. "We will win," she murmured. "We will win!"

"Well, uh, with all due respect to your Majesty, uh, it might be a trifle more correct to say we stand an even chance."

Breden Plain was a delta, open to the south but closed on the north by the meeting of two rivers. A dense thicket of trees ran along each river, bordering the field. The field itself was tall grass and lavender.

Not that they could see much of it, Rod thought as he squatted by a campfire. A thick, chill mist covered the field; at least Rod, who had seen something of civilized smog, would have called it a mist; but Tuan, chafing his hands across the fire from Rod, shook his head and muttered, "A most dense and unclement fog, Master Gallowglass! 'Twill weigh heavily on the spirit of the troops!"

Rod cocked an eyebrow at him and listened to the sounds of revelry drifting over the field from the beggars' pickets. The witches were at it, too; the usual party had started at noon today, out of respect for the weather.

His shoulders shrugged with a snort of laughter. "Well,

don't let it worry you, Tuan. The precog—uh, witches, say it'll be a beautiful, sunny day, tomorrow."

"And St. George be praised, we will not have to fight until then!" Tuan drew his cloak about him, shivering.

The latest word from Brom's miniature spies—whom Rod had immediately dubbed the Hobgoblin Associated Reconnaissance Korps—was that the Southern troops were just half a day away. Catharine had arrived with Brom and her army the preceding evening, and the beggars had been resting a full day already. They were, in fact, so primed and ready that Tuan was having a little trouble holding them in check; they were all for marching south and attacking the noblemen on the run.

"Still," said Rod, tugging at his lip, "I don't see why we should wait for morning to do the fighting. We could ambush them tonight, when they're drawing up their troops."

"Attack at night!" Tuan gasped, horrified.

Rod shrugged. "Sure, why not? They'll be tired from a day's march, and won't know where we are. We'd stand a much better chance of winning."

"Aye, and you would stand a better chance of killing a man if you kicked at his head while he was down!"

Rod sighed and forebore saying that he had once done exactly that, when the man was one of five excellently trained, seasoned killers who'd ambushed him. As a matter of fact, he'd fought dirtier than that with a lot less justification; but this didn't seem quite the time for telling it.

He did say, "I thought the point in fighting was to win."

"Aye," Tuan agreed, staring out into the fog toward the south end of the meadow, "but not by such foul means. Who would be loyal to a Queen who maintained her power thus?"

And that, Rod admitted, was the kernel of it. Prestige was everything on this world; and honor was the cornerstone of prestige.

"Well," he sighed, "you're the doctor."

Tuan frowned at him. "Doctor? I have no skill in healing."

"No, but you're an excellent practical psychologist. So I'll follow your lead when it comes to handling people."

Tuan smiled sadly, shaking his head. "Friend Rod, I have no skill at ruling."

Rod allowed himself a skeptical look. "Well, maybe not, but you're one hell of a leader."

"Ho!" a voice bellowed.

Rod turned and grinned at the huge shape that loomed in the fog. "Everyone happy over there?"

Big Tom shouldered his way out of the mist, grinning. "Most happy, master. They've ne'er in their lives drunk such wine, or so much of it."

"Hmmm." Rod tugged at his lip. "Better roll the wine away in a little while. We don't want them drunk so soon before battle."

But, "Nay," Tuan corrected, almost automatically, Rod noticed. "Let them drink their fill; 'twill put them abed sooner. Then rouse them early in the morning and give each a tankard or two—then they'll fight like the very demons."

Well, Rod had to allow that was true. They weren't asking precision from the beggars, just wanted them to get out and beat up the enemy.

The night was pricked with the pinholes of watch-fires, softened by the lifting mist.

More dots of light sprang up to the south, where the noblemen and councillors were bringing up their army.

In the northern meadow, there was bawdy laughter and shouting, and the din of music, where the beggars were in the last stages of gleeful compliance with the order to get drunk as fast as possible.

On the hillside across the river there was a stern, disapproving silence, and the gentle glow of lamps within silken tents, where Catharine and her army of regulars went sober to bed.

But in the largest tent, Catharine's, things were anything but quiet.

"Nay, nay, and again I say nay!" she cried, angrily pacing the floor.

She swung about, clapping her hands sharply. "I shall have no more of your arguments! Have done, have done; for I *will* ride tomorrow at the head of my armies! I shall brook no further objection!"

Rod and Brom exchanged glances.

Tuan's face was beet-red with anger, frustration, and worry.

"Begone," snapped Catharine, and turned her back.

Reluctantly, the three men bowed, and filed out of the tent.

"What she will, she will," Brom growled. "We three must

guard her, then, and leave the plan of the battle to Sir Maris."

"That's one sure road to defeat," Rod growled. "His way of running a battle is as outdated as the phalanx."

Brom sighed and rubbed his eyes. "But as I have said, I will die by her. Yet mayhap we shall live, for I have a slight plan."

He stumped away into the darkness before they could question him, from which Rod inferred that his "plan" was limited to buoying up Rod's and Tuan's spirits by insinuating that there was yet hope.

"We shall die in her defense," Tuan whispered, drawn and pale. "Yet when we are gone, she will die too, and for that I am loath." He spread his hands helplessly. "But what can I do?"

"Well . . ." Rod pursed his lips, and looked back over his shoulder at the lighted tent. "I know one way to make sure she won't ride tomorrow. . . ."

"Tell it, then!" Tuan's face lit with frantic eagerness.

"Make sure she won't be able to sit down in the morning."

Tuan stared. A slow flush crept into his face, then drained away, leaving him pale and trembling. "What . . . dost . . . thou mean?" His voice was choked and threatening. He lifted a clenched, trembling fist.

Rod looked at him, frowned. "Why, spank her. Smack her so hard she'll have to stand till next Sunday. How else would you do it?"

Tuan's fist slowly dropped; the color came back to his face in a blush. "Oh," he said, and turned away. "I' truth," he said. " 'twould be well done."

"It's that, or let her die."

Tuan nodded, life coming back to him. He turned to the Queen's tent, paused a minute, then squared his shoulders. "That shall I do, then. Pardon me, friend Gallowglass, for my anger; for a moment I had thought you meant . . . something else."

He took a deep breath and stepped off briskly toward the tent.

He paused at the entrance, nodded at the guards, squared his shoulders again, and marched in.

Rod smiled, amused. "And I thought I had a dirty mind!"

He chuckled, shaking his head, and turned toward the witches' campfires, reflecting that Tuan's years in the House of Clovis had taught him a lot about life.

Gwendylon materialized out of the darkness (literally). She smiled shyly. "What amuses my lord?"

Rod grinned, caught her by the waist, and swung her up for a kiss, a warm kiss, and lasting.

"My lord!" she said, blushing prettily, patting her hair back into place.

The night breeze wafted a sudden slapping sound to them, accompanied by squeals and cries.

The guards at the tent jerked bolt upright, then swung toward the tent. One put up a hand to swing aside the cloth of the doorway; but the second caught the hand and cried, "Does your Majesty require aid?"

"Stay out!" squealed an agonized voice. "On pain of your life, do not enter!"

The sentries exchanged puzzled looks, then shrugged and turned back to their posts, albeit with some nervous looks over their shoulders.

The squeals became muffled, then turned into sobs. The slapping sounds ceased.

Then all was still.

Rod looked down at Gwen. "What are you grinning about?"

She looked up at him out of the corner of her eyes. "I ha' told you, my lord, that I can hear all thoughts but yours."

"Oh?"

"Aye. And there are most goodly thoughts in that tent at this moment."

The lights in the tent went out.

Gwendylon giggled and turned away. "Come, my lord. 'Twould be most improper to listen further. Come. Thou must be early abed this night."

"Waken, Rod Gallowglass!"

Something jarred his shoulder.

Rod growled and levered his eyes open. "What the hell do you think . . ."

He stopped as he saw the look on Brom's face.

"Aye," Brom growled. "Now robe thyself and come with me."

"I don't sleep naked on battle nights," Rod growled, and rose very carefully, so as not to disturb Gwendylon.

His face softened for a moment as he looked down at her. He touched his lips to her cheek. She stirred, murmured in her sleep, and smiled.

Then he rose, his face hardening.

Brom was already striding away through the chill pre-dawn mist, beckoning curtly.

"All right, what's happened?" Rod growled as he caught up with Brom.

"Nay, be still!" Brom snapped, and was silent till they had climbed the hillside far above the tents.

Then he swung on Rod and snapped, "Now tell me! Dost thou love her?"

Rod's face emptied.

Then he said, softly, "You woke me just to ask that?"

"It is of some importance to me," Brom snapped. "Dost thou love her!"

Rod folded his arms, leaning back on one hip. "Just what the hell business is it of yours? What right have you to know my soul?"

Brom looked away, his face working; and when he spoke, the words seemed almost dragged out of him.

"She is my daughter, Rod Gallowglass."

He glanced up at Rod's stunned face, and a sardonic gleam came into his eye. "Aye. Thou scarce can credit it, canst thou?"

He turned away, looking out over the valley. His voice softened with memory and musing.

"She was naught but a servant-wench in the King's halls, Rod Gallowglass—yet I loved her. She was small, scarce half the height of another woman, yet still a head taller than I. And mortal, much too mortal.

"And she was beautiful, ah, so beautiful! And, strange though it may seem, highly desired by the men of the court. And yet"—Brom's voice took on a tone of wonder and awe—"yet she loved me. She alone, of all women living, elf or mortal, saw me not as dwarf, elf, or Prince—but only as a man.

"And desired me . . .

"And loved me . . ."

He broke off, shaking his head in wonder.

He sighed. "I loved her, Rod Gallowglass, I loved her only, and begat a child within her."

His face darkened. He locked his hands behind his back and scowled at the ground. "When she proved by child, and her time grew apace, and she would soon be so swollen that all would know, and would shame her with cruel jests, though we were wed, I sent her away to the wild wood, to my people. And there, midwived by elves and leprechauns, she birthed a beautiful, laughing, part-elven child."

His eyes misted over. He lifted his head, staring through Rod. "She died. When her daughter was aged of two years, she died of a chill. And we buried her there, 'neath a tree in the forest. And yearly I come there . . ."

His eyes focused on Rod again. "But I had, still, the child."

He turned away, restless. "Yet what should I do? Raise her near me, and have her know her father for a gnarled thing, and the butt of bad jests? Raise her to shame of me?

"She was raised in the woods, therefore, knowing her mother's grave and the elves, but never her father."

Rod started to protest, but Brom waved him silent. "Be still! 'Twas better so!"

He turned slowly, murder in his eyes. "As 'tis still. And if ever she learns of it from thee, Rod Gallowglass, I'll hale out thy tongue by its roots, and lop off thy ears."

Stone-faced, Rod studied him, and found nothing to say.

"And therefore, now tell me!" Brom slammed his fists against his hips and lifted his chin. "For know this: half-mortal am I, and may therefore be slain; and it may be that this day I shall die."

His voice lowered. "So tell me, tell a poor, anxious father, an thou wilt: dost thou love my child?"

"Yes," Rod said, low. Then, "So it was no accident that I met her on my ride south?"

Brom smiled, sourly. "Nay, of course not. Couldst thou ever have thought that it was?"

The east was reddening, embarrassed with dawn, and the mist lifting as Rod rode into the beggars' camp to waken them.

But Tuan was there before him, going from pallet to pallet, shaking the beggars awake. A soldier was with him, placing a mug of hot mulled wine by each pallet.

Tuan looked up, saw Rod, and came up to him with arms outstretched and a grin a yard wide.

He clapped Rod on the shoulder, gripped his hand in a crushing shake. There was a deep, almost intoxicated quiet content in his eyes.

"My thanks, friend Rod," he said simply. "Dost thou wish my life? Thou mayst have it! Such is the debt that I owe."

Rod smiled slyly. "So you made double sure, did you? Well, all the better."

Tuan seemed to have things well in hand in the beggars' camp, so Rod turned Fess's steps toward the witches' lines.

All was in good order there; the baskets with ropes and harnesses stood ready; and the morning brew was passing from hand to hand. It was a potent beverage, something like concentrated tea with a touch of brandy, and served much the same purpose: a stimulant, to bring the witch powers to their peak.

Elves were underfoot everywhere about the camp, distributing good luck tokens and preventive-magic charms to all who would take them. Witches or no witches, the little folk argued, it never hurt to be sure. The charms could do no harm, and they might . . .

There was nothing for Rod to do there, either, so he rode in search of Gwendylon.

He found her seated in the midst of a knot of witches, old ones, as Gramarye witches went; they must have been into their twenties.

Gwendylon seemed to be explaining something to them with great earnestness, marking diagrams in the dust with a pointed stick. They were hanging on her words as though every syllable might mean life or death.

It didn't look like a good time to interrupt.

Rod turned and rode through a maze of scurrying forms, cooking smells, clamor of voices and discordant bugle calls, out past the pickets into Breden Plain.

The first rays of sunlight slanted through the meadow now, burning away the last tatters of mist. The long grass was moist and chill with the dew, the sky clear and blue.

And the glitter of spear-points flashed from the south verge of the field. Sun gleamed off burnished armor. The wind blew him the metallic din, the horse-cries, and the mutter of a war-camp awaking. The councillors, too, were awake early.

Hooves approaching; Rod turned to see a page pelting across the meadows toward him.

"How now, my lad?" Rod called, grinning and waving for appearances.

"Thou must come to the Queen, Master Gallowglass," the page gasped, out of breath, as he clutched at Rod's stirrup. "My Lord O'Berin and the Lords Loguire are there already before you. 'Tis a council of war!"

The council of war was quickly over, no more than a

summary of existent plans, and a brief prayer, plus the news that Catharine wouldn't ride after all. Rod had noticed that Catharine had stood through the meeting.

Then they were up and away, each to his station: Sir Maris to the center, old Duke Loguire to the right flank, and Rod to the left flank. Brom would stay high on the hillside with Catharine and Gwendylon, to direct the whole battle, an innovation Rod had recommended, and which Brom had accepted without reservation: the little man was a mighty fighter, but his legs weren't long enough to hold his seat in a joust.

Tom, offered the option of fighting with the beggars or staying by Rod, had chosen the latter option, probably because he wanted to be in the thick of the battle.

Tuan, of course, would stay with his beggars.

As Tuan swung into the saddle, Catharine stopped him with a hand on his knee. Rod saw her tie a veil of silk about Tuan's upper arm.

Then her hands lifted to him, pleading. Tuan caught them and pressed them to his mouth, bowed to kiss her lips, then wheeled his horse away, rode perhaps ten yards forward, then wheeled again.

They stood frozen a moment, the young Queen and the white knight. Then Tuan reared his horse, pivoted, and galloped after his ragtag-and-patchwork troops.

Rod smiled covertly.

"The time to feel smug is not yet, Rod," Fess reminded him.

Rod made a face. "Who do you think you are, Pinocchio's Cricket?"

He turned back for one last look at Gwendylon, standing near the Queen's tent; then he rode for the left flank.

He was the only horseman who rode without armor.

It was full, 14th Century plate armor, on both sides of the field; but the Southern armor was massed together in a solid, glaring wall, while Catharine's knights were spaced out, twenty yards apart, over the length of the enemy line.

Yes, there are a few holes, Rod thought. And the single line of foot soldiers behind the Queen's knights didn't compare too favorably with the packed masses that backed the rebel lords. No, it was not a sight to inspire confidence.

But the beggars weren't in sight. Nor, for that matter, were the witches. Or the elves.

The rebels were in for some very unpleasant surprises.

At the southern end of the field, a bugle called.

The rebel knights couched their lances.

The Queen's knights followed suit.

There was a long, straining, pause; then the horses plunged forward.

Horses' hooves muttered and rose to the roar of an avalanche as the two metal lines fell toward each other.

And as they fell, the North's line drew it upon itself till the knights rode shoulder to shoulder in the center.

A cheer went up from the rebel line as they saw easy victory coming; it would be easy for the rebel flanks to sweep around the Northern line and trap the Queen's forces.

The Queen's knights met the center of the rebel line with a grinding crash. Knights were unhorsed and blood spurted, but the center of the line held.

And with a victorious roar the rebels swung about to outflank the North. . . .

The yell broke into wild screams as the ground fell away beneath their mounts.

Knights and horses floundered in a six-foot trench.

The elves had done a good night's work.

The footmen came running up to their masters' rescue; but now the beggars broke howling from the trees at the sides of the field, with knife and sword and bludgeon, and fell on the footmen with extreme good will.

Still, they were vastly outnumbered.

But now the aerial arm got into the action. Teams of four levitating, fuzz-cheeked warlocks supported a swinging basket beneath them; and in each basket was a telekinetic witch. The warlocks fired arrows into the scrimmage at random, their hands freed by the leather harness at their waists; and pebbles flew out of the baskets, guided by the witches, to strike with more than enough impact to stun. Arrows speared up at them out of the Southern ranks; but the witches deflected them, and sometimes even managed to turn them back on their owners.

The simple, orderly battle deteriorated into hand-to-hand chaos.

But the Southern knights were still overly busy. The Code dictated that only a knight could fight another knight—a foot soldier could be killed just for trying it, and Heaven help him if he tried and won!

So Catharine's knights worked their way outward from the center along the rebel lines, a large percentage of them dying on the way. But the percentage of rebels was greater, for Catharine, like her father before her, had seen fit to give her knights a little extra in the way of training.

Toby, the young warlock, suddenly appeared in the air just above Rod. "Master Gallowglass! The Duke Loguire is sorely pressed; you must come to him!"

He disappeared as abruptly as he had come. It might not have been the greatest form of military communication, but it was better than the rebels had.

Rod dispatched his current preoccupation with a parry and a thrust between breastplate and helmet and backed Fess out of the melee.

He ran around the lines to the other end of the line, where a spindly, armored-clad form with a glowing sword had just finished cutting its way through the troops to Loguire. One of the councillors was trying to save the day by eliminating the leadership. The sword had a strange, radiant qualit. Rod didn't know what it was, but it was something mighty potent disguised as a sword.

Rod sailed into the ruckus, bulldozing his way through grappling pairs of beggars and soldiers, slipping in blood and loose heads.

Loguire saw the blow coming and threw up his shield to ward it off. The councillor's sword sheared through it silently, but missed Loguire. The old Duke yelled in pain as the heat was conducted through shield and armor to his skin and momentarily dropped his guard.

The councillor swung the sword up for the final blow.

Fess slammed full tilt into the councillor's horse. The animal went down and the councillor went flying with a scream of terror, sword flinging wide from his grasp.

Soldiers scurried back to be clear when the magic sword fell.

Rod, without the slightest tremor of conscience, wheeled about and trampled the councillor under Fess's iron hooves. The man gave a bubbling scream, choked off; and the scream rang on in Rod's mind.

Now his conscience began to clamor; but he locked it away till the battle was done.

He whirled about toward the sword, hearing the soldiers gasp "Witchcraft!"

"No, just magic," Rod shouted as he swung down, caught the sword, and remounted. "That's not so strange, is it?"

He threw the sword to Loguire hilt-first; the old nobleman

265

caught it and saluted him, and Rod broke out of the lines again.

The battle clamored about him, steel on steel and bone and gristle, no quarter asked. The locked armies lay in the middle of the field like some great, pulsing, obscene amoeba.

Overhead the esper-witches turned and wheeled home, no longer able to tell friend from foe.

Rod charged back and forth through the battle-lines—Fess plowing his way easily through mere mortal flesh—guarding the three generals and as many knights as he could; directing the clearing of the wounded when he could, adding the weight of his arm to break deadlocks.

The beggars seemed to have the soldiers hopelessly outclassed; this was their kind of fighting. Many of them were killed, but seldom without having first accounted for six or more of the enemy, with wooden staves, rusty swords, keen knives, and total disrespect for age and/or rank.

Rod thought of Karl Marx and winced.

Big Tom had long since gotten lost in the battle. Rod hoped he was all right.

Then at the back of the rebel line, Big Tom rose up roaring "To me! To me!"

A thousand beggars rallied to him and began to chop their way through the Southern ranks.

The idea spread; beggar groups sprang up all along the line, and began to press the amoeba of war in on itself.

Big Tom was hewing his way through to a very definite goal.

Rod frowned and stood up in his stirrups, trying to plot Big Tom's course.

There, in the center of the battle, twenty frantic scarecrows labored furiously to construct some sort of machine: a spidery tripod topped by a wasp-waisted contraption with alien curves. It was the councillors, with their last hope.

Rod rapped with his heels, and Fess leaped—but the robot had responded a touch slow. With a sense of dread, Rod realized that the strain of battle was beginning to tell on Fess.

The horse bounded over the heads of the army and plowed through to the force of councillors, just as Tom broke through from the other side, with only a fraction of his beggar troops.

A long, lurking moment of silence filled the little circle as the councillors saw their executors.

Then the councillors howled, drawing back into a tight

circle about the machine, the ferocity of despair in their eyes, their glowing swords leaping out.

Tom's boys circled out around the councillors and closed in.

The councillors' swords were deadly; but they had to hit to be effective, and the beggars were good at hitting and getting clear.

A lot of beggars dropped, cut in half; but a lot more lived. They outnumbered the councillors four to one. They whittled away at the ranks.

The councillors screamed, chopping, and died.

In the center of the circle, Rod could make out one lonely figure still working frantically at the machine—Durer.

Then, suddenly, there were only five councillors left.

Durer spun away from the machine with a shriek of despair and lugged something out of his wallet-pouch.

A laser pistol.

Rod dropped down to Fess's far side, the bulk of the horse between him and the councillors, knowing that only a head shot could hurt the robot, and snapped open a hidden panel in his horse's side. In it was his last-ditch defense: the latest-issue DDT laser pistol.

He fumbled the weapon out, hearing the screams of the the beggars as their legs were sheared off at the knee, and shot around under Fess's neck.

His shot creased Durer's leg. The scarecrow-man clasped his knee and fell, howling.

Tom bellowed.

The beggars stepped in. Oaken staves whirled, knocking the remaining councillors off their feet.

The staves rose high, poised a moment, and fell with a sickening, moist crunch.

Big Tom bellowed victorious laughter and scooped up a fallen councillor's sword.

Durer rolled back up to one knee and fired.

The red pencil of light caught Tom in the shoulder. He roared, spinning, and fell.

Half-crawling, half-leaping, Durer went for him, struggling to get a clear shot.

Rod snapped a shot at him, and missed.

Durer howled and dove behind a fallen body.

Rod slammed his heels into Fess. "Quick! Before he can recover to shoot!"

The horse leaped; the laser beam caught it in the belly—a hollow steel belly, no harm.

But the robot's legs stiffened, its head lolled forward, even while it was in the air.

Rod sprang free as Fess landed, crumpled, rolled.

Rod rolled too, came up to see Durer, risen to one knee, level the pistol at him.

Tom's huge body smashed into him.

Durer caromed away, pistol flying wide from his hand. The same had happened to Rod's. He cast about him, frantically searching.

Tom rolled, came to his feet, lurched after Durer, catching up a fallen councillor's sword . . . and tripped over a body.

Quick as an eel, Durer was up, catching Tom's fallen sword, chopping down . . .

Rod dove.

His shoulder caught Durer in the belly, whipped the little man around; the sword landed harmlessly in the earth.

Durer leaned on the sword, kept his feet, and swung the sword up, turning to Rod.

Rod rolled to his knees, saw the sword coming. . . . .

Tom bellowed, slammed into Rod, striking him out of the sword's path.

The glowing sword fell, shearing off Tom's shoulder and a third of his rib cage.

Rod screamed as he rolled to his feet and swung around. His arm locked around Durer's throat, his knee came up into the small of the back. Something snapped.

Durer screamed and went limp, screaming still, the sword falling from his fingers.

Rod threw him down.

Still screaming, the scarecrow groped for the sword.

Rod dropped to his knee and chopped down.

The callused edge of his hand smashed larynx and vertebrae.

Durer gurgled, convulsed, and lay still.

Rod stood, gasping, and turned, to see Tom's shoulder pumping blood in great gouts, the big man's face contorted in a silent grimace.

Rod was down again, groping frantically in the welter of blood and spare bodies.

He came up with the laser pistol and swung back to Tom.

The remaining beggars lurched forward, too slow; before they could reach him, Rod pulled the trigger and, holding it down, sliced off another half-inch along Tom's wound. Tom screamed.

Then they were on Rod, mauling and clubbing.

"Nay!" Tom rasped, a sickening parody of his former bellow. "Fools, let him be! Do y' not see! He stopped the blood!"

He sank back as the grasping hands hesitated, then loosened. Rod limped back to him, bruised on face and body, rubbing the worst of them—his scarcely-healed shoulder.

He sank to one knee by the gasping hulk of a man, face still wrenched with pain. The stink of cauterized flesh filled his head.

Tom forced his eyes open a fraction and tried to grin. " 'Twas . . . well meant . . . master. Two minutes ago, it . . . might ha' saved me."

Rod jerked off his cloak, balled it up, thrust it under Tom's head. "Lie back and rest," he growled through a tight throat. "You're a healthy hunk, you'll make it. You haven't lost all that much blood."

"Nay," Tom panted, "too much . . . lost. And the . . . body's shock . . ."

His face twisted with a spasm of pain. Rod turned away to Fess, slapped the reset switch and fumbled in one of the horse's hidden pockets for an ampul.

He limped back to Tom, slapped the ampul against the burned flesh.

Tom relaxed with a huge sigh as the anesthetic took hold. "My thanks, master," he murmured weakly. "Tha hast given me, at least, painless death."

"Don't talk that way." Rod's face was frozen. "There's many a roll in the hay for you yet."

"Nay, master." Tom shook his head, closing his eyes. "My time is nigh."

"You're not going to die. You'll leave me in your debt if you do. I won't have it."

"A pox on what thou wilt or wilt not!" Tom spat, with a touch of life again. "I am not thine to command or deny now, lordling. He who now hath me in thrall is far more puissant than thou, and will one day command thee also."

He sagged back on the pillow, heaving gasps of air. Rod knelt silent by his side.

Tom's remaining hand groped over his belly to catch Rod's forearm. "Aye, thou'rt now in my debt, though 'twas not of my choice."

"Not your choice?" Rod scowled. "What are you talking about? You saved my life!"

"Aye, and thereby lost my own. But I would never ha' done so with a clear head."

"Clear head?"

"Aye. In battle, one sees and one does, whatever comes first to mind. 'Twas thee, or living my life longer to serve the House of Clovis; and in the heat of the battle I chose thee, in my folly!"

He was silent a moment, breathing hoarsely; then his hands tightened again. "Yet while I die, thou wilt live in my debt! And what thou canst not pay to me, thou must pay to my people."

Rod tried to draw his hand back. "No!"

"Aye!" Tom's eyes flew wide, glaring, angry. " 'Tis the payment I demand! Thy life for mine, thy life spent here on Gramarye, to work for the good of my people!"

"I'm not my own master . . ."

"Nay, thou art." Tom sank back, weary. "Thou art, and if thou knowest it not, thou'rt true fool."

"The price is too high, Tom. My death in battle, yes, gladly. But living here, all my days, I cannot. I too serve a dream. . . ."

" 'Twas my choice, also," Tom sighed, "the dream or the man. Nay, then, choose what thou wilt."

"I'm under a geas . . ."

"Then my geas also is on thee, freeing thee from the other. Thou must serve me and mine now . . ."

The dying face darkened. "I had thought I knew what was best for them . . . but now, as all darkens about me . . ."

He heaved up suddenly, body wracked with a spasm, coughing blood. Rod threw his arms about the big man, holding him up.

The spasm passed. Tom clutched weakly at Rod's arm, gasping. "Nay, then . . . thy mind is . . . clearer . . . thou must decide . . ."

"Be still," Rod pleaded, trying to lower him again. "Don't waste what little life is left—"

"Nay!" Tom clutched at him. "Let me speak! Espers . . . Tribunal . . . they'll make it . . . work . . . We . . . fight them . . . here . . . in the . . ."

"Be still," Rod pleaded. "Save your breath, I know what you're saying."

Tom craned his neck to look up at him. "You . . . ?"

Rod nodded. "Yes. You told me the last little bit I needed, just now. Now lie down."

Tom sagged in his arms. Rod lowered him gently, letting his head rest in the blood-soaked cape.

Tom lay panting. "Tell me . . . I must know . . . if you know . . ."

"Yes, I know," Rod murmured. "The DDT will win out. You can only fight it back here. And you fight each other as well."

"Aye." Tom nodded, a barely perceptible movement. "Thou . . . must decide . . . now . . . and . . . master . . ."

He mumbled, too soft to hear, and labored for another breath, eyes opening, anxious.

Rod bent forward, putting his ear to Tom's lips.

"Don't die for . . . a dream . . ."

Rod frowned. "I don't understand."

He waited, then said, "What do you mean, Tom?"

There was no answer.

Rod straightened slowly, looking down at the vacant eyes, the loose mouth.

He touched the base of the throat, the jugular.

He let his fingertips rest there long minutes, then slowly reached up to close the man's eyes.

He stood, slowly, and turned away, his eyes not seeing.

Then, slowly, his eyes focused. He looked around at the staring, pathetic beggars, their eyes fixed on the huge body.

A slight, slender shape stepped hesitantly into the ring. "M-master Gallowglass?"

Rod turned, saw, and stepped forward as the beggars began to move in, to kneel by Tom's body.

Rod moved away from them, head hanging heavily.

He raised his eyes. "What is it, Toby?"

"Milord . . ." Toby's face was strangely tragic in its confusion as he looked at the group of beggars, distrubed without knowing why. "Milord, they . . . They cry for quarter, milord. Shall we give it them?"

"Quarter? Oh, yes. They want to surrender." Rod nodded, closing his eyes.

He turned and looked at the group of beggars. "Oh, I don't know. What does Brom say?"

"My lord O'Berin says, aye, grant it them, but the Queen says nay. The Lords Loguire are with Brom."

"And still the Queen says nay." Rod nodded, bitterness

tightening his mouth. "And they want me to break the dead-lock, is that it?"

"Aye, milord."

The circle of beggars parted a little. Rod saw Tom's waxen, still face.

He turned back to Toby. "Hell, yes. Give 'em quarter."

The sun had sunk behind the hills, leaving the sky a pale rose, darkening to the east.

The twelve Great Lords stood, bound in chains, before Catharine.

Near her sat Loguire and Tuan, Brom and Sir Maris.

Rod stood a little distance away, leaning back against Fess, arms folded, chin sunk on his breast.

The old Duke Loguire's head was also bowed, deep misery in his eyes, for his son Anselm stood a pace in advance of the rest of the lords, directly before the Queen.

Catharine held her head high, eyes shining with triumph and pride, face flushed with the joy of her power.

Rod looked at her and felt a twist of disgust in his belly; her arrogance had returned with her victory.

At a sign from Brom O'Berin, two heralds blew a flourish. The trumpets whirled away from their lips, and a third herald stepped forward, loosening a scroll.

"Be it known to all by these presents, that on this day the miscreant vassal, Anselm, son of Loguire, did rise in most vicious rebellion against Catharine, Queen of Gramarye, and is therefore liable to the judgment of the Crown, even unto death, for the crime of high treason!"

He rolled the scroll and slapped it to his side. "Who speaks in defense of Anselm, chief of the rebels?"

There was a silence.

Then old Loguire rose.

He bowed gravely to Catharine. She returned his courtesy with a glare, astonished and angry.

"Naught can be said in defense of a rebel," Loguire rumbled. "Yet for a man who, in the haste of hot blood, rises to avenge what he may consider to be insults to his father and house, much may be said; for, though his actions were rash and, aye, even treacherous, still he was moved by honor, and filial piety. Moreover, having seen the outcome of rash action, and being under the tutelage of his duke and his father, might well again realize his true loyalties and duties to his sovereign."

Catharine smiled; her voice was syrup and honey. "You would then, milord, have me enlarge this man, upon whose head must be laid the deaths of some several thousand, once again to your protection and discipline; to you who have, as this day has proved, failed once already in these duties?"

Loguire winced.

"Nay, good milord!" she snapped, face paling, lips drawing thin. "Thou hast fostered rebels against me before, and now seek to do it again!"

Loguire's face hardened.

Tuan half-bolted from his chair, flushed with anger. She turned to him with a haughty, imperious look. "Has milord of the beggars aught to say?"

Tuan fought for calm, grinding his teeth. He straightened and bowed gravely. "My Queen, father and son have this day battled valiantly for you. Will you not, therefore, grant us the life of our son and our brother?"

Catharine's face paled further, eyes narrowing.

"I thank my father and brother," said Anselm, in a clear, level voice.

"Be still!" Catharine fairly shrieked, turning on him. "Treacherous, villainous, thrice-hated dog!"

Rage came into the Loguires' eyes; still they held themselves silent.

Catharine sat back in her chair, gasping, clasping the arms tight, that her hands might not tremble. "Thou wilt speak when I ask thee, traitor," she snapped. "Till then, hold thy peace!"

"I will not hold my peace! Thou canst not hurt me more; I will have my say! Thou, vile Quuen, hast determined I shall die, and nothing will sway thee! Why, then, slay me!" he shouted. "The penalty for treason is death! I had known as much before I rebelled; slay me and be done with it!"

Catharine sat back, relaxing a trifle. "He is sentenced by his own mouth," she said. "It is the law of the land that a rebel shall die."

"The law of the land is the Queen," rumbled Brom. "If she says a traitor shall live he shall live."

She spun to him, staring in horror. "Wilt thou, too, betray me? Will not one of my generals stand beside me this day?"

"Oh, be done with it!" Rod stormed, looming up over the throne. "No, not one of your generals will support you now, and it seems to me that might give you some slight hint you're in the wrong. But oh, no, not the Queen! Why hold a trial?

You've already decided he'll die!" He turned away and spat. "Come on, get this farce of a trial over with," he growled.

"Thou, too?" she gasped. "Wilt thou also defend a traitor, one who hath caused death to three thousand . . ."

"*You* have caused the death of three thousand," Rod bellowed. "A noble man of low birth lies dead in that field, his right side torn away, the birds pecking at him, and why? To defend a willful child who sits on a throne, not worth the life of a beggar! A child who is so poor a queen she gave birth to rebellion!"

Catharine cowered back in her throne, trembling. "Be still!" she gasped. "Was it I who rebelled?"

"Who was it gave the nobles cause to rebel by too-hasty reforms and too-lofty manner? Cause, Catharine, cause! There is no rebellion without it; and who but the Queen has given it?"

"Be still, oh be still!" The back of her hand to her mouth, as though she would scream. "You may not speak so to a Queen!"

Rod looked down at the cowering Queen. His face twisted with disgust.

He turned away. "Ah, I'm sick to the belly! Let them live; there has been too much death this day already. Let them live. They'll be loyal, without their councillors to needle them. Let them live, let them all live. They're schooled now, even if you're not."

"This cannot be true!" Catharine gasped.

"It is not!" Tuan stepped forward, his hand going to his sword. "The Queen gave cause, aye, but she did not make the rebellion."

Catharine's eyes leaped up to him with a look of radiant gratitude.

"Speak truth," Tuan went on, "and you may chastise her. But when you charge her with that which she hath not done" —he shook his head slowly—"I cannot let you speak."

Rod ached to spit in his face.

Instead, he turned again to Catharine, who sat straight again, regaining her haughty look.

"Do not forget," he said, "that a queen who cannot control her own whims is a weak queen."

She paled again, and "Walk wary!" Tuan snapped.

Rage surged up in Rod, higher and higher as he stood rigid against it, till it broke some bond within him and drained away, leaving an icy calm and a great clearity, a clarity in which he saw what he must do and why . . . and what the consequences to himself must needs be.

Catharine was almost smiling now, smug and haughty again, seeing Rod hesitate at Tuan's threat.

"Has more to say, sirrah?" she demanded, lifting her chin.

"Yes," Rod said between his teeth. "What kind of queen is it who betrays her own people?"

His hand whipped out and slapped her.

She screamed, falling back in the chair, and Tuan was on him, fist swinging square into Rod's face.

Rod ducked under the blow and grappled Tuan to him, shouting "Fess!"

Tuan's fists slammed into his belly, trip-hammer blows; but Rod held on, seeing the other generals rushing up.

But Fess got there first.

Rod tried to forget what a nice, clean young kid Tuan was and drove his knee into Tuan's groin.

He let go and leaped to the saddle as Tuan fell, doubled with pain, rattling in his throat.

Fess spun and leaped over the heads of the approaching Guardsmen.

He landed and stretched into a gallop. Rod heard Catharine screaming Tuan's name and grinned savagely.

Then his grin stretched into a silent scream as pain exploded in his wounded shoulder.

Turning, he saw the nock of a crossbow bolt sticking out of his shoulder.

And, beyond the bouncing shoulder, in the midst of the circle of Guardsmen around the throne, Catharine bending over Tuan, who knelt, still curled around his pain, with a Guardsman's crossbow dropping from his hand.

They came back to a hill overlooking the field as dusk gathered, having run a long circle through wood and field and waded a mile of stream to hide their trail.

Rod slumped out of the saddle as Fess came to the edge of a grove. He limped to a large tree and sat, leaning back against the trunk, hidden from eyes in the field below by the gathering gloom.

He looked down over the glowing fires on the field, listening to the faint sounds of the victory merry-making.

He sighed and turned to the problem at hand, or more accurately, at shoulder. He opened his doublet and probed the shoulder gently, wincing with the pain that he felt even through the anesthetic he'd applied on the run.

The barbed bolt-head seemed buried just in front of collarbone and joint; by some miracle, it had missed both bone and artery.

There was a faint puff of air, like a miniature shockwave, and he looked up to see Gwendylon bending toward him, tears welling from her eyes. "My lord, my lord! Art badly hurt?"

Rod smiled and reached up to pull her head down to his. He held her against him for a good, long time.

"Nay, then," she said, blushing as she drew away, "I warrant thou'rt not so sorely wounded as I had feared."

"Ah, lass, lass!" Rod leaned back, cradling her in his arm. "I was lonely, on that ride."

"I'd ha' come to you sooner, lord," she said apologetically, "but I must needs wait till you'd come to rest.

"Now to that shoulder." She took on a brisk, almost business-like air. " 'Twill hurt some, my lord."

Rod ground his teeth as she stripped the blood-soaked tunic off his shoulder. "Bandages in the saddlebag," he gritted as she finished.

She turned to Fess, brought out the small metal box, frowned. "What is this red cross here, my lord?"

"Just a symbol," Rod wheezed. "Means it's a, uh, healing kit."

She knelt by his side again, very still.

Rod frowned, wondering what she was doing.

Then pain lanced him again, and he felt the bolt-head receding, withdrawing slowly along the channel it had cut on its way in, and, seemingly, all of its own accord.

Through a pain-blurred haze, a random thought burrowed: these witches were the answer to the surgeon's prayer.

The bolt-head eased itself past his skin, then suddenly whirled spinning through the air to smash itself against a stone.

"Thus," she hissed, "may I serve all who would harm thee, my lord."

Rod shivered as he realized the extent of the power he'd been dallying with.

She reached for the bandages.

"No, no!" Rod touched her arm with his good hand. "The powder in the silver envelope first. It'll stop the bleeding."

"I would rather use compress of herbs," she said dubiously. "But as thou wilt have it, my lord."

Rod shuddered as the sulfa bit into him.

Then the pain numbed, and she was winding the bandage.

"It seems you're always bandaging that shoulder," Rod muttered.

"Aye, my lord. I would that thou wert more chary of it."

Someone coughed, somewhat delicately, nearby.

Rod looked up and saw a squat silhouette lurking in the shadows.

Rod's mouth tightened. "Well, if it isn't the Atrophied Ajax himself!"

Gwendylon laid a reproving finger gently on his lips.

Rod gave a short nod, irritated at himself; the fingers lifted away.

He beckoned with his good arm. "Well, come on and join the party, Brom. But be careful; the fruits of victory are sour tonight."

Brom came forward, hands locked behind him, head bowed, and sat on a nearby root.

Rod frowned. There was something sheepish, almost furtive, in the dwarf's manner. "What's eating you?" he growled.

Brom sighed and rested his hands on his knees. "Thou hast caused me much heartache this day, Rod Gallowglass."

Rod smiled, one-sided. "Sounds more like a bellyache. I take it you weren't too pleased at the way things went?"

"Oh, nay, I was most enormously pleased! And yet"—Brom rested his chin on his clenched hands, looking sheepish again —"I confess that at first I was somewhat wroth with thee."

"You don't say!"

"Aye; but that was before I realized your plan."

"Oh?" Rod raised one eyebrow. "But you did figure out what I was up to?"

"Nay. I grow old, Rod Gallowglass . . ."

Rod snorted.

"My thanks." Brom inclined his head. "But 'tis truth; I grow old, and must needs be shown."

"And what were you shown?"

"Oh, 'twas a most touching scene!" Brom smiled with a touch of sarcasm. "At first Catharine could but cry, 'My love, thou'rt hurt!' and call for doctors and herbs, till Tuan managed to rise, saying his hurt was but slight; and then she fell to weeping on his shoulder, the while crying him her lord and protector and the guard of her honor, and would

not be comforted till he'd swore he would wed her!"
Brom's smile softened, "Aye, 'twas most tender to look upon."

Rod nodded wearily, closing his eyes. "When's the wedding?"

"As soon as they shall be thrice called in a church. Catharine would have had it right then, but Tuan cried no, that she was Queen and the flower of womanhood, and must be wed as befitted her estate."

"A promising beginning."

"Oh, 'twas more promising still! For Tuan then turned to the twelve lords and, quoth he, 'And how shall we deal with these?' And Catharine cried, 'Oh, as thou wilt, my lord, as thou wilt! But be done with them right quickly, and come away!' "

"Very auspicious," Rod agreed. "What did he do with them?"

"Struck off their chains, and bade them once more take up the care of their demesnes. But he required of them each a hostage, of twelve years old or less, of their blood and body and legitimate household, to dwell in the Queen's castle."

Rod frowned, nodded. "Should work. He gets a deterrent, and a chance to raise a new generation very loyal to the throne."

He leaned back against the rough bark, feeling totally drained. "Glad it worked."

"Aye." Brom's eyes glowed. "This land shall stand ever in thy debt, Rod Gallowglass. Thou hast saved us our Crown, and banished the ghost of a long and full bloody civil war; and, moreover, thou hast given us a King."

"And a Public Enemy No. 1," Rod said bitterly.

A shadow darkened Brom's face.

Rod lifted an eye to him. "You must admit that I'm slightly *persona non grata*."

"Aye," Brom growled, "yet ever wilt thou find sanctuary in the land of the elves."

Rod smiled weakly. "Thanks, Brom."

"Yet tell me!" Brom hunched forward, frowning. "How is it thou hast come? When all looked bleak in our land, and hope had been exiled, then did you come, falling from the skies like an answer to prayer—you, who had no stake in our countryside, no manor to defend. Our cares were not yours, yet you made them so."

He thrust his head forward, eyes burning. "Why hast thou saved us?"

Rod's smile soured. "For the Dream."

Brom frowned. "How . . . ?"

Rod looked up at the stars. He hesitated a moment, then said, "Fess, record this."

He turned to Brom, then to Gwendylon, lifting his good arm to point to the sky.

"Look up there. See those stars? Each one has worlds circling about it, worlds like this one, where lovers meet and men feud, and kings topple.

"But most of them are united under one rule, one government—the Decentralized Democratic Tribunal. And the voice that commands is that of the people themselves."

"Nay!" Brom boomed. "How can that be?"

"Because each man's voice can be heard, his opinions adding weight to those of his fellows. That's the key, communications. You can't have that kind of government here because your communications are lousy, which is strange, because you've got the potential for the best system, if you'd just use it."

He folded his arms and leaned back. "But they've got bad trouble up there. They're growing, you see. Every day, at least one new world joins the Tribunal. At that rate, they'll have reached the limit of their communications. After that, they'll start running downhill to dictatorship."

"But how is this thy concern?" Brom growled.

"I work for them. I'm the salesman. I'm the boy who goes out and gets new planets ready for membership . . . if they want it, which they always do, *once they're ready!*"

"And what is this readiness?" Brom smiled, fighting for tolerance.

"Communications, as I told you, but even more than that, learning. Education."

He sighed. "The education, we've got licked. Took a long while, but it's licked. Communications, though, that's another matter.

" 'Cause there's one other ingredient to freedom: a frontier. It prevents a stratified society—never mind what that is, my Lord O'Berin, King of the Elves—and a stratified society is another road to totalitarianism.

"So the Tribunal's got to keep growing. But if it grows much more, slowing communications will be its death. And I, very personally, don't want that. Because the Dream has a name, you see—Freedom. That's my Dream. And that's why Gramarye means so much to me."

Brom scowled. "I do not comprehend."

Rod turned to him, smiling. "The witches. Their power to hear thoughts. That's the communications system we need."

He watched understanding, and a certain dread, dawn in Brom's face, then turned away.

"We need them," he said, "we need lots of them. Up till now, their numbers have been growing slowly. But, under Catharine's protection, they'll grow faster; and from their winning in today's battle, they'll begin to be respected, and before too long, every parent will be hoping for a witch to be born in the family. Then their numbers will soar."

Brom scowled. "But how is it this world alone, of all the ones you speak of, hath witches?"

"Because the men who brought life to this land, your ancestors, who dropped from the skies, selected only those persons who had at least a trace of witch-power in them, to come here. They didn't know they had it, it was too little, and hidden too deeply, to be seen; but as the generations rolled and they married one another again and again, that little bit grew and grew, until at last a witch was born."

"And when was that?" Brom smiled tolerantly.

"When the elves appeared. Also the banshees, werewolves, and other supernatural fauna. Because there's a strange substance on this planet, called witch-moss, that shapes itself to the forms a witch thinks of. If the witch thinks of an elf, the moss turns into an elf."

Brom paled. "Dost thou say . . ."

"Don't feel bad about it, Brom," Rod said quickly. "All men were once just pulsing blobs floating in the sea; it's just that in your remote ancestor's case, the process was speeded up a trifle, through the witches. And it was your first ancestor, not you; my guess is that the critter formed out of the moss is such a perfect copy, it can breed true—and even cross-breed with mortal men."

He leaned back and sighed. "Be proud, Brom. You and your people are the only ones who can claim to be real native citizens."

Brom was silent a long moment; then he growled, "Aye, then, this is our land. And what wouldst thou do with it, warlock from the skies?"

"Do?" Rod cocked an eye. "Only what you yourself are trying to do, Brom, through the reforms you've suggested to

Catharine. Equality before the law, isn't that your aim?"

"It is, aye."

"Well, it's mine, too. And my job is to show you the least bloody road to it, which job I have just finished."

He scowled, suddenly brooding.

Brom studied him. Gwendylon touched his head, stroking the hair, worried.

Rod looked up at her and tried to smile.

He turned to Brom. "That's why I fought for Catharine, you see: because she protects the witches, and because she's a reformer; and so is Tuan, thank Heaven.

"And that's why the councillors and the Mocker fought against her."

Brom scowled. "I am old, Rod Gallowglass. Show me."

Rod looked up at the stars again. "Someday the Tribunal will govern all the stars you can see, and a lot more that you can't. And almost all the people who live on those worlds will be witches, because they'll have the blood of Gramarye flowing in their veins.

"How's that for a laurel wreath, Brom? 'Father to a Galaxy . . .'

"But some people won't be witches. And because they're not, they'll hate the witches, and their government, more violently than you can imagine. That kind is called a fanatic.

"And they'll go for any system of government, any, as long as it isn't democracy. And they'll fight democracy with every breath in their bodies."

"If it is to be as you say," growled Brom, "these men will lose; for how could they fight so many worlds?"

"They can't," Rod answered, "unless they kill it before it's born."

"But how shall they do that? For to kill the witch in the womb, they must come to the womb, here to Gramarye, and try to . . . why . . . to slay . . ."

Brom stared, horrified.

"Catharine," Rod finished for him, nodding sourly. "Right, Brom. The councillors and the leader cadre of the House of Clovis are somebody's great-great-fifty-times-great-grand-children."

"But how could that be?" Brom gasped. "What man can visit his ancestors?"

"They can. They've got a thing called a time machine. There's one of them hidden somewhere in the House of

Clovis, and another in the haunted tunnels of the Castle Loguire.

"So guard those four men in your dungeon very carefully, Brom. They might have a few surprises in store."

"Be assured that I will!"

"And the councillors are all dead." Rod leaned back, eyes closing. "Which nicely wraps up the report. Send it home, Fess. Oh, and corroborative material: a description of the time machine, and descriptions of the witches' main tricks—you know, telekinesis, levitation, telepor—"

"I do know, Rod," the robot's voice reminded him.

"Umph. Some self-effacing retainer *you* are. Well, send it home."

The warp transmitter deep within Fess's basketball brain spat a two-second squeal at the stars.

All was silent a moment; then Gwendylon said, hesitantly, "My lord?"

Rod lifted an eyelid and smiled. "You shouldn't call me that. But I like it."

She smiled, shyly. "My lord, you ha' finished your work here . . ."

Rod's face darkened.

He turnd away, glowering down at the earth.

"Where will you go now, Rod Warlock?" Brom murmured.

"Oh, cut it out!" Rod snapped.

He turned away again, sullen. "I'm not a warlock," he growled. "I'm an agent from a very advanced technology, and as such have a bag of tricks like you wouldn't believe, but they're all cold iron and its breed. I haven't a witch trick to my name, and I certainly don't have the tiniest shred of witch power."

He lifted his eyes to the stars again. "I'm not a warlock, not the slightest bit, not so much as the meanest of your peasants. I don't belong here."

He felt a tearing in him as he said it.

"I don't belong here. I belong out there, chasing a dream."

He looked down at the earth and said heavily, "The men of the Tribunal will tell Fess, and Fess will tell me. I'll go where they send me."

Brom was very quiet for a moment.

Then he plucked a blade of grass and tore it between his fingers. "You are not your own master, Rod Gallowglass?"

"I chose this life," Rod growled. "I take orders, yes, but I do it voluntarily."

"A point," Brom admitted, "but a weak one. By choice or not by choice, thou'rt still enslaved."

"Yes," Rod admitted. "But some must give up their freedom, so that their children may have it."

But it didn't even sound convincing to him.

Brom gusted a sigh and slapped his thighs, standing. He gazed at Rod, his eyes weary and old.

"If thou must go, thou must go; a geas is a thing no man can deny. Go on to the stars, Rod Gallowglass, but be mindful: if ever thou seekest a haven, 'tis here."

He turned and strode away, down the hillside.

Gwendylon sat quietly beside him, clasping his hand.

"Tell me," she said after a little while, "is it only one dream that takes you away from me?"

"Yes. Oh, yes." Rod's hand tightened on hers. "You sort of blotted out any other dreams."

She turned, smiling tremulously, tears glittering on her lashes. "Then may not I accompany you to the stars, good my lord?"

Rod clamped down on her hand, throat tightening. "I wish that you could; but you'd wither and die there, like an uprooted flower. You belong here, where they need you. I belong there. It's as simple as that."

"No." She shook her head sadly. "You go not for belonging, but for a geas. But, good my lord"—she turned, tears flowing now—"is not my geas as strong as your dream?"

"Look," he said tightly, "try to understand. A man has to have a dream. That's the difference between animals and man, a dream. And a man who's lost his dream is something less than a man, and worthy of no woman. How could I dare claim you if I wasn't a man?

"A man has to prove his worth to himself, before he can claim a woman, and the dream is the proof. As long as he's working for it, he's got a right to her, because he's worth something. I could stay here and be very, very happy with you. But in my depths I'd know I didn't deserve you. Because I'd be a drone, a male with no purpose. How could I father children if I knew their mother was more valuable to the world than I am?"

"Then it wouldst be thou who wouldst wither and die?" she murmured.

Rod nodded.

"But the geas, my lord, if not mine alone, is not Big Tom's geas added to it, and the old Duke Loguire's enough to balance the geas of the stars?"

Rod sat rigid.

"They bade you watch over their people," she murmured. "And what would become of them, lord, if these fiends from tomorrow come again? As surely they will, if they hate as deep as thou say."

Rod nodded, very slowly.

"And what of the Dream then, my lord?" she murmured.

Rod sat rock-still for a moment.

"Fess," he said quietly.

"Yes, Rod?"

"Fess, send them my resignation."

"Your *what?*"

"My resignation!" Rod snapped. "And hurry it up!"

"But, Rod, your duty . . . the honor of your house . . ."

"Oh, stuff it! The councillors might be back, Fess, even if we smash the time machines. They did it once, they can do it again. Send it!"

Fess obediantly beeped at the stars.

Then, slowly, Rod's head lolled forward.

"My lord?" Gwendylon gasped.

Rod raised a hand weakly. "I'm all right. I've done the right thing, and the one that'll make me happiest. For the first time in my life, I'm working on my own.

"And that's it. I've cut myself off. They're not backing me anymore—the house, the clan, Big Brother watching over me . . ."

"Thou hast a house here, lord," she murmured.

"I know, I know. And in a little while this'll pass, and I'll be happier than I ever have been. But now . . ."

He looked up at her, smiled weakly. "I'll be all right."

"Rod," Fess murmured.

He lifted his head. "Yes, Fess?"

"They have replied, Rod."

Rod tensed. "Read it."

"*Report accepted. Request send coordinates for verifying expedition.*"

Rod nodded, mouth twisting back with bitterness. "Send 'em. Go on."

"*Request you reconsider resignation. Accept permanent assignment planet Gramarye guard against further infiltration-subversion.*"

284

Rod straightened, staring. "What?"

"They would like to make your chosen position official, Rod," the robot replied.

"What is it, my lord?"

"They want me to stay on," Rod answered mechanically. He turned to her, life replacing the stunned look. "They want me to stay on!"

"Stay on where, my lord?" she asked, catching the first traces of his enthusiasm.

"Stay on here!" he bellowed, jumping to his feet and flinging his arm wide to include the whole planet. "Here on Gramarye! As an agent! Gwen, I'm free! And I'm home!"

He dropped to his knees, spinning to face her, hands biting into her shoulders.

"I love you!" he bellowed. "Marry me!"

"At once and forever, my lord!" she cried, clasping his face in her hands, and the tears poured.

He grabbed for her, but she held him off with a palm over his lips. "Nay, my lord. Only a warlock may kiss a witch."

"All right, I'm a warlock, I'm a warlock! Just kiss me, will you?"

She did.

He locked his hands in the small of her back, grinning.

"Hey," he said, "is it true, what they say about farm girls?"

"Aye, my lord." She lowered her eyes and began unbuttoning his doublet. "You'll never be rid of me now."